## WAVE OF DESIRE

As the waning candlelight illuminated Juan's masculine countenance, Raven searched for the lover's compassion in his eyes. Then she pulled his head down to hers and covered his lips with feverish kisses. "Please, Juan," she begged, "let me journey with you. I can't bear to be away from you again."

"No, Raven. This is a dangerous voyage, and I won't risk losing you a second time. But let's not speak of this now. We have the rest of the night to remain in each other's embrace."

Reluctantly, Raven relented and eased Juan into the bed with her. Then, intoxicated by the surgings of desire running through her, Raven conquered Juan's mouth with her own while nimble fingers worked at unbuttoning his shirt.

"What have I created?" he joked.

"A wanton wench," she declared smugly. "One whose fire for love matches your own!"

# HISTORICAL ROMANCE IN THE MAKING!

# BAHAMA RAPTURE

BY JOLENE PREWIT-PARKER

**ZEBRA BOOKS**
**KENSINGTON PUBLISHING CORP.**

ZEBRA BOOKS

are published by

KENSINGTON PUBLISHING CORP.
475 Park Avenue South
New York, N.Y. 10016

Printed in the United States of America

# *Chapter One*

Raven was surprised by her Aunt Martha's unusually good humor as the fleshy woman happily gorged herself with squab and bread pudding. Even her husband, John, who Raven suspected preferred spending his evenings in town flirting with the tavern wenches as he squandered money at the gaming tables, had graced the cheerless dining hall with his portly presence.

"What's the matter, Raven?" demanded Martha, peering longingly at her niece's untouched plate. "You've hardly eaten at all. Are you feeling ill?"

"No, Aunt. I am not ill," mumbled Raven, staring down at her hands folded demurely on her lap. "I am just not very hungry this evening."

"Mustn't let all that good food go to waste," she remarked, reaching across the wine-splattered table linen.

Raven stared loathingly as her aunt greedily grabbed the plate and attacked the food with ravenous vigor. How I abhor that woman, she thought contemptfully. She is utterly incorrigible! I despised her from the very onset of her arrival at Ravenwood, and my feelings for that abominable creature have not altered since. I am nineteen years old! Why must I still have a guardian? I am perfectly capable of caring for myself. There was no reason for that stupid Mr. Bentley to contact the Meyers after Mama died. I would have been content to live here with our house servants. Papa would not have objected since Mattie and her husband have been with the Gatewood family for years and years. Had it not been for my afternoon rides on Sheik and being able to lock myself in Papa's library to read, I would have surely gone mad by now! Aunt Martha must have been overjoyed with the prospect of living on a grand country estate and mingling with the landed gentry, even though she never fails to remind me of how she gladly left the civilized life of London in order to come to the country and fulfill her Christian obligation to her dead sister.

Raven could not help but snicker softly to herself. What a shame the society to which she so desperately wanted to belong snubbed her unmercifully! Not even elegant clothing and a fine home could conceal her garishly vulgar tastes and peasant manners. How much more morose her already foul disposition had become after being rebuffed by the affluent and the elite time and time again.

Raven surveyed the ornately decorated room and cringed. She quickly blinked her long, uplifted lashes to prevent tears from falling from her emerald-colored eyes. The audacity of that woman! How dare she toss my Mama's treasured heirlooms into the cellar and replace them with such hideously obese pieces of furniture! I shall never forget that afternoon I stood outside my mother's dressing room, she silently recollected, and watched speechlessly as that horrible woman strutted in front of the mirror admiring the emerald and diamond necklace that adorned her squatty neck. The necklace Papa had given Mama on the day of my birth! I can still hear her ranting and raving when she discovered its absence from her jewel chest. Poor Uncle John! How befuddled he was when she accused him of stealing it for one of his shameless hussies or selling it to pay off one of his many gambling debts.

Martha completed her third generous portion with a resounding belch. "Raven, darling, why don't you join us for an after-dinner brandy?" she suggested sweetly while glancing knowingly at her husband. Noticing her niece's reluctance, she urged, "There's a matter of importance that John and I feel must be discussed with you immediately."

Raven nodded in defeated acquiescence and followed the pair into the library.

That girl's resemblance to Elizabeth is morbid, reflected Martha bitterly. Sometimes I feel as though Elizabeth has returned from the grave to haunt me. Those sickening green eyes! How could Robert have ever chosen my whining, sickly sister over me?

While John was pouring the brandy from a tall crystal decanter, Martha removed a letter from between her sagging, freckled bosom and handed it to her astonished niece. "This came for you this afternoon while you were out. I could not help but notice the unfamiliar posting. Perhaps it contains news of your father," she suggested with mild interest.

A foreboding expression clouded Raven's face. "News of Papa? After four years? Why that hardly seems possible."

When Raven was fourteen years old, Sir Robert Gatewood, an anthropologist for King George, had been assigned to research the nearly extinct Lucayan Indians on the Bahama Islands. The Lucayans, Raven learned, were an Indian tribe that had once populated the Bahamas. But at the time of her father's expedition only fifty members of that happy, carefree tribe still existed. Those who had survived frequent massacres by marauding cannibals were enslaved by the Spanish and forced to labor in foreign mines. He had returned from his expedition six months later, during Christmas, then resumed his search in January of 1716 with the promise that when his work was completed in the spring, he would return home and devote himself entirely to his wife and only child. Shortly after his departure, Raven's mother had contracted pneumonia and had died. Word of the death of his wife had been sent by the Crown, but Sir Robert failed to return home, and Raven sadly resigned herself to being an orphan.

Raven was so bewildered by the arrival of the letter that she did not notice that the seal had already been broken. She delayed opening it, for she feared that her worst thoughts about her father would be confirmed.

"Go on, child, open it," encouraged John with smooth gentleness. "We are most anxious to hear news of your father."

Raven nodded obediently and tore open the envelope's flap.

"Don't just stand there dumbfounded. Read it aloud," insisted her aunt harshly.

8

Raven's voice quivered with anticipation as she began.

Dear Miss Gatewood: My name is Morgan Taylor, and I am a close friend of your fathers. I met Sir Robert on one of the Bahamian islands where I was surveying the prospect of cotton production two years ago. At that time, he was gravely ill, due to an outbreak of malaria the year before. Because he had remained delirious with the island fever for such an extended period, he could recollect very little of his past. From old letters and government documents, we were able to determine his identity and reconstruct his past. When I found him, an elderly Lucayan woman was caring for Sir Robert, but he needed far more professional attention than her medicinal herbs and love vine tea. It is on your father's behalf that I am writing to you. He begs your forgiveness for not returning home after your mother's death. Notification of such did not reach him until the early part of the spring, and when he attempted to return home, he discovered that because of Spanish infiltration of our waters, transportation would not be available until July. By then, he was too ill to carry on with his plans. I stayed with your father until he was well enough to travel to Nassau, New Providence Island, where he has remained under the very competent supervision of my good friend Dr. Henry Lightbourne. You may rest assured that your father has received expert medical attention. By the time my letter reaches you, I am confident that Robert will have regained sufficient strength to travel to my home on Eleuthera, as Nassau does not offer the healthy atmosphere needed for his complete recovery. Before this year's end, it is imperative that I travel to England, and your father intends to accompany me at such time. He asks that I convey to you his love and concern for your well-being. Sir Robert is most anxious to receive some word from you and asks that any correspondence be directed to Dr. Lightbourne. If I may say so, Miss Gatewood, I feel that any message from you would greatly speed his recovery, for his heart is heavily burdened with tremendous guilt concerning the circumstances of his involuntary abandonment of you.

Forgetting her dislike of her guardians, Raven flung both arms around her aunt's corpulent neck and cried, "Oh, isn't it wonderful that Papa is alive? I cannot believe it! How the poor dear must have suffered! I cannot wait for him to come home!"

"Do sit down, Raven," cooed Martha. "Why, you're quite flushed! I am afraid the excitement has proven too much for you. You look as though you are about to faint." She fanned her niece with her embroidered silk handkerchief.

"He's alive! And he's coming home!" shouted the jubilant girl as she gleefully grabbed her uncle's fleshy arm, swinging him around the room with her.

Martha began her well-planned discussion, cautious not to have Raven suspect her underlying intentions. "Darling, a lot may happen between now and the time your father is able to travel. So please, dearest, for your own sake, do not get your hopes up only to be disappointed."

"What do you mean?" questioned Raven, an uncertain expression shadowing her fine featured face.

John ceremoniously cleared his throat and made a show of sincerity. "All your aunt is saying, dear, is that you mustn't be too optimistic about your father's return. What I mean to say is that I want you to look forward to it, of course, but do not dwell on it in case, well ummm . . ." He gave his niece a fatherly pat on her shoulder. "Honey, after your mother died and your father failed to return home, it grieved your aunt and I so much to see you so despondent. We could tell that your little heart was wracked with grief even though you chose not to discuss your sorrow with us."

"Exactly what is it you're trying to say, Uncle?"

Martha callously interjected. "Both of us hope that everything will work out well, just as God intends it to, but do not permit yourself to become so broken-hearted again if something hinders his return."

After a moment of thought, Raven conceded sadly. "I know that what you say is true. I could not bear the thought of something else happening to him now that I know he is alive. Oh, it is such a long time for me to have to wait to see him. These next months will pass so slowly," she wailed.

Martha gently stroked Raven's head with her icy fingers, grimacing the entire time. "I know, dear. Why, it would be frightful to think that Robert may never see you, especially now that you have grown up to look so much like our darling Elizabeth." She cringed at the mention of her dead sister's name, aware of the bitter taste in her mouth after having said it. Martha swallowed hard and tried to compose herself, knowing that her performance at that moment would determine her own future at Ravenwood. "Oh niece, if only you were a few years older, then . . ." she purposely hesitated. "No, that cannot even be considered."

"What Aunt Martha? Please tell me!" she implored.

"No, no dear," she shrewdly refused. "It was just a silly notion. I do not know why something like that would have even occurred to me," she scoffed, coldly eyeing her niece out of the corner of her beady eye. "Such an undertaking would be far too dangerous, even for a young woman of your maturity and intellect. Your father would never forgive me if he even thought I had suggested something like that to you."

"Whatever are you gibbering about, Martha? I insist you tell us," innocently persisted John, pretending to be as perplexed as Raven even though he had rehearsed this scene many times with his wife.

Martha finally relented. "Oh, all right, if you must know. I was going to suggest that . . . no, it is so foolish. I would never agree to letting her do it."

"Letting me do what?" prodded Raven with impatient curiosity.

"Since you must know, I was going to recommend that you go to New Providence and find your dear father in case he does not—I mean—to make certain that his return trip is a comfortable one." She paused long enough to study her niece's impassive countenance. "But I think it is a far better idea for you to wait here patiently, praying all the while that in due time Robert will return to us healthy and . . . alive."

The bland expression on Raven's face slowly transformed into sudden realization that her aunt's suggestion was the only solution to her dilemma. "No, Aunt Martha. That is a splendid idea, and I shall do just that! I am a woman, and my Papa needs me by his side." Raven had obviously fallen prey to the Meyers' carefully devised scheme.

Martha approached her niece, her eyes squinted in worry. "But darling, if something were to happen to you, your father would most definitely hold us responsible. Please, for our sakes, do reconsider."

"I am old enough to make my own decisions. I am quite certain Father would appreciate your trying to stop me, but it is useless for you to attempt to do so," she said staunchly.

John wiped beads of perspiration from his wrinkled forehead and nervously cracked his knuckles. "Raven, I know I have not been the guardian uncle to you I should have been, for having no children myself, I was quite awkward in your presence. But I simply cannot allow you to undertake such a dangerous sea voyage. Why, a girl of your youth is vulnerable to all sorts of problems. I beg you, niece, remain here with us and wait for your father's return. Six or seven months isn't an eternity. And it would take such a worry from my mind."

Raven was more determined than ever to proceed with her plans. "Nothing you can say will make me change my mind. I intend to go. I trust you will make the necessary arrangements for me, Uncle. My passage must be booked as soon as possible!" The determined young woman left the room, resolved to remain steadfast in her decision. Her two relatives smirked guilefully as they exchanged cunning winks.

"Well done, my dear," congratulated John after a brief silence.

"Hush, you fool!" snarled Martha viciously. "Do you want her to hear you? Here, pour me another," she demanded, shoving her empty brandy snifter at him.

"Whatever you say, dearest," replied John with mocking adoration.

After a few more minutes, Martha's wine-flushed face relaxed into a cynical grin. She conceitedly patted a tawdry silk rose that was perched crookedly in her coarse, frizzy hair. "An ingenious plan, wouldn't you say, John?"

"Absolutely! And executed magnificently!"

"Quite a stroke of luck," continued Martha. "For four years I have patiently waited for such an opportune moment. No longer will I be forced to contend with that sniveling whelp. You and I shall be the master and mistress of Ravenwood."

"But what if—" began John hesitantly, for he did not wish to upset his wife and bring an end to her uncharacteristically good humor. "What I mean to say is, in the event that she does reach Robert, what do you suppose will happen to us?"

Martha's smile was one of smug confidence. "I doubt that ever happening. Even if she was to survive a three week voyage among a group of lusty sailors, and even if Robert does survive his bout with island fever, we will not be subjected to his wrath. After all, did we not expressly forbid Raven to make such a journey? Even she will attest to our reluctance in permitting her to travel to New Providence."

"I suppose you are right. All sorts of things could happen to a virginal young woman before she reaches her destination. And people have been known to have fatal relapses even after a seemingly smooth recovery from malaria," mentioned John hopefully.

"And now, my darling husband, I would like to propose a toast," suggested Martha gaily. "To the Spanish and to pirates. To foul weather and hungry sharks!"

"To our niece's misfortunes at sea," concluded John as their glasses clicked together.

## Chapter Two

Raven gazed absently into the murky waters below, too deeply absorbed in her own weary thoughts to notice the boisterous, brawny sailors who were hoisting weighty casks of cargo onto the deck of the *Fancy Free*. Frigid winds blustered threateningly across Plymouth Harbor, ripping underneath the thick, gray brocade the young woman wore and forcing her to draw the ruffled, velvet cloak even tighter around her shivering body. Tears surfaced in her eyes as flurried thoughts of leaving her beloved homeland clouded her mind. Her heart was filled with anger and malice for the guardians who had professed such concern for her well-being, and she deliberately ignored the hypocritical farewells and the pretentious exclamations of "Best wishes," and "Safe journey," from her aunt and uncle, who were standing on the dock below.

Her troubled thoughts returned to the evening she had disclosed the contents of Morgan Taylor's letter. She had returned to the library several minutes after her hasty departure to retrieve the letter she had left on the sofa. Unbeknown to her aunt and uncle, she had overheard them discussing how well they would prosper once the problem of their niece's disposal had been so shrewdly solved. Upon listening to them laughingly toast to her misfortunes at sea, she had realized that she had unknowingly been ensnared by the insidious trap. She glared stonily at the jubilant pair as they turned to leave. "You may think yourselves rid of me, but your victory will be short-lived. When Papa and I return home, you will rue the day you ever set foot on my father's estate," she vowed ardently.

When the sight of land completely disappeared Raven became uneasy, for it was then that she realized the creaking, four-masted ship would be her home for the next twenty-one days.

"What's the matter, lass? You look like you haven't a friend in the world."

Raven's fears were temporarily forgotten when she looked upon the tanned, weather-beaten face of Captain Horatio Mabry.

He decorously introduced himself. "And as captain of this ship, I can assure you that she is very sound. I would say that the *Fancy Free* is one of the most seaworthy vessels in the entire British merchant fleet."

She blushed ingenuously. "Is it that noticeable that I am scared out of my wits?"

"Well, Miss . . . uh?"

"Gatewood, sir, Raven Gatewood. I shall be traveling with you as far as New Providence."

The captain bowed ceremoniously. "I am very pleased to make your acquaintance. You had such a forlorn look on your pretty face that I knew it must be from dread of the sea. Your first time, of course?" His soothing cockney tone calmed her uneasiness.

She explained her situation lamely, trying to control

the contortions within her, for she felt her stomach heave unmercifully with each wave. She felt dizzy. "I have never been away from land before. Or, for that matter, away from home."

"Perfectly understandable, I assure you. It will take you some time to get your sea legs about you."

Raven gave him a questioning look, never having heard such an expression.

"It means to become used to the motion of the waves," translated the captain to his companion, who was turning a greenish hue. He was helpless to comfort her, but he knew that she would stand a better chance of a quick recovery if she stayed a little longer on deck.

"I certainly hope it comes soon!" Raven steadied herself against the railing. Soon she felt the color creeping back into her wan cheeks. "She certainly is a magnificent ship, Captain Mabry. I must admit, she is not at all what I expected."

"Aye, lass. And stout, too. I have been sailing her to the colonies nigh on five years. She's a grand lady, one of England's finest!"

The wind and sun had etched many impressions on the kindly captain's face, giving him a wrinkled, harsh appearance, and making it most difficult to judge his age. Probably between forty and sixty, decided Raven. Even though she had been cautioned at an early age against associating with strangers without proper introduction, Mabry's gentleness and genuine show of concern for her welfare made Raven feel completely at ease in his presence.

"I am sure you are rather fatigued, Miss Gatewood, so I will not detain you. We shall have a better chance to continue our conversation later in the day. In the meantime, allow me to show you to your quarters. I hope you will find them to your liking—quite comfortable, a wee bit small, perhaps." He offered her his arm, and smiling demurely, she graciously accepted it.

The size of her accommodations for the next three weeks was a fraction of the size of her room at home. Extending from one wall was a narrow, shelflike bed; from the other a dressing table of equal length with three drawers. Seeing that her two trunks had been promptly delivered and stowed underneath her berth, she decided to take a nap before beginning the tedious task of unpacking. The gentle undulation of the waves lulled her to sleep, and Raven dreamed she and her father were on a ship bound for home.

For dinner that evening Raven chose to wear a simple, modestly cut, pale yellow gown. The loose-twilled silk accentuated the female endowments that had emerged from her boyish figure just this past year. After much time looking at her reflection in the tarnished, unframed mirror above the dressing table, she decided to wear her hair loosely gathered on each side of her face with combs, instead of pinning it up in a tight, severe knot. Opening her mother's alabaster jewel case, she removed a small cameo broach attached to a strip of black velvet and fastened it around her slender, cream-colored neck. Stepping back from the mirror, she once again studied her image and marveled admiringly at her likeness to her mother. She reminded herself to guard against vanity, even though she was sure her father would be pleased at the similarity.

Raven had already formulated plans of how she would locate her father. After her arrival in Nassau, she would find the Dr. Lightbourne of Mr. Taylor's letter, who would no doubt be able to direct her to her father, even if he were no longer under his supervision. If her father had already left for Eleuthera with Taylor she would have to wait in Nassau until she would be able to board a boat for the outer island. She brought with her a tidy sum of money just for such an emergency.

The entire day's journey from Saxton to Plymouth Harbor by coach had been most exciting, even though her aunt complained about her poor back's discomfort the entire distance. The friendly simplicity of the country folk, their quaint way of life, and the unfamiliar sites of the sleepy coastal town fascinated Raven.

Leaving the tiny room, Raven cautiously made her way down the narrow corridor, steadying herself with outstretched hands on the polished cedar walls, to the dining room beside the captain's quarters. What was that funny comment Captain Mabry made? she mused. Oh yes, I shall have my sea legs in due time.

The room was not nearly as large as she had imagined. Most of its space was taken up by a long, mahogany table with nine slender chairs, four on each side plus one at the head of the table. Apparently the room was intended only for the use of the captain and his guests since the crew members ate their meals at their posts. Maps and charts covered each of the walls. Already seated at the table were the captain and a young couple.

The captain's raucous voice echoed in the small room. "Ah, Raven. I am so pleased to see you are looking so much better! It would have been a terrible blow to my reputation to lose a passenger so soon after having set sail!" He and the young gentleman both stood as she entered. Blushing noticeably at his remark about her sea sickness, she seated herself to the left of Mabry, across from the others.

"Raven," began the captain in his booming voice, "allow me to introduce Dr. Roscoe Fairmont, who is traveling with his sister Lucy."

"I am so pleased to meet you both," replied Raven charmingly, but with reserved enthusiasm.

"It is so nice having another female on board. I am sure that we shall become fast friends. Are you going to Charleston also?" Lucy was, by nature, very inquisitive, and was often dubbed cheeky by those who did not know her.

Raven took an immediate liking to the pert, auburn-haired girl. "No, I am going only as far as Nassau. My father has been rather ill for some time, and I intend to join him there and accompany him back to England on Captain Mabry's return voyage."

"When will your chaperon be joining us, Raven?" asked Lucy, assuming that a girl of her own age would have an older matron traveling with her.

"I am traveling alone. My mother is dead, and there was no one who could make the trip with me."

The young doctor had been staring intently at Raven from the moment she entered the room. He studied her completely, totally captivated by the emerald forests of her eyes. "Do you think that is wise, Miss Gatewood?"

"My brother has some rather archaic ideas about women." She stung Ross with a dartling glare.

Raven sensed some sort of family problem and decided it best to ignore Lucy's comment. "Actually,

Dr. Fairmont, there is very little trouble I could encounter on this ship, and once we arrive in Nassau, I shall be under the supervision of my father. I am sure convention can be forgotten this one time." Then she tactfully attempted to divert the conversation to something other than herself. "Do you plan to reside in Charleston, or are you visiting relatives there?"

"We shall be living there," answered Ross, giving his sister a sidelong glance.

She was quick to retort. "But only for a year. Ross has volunteered his medical services in the colonies until next March. He just completed his studies at Oxford and felt that a year away from London would be most beneficial to his career."

"And you chose to accompany your brother?" inquired Mabry, who had said very little, giving the younger ones a better chance to get acquainted.

Lucy's face lowered, and her eyes clouded with tears. Ross hastened to explain. "I am afraid it was not much of a choice on Lucy's part, sir. Our parents were both killed in a fire last year, and since we've no relatives, the only solution was for us to remain together."

Lucy's disheartened attitude slowly vanished, and she forced herself to smile. "So we are off to the New World to seek our fortunes." Then she became even more spirited as she boasted about her brother. "I am sure Ross will be the best physician Charleston ever hoped to have. Why, at the university, Dr. Farrow told him that he had never had a student with so much natural ability."

"Ah, here are the other passengers now," Mabry announced as two middle-aged men entered the room. "Mr. Baxter and Mr. Phillips."

Lionel Baxter, an epicure of delectable foods and fine port, was a heavy man whose protruding stomach served as a rest for his puffy, folded hands. His rubicund neck was hidden by the last fold of a three-layered chin, causing the buttoning of his French laced shirt to be a most uncomfortable chore.

Mathew Phillips, his contrasted companion, appeared to have missed as many meals as Baxter had overindulged in. He was skinny, almost birdlike, with an aquiline nose extending from between popping, myopic eyes.

Once again, courtesies were exchanged, introductions made, and the newcomers were seated; Baxter beside Raven and Phillips beside Ross. Polite conversation ensued. Soon the meal was served by a short, squatty cabin boy named Benjy, who did not look a day over thirteen years old.

"Tell Cookie he's going to spoil us before the voyage is barely underway!" bellowed the captain. Baked chicken, pearl onions in cream sauce, and a dish of steaming hot red potatoes were placed in the center of the table. Mabry's voice lowered to barely a whisper. "You'll do well to enjoy the feast tonight, folks, for the meals do get progressively, uh, less appetizing."

Ross, passing the chicken first to Raven and then to Lucy, curiously inquired of the captain. "How do you manage to store enough food for your sailors and passengers without the food spoiling, sir?"

"Perhaps you saw cages of chickens and pigeons and our goats as they were loaded aboard. We have pens for the animals at the rear of the forequarter, thus our supply of eggs, milk, meat and squab. Potatoes, onions, and cabbages last for several weeks in bins in the galley, along with dried beans and dried fruits. You shall not want for food on my ship, for despite my little joke about the meals, everyone is well fed. There is a more than adequate supply of dried cod, bully beef, and salt tack."

He noticed the passengers' puzzled glances at the containers of juice beside their water glasses. "Lime juice, preserved with salt, ladies and gentlemen. I insist that passengers and crew alike drink the juice every day to ward off scurvy. A simple precaution!" He lifted his glass of juice and toasted to the passengers.

"What about fresh water?" questioned Baxter, in between large mouthfuls of food. "Is there enough on board to last the duration of the journey?"

"We have a more than sufficient amount, sir. During our first rainfall, we shall replenish our supply. Of course, if the supply of water diminishes faster than we figured, we have full casks of brandy and rum in the ship's hole."

The audience chuckled at his joke, their captain obviously had a keen sense of humor. He encouraged their questions throughout the meal, even though his answering them allowed him very little time to enjoy his food. He relished being able to entertain his guests, the opportunity to put on his dress uniform and use refined manners, being in the company of women, and engaging the men in interesting conversation. He usually ate with his crew on deck rather than dining alone. He informed his guests of his responsibilities as captain in the British merchant fleet. It was his obligation to transport tea and brandy to New Providence and then to Charleston. In Nassau he would exchange some of the load for tortoise shells and indigo, which he would later use for bartering with the colonists.

"What about pirates, captain? Are you aware that our government is still apprehensive about them?" asked Baxter, peering over his plateful of food while fastidiously removing the skins from the potatoes. He was an advisor to King George, en route to the colonies to view the living conditions and to report back to the Crown on the colonists' loyalty: an assignment for which he lacked enthusiasm.

"I am not worried about those cutthroats," Mabry replied confidently, "for our cargo ships are four-masted and can easily outrun their leaky, rotten boats. Why, their crews are just a bunch of ill-nurtured, drunken outcasts."

Such talk made Raven and Lucy visibly nervous, and they exchanged worried, questioning looks. Even Mr. Phillips fidgeted uncomfortably in his seat.

Ross tried to dispel their fears. "We are on a fast ship which is manned by capable, experienced mariners. So there is no need for you all to look so distraught."

"The doctor's right, ladies. There is no need for any worry on that account. We will not fall easy prey to that scummy lot. Besides, many of them have abandoned their profession. The punishment of death by the gallows is strictly enforced. Eat up," he encouraged, as Benjy brought in trays of dried fruit and cheese for their dessert.

Phillips, a botanist who was to do extensive research on the flora of the Carolinas for the Crown, inquired, "Piracy used to be a very honorable profession, did it not captain? Quite a gentleman's calling, I believe."

"Indeed it was," answered Mabry, who had a flair for history and a willingness to share his knowledge with others. "At one time, kings encouraged private vessels to wage war against enemy countries. It cost the government nothing to inflict such injury. The privateers were allowed to keep most of the captured booty in return for their service. Each captain carried with him a letter of marque from the ruler of his country that was his protection against the gallows."

Lucy, who thought the idea of privateering romantic and adventurous, was confused. "How did they get such a bad reputation if they were helping to protect their countries?"

"In 1713," began Mabry, "the peace of Utrecht was signed, establishing bonds of friendship throughout Europe. Privateers began attacking friendly vessels since there were no more rivalries between countries."

"What about now, captain? Are we in great danger of pirates?" Raven was duly concerned since John and Martha had discussed them as being one possible means of Raven never reaching New Providence.

"We are in very little danger, my girl, even though we will be in Bahamian waters. You see, the Bahamas used to be a favored place among the pirates because of its hundreds of harbors and hidden creeks that could protect them from storms or government troops. Woodes Rogers, the governor there now, is trying to supress piracy. He offered amnesty to all those who would surrender to him by September fifth, 1718, this past year. Those who did give up their plundering were hired to clean up Nassau and to assist in bringing renegade pirates to trial. Actually, very few are left of that whole motley lot. And my men are expertly versed

26

in the use of their muskets, pistols, and cutlasses. They're just itching for a chance to settle some old scores with any of those scoundrels who may try to waylay this ship!" The captain winked triumphantly at his audience and patted the cutlass hanging from his belt.

With their dinner and conversation ending on a more promising tone, the men excused themselves, deciding to accompany the captain to his adjoining cabin for an after-dinner smoke and brandy and left Raven and Lucy to entertain themselves.

A faint tapping on the door roused Raven from her placid slumber some nights later. After calling out "Who is it?" to be answered by a despondent "It's me," she stumbled, half-awake, to the arched entrance. "Good heavens, Lucy. What time is it?" she asked incredulously, opening the door to a tearful, dishevelled Lucy.

"Please, let me stay with you for a while. I have to talk to someone or I shall go mad!" pleaded the hysterical girl.

"Of course. Come on in," said Raven gently, arm around her sobbing companion as she led the girl over to the tiny bed.

During the past twelve days at sea the two young women had developed a warm-hearted fondness for each other, the only closeness Raven had ever experienced for anyone other than her parents. Even though the two girls were within days of being the same age, Raven felt very protective of Lucy and could sense her sorrow and anxiety, even though the auburn-haired girl had chosen not to disclose her problems.

Lucy sat on the edge of the bed in Raven's embrace, her tears unrelenting. After several minutes she was able to partially compose herself, and wincing, told Raven of her dilemma.

"I love Ross so much, and I tried to be a good sister to him, but I refuse to continue this charade, even for him," she blurted.

"Charade? Whatever are you talking about, Lucy?"

Lucy tried to explain. "I am in love with someone of whom Ross does not approve. I tried to convince him to allow Jean-Claude and I to marry, but he would hear nothing of it. He said that since Jean-Claude's mother was a French actress, he is a philanderer and lacks ambition, and that he's only interested in marrying me because he thinks my parents left us vast wealth." She wiped the tears with the sleeve of her flannel nightgown. "I think keeping me away from him was the real reason Ross wanted to go to the Carolinas."

Raven objectively tried to reason with Lucy. "Ross must certainly have had other objections to Jean-Claude besides his heritage. Perhaps he knows something bad about him and does not wish to disclose his true reasons for fear of hurting you."

Lucy quickly disagreed. "No, Raven. There can be nothing detrimental in Jean-Claude's character. He's so handsome, ever so kind, and would do nothing to hurt me. I am confident he loves me as much as I love him." At the mention of her lover's name, Lucy's eyes sparkled through the tears. "The real reason Ross hates Jean-Claude is because of his sister, Louisa. They were engaged to be married, but she eloped with Ross's closest friend instead. And now I am being punished for his unhappiness.

"Surely Ross does not begrudge the love you and Jean-Claude have for each other because of something his sister did. He seems much too sensible for that," remarked Raven, feeling that Ross's concern for Lucy was genuine and typically brotherly.

"Oh, but he does. He even refused to let me see Jean-Claude before we left. I love him so much, Raven, but I cannot bear the thought of Ross hating me for it. I just don't see how I can exist without Jean-Claude. I am going to be so miserable during the entire year we spend in Charleston. He's promised to wait for me to return to London, but a year is so long for a man to wait. Besides, in a year, I wi— Uh . . . uh . . ." She began sobbing rapidly, her tears falling freely.

Raven attempted to console her friend. "Cheer up, Lucy. If your beau loves you as much as you love him, then a year's separation will only strengthen that love. Goodness, I'm a fine one to give advice on such matters. I've never even had a boy walk in the garden with me," she admitted sadly. "I guess your brother is the only young man I've ever had a chance to talk with." But Lucy was not listening to her comforter's problems.

"It is as though I am going to waste an entire year of my life in Charleston. Jean-Claude promised to come at Christmas and try to convince Ross that his intentions are indeed honorable, but I know it will do no good. Had it not been for that flighty sister, Ross would never have left London, and I could still be in Jean-Claude's arms!" She wailed endlessly, throwing her head onto the bed and burying her face in the pillow.

"There, there Lucy," whispered Raven, stroking

Lucy's long, red curls. "If Jean-Claude is the kind of man you think him to be, he will wait for you. And if he is not, it would be so much better for you to find out now. Besides, Charleston must be overflowing with handsome, eligible men who would welcome the chance to court you."

Lucy's tense body relaxed, and she looked at Raven shamefacedly. "I suppose you think I am terribly selfish, thinking only of my own happiness with no consideration for Ross." She rubbed her eyes, swollen and red from too many tears, waiting for Raven's judgment.

"Of course not, Lucy. As a matter of fact, I think you are the most unselfish person I know. You care about how others feel. If you didn't you would have disobeyed Ross with no regard for his feelings. You're a woman who is obviously in love. No one can fault you for that." She patted Lucy's hands and rubbed her fingertips across Lucy's gnawed nails. "All this worry isn't going to change anything. Now, it's almost dawn. Why don't you try to get some sleep before breakfast, then later in the day you can tell me all about the plans you and your fiancé have made." She gave Lucy a reassuring pat on the back as she helped her to the door.

After Lucy had returned to her own cabin, Raven lie awake, unable to return to her peaceful slumber. Instead she thought about the love Lucy shared with Jean-Claude. In a way, she envied her troubled friend. How wonderful it must feel to have a man's strong arms encompassing your body, to be tenderly kissed and protectively held. A strange desire began to rouse in Raven, and she knew instinctively that if she were to get any more rest such thoughts must vanish.

That morning, after a breakfast of tea and crumpets in her room, Raven decided to go for an airing on the top deck. The warm, early morning sun and the balmy ocean breeze never failed to make her feel vibrant and wonderfully alive. How she loved the feel of salty water spraying her face as she watched the whitecaps of the waves disappear as the majestic ship glided effortlessly through the azure water! She could amuse herself on the deck for hours on end. She now laughed aloud at her earlier inhibitions and fears of being confined on a "Leaky, worn ship in the middle of the ocean." She now viewed the *Fancy Free* as her protective fortress, sheltering her from the greed and malice of her relatives and the uncertainty of venturing alone into an unknown land. She was truly happy, completely at ease with herself and content to be at sea enjoying the company of the other passengers. She and Lucy had attained a kindred closeness, and a strange, never before felt attraction had developed between she and Ross. Captain Mabry was always joking with her, teasing her and calling her affectionately "My girl" and never seemed to tire of her unending questions about the ship's routine operations.

Raven looked upon her new adventure the way her father had encouraged her to view any unusual situation; as a learning experience. Her studies had never been neglected; Sir Robert had seen to that, even though the consensus of their society was that females had little need of formal learning. A governess had resided at Ravenwood until Raven turned twelve, teaching her quick-minded pupil basic grammar, numbers, and French. Then Raven's mother patiently

31

nurtured her in deportment, the necessary accomplishments of any young lady of good breeding: art, conversation, music, needlepoint, and the social graces required of their aristocratic society. Later, Sir Robert had instilled in her grasping mind a youthful appreciation for great works of literature and an understanding of the lessons to be learned from Chaucer's worldly travelers, Shakespeare's tragically flawed characters, and Milton's profound Puritan wisdom. Raven was determined not to flinch in her desire for knowledge. Mr. Baxter and Mr. Phillips both offered her opportunities to further enhance her educational growth. From Baxter she learned much of government affairs. He delighted in their afternoon discussions about the Hanover king who was frequently absent from his Cabinet meetings because he did not understand the English language or conventions and made little effort to do so, preferring to remain in his small province in Germany instead of ruling England. Mr. Baxter seemed certain that because King George left that chore to his various advisors, problems and dissension would be the downfall of this monarch; many of his trusted advisors were corrupt and ruthless. And from Mr. Phillips Raven learned an appreciation of nature. He saw in her an avid botany student. She had a flair for remembering the Latin names and the characteristics of the plants and flowers he discussed with her.

"Do you mind sharing some of your scenery with me?" asked Ross, who had been observing her morning meditation for the past half hour. "Or if I am disturbing your solitude, I will leave." The young man was, by nature, a reluctant conversationalist in the presence of women. This timidity worsened after his shattered romance with Louisa.

"Of course you are not disturbing me," was her prompt answer. She held out her hand, beckoning him to join her. Ross stood with his hands in his pockets, looking out over the waters, wondering what would be an opportune time to reveal his feelings for her.

"I was just thinking of how fortunate I have been in meeting so many wonderful people," she said, sensing his nervousness. "Before the trip, I had convinced myself that the voyage would be dull and the ship cramped, but things are not like that at all. I quite dread the prospect of leaving the ship when I arrive in Nassau and saying good-bye to all of my new-found friends, especially to you and Lucy."

Her words furnished the bashful young man with a surge of confidence and courage. He spoke eagerly. "That is exactly how I feel, Raven. It was fate that brought us all here together like this, and in another ten days we must part, perhaps never to see one another again." Ross took Raven's hand and tenderly brushed his lips across her fingertips.

She blushed uncomfortably for fear that Ross had misunderstood her meaning. She liked Ross as a dear friend, and she admitted to herself, on several occasions, she had even thought of him romantically. But such fantasies failed to provide the tingling sensations she felt were sure to accompany such speculations. He was certainly handsome, though not much taller than she, with wavy blond hair that curled in ringlets around his deep-set temples, and agate, incandescent eyes that pondered every situation with intense objectivity.

Ross assumed her reserved attitude stemmed from

being bashfully shy in the company of the opposite sex. How unlike Louisa, who flitted about boldly from man to man! He resolved to convince Raven of his sentiments. "I know, Raven, that it is too soon for either of us to reveal our true emotions, but I am compelled to be forthright. I feel certain that I am falling in love with you for you are constantly in my thoughts. You are the kind of woman I have hoped for for so long, and I want you to know of my adoration of you. Before you speak, I realize that by so suddenly pouring out my heart to you I am placing myself in a very vulnerable position, but I do not believe that you would use the situation to your advantage. You are too much of a lady to be so callously cruel."

Raven faltered, not knowing what must be said. "Ross, I am truly honored that you feel so for me, but I—" she hesitated, not wishing to hurt him, or even worse, make him feel foolish.

"What is it, Raven?" he implored, then with the realization that perhaps she was engaged to someone else, he dropped her hand from his hold. "There's someone else isn't there? He's waiting for you to return to England to him," he bitterly surmised.

She answered quickly, smiling slightly at such a thought. "Heavens no, Ross. There truly isn't anyone. Everything has happened so quickly that I am just unsure of my feelings. And until I can be perfectly honest with you, it would not be fair for me to encourage your attentions."

"Oh, my sweet girl, I understand." His eyes were full of hope. "I do not ask you to make any rash decision about us, just to think pleasantly of what I have said.

For the next year both of us have totally different intentions, and we each must do what is important; you with your father and me with my career. Perhaps during that year we may correspond, and then when we have both returned to England, you will allow me to come visit you from time to time. We shall give our feelings the opportunity to grow and become stronger," assured Ross, drawing Raven into his stiff, unsure arms. "I can honestly say that I have never known anyone like you: so beautiful, so demure. You possess an aura of goodness that most women lack. So kind, wonderful. . . ." His lips nervously sought Raven's heart-shaped ones, and Raven, at first with a timid uncertainly, experienced the sweet joy of her first kiss. They became totally engrossed in each other, exchanging long, lingering kisses in the salty air.

After a while, their bodies separated, and Ross, in an effort to restrain himself, asked Raven to tell him about the circumstances leading up to her voyage. He had heard only bits and pieces from Lucy and admitted that his sister had a tendency to be overly imaginative. She reluctantly told her suitor of her mother's death, the unpleasantness of living with relatives who sought only to control Ravenwood, and of the letter from Morgan Taylor. Seeing the sorrowful effect such reminiscing had on her, he diverted her thoughts elsewhere.

"Ravenwood. What an unusual name. How did it get its name?" asked Ross, gently grasping Raven's hands and stroking her long, pointed fingers.

The girl proudly told him of her great-grandfather's building of the gray stone home in the mid fifteen hundreds, after receiving a crown grant from King

Richard, and of his naming the estate after the jet-black crowlike birds that covered the meadows at dusk every evening.

"And were you named for the bird as well?" he teased, wishing once more to feel the silkiness of her ebony tresses against his face.

"Indirectly so, I suppose. To see a raven was a reminder of impending doom, but to my family, it has always proven to be an omen of good luck."

From behind them came the familiar clearing of a harsh, low voice. Both Ross and Raven flushed and turned abruptly to see Captain Mabry pleasantly eyeing them.

"Sorry to interrupt your conversation, but I'm in bad need of your services, Doctor. One of the mates fell below. I think his foot is broken and it'll need setting." Mabry had hoped that a romance would flourish between the two young passengers, and he was pleased that the shy doctor had finally made the move in that direction.

"Of course, Captain. Just allow me to get my supplies," Ross replied professionally. Glancing over his shoulder, he added questioningly. "Perhaps we may continue our conversation after awhile?"

Raven nodded in reply and watched Mabry and Ross disappear into the passenger's area below. I really do like Ross, she thought, but she was not sure of any serious inclinations. Making plans for next year was much too hasty. Still, Ross had awakened in her a woman's desire, and she shivered remembering the searching kisses of her cherubic-faced wooer.

The wind gustily picked up speed, and Raven decided to go to her cabin before being swept overboard by the mid-March gale. Settling comfortably on her berth with *The Canterbury Tales* propped on her lap, she tried to concentrate on the three roisters' search for death but found it increasingly difficult to erase Ross's touch from her mind.

During the noon meal, the skipper informed the passengers of their progress at sea. Because of very favorable winds, the ship was able to maintain a constant speed of seven knots. If such conditions continued, their arrival date in Nassau would be in nine days, on the twenty-ninth of the month. Everyone knew of Raven's excitement over the prospect of seeing her father for the first time in four years, but by Ross's dejected countenance, she could tell that he did not relish the thought of her departure. She had never intended to be flighty and toy with his emotions the way Louisa had done, and she hoped that he did not view her as such a person. She had silently admitted her selfish thoughts about Ross. It was indeed invigorating knowing that someone had professed his love for her and would be willing to wait an entire year for her to decide her feelings. She decided to give his proposal ample consideration, reasoning that perhaps in a year, when they had returned to England, she could honestly return his affections. What harm was there in a few innocent kisses now and then, she reasoned.

Lucy's absence from the table worried the others, for even Ross did not know her whereabouts. Raven hoped she wasn't in another of her melancholic states, languishing in pity over her separation from Jean-Claude. She decided to check in on Lucy afterward, taking with her a slight snack prepared by the cook.

"Lucy, I've brought a tray for you. May I come in?"

she called, unable to balance the tray with one hand and open the door with the other. "You'll have to open the door for me."

Raven saw immediately that Lucy had indeed been wallowing in tears. She placed the tray on the dressing table. Instead of comforting her in her sorrow, she scolded harshly. "I thought you promised there would be no more of this nonsense. You have to accept things the way they are and not continue to sit alone in this stuffy cabin brooding your life away."

Lucy made a genuine attempt to compose herself. "I know I cannot sit in here all the time Raven, and I really had no intention of doing that this afternoon. But right before noon I decided to write another letter to Jean-Claude. Captain Mabry promised to post them the moment he returned to Plymouth. Anyway, as silly as it may sound, the more I wrote, the sadder I became. I couldn't let everyone see me like this." She wiped the remnants of her sadness from her dark, narrow eyes. "Anyway, thanks for bringing me some food. I was becoming ravenous."

Raven was pleased to see her friend in better spirits and decided from now on she could achieve more by scolding Lucy in her fits of moodiness instead of sympathizing with her. "Alright, you silly twit. You had better eat before you faint from hunger."

In between bits of biscuits and bully beef, Lucy questioned Raven about her feelings toward her brother. "It's so obvious that Ross is enamoured of you. I'm sure everyone has noticed those cow-eyed expressions of his when you are around." She giggled.

Raven embarrasingly shrugged at Lucy's comments. "Ross and I are friends, Lucy, just as you and I are.

38

Your brother is very handsome and extremely talented, with an excellent future ahead of him. He is the only man who has ever paid the slightest attention to me. I am grateful of his concern and interest in me, but I am not sure what else I feel. You know as well as I that Ross is just recovering from a cruel love affair, and I do not want to be someone to whom those emotions can be transferred. Please don't think I'm leading him on, Lucy, because I truly am not. Earlier this morning I explained my reservations to him, and we agreed to wait and see how our feelings will progress when the two of you return to England."

For once, it was Lucy who spoke reassuringly. "I know you would never deliberately hurt anyone, Raven. I was just curious; actually a little nosy. Ross refuses to discuss affairs of the heart with little sister." Lucy grinned at the crimson color that flushed Raven's high, dimpled cheeks. "What plans have you for later on?"

"Oh, I was going to read for a while, perhaps work on some embroidery. Later, Mr. Phillips promised to show me some more sketches of flora. And you?"

"I believe I will go see Ross. I have been absolutely wretched to him lately. Maybe since he's so in love with you, I will be more successful in convincing him to allow Jean-Claude to visit us at Christmas." She hesitated for a moment before suggesting, "Perhaps I shall come by your cabin later, if you are free, and we can talk a bit before meeting the others for dinner."

Raven nodded her approval. "That sounds grand, Lucy. See you then." She waved good-bye and left the small cabin. She was glad that Lucy respected her need for privacy and did not insist that she follow her friend about all day. Lucy truly was a wonderful companion, even with her momentary lapses of melancholia. Raven missed the warm vivacity of her friendship with Lucy already. Perhaps, once arriving on New Providence, she would also miss her newly found admirer.

## Chapter Three

Three days later drenching rains began pelting the ship, and by the seventeenth day of the voyage, the languid seas had suddenly transformed into raging torrents. Huge thunderheads formed in the usually clear skies, and the once foam-figured waves weltered bellowingly over the decks of the tossing ship. Despite her closely furled sails, the *Fancy Free* was at the storm's mercy, and she was heaved about directionless in the waters. The darkened, treacherous sea was illuminated only by arrowy bolts of glaring lightning that accompanied the unending thundery roars. It became increasingly difficult for the crew to hold the ship on her charted course. With each enormous wave the stern of the vessel was lifted out of the water, lunging the bow forward into the salty depths of the wave's valley until the wave outdistanced the ship. Fifteen-foot waves encompassed the deck frequently, plunging the ship headlong into violent surges.

At the onset of the tumultuous commotion, the captain ordered all passengers to the ship's chartroom, reasoning they would feel safer in numbers and would be less likely to interfere with his men's duties. Even though he was worried about the effects of the storm, he assured his petrified group that he had successfully weathered storms far worse than this.

Lucy and Raven sat huddled in one corner of the chartroom, both frantically praying for a safe delivery from the deadly grasp of the sea. On the other side of the room, Ross and Mr. Phillips were busy comforting Baxter, who was wretching with the agony of sea sickness.

At midnight the hull of the ship rammed headlong into a reef with such an impact that it sounded as though the great ship would break in half. It violently rolled with each wave, crashing upon the reef time and time again. After what seemed to be hundreds of such rolls, a monstrous wave lifted the *Fancy Free* clear of the reef and laid it into shallow, calmer waters inside the reef, protected from the ferocious, open seas.

Several hours later the first mate came below with a message from Captain Mabry. He told them that after hitting the reef the ship was swept to the lee side of the southern tip of Abaco, a point some fifty miles northeast of New Providence. He assured them that this position afforded relief from the mountainous southeasterly seas, and suggested that they all return to their cabins, for each person's help would be needed early the following day to help ready the ship for her continuing voyage.

"Excuse me, Mr. Heimes." Phillips stepped timidly forward. "Before you return to your post, may I inquire as to how extensive our damages are?"

"That cannot be determined until morning when we have enough light to thoroughly inspect the ship. I will say though that any ship that can withstand such a storm as the one we've just experienced must be extremely fit and sound," replied the first mate.

Phillips helped an embarrassed Mr. Baxter to his feet and supported his companion's massive bulk with very little difficulty as he assisted him to his cabin.

"I am still shaking, Ross," said Raven as the young doctor escorted his sister and Raven to their cabins. "I thought for sure we would all be killed. I cannot believe I was so naive as to think the seas would be smooth and calm the entire time. Were you not frightened the least bit? You looked so assured and acted so gallantly in trying to make the rest of us comfortable," she complimented.

The word "gallantly" obviously pleased Ross, and he drew himself up to his full height, wanting Raven to view him as a brave, dashing hero. "I would be a liar to say I was not scared, Raven," he replied matter-of-factly, placing an arm around both girls' shoulders, "but I was trying to do my best to see to it that no one panicked during that ordeal. Poor Mr. Baxter. I do not believe I have ever seen anyone in such discomfort. As a doctor, I had a duty to all of you, but as a man, my particular responsibility was to you and Lucy," he said, holding Raven tightly against him. Suddenly he became aware of his sister's silence. "Lucy, dear, you are all right, aren't you? I don't believe you've uttered a single word since we left the chartroom."

She answered her brother coolly. "Of course I am all right, Ross. I'm walking, aren't I?"

"Then why the long face, sissy? We've survived the worst of the voyage. I promise you that all will be smooth from now on into Nassau," he assured his sister, tousling her curls. "Why, we should be celebrating this very hour!" he added, trying to spark his sister into a better mood.

Lucy peered at him cheerlessly. "Why should we celebrate?" she scoffed. "During these past few hours, I have learned a very important lesson. It seems that death is always lurking about us. It is ludicrous to make any plans for tomorrow, or even for one hour from now, for there's no guarantee we shall exist a half a second from now."

Ross nodded pensively. He understood exactly what Lucy was referring to. If she were to die because of his insistence that she accompany him to the colonies, the guilt would be forever on his shoulders. He vowed silently that the next morning he would speak with her and ask her forgiveness for his callous treatment of Jean-Claude. Perhaps he would even submit to having Louisa's brother visit them at the end of the year. If the young scholar was indeed serious in his intent to marry Lucy, then Ross had no other choice but to relent.

"I know exactly how you feel, Lucy, and tomorrow I promise we shall discuss the entire matter. But for now, you do need your rest. Don't worry anymore. Everything will be all right." He gave his sister a reassuring pat on the cheek, which she regarded with indifference, and squeezed Raven's hand longingly. "Good night, girls. Remember we're all to be up before dawn to check out the ship."

Lucy's morbid attitude concerned Raven, so she offered to spend the remainder of the night in her friend's room. Solemnly, Lucy agreed to the suggestion and, arm in arm, they entered the damp, musty room. "What were you thinking about in there, Raven, when the ship was tossing about so?"

Raven did not feel such talk would calm Lucy's nerves, but seeing the insistence on her friend's face decided nevertheless to humor her. She thought for a moment before answering. "Oh, I suppose I just sat there most of the time with no thoughts at all, Lucy. I was too scared to think much. I remember worrying a lot about my father. He has no way of knowing that I am on my way to him. Had I been lost at sea it would have taken many months before he would have discovered what had happened to me. And after it was all over, I thought about how pleased my relatives would have been had something fatal happened." She began unbuttoning her wet, torn muslin dress.

Lucy stared glassily at Raven. When she finally spoke, her voice was unvaried in tone. "Do you know what I thought of, Raven? All I thought about was how much I hated my brother for taking me away from Jean-Claude."

"You mustn't be too harsh with Ross, Lucy. He had your better interests at heart, I'm sure. He's probably just as miserable as you right now, imagining all sorts of things that might have happened to you and blaming himself for ever subjecting you to such dangers." She helped Lucy out of her dress and tucked the girl in bed. After a bit Lucy fell asleep, more mentally exhausted than physically.

Trying to balance her body on the edge of the bed, Raven pulled the covers tight around her neck, and reassuringly hugged the whimpering body beside her. Finally, Raven drifted off into a slumber, only to be awakened from her sleep by golden rays of sunshine streaming in through the porthole above the bed. The robust voices of the sailors sounded loud as they called out the reports of their inspection tour. Raven borrowed a dressing gown from Lucy and quickly slipped out of the stuffy room, cautious not to disturb her friend's sleep. When in her own cabin, Raven had to wade across small puddles that dotted the floor. After having dressed standing atop her bed, she ventured up to the top deck.

"Good morning, Captain!" she shouted cheerfully to the gray-whiskered man who was yelling instructions to his burly seamen. Perhaps because of the sun, but more likely due to the experience of last night, the man looked as though he had aged several years and acquired at least a dozen more wrinkles on his haggard face. Standing there, watching him issue commands to his men, Raven remembered how she had taken an immediate liking to him the first time she met the skipper, and her fondness for him had grown quickly. He was not at all as she had imagined a captain of the British merchant fleet to be: no dignified, brass-buttoned uniform, clean shaven face, or immaculately groomed commander, and yet his men and passengers had the utmost confidence in his capabilities. He dressed in the same uniform as his sailors; a simple, linen shirt and trousers and a close-fitting wool cap pulled tight over his head.

Mabry saluted her smiling, but the usual joviality was absent from his worried face. "Raven, darlin', how are you?"

Raven grinned. "Much better, now that we're not being tossed around helplessly in the ocean." She surveyed the land mass ahead of them. "Where are we, Sir?"

"We are on the southern end of Abaco. The storm

brought us over that reef and into shallower waters."
He pointed to a coral, wall-like formation extending a
mile in length and rising to a height of forty-five feet.
"Ain't that a magnificent piece of God's sculpturing?
That wall marks the entrance into New Providence
Channel. I'd say we're within fifty miles of Nassau."

The massive rock barrier made Raven feel small and
insignificant. She shook her head. "I still cannot
believe that we survived that storm. It seemed that at
any moment we would all be hurled out into the water.
And yet, look how calm and clear the ocean is today.
Hardly a ripple! Not at all threatening!"

"Aye, Raven. 'Tis always like this right after a storm.
The ocean is very deceptive. Like a woman, she has
many faces: angry and striking out with her wrath one
moment, the next, subdued and loving."

How odd, comparing the ocean to a woman, thought
Raven. Perhaps it was this comparison that prompted
her next question. "Are you married, Captain Mabry?
Uh, I'm sorry. It really is none of my business."
Ashamed of herself, she added, "I guess my manners as
well as my good sense were jiggled a bit too much last
night. Please, forgive my—"

He waved his hand, hushing her apologies. "No need
for being sorry, gal. It's a perfectly reasonable
question. I was married once. She was a beautiful lass."
His voice became soft, and a distant glow shone in his
eyes. "She died giving birth to our babe. He died, too.
Never could forgive myself for not being there when
she needed me. I remember she used to beg me time and
time again to quit the sea and take a job as a ship
builder in her father's yard. But I always had some
excuse or another. Salt water has flowed through my

47

family's blood for years and years: my father was a seaman as was his father, and his father before him. I reckon the ocean's the only mate for me."

Remembering his loneliness was still very painful for Mabry, and even now he blamed himself for his wife's death twenty years earlier. Turning his back to the silent girl, he wiped his eyes and blew his nose into his worn, red bandanna, complaining of the moisture in the air after a tropical gale. He cleared his throat loudly before speaking. "I'll be taking a boat over later to explore the island a bit. I'll be needing to find some yellow pine timber to mend one of the broken masts. Know anybody that might be interested in going along to bail water?" He gave her an impish grin.

"Bail water?" she asked. "It sounds as though we would sink before reaching shore."

"No need to worry about that. The skiff's been out of the water for some time. Her planking has shrunk and a little water may come in. No danger, though, I assure you."

"All right," she agreed. "I'd enjoy that, Captain."

Mabry ordered his men to lower the dinghy from the side of the *Fancy Free,* and Raven, after discovering that maintaining her balance on the rope ladder that scaled the ship's starboard side was more difficult than she had expected, cautiously seated herself in the small craft. The brown gourd the captain had given her for bailing out water rested on her lap.

As Mabry rowed the dinghy toward the jagged shoreline he told her that the name of the group of islands, Bahamas, was derived from a Spanish word, *bajamar,* meaning "shallow waters."

Raven nodded, remembering that her father had

48

mentioned the same thing to her several years earlier when telling her stories of how the Spanish, in their quest for the fountain of youth, had exploited the islands and the friendly inhabitants. She noticed the boat was beginning to take on water, so she hurriedly began bailing it out.

·"I hope we can get a closer look at that cliff. I have never seen anything quite like it. It's so . . . so overpowering!"

Mabry paused long enough to scratch his bristly whiskers. "I was as close to it last night as I care to get."

Raven looked at him in shocked confusion. "What do you mean? Just how close were we, Captain Mabry?"

He continued rowing and shook his head in disbelief that they had all not been crushed by the rocks. "The force of the wind combined with the power of the waves swept us right up to the edge of that cliff. It was frightening! Sounded like the end of the world! Even above the storm's fury, I could still hear those waves crashing against the rocks. When lightning bolts lit up the sky, I even saw those waves push right over the top of the cliff's peak. Why, had we hit those rocks like the waves did, we would have all been beaten unmercifully against those boulders. The ship would have splintered in a matter of a few short seconds."

Raven shuddered at such a thought. She had not realized just how close their brush with death had been last night. Lucy need never know just how accurate her observation last night about death had been, resolved Raven. A gap at the end of the wall caught her eye, and she asked the skipper about it.

"Sailors call it 'hole in the wall,'" he replied. "It

doesn't look nearly as menacing now as it did last night. You're shirking from your duties, sailor." He pointed to the water oozing in through the boards, and Raven immediately got to work.

"The ocean is a myriad of brilliant colors," she observed wistfully. "Look at all the various hues of the same color. Isn't that unusual? I wonder why it is. This morning the waters around us were a bright green, but farther out I could see patches of brown, light green, and even black. Why is that?"

The captain smiled knowingly. What a good sailor I could have made out of this one had she only been a lad, he thought. "Those colors are very important to us seamen, for that is how we read the sea's depth. A bright green shows a shallow, sandy bottom, while the darker green shows a deeper sand bottom. Black water is nothing more than sea weed on the bottom. When the water looks a reddish brown is when you have to worry, for that indicates reefs and shoals." He then pointed out the various spots in the water where the different hues were most distinguishable.

Raven leaned over the edge. "Look, it's so clear I can see the shells on the bottom. Why, it looks as though I could put my hand down and scoop them up."

Mabry cautioned her against doing so. "It may look that way but it's at least four fathoms deep. If you can't swim, I'd have an awfully hard time pulling you out of there."

Closer to their destination, the captain guided the dinghy through the shallower waters up to the sandy point, and the two explorers pulled it inland, out of reach of the incoming tide. Raven gathered her full skirts around her knees, removed her black, low-heeled slippers, which were already saturated with salt water, and rolled down her heavy woolen stockings, tossing them both into the boat. Mabry was quick to retrieve the shoes, explaining, "You had best take these, lassie. Those sharp shells and pine burrs have no compassion for tender feet."

She blushingly scoffed at her childish behavior, thinking of how her mother used to reprimand her when she found out that her unladylike daughter insisted upon running barefoot through the woods. Raven closed her eyes and began to run. Her lustrous black mane waved behind her in the arid breeze. How good the warm, moist sand felt oozing in between her toes! She trotted faster and faster in the direction of the cliff, but because of her lack of exercise, being confined to the ship's deck, she found herself short-winded and paused to rest. She wanted to kiss the sun-drenched ground beneath her shaky legs, for not too many hours ago she had feared never again setting foot on steady ground. Raven sat down in the sand and watched as the waves gently lapped against the rocks. She was awestruck, for never had she seen anything quite so magnificent as the cliff.

"Don't get any closer to those rocks," warned Mabry, huffing and puffing after catching up with her. "They're very slippery, and you're liable to fall and hurt yourself." He collapsed wearily beside her, wiping his perspiring face with the faded bandanna.

Raven turned apologetically to her comrade. "Oh, I'm so sorry I ran off and left you Captain Mabry, but the beauty of this place completely overwhelmed me. I never imagined the Bahamas to be so very lovely."

"Breathtaking, isn't it?" asked Mabry. "Completely untamed. A virginal Garden of Eden."

"It truly is a paradise. Now I can understand why my father loved these islands so. Many times he tried to convey their splendor to Mother and me, but mere words were not enough. You have to set foot on this place to know that it really exists and to appreciate its grandeur. No words can ever describe the warmth of the sun as it bathes your body, or the way the waves bellow over the rocks, or even the feel of the sandy grains on your bare feet."

"Aye, lass, it is indescribable. None of them fancy poets could ever capture its beauty with words," Mabry said softly. He allowed his spellbound companion several more minutes to survey the pristine surroundings in silent meditation before interrupting her thoughts. "Come on, gal. We need to hurry about our chores before the midday sun hits us. Come along. I'll show you some other interesting sights."

Raven took his outstretched arm as he led her a hundred feet away from the beach to a less sandy, sparsely grassed area populated with towering coconut and cabbage palms and yellow, long-leafed pines. Pointing to one such pine the captain told her that its timber would be suitable for use in mending the broken mast. He then stooped down to examine the fiber of the trunk of the coconut tree. Nodding his approval, he revealed, "When we were being hurled across the reef, a great deal of water seeped in between the plankings of the ship. This fiber will make a good substitute for the oak caulking used originally to seal the boards. I shall send some of the men over later to get the necessary wood and fibers for repairs."

Raven picked up a coconut that had just fallen from one of the trees and solemnly studied the green, oval hardness as she felt the smoothness of its shell.

Mabry enjoyed the intense way Raven studied her discovery. Grinning at her seriousness, he took the fruit from her hand. "You've never tasted anything so sweet as its water. Let me show you." Stepping back to a safe distance, he raised the cutlass that had been attached to his braided belt and chopped away the top of the coconut, revealing three eyelets. After rounding out a hole in two of the black eyelets, he offered it to Raven. "Drink some. You'll find it to be cool and sweet, most refreshing."

"It is delicious!" exclaimed Raven after a large swallow. "So unusual tasting. I was getting quite thirsty and not so sure if I could wait until we got back to the ship for water."

"You should have told me. No need to have waited. Why, look, there's fresh water right here." He dipped the gourd into a pothole in one of the coral rocks. Raven reluctantly sipped a small amount, expecting the taste to be salty, but it was definitely not. "When me and some of the crew come over later," he told her, "we'll fill up the empty water barrels with this."

"With fresh water, and the sea's bounty of fish, someone could actually exist here if need be." She hoped there were no Indians staring at her at that moment, but Mabry eased her worry by assuring her the island was uninhabited even before she had a chance to ask him.

He cracked the top of the discarded coconut with the edge of the cutlass and, reaching inside with his hand, scraped out some soft, jellylike meat from within. He offered some to his young companion who, much to his surprise, delighted in its taste. "Now, rub some of that on your face," he instructed. "It will guard against sunburning. We'll have to purchase you a wide-brimmed straw hat the moment we reach port. I won't have you exposing your face in that hot sun," he added in a fatherly, concerned manner. "Why, you'd look like me in no time."

Their mission accomplished, Raven and Mabry headed toward the dinghy, stopping only long enough for Raven to scoop up some pale-colored shells from the ivory sands. "Look, Captain, this one has a hole at the top. If I put it on a chain, it will make a lovely necklace; perhaps a going-away present for Lucy." She held out the fan-shaped shell for him to see, but the skipper was too busy concentrating on a huge sea turtle sliding into the water.

"Folks say that the sea turtle is one of the few things that have managed to survive through the centuries." Mabry's storehouse of knowledge never ceased to amaze Raven and the other passengers, even though he had told them time and time again that the only reason he knew so much was that his time at sea afforded him with infinite opportunities to read and study. "Tonight, young lady, we will all have quite a treat for supper: fresh coconut pie, turtle meat that tastes every bit as good as English beef, heart of palm, and conch. I can hardly wait." He smacked his lips in anticipation.

The pair pushed the dinghy into the water, and Mabry paused for a moment, reaching down in the knee-deep surf and scooped up a large, brown shell. He turned it over in his hand and revealed to Raven the soft pinkness of the lips of the shell. "This is conch.

Inside it is some of the juiciest meat you will ever have the pleasure of tasting. Deliciously succulent! It also contains a rare pink pearl. Quite a treasure in the Bahamas, and a most sought after gem in London."

Raven was tempted to tell Mabry of the one her father had had mounted onto a pendant for her. An Indian friend whose life he had saved found the pearl and gave it to him as a token of his appreciation. But she decided that if she did, Mabry might mistake her pride in her father for boasting.

They rowed slowly back to the *Fancy Free;* the scorching sun was now at its midday peak, making even the slightest physical effort strenuously difficult. The captain whistled an old seafarer's chantey, and Raven imagined she was an adventurer, an explorer, returning to her ship after having set foot on a land never before seen by man. Perhaps, she mused, this was how Columbus felt when he landed on San Salvador in 1492.

## Chapter Four

That evening, just as Mabry had promised, passengers and crew alike feasted on the island delicacies brought back to the ship: coconut pies, salads made from the heart of cabbage palm, turtle steak, and cracked conch battered in freshly ground meal and fried to a crunchy thickness. Raven showed her shells to Ross and gave the necklace to Lucy. Mabry promised that tomorrow he would take all who were interested to the island for several hours of exploring while the crew tended to the repairs. Timid Mr. Phillips was exhilarated since it afforded him the chance to study tropical plant life never before recorded at the university. Lucy could hardly wait for her first chance to comb the island for hidden treasures and Indian artifacts, while Ross, elated that his sister's faded spirit was lifting, agreed whole-heartedly to join them. He hoped to talk to his sister about Jean-Claude since she had avoided him most of the day. Baxter murmured deprecatingly about the torrid weather and tried to beg off from the outing, but after Raven's insistence that he accompany them, he good-naturedly concurred that even he could do with a bit of exercise.

The lively discussion of the following day's plans and of the delightful imaginings of what might be found on the island was interrupted when the second mate entered the room, a harried look on his face. "Pardon me, sir, but Jenkins reports from the nest that a small sloop is headed toward us."

Alarmed glances were exchanged across the table, and Mabry quickly assured them there was no cause to worry. Knowing that their immediate assumption would be that pirates were on that sloop, he added that sea rogues would not dare attempt an attack from a small vessel. He then hurriedly excused himself and joined his crew above. The gaiety of the meal subsided, for in their minds each of the five passengers was imagining the worst of possible fates. No more efforts were made to continue the delicious island repast, or to enjoy the taste of the tropical punch Cookie had made from fresh coconut water and rum that had just been tapped from one of the casks in the hold. They waited anxiously and silently for some word from their captain.

"What do you suppose is going on up on deck?" whispered Lucy timorously. Her tiny fingers reached across the table to lock onto Raven's hand. Both girls had turned a waxen white, their pallor betrayed their fear, the unmentionable fear that the ship was about to be attacked by pirates.

"Easy, Lucy," encouraged Ross, wrapping his arm around her soft shoulders. His overly confident words were an effort to calm himself as well as the others. "Most likely, another merchant ship encountered problems similar to ours last night. They may have anchored on the other side of the island. Perhaps its skipper is trying to enlist Mabry's aid or maybe offering his assistance to us."

After a half hour's solemnity, the captain's resonant, hearty laughter boomed outside in the hallway. Sighs of relief relaxed the strained atmosphere. Ross's protective embrace of his sister loosened, and Raven sat curiously alert in her chair. Baxter eased the choking hold of his tight-fitting collar while Phillips wiped beads of moisture from his hairless brow. The door opened, revealing that the captain was accompanied by a handsome, bearded stranger.

"Folks, this is Captain Perez. I have invited him to share our supper." The captain motioned to the empty chair next to Raven, and after having made the necessary introductions, called for Benjy to bring out another plate and some more hot food. Once the uneasiness of a stranger's intrusion into the tightly knit group had vanished, everyone continued to enjoy their meal.

Perez appeared completely at ease and was immediately included in the conversation by the men. Raven, however, picked over her food, while the others talked of the storm. She was baffled by the stranger. Perez was most definitely not an English name, yet his unblemished command of the language was definitely British. His manners were impeccable; he behaved more like a member of the landed gentry than a sailor. She surreptitiously studied him from the corner of her eye. His clothes were the same texture worn by all sailors. The pale blueness of the material accentuated the bronzeness of his hard-muscled body. A tattered linen shirt stretched across his massive shoulders, and his tight-fitting trousers outlined the prominent muscular bulges of his sinewy thighs. While pretending to press out the creases in her green twilled silk gown with the palm of her hand, she stole a more deliberate look at his face, only to be received by laughing eyes and a questioning arch of his brow.

Raven heard her name and abruptly looked up, feeling her cheeks flush. "I am sorry. I haven't been listening very closely. What was that you said?" She stammered, unable to speak coherently, and knew that she must look as inept as she felt.

Mabry was concerned. "I only asked if you were feeling well. You have hardly spoken a word during the last hour."

Trying to compose herself and think of a valid excuse for her much noticed despondency, she stuttered a lame excuse. "Oh, yes. I'm fine. Really I am. I . . . I fear that perhaps all of the day's activities have quite worn me down. If you all will excuse me, I believe I will retire to my cabin." She spoke in a disconcerted tone, immediately regretting the words spoken in haste, for now she would have to follow through with her blurted declaration lest she look utterly foolish in front of everyone. She dared not meet Perez's glance for fear that she would see him scowling disapprovingly at her. The five men stood, and Perez gallantly pulled her chair away from the table. She mumbled a barely distinguishable "Thank you" and left the room, her eyes holding steadfast on the oak floor.

Oh, why did his presence affect me like that, she reflected grimly once out in the hall. Why, I acted like a giddy young woman who had never before had a handsome man seated beside her. Such sensations I have never before felt! Just his sitting beside me and accidentally brushing against my arm as he ate made warm tinglings surge throughout my body.

She nervously ran her hand through her ebony curls, wondering how it would feel to have a man like Perez hold her in his embrace. Would his kisses betray his experiences with other women, or would he be awkward and groping like Ross. She guiltily scolded herself for belittling Ross so since she had enjoyed her first taste of romance with the blond doctor. And yet, she admitted, something had been missing. I surely never felt like this when I was with him.

Remembering that the captain had cautioned them against opening their small portholes at night because of the abundance of mosquitoes in the tropics, she delayed returning to her humid cabin, which still smelled of the damp mustiness of the storm. She found herself looking over the railing of the ship's deck; her own retreat of solace and solitude, the spot from which she had tearfully watched her aunt's feigned good-byes, and the spot where Ross had first declared his love for her.

The luminous, full-orbed moon, suspended omnipotently among millions of twinkling lights, cast an eerie reflection on the opaline waters, clearly outlining the jagged, ivory-sanded beach of Abaco. The night exaggerated the ordinary evening sounds: the quick splash of fish striking the surface, the bellowing of a herd of monk seals in the shallows, and the distant haunting hum of a lone hump-backed whale searching for its mate. Raven paced along the length of the railing with heavy, deliberate steps, hands clasped behind her back, mouth pursed, and brows knitted in deep thought, unaware that she was being observed by

Perez, who was lurking in the shadows marveling at her beauty. He stepped out of the darkness at the same instant Raven was across from him. She gasped, involuntarily raising her hand to her mouth as if to stifle a near scream.

"I am sorry if I frightened you, Miss Gatewood," said Perez stiffly. "I was returning to my skiff when I saw you, and I wanted to apologize to you." He rubbed his palm against his mouth, trying to hide his amusement of the wide-eyed girl's shocked expression.

"You owe me no apology, Captain Perez," meekly answered Raven. She sought to choose her words carefully, not wanting Perez to sense her uneasiness in his presence. How glad she was that she had kept her thoughts, about him to herself instead of her usual method of rationalizing problems by talking aloud to herself!

Perez leaned his manly form against the railing, his back erect and his eyes penetrating appreciatively the softness of Raven's flushed face. Her wavering eyes were unwilling to meet his, resting instead on the railing beside him. "Oh, but I am afraid I do, Miss Gatewood. I fear my presence at your table this evening was distasteful to you and caused you much discomfort. I am truly sorry if I caused you any undue anxiety."

Because of the mocking intonation of his voice and the void look on his impassive face, Raven could not decide if he was being sarcastic or attempting a sincere, though unnecessary, apology.

The glossy light of the moon slightly illuminated the stalwartness of Perez's bearded visage, sinisterly tracing a thin, vertical scar on his left cheekbone. In a derisive tone, he bluntly suggested, "Perhaps I should leave rather than risk tarnishing the reputation of a lady of your stature."

"Oh, no! Don't leave!" she blurted before gaining control of herself. "What I mean to say is that it seems that you have gotten the wrong impression of me. It is quite clear that you think I considered myself too good to dine with you this evening and was rude enough to let my feelings be known to the others." She waited for a response from him, but Perez remained silent. "And you are very wrong. If I did appear rude, it was because I was tired and had not completely recovered from that dreadful storm. And then when word arrived that another vessel had been sighted we were all frightened out of our wits for fear pirates were attacking us. Perhaps it is I who should apologize to you," she amicably concluded. "I certainly did not wish to give you the impression that I am a snob." With a benign smile, her gaze returned to the rail.

As though the words Raven had spoken had laid deaf on his ears, Perez casually asked, "Why do you avoid my eyes when you speak to me? It makes me feel as though you have something to hide. Or perhaps that you are not sincere about what you have just said." Perez brushed the tip of his finger against Raven's cheek, and resting it on her chin, turned her face upward, forcing her to look into his eyes. At first she responded with a blinking uncertainty, then with an acquiescing boldness. "Now, that is much better," he praised, as though she were a child. "A man can tell much from a woman's eyes."

For one brief moment the position held, and Raven's eyes were locked onto Perez's. His eyes were even more unusual than her own: a yellowish green that reminded her of the sea grapes on the island. Eyes the color of a cat's! She longed to reach out and trace the border of his scar with her fingertips, just as Perez ached to kiss her full, pink lips that had parted instantly at his touch. Trying to control his mounting desire, he stepped away from her, and turning his frame sideways to hers, stared into the listless waters below.

"Captain Mabry tells me you are going to Nassau and that you are unescorted for the voyage."

"Yes. Yes, that is correct," she replied nervously, uncertain as to what sort of feelings were encompassing her.

"Whatever prompted you to book passage for there?" he demanded roughly, then in a quieter tone added, "Nassau is no place for a beautiful, unchaperoned woman."

Raven regained her composure, and feeling more at ease with him, told Perez about her father's illness and how her aunt and uncle successfully connived to use that as a means of ridding themselves of her and gaining control of the family estate. She found that she could confide in him as easily as she could Ross or Captain Mabry.

"Gatewood," remarked Perez, more of a statement than a question. "Robert Gatewood is your father?" His puzzled face clearly revealed his surprise.

"Yes, yes he is," answered Raven hopefully. "Then you know my father?"

"No, I only know that he is a friend of a man I know; Morgan Taylor," he hurriedly explained. "I regret that I have never had the occasion to meet him."

The hopeful delight in her voice was quickly replaced

with grim despair. "Oh, so you would not know where my father is now?"

Perez hesitantly shook his head.

"I received a letter from this Mr. Taylor back in January. He told me that he had taken my father to New Providence where he is being treated by a Dr. Lightbourne. I have hopes of finding my father there."

"Suppose your father is no longer under Lightbourne's supervision? What do you propose to do then?" he persisted.

Raven's posture became resolvedly erect. Determination was evident in her voice. "If my father is no longer there, I shall have Dr. Lightbourne direct me to Eleuthera. I understand that that is where my father intended to recoup." When Perez did not speak to either encourage or discourage her plans, she blandly implored. "No doubt you think I'm a bit foolish, do you not?"

His stern lips spread in an affable smile. "No, not foolish. Perhaps just a bit too naive for your own good. You knew nothing about the dangers of the sea until you undertook this voyage, and just as blindly, you go to Nassau. And you will be in for a rude awakening there. Why, the streets are filthy, and smelly, drunken seamen lurk in every dark shadow. It is definitely no place for a lady!" Seeing her disheartened look and not intending to upset her, his tone mellowed. "Your intentions warrant praise, but you have no idea of the jeopardy involved. You yourself must admit that you were foolish to allow your aunt to use such an opportunity to her own advantage." For a moment he regarded her with vexation and dismay. Then he reached for her hands, massaging each curve of her fragile fingers with his own roughened ones.

She was anxious to offer some type of excuse, not wanting him to think that her actions were merely a foolish girl's whims. "I understand, Captain Perez, that I was just a pawn in my aunt's scheme, and I know also that I must be very careful in Nassau. Once the ship has docked Captain Mabry promises me that he will personally see to it that I am escorted to the doctor's home."

Perez was not easily satisfied. "What if Lightbourne is away? What do you propose to do then?" He paused questioningly. "Wait on his doorstep until he returns?"

Raven was glad that she had the foresight to plan for such a crisis, and she hoped that her prudence would convince Perez that she was a sensible woman, not a flighty, empty-headed girl. "Captain Mabry knows of a rooming house there that is owned by two respected widows. I shall seek lodging there if I must stay any length of time."

Perez grinned reluctantly. "You certainly seem to have thought everything out completely."

Raven pleasantly acknowledged his slight compliment and deliberately changed the subject before he could conceive any other hypothetical situations concerning her safety. "Captain Mabry told us that the governor of the Bahamas is making quite a name for himself here with his efforts to civilize Nassau by punishing those who insist upon plundering for their livelihood."

"Indeed he is," agreed Perez. "He's even been able to recruit quite a few former pirates to help in his reconstruction campaign. He has great dreams for these islands. Buildings that were burned and sacked by raiding French and Spanish forces through the years are being cleared away and others erected. Nassau's been given a fresh coat of paint, and a competent militia constantly patrols the streets, making sure drunken brawls do not result in total destruction of property."

"Then pirates no longer frequent Nassau?" asked Raven, hopeful that that was one worry she would not have to concern herself with.

"I'm afraid they do. The ones who have not surrendered and who want nothing of Roger's royal pardon pose the real threat to these islands." Seeing that he had alarmed the young woman, he quickly added. "But with a well-trained army and a strong fortress surrounding the city, Nassau should be fairly safe. There is of course one pirate who warrants fear and concern, and unfortunately he is still in hiding. Red Ames is his name. If only we could capture him, I am sure those remaining would quickly give themselves up. I hope I have not frightened you by my monologue about pirates."

Raven was quick to reply. "No, not at all," she said a bit too rapidly. A brief silence ensued, and Raven, afraid that Perez would use it as an opportunity to excuse himself, attempted to involve him in another discussion. "Why did you visit our ship this evening, Captain Perez?" She wished she knew his first name for "Captain Perez" sounded so stiff and formal, but she lacked the tart impertinence to ask.

Perez sighed cautiously and tried to chose his words carefully. "When the storm commenced we sought refuge on the other side of the island where the area is well concealed by mangroves we thought would protect us from the gigantic waves and from unwelcomed intruders. Early this morning my men reported seeing the mast of another ship. I rowed ashore and stood on the cliff's edge to get a better look. I decided that yours was a merchant ship, and that you were probably in need of assistance." He pondered for a moment before continuing. "And I felt it my responsibility to warn your skipper to return to the open seas as soon as possible. You see in your present anchored position, your ship is vulnerable to an attack by Red Ames."

Raven gasped, startled at Perez's words. "That is the pirate you were just talking about, isn't it? Do you think he is in this area? Are we in danger? Where was he last sighted?" Questions tumbled from her mouth. "Are you certain he is in this vicinity? What will he do to us if he finds our ship here?"

Perez tried to mollify her. "I see I have caused you undue alarm. By now, I suspect, Ames knows that I am looking for him, and he has most likely fled to some obscure cay."

"You are looking for him? Why?" asked Raven, recovering finally from the surprise of knowing that their voyage was a long way from being safely completed.

The strong Captain Perez saw no way to avoid the involved explanation Raven demanded. "Red Ames's true name is Henri L'Ameur. He is a former French naval commander who absconded with his vessel almost ten years ago when he received word that he was to be relieved of his command because of his many heinous crimes at sea. He replaced the tricolored flag of France with the skull and crossbones. No ship is safe

67

with his crew of scoundrels manning the twenty gun corvette. Governor Rogers is well aware that if he is to succeed in repressing piracy once and for all, it is imperative that Ames be captured. Others have failed tragically in this mission, so I was commissioned to bring Ames to justice."

Raven's face turned a pallid white. "But are you not placing your life in a lot of danger?"

He shrugged his shoulders. "No more danger than many innocent people who sail these waters if Ames goes unpunished for his crimes and is allowed to continue his raids. Besides, I respect Rogers's motives. Through his leadership our islands could become a prominent center for commerce instead of a haven for renegades. The only way to guarantee safe passage to any ship in our waters is to rid the area of such barbarians. If Ames is apprehended and hanged the others will gladly surrender lest the same fate be theirs."

In her mind Raven had already begun to romanticize Perez as being some sort of national hero. She urged him to tell her more, and he obliged willingly.

"I have been pursuing Ames since the earlier part of this year. So far he has been successful in eluding me. Sly as a fox that red-haired demon is! I was led to believe that he was hiding out here on Abaco, but after a thorough investigation, it seems my sources have proven incorrect. It seems impossible for me to search every cay in this area, but I must do just that before I return to Nassau." Once again he held Raven's hands tightly. She hoped he could not fell the surge of her rapidly beating heart. "I do not feel there is any immediate danger or any reason either you or the others should be worried. Ames may be nowhere near here. If he is, he would be foolish to attempt an attack with me so close. Your captain has assured me that the repairs on your ship will be completed by tomorrow afternoon, and with a strong evening breeze, you can pull anchor and be on the Nassau bar by dawn."

"Once you are successful bringing Ames to trial, do you plan to continue with Rogers's navy?" asked Raven curiously.

He shook his head emphatically and grinned to himself that the young woman had complete confidence that virtue would defeat vice. "No, I was never a member of the Royal Navy. I agreed to help Rogers because I respect his friendship and his motives. And I suppose I had selfish interests as well. I . . . I captain a ship that transports cotton from the outer islands to Nassau for export to England. Without the constant threat of piracy, my job would be made much safer and a lot easier."

"Oh, so that is how you know Mr. Taylor," she deduced confidently. "He's a cotton grower, you know. How about your crew for this search? Are they the same men you usually command?"

Perez laughed heartily. "No, no. These men were handpicked for this mission. They have all been involved with pirating at one time or another but were wise enough to accept Rogers's promise of amnesty. They have sworn their loyalty to the cause."

Raven gaped in wide-mouthed astonishment. "But you must be afraid that these men will return to their previous way of life once you have armed them."

Perez disagreed. "Even though we undertook this assignment as strangers, I trust my men completely.

They are intelligent enough to realize that their days of pilfering are over and that it would only be a matter of time before they are hanged. This way they are given a chance to earn a future. Rogers has promised to each man who aids in capturing Ames a tract of land that he can develop into a farm."

"How can you be certain these rogues will not betray you?" asked Raven. "Surely they realize that it is the lot of them against you if ever there was trouble."

"I honestly do not believe I have anything to fear. I have gotten extremely close with some of them, and I am certain they would risk their own lives rather than have any harm befall me. One young boy, an eighteen-year-old, ran away from home when he was just a lad and joined Ames's group. He wanted adventure and excitement. He was caught several months ago and sentenced to hang alongside the worst of those murderers and cutthroats. As the noose was being tightened about his neck, Rogers pardoned him. The boy then swore life-long allegiance to Rogers for sparing his life. He's sailing with me now. A trustier lad could not be found in all of these islands."

"You are a very brave man, Captain Perez," Raven languorously murmured. "So brave to attempt such a feat."

In the few moments that followed, thoughts of Ames, of Raven's sick father, and of the dangers lurking in Nassau were temporarily forgotten. As far as they were concerned, no one else existed. Each other's company offered refuge enough from the problems confronting them. Their eyes spoke distinctly the words that were unnecessary to say. Slowly and deliberately Perez unfastened the pins that held her hair tightly about the nape of her neck, his eyes never straying from her for an instant. Raven's blue black, waist-length tresses cascaded down her back. Perez caressed her temples, traced an imaginary line down the path of her high cheekbones, and stroked her delicate nose and demure, dimpled chin, fondling her face as though she were a fragile porcelain figurine. His hand brushed her mouth; her lips followed its movement. Perez drew her trembling body closer, and she quivered, not from fear but from anxious anticipation. Her eyes fluttered, her mouth parted slightly. Their lips sought ecstasy, and their palpitating bodies awakened with burning desire. The kiss was at first frantic, and he bruised her tender, yielding lips. Then Perez soothed the pain with honeyed tenderness.

"Oh, Raven," he moaned. "I have longed to embrace you from the very moment I entered the galley and saw your sweet face looking into mine."

Without the least bit of shyness, she responded. "That is why I had to leave the table. The feel of your leg pressing against mine and your arm brushing my shoulder made me feel strange surges of emotion that I have never before experienced. I know I should pretend to be coy, but I am at a loss to find the words to express myself. Please, just kiss me."

He was all too anxious to obey her shaky command. Then he brusquely stopped, and Raven surveyed him questioningly.

"What is wrong? Do you not enjoy my kisses as much as I enjoy the feel of yours?" After no reply, she turned embarrassedly away, unable to look at him. "By my behavior, you think me to be a shameless strumpet, do you not?" Still there was no response. "I do not know whatever possessed me to so . . . so easily succumb to your touch. Please go!"

*"Shh,* my darling," comforted Perez, massaging the tightness from her bare shoulders. "I know you are no strumpet. I am honored that you feel the same longing for me as I do for you. This is nothing to be ashamed of. I want to woo you slowly, when I have hours to devote to you, not minutes. I have stayed on your ship longer than was my intention, but my urgency to stand in the moonlight with you far surpassed my sense of duty and obligation." He was content to hold her closely to him and bury his unshaven face in the silky softness of her lustrous hair.

"Tell me about yourself," urged Raven sedately. "For I know I shall think of you often after you depart, and I would like to know all there is about you." She did not reveal that she would relive these moments over and over again each day, cherishing every thought of their lusty kisses, the thrilling warmth of his hands on her flesh, and the confident sound of his words.

"I would much rather concentrate on you, Raven," he complacently objected. "I want to implant your image in my mind forever so that I can but close my eyes and your face will appear."

But Raven was not to be discouraged. "How can I feel such things when I know so little about you. Why I know nothing of your family. I do not even know your given name!"

Perez relented and awkwardly began, groping at first for just the right words to explain himself. "Let me see now. My Christian name is Juan Roberto Perez. My father was English, my mother Spanish. When he was still a young man, sixteen or so, he disobeyed his father and left England with seventy other refugees who sought freedom from the religious intolerance of the Royalists. The group was led by William Sayle and they came here to the Bahamas and settled on an island called Segatoo. Later they renamed it Eleuthera, which is Greek for 'freedom.' That signified their intent, to establish a colony free from religious persecution. It became apparent from the start that the settlement would fail, for the colonists knew nothing about farming the rocky soil. Most of their animals, as well as a lot of the men, died from heat exhaustion."

"How dreadful," interrupted Raven. "What happened to them after that?"

"Well, as a last resort, Sayle ventured to a British colony in Boston, and his pleas for food and supplies were heeded by the people there; they remembered the struggles they themselves had to endure. Even though they were given adequate supplies to last through the winter months, the colony did fail, and my father returned to England. He studied law and became a prominent barrister and married the daughter of one of his senior partners."

"And did you come to the Bahamas because he had come as a young man?" she inquired.

"No. You see, my father eventually came back to the island of his youth. His parents were victims of the Plague, then his wife and children died in the fire of London. I suspect he wanted to return here as an escape from the tragedy that had surrounded his life in London."

"What happened to your father? Is he still living?"

"No, he's been dead since I was a child. Apparently after returning to Eleuthera he was content to eke out

73

an existence through farming and fishing. Then when Charles the second granted a charter to the Lord Proprietors of the Carolinas he established an agreement of trade with both England and America and exchanged brazilwood for tobacco and sea cotton, which he would in turn sell to England. Are you sure I am not boring you, Raven?"

Raven urged him to continue. "Of course you are not boring me. I could never grow weary of listening to you."

"Fourteen years later the Spanish burned and plundered Governor's Harbor, and his tiny trade empire crumbled. Some months passed and a second Spanish ship came to Eleuthera, this one carrying the exiled Cuban governor and his family. The ship broke up on a reef several hundred feet from shore, and the next day my father found a half-drowned young woman washed up on the beach. He nursed her back to health, they were married, and she died a year later giving birth to me. My father became a very bitter man. He could not understand why she had survived the wreck only to die in childbirth. And I suppose he could never have forgiven me for living while his wife died. Anyway, the afternoon of my birth, my father walked into the ocean carrying the body of his wife."

"Oh, Juan, how terrible for you," she comforted, kissing his cheek. "How did you survive without a mother or a father?"

"My father's old Indian housekeeper nursed me with goat's milk until she found a native girl whose own child was born dead. Then when I got older I went to the home of Anthony Caldwell, a Presbyterian layman who had fled England during the Puritan supression.

He educated me and taught me the ways of the English. Even though he was extremely stern and pious, he loved me as his own son, and he was the closest thing to a father I ever had. When I was fourteen he became very ill, and knowing that he was about to die gave me a diary my father's housekeeper had entrusted to him, saying that I had a right to know something of my parentage."

"And after that, what did you do?"

"Oh, I signed on with numerous cargo ships, traveled quite a bit for a lad of my age, and then decided to make my home in these islands."

Raven was practically in tears. "Juan, please forgive me for insisting that you tell me of your family. Had I known, I—"

He hushed her regrets. "There is no reason for you to feel so bad about it. Sometimes it is even good for me to talk of such things. I know nothing whatsoever of my mother or father except what I read in his journal. You see Raven, it is difficult to mourn someone whose face you have never touched or whose voice you have never heard."

"But why did you not take the English name of your father?" she asked.

A shrill whistle prevented Perez from answering. "I must go now, dearest. My men grow impatient. When you arrive in Nassau go to Lightbourne and tell him that Juan Perez requests that he take care of you until I return to New Providence. Then, I promise, I shall take you to your father."

"But when. When will that be," inquired Raven, her eyes filling with tears. "When will I see you again?"

"Hopefully, in four days I will be able to return to

New Providence. Quickly, my darling, one more kiss, then I must join the others. In Nassau, my dearest," he promised, sealing the vow with a light touch of his fingertip against her lower lip. "In Nassau, we shall have time to discuss that which we cannot now. Until then, darling."

Raven watched as he and his three men rowed away into the darkness. Even when she no longer heard the splash of the oars chopping the water, she remained fixed, her mouth shaping the same words over and over again. Juan Perez! Juan Perez! Closing her eyes, she felt the pressure of his lips surrounding hers, the heat of his body against her own pulsating form, and the sensation within her breasts when he had slightly grazed against their creamy silkiness.

The four days would not pass quickly enough for her until she could be in his embrace once more. He will take me to Father, she thought, and then . . . and then what?

The stark realization that at that point all must end dissuaded any further romantic longings. She and her father would return to England, and Juan would be left to his islands. Two different parts of the world, two totally different people, and two opposite lifestyles, she admitted dismally. It could never work out, regardless of the love she already felt for him. As Mabry had once told her, a sailor's only love is the sea. Nothing can ever change that. Once that salty water's inhaled in a man's lungs, it stays in his blood until he dies. And even if Juan were to give up the sea, what then, she asked herself. Father would certainly never approve of him because of his mixed heritage. Oh, after experiencing the sweet taste of his kisses, she groaned, how can I possibly live without him?

Raven was suddenly jerked back to her senses and regained the logic that had temporarily given way to her heart. She scolded herself for such actions against her sensible intellect. Why, how ridiculous I am! After acting like a wanton tart for an hour, I have begun imagining all sorts of things, she thought.

She straightened her rumpled dress, smoothed her mussed hair, and attempted to regain her austere composure. No doubt, the captain will forget the promise that he made to me. Even if he does seek me out in Nassau, why should I think it would be for anything more than a quick romance? After all, he has been at sea for a while and did need the soft companionship of a woman—which you so brazenly gave him, Raven Gatewood! Why, he probably has a wife and a family waiting for his return. What have I done? How could I have gotten myself so involved in such a short time? How could I allow myself to feel such uncontrollable passion, especially for a man with whom I could never have a future. I am a lady, and I must remember to act as one in the future. A lady first, a woman second!

Such frustrating thoughts persisted as long as Raven tried to verbalize the turmoil swelling in her heart. So much had happened these past weeks. And it all happened much too fast, she decided wearily. At home I could find satisfaction in rides over the meadows and amusement in reading about foreign places and someone else's romance. What a sheltered existence I have led! And now, less than a month away from the secure confines of Ravenwood, so much has happened: A young doctor proposed marriage to me, I survived a near shipwreck, and afterward melt in the arms of a common sailor who enslaved me by his touch. Oh, Raven, a sailor, mind you.

Why could you not be sensible and return Ross's affection, no matter how tepid he makes you feel! Instead, you must fall in love with a man you may never again see. Why, if I were as level-headed as I pride myself in being, I would rush into Ross's arms this very moment and accept his proposal. Then I would be able to carefully guard against Juan Perez if ever we were to meet again. Oh, but I don't love Ross. I love Juan. Of that I am certain. Regardless of all the unsolvable problems, the fact remains; I do love him! What he's doing for the governor is a very brave undertaking. I cannot help but admire his boldness, his sense of duty and honor in doing what he feels is right. A man cannot be faulted for his heritage; neither can he be blamed for his profession.

My mind is so disoriented; all these jumbled thoughts are giving me a headache. What am I to do? If only I had someone to talk with. Lucy would understand how I feel, but her loyalty is with her brother. Ross would be shattered if he knew I favored Juan's impassioned lovemaking over his barren hugs and wet kisses. Poor Ross, you are but a boy in comparison to that man. No doubt he would accuse me of being another Louisa, and rightly so I suppose, but it was not my intent to cruely string him along.

Such confusion I have never known. My mind is wracked with it! My head tells me to do one thing, my heart another. Perhaps tomorrow's dawn will offer a solution to all of my misgivings and problems. Ah, such desolate situations! I must not feel shamed by my liaison with Juan or for the stirrings that mounted inside me as our bodies pressed together. Oh, I cannot think such thoughts any longer. I must try and get some rest. Surely things will all work themselves out tomorrow. They must!

## Chapter Five

Only those crew members who had been assigned to mending the top mast at dawn's early awakening saw the billowing, unfurled sails of the *Falcon,* as Perez and his band of reformed renegades sailed north along the eastern coast of Abaco in search of the infamous Red Ames.

Nearly two hours later five zealous explorers were impatiently waiting in the chartroom for Captain Mabry to conclude his morning instructions to the crew: Raven and Lucy had bags slung over their shoulders into which their treasures would be carried, Phillips had his sketchbook tucked securely under his arm, and Ross and Baxter had their leather journals stuffed underneath their shirts. Finally, at half past seven, Mabry was free to keep his promise of taking the passengers ashore to explore the island. He met them in the chartroom where he had ordered Cookie to leave two large straw baskets, which he intended to fill with coconuts, wild fruits, and yams.

The spectacular panorama of the ocean, framed by the cottony whiteness of the low-hanging clouds, evoked silence from the sojourners as Mabry rowed the skiff to shore. They were totally awed by the splendor of the radiant, sparkling hues of the early morning's blues and greens.

Baxter, appropriately quoting Columbus after he had first laid eyes on the islands, remarked contemplatively, "This country excels all others as far as the day surpassed the night in splendor."

Mabry patiently explained to his attentive listeners many of the things he had told Raven the day before, and he startled them when he pointed out the ship's closeness to hole-in-the-wall during the fury of the storm. Phillips, having spent most of his youth on the western coast of England, quickly noted in surprised discovery the absence of rocks and small pebbles from Abaco's shore. As the boat was pulled onto the sandy point by the men, Lucy asked Mabry about the possibility of island inhabitants, and he told her of an unsuccessful attempt of the French to settle Abaco in 1625.

Once ashore, the skipper cautioned them to remain together. After taking a closer look at the massive cliff with its threatening hole, Phillips asked if they might venture farther into the interior of the island. He had already sketched the soaring palms and the wide-trunk yellow pines along the coast, which, he remarked, seemed to grow out of the rocks instead of the grainy sand.

Using his cutlass to chop through the thick undergrowth, the captain warned them against touching the white leaflets of the poisonwood shrub that dotted both sides of the narrow path. The denseness gradually opened into the verdant surroundings of a tropical Eden.

Everyone was delighted at the array of colorful plants and flowers blooming in the bower away from the pine hammocks, where the only flowers seen had been lavender ground orchids at the pines' bases. Clusters of yellow hibiscus, purple bougainvillea, and the pink, waxy balsa erupted into full glory, as did the yellow- and white-stemmed flowers of the wild guava tree. A cawing sound prompted everyone to look high above their heads into the limbs of an alamanda tree, where among the golden blossoms sat a fearless, hooked-beak bird of magnificent orange, red, green, and gold plumage.

"A parrot," informed Mabry to his awe-striken guests.

"Nothing I have ever seen could compare with the beauty of this spot," commented Phillips, who was busy drawing a tiny green-feathered bird that was buzzing around the center of a red, long-leafed poinsettia.

Raven and Lucy were braiding each other's hair with the abundant bougainvilleas when both shrieked in horror. Mabry rushed to their side in time to see a curly-tailed lizard scampering into the brush. Stiffling his impulse to burst into laughter, he assured them soothingly, "No reason for panic, ladies. The little fellow is quite harmless, probably more afraid of you than you of it. Don't be surprised if you see some two or three feet long."

"Surely you cannot be serious!" piped Lucy. "That must be an exaggeration!"

Baxter joined in. "No, he's quite right. The larger ones are called iguanas. The Indians used to roast them—quite a delicacy I understand."

Mabry could not resist the temptation to have a bit of fun. With a straight face, he facetiously informed Baxter that, if he so desired, he might catch some so Cookie could prepare them at noon for everyone to sample.

"No, thank you, sir," replied Baxter. "That would be one of your island treats that would not tempt me the least!"

Nearing a strand of trees that had recently regenerated new foliage, the explorers noticed that an aromatic fragrance suddenly drifted through the air. Raven picked a full white flower from a low limb, put it to her nose, and revealed to the others that it was the source of the scent. None of the other flowering trees had emitted such a distinct aroma.

"This must be the frangipani tree," she told the others as Mabry nodded in confirmation. "My father described it to me and said that the Indian women rubbed the flower over their bodies as a perfume. Here, smell!" She dabbed her wrist with the scent of the soft petals and held it out for the others to sniff.

"I have found that those Indians were able to utilize most all of these plants and trees. Quite remarkable. Step over here a moment, please. And you, Dr. Fairmont, pay particular attention to this. I doubt they taught you about this little plant in medical training." He broke off a piece of a sprawling green vine that wound itself tightly around a tree. "Love vine. For many years, the Indians used this as a remedy for every imaginable ailment. They would boil it and make the patient drink the tea."

"That's what you said the Lucayans were using to cure your father, didn't you Raven?" asked Lucy. Her

83

friend nodded.

Ross shook his head in disbelief. "I wonder what could possibly be contained in that plant that would serve as medicine. I must make a note to ask Dr. Farrow about it when I return to Oxford next spring." Scribbling a reminder in his journal, he asked if any of the other plants served a medicinal purpose.

Mabry scratched his whiskered chin as he deliberated on the question. "I am sure that all of them have some sort of use. The good Lord wouldn't just put them here for our enjoyment. They must have a purpose; all of them. Did I tell you that coconut water is used to prevent sunburn? The juice of the lime for mosquito bites? Hmm. . . . Ah yes, let me see if I can find some aloe vera."

"Aloe vera?" questioned Lucy curiously. "I've never heard of such a plant." The pert, auburn-haired girl had never found the botany lessons prepared by her tutor particularly stimulating, but she listened closely to Mabry and tried to remember all of the names of the flowers and plants he introduced to them.

The captain of the *Fancy Free* looked closely through the foliage in search of the prickled-leaf green cactus growing close to the ground. Breaking off a piece of its many thick leaves, he squeezed a jellylike substance onto his palm while Phillips outlined the odd-shaped plant on his pad and Ross recorded the captain's explanation of the plant's origin in his journal.

"I told you already of the attempted French settlement here in 1625. This verifies that fact, for it shows that the French brought their African slaves here with them."

"I don't understand, Captain," interrupted Raven. "What does the presence of that plant on the island have to do with Africans?"

"Their slaves brought this plant from Africa when the poor devils were first captured and brought to civilization to work. Around their necks were worn leaves from this plant. When his master would beat him, the liquid found inside here was used by the slave as an ointment for the wound. It would soothe the pain and cleanse the sore. When they were brought to Abaco, the slaves had the good sense to plant their medicine, certain they would eventually make use of its healing powers. Legend has it that aloe was the only plant Adam took from the Garden when he and Eve were expelled from Paradise," Mabry solemnly concluded.

Ross, turning the leaf over and over in his hand, carefully examined the miracle cure. "I hope I shall be able to find similar species once I arrive in Charleston. They would be most interesting to study. Why, I would even wager that the cures for most of the diseases known to both man and animal could be found in nature, right under our noses!"

Baxter liked the young doctor Fairmont, but he held the medical profession in general in very low esteem ever since the court physician practically bled him to death in order to cure an unsightly pimple on his nose. He sarcastically added to Ross's comment. "Yes, and ever so much pleasanter than inserting knives or leeches into the skin!"

Ross ignored Baxter's wry humor and queried Mabry further. "Are there any others you can think of, sir? That is, plants that have been known to be remedies for certain diseases?"

After deliberating for a moment, the captain told him that the sap of the cedar bark could be used as an effective insect repellent. Glancing over his shoulder to make sure the two ladies were out of hearing distance, he continued softly. "I shall try to remember to point out the lignum vitae tree to you on the way back. Its juice has been known to be remarkably effective in the treatment of the sailor's curse."

Ross knitted his eyebrows together in confusion until it occurred to him that Mabry was referring to syphilis. "Ah yes, the sailor's curse." He nodded. "If that's the case, then it could no doubt be used equally as well for the treatment of less severe infections."

Mabry shrugged his shoulders and strolled over to Raven and Lucy who were on their knees examining bits of leaves. "What have you discovered, lassies?" he asked, bending down for a closer look himself.

"It looks like animal tracks," said Raven, studying the marks closely. "What other animals are here, besides birds and lizards? See how the foliage has been nibbled away?"

"Yes, I see. Well now, I suppose there might be some chickens here, a few wild pigs, perhaps even a goat or two," surmised Mabry thoughtfully.

"There must be," speculated Baxter knowingly. "If the French brought their slaves to a settlement, it stands to reason they would bring animals for food and herding as well. Most likely, when they abandoned their project, they left the animals here to roam wild."

"There may even be horses on the island," commented Mabry. "I understand several Spanish ships have shipwrecked in this area. One in particular during the mid-sixteen hundreds was thrown against the hole-in-the-wall during a violent winter storm. The sister ship was able to anchor inside the reef until the weather cleared. After the storm ended the island was combed for survivors, but none were found. We do know, however, that the Spaniards had a passion for their mounts and frequently took the steeds with them."

Raven was intrigued by this remark, and she found herself sadly longing for her morning jaunts across the hills astride her own faithful mount.

"But what happened to the wrecked ship?" inquired Ross.

"The accompanying ship salvaged everything of value from it, and eventually the wreck sunk to the bottom. It's hard tellin' just how many vessels and their men lie in that watery grave."

A moment of silent meditation followed Mabry's woeful words. Several shook their heads, grateful that theirs had not been a similar fate.

"Look, another contribution from Spain." Phillips motioned them over to the spot where he stood. "Seville oranges." He picked a thick-skinned orange from the scraggly tree, peeled it, and divided it into six slices. Then he distributed a piece to each of his companions.

Lucy puckered distastefully, causing her friends to laugh. "Ugh, it's sour!"

Mabry began filling his baskets with the oranges, and after plucking nearly two dozen of the citrus suggested that they make their way back through the pine hammock to the beach. Raven and Lucy carried with them bouquets of fresh flowers to brighten up the galley, Ross had samples of aloe and love vine, and

Phillips protectively clutched his much-valued sketch-book.

Mabry stooped beside a coral rock before leaving the hammock and scooped fresh water out of the potholes. The others followed suit and soon quenched the thirst brought on by the blazing noon sun.

Baxter, who was not easily excited, ranted on and on of the availability of food and fresh water on the island. "If there were any survivors here, they could exist quite comfortably! How very remarkable!"

At the edge of the pines Mabry discreetly nudged Ross and pointed out the lignum vitae tree. Spying fallen coconuts nearby, he asked for Phillips's assistance in gathering them. Lucy collected some of the brightly colored shells, which had been embedded in the ribbed, sun-bleached sand while Baxter speculatively eyed an indention in the ground. Ross and Raven were left alone for the first time all morning, and he led his adored over to a shady area underneath a cabbage palm, his arm resting possessively on her stiffened shoulder.

"What's wrong with you today?" he huskily demanded as she deliberately stepped out of his grasp. "All day I've been trying to get you alone, but Lucy or someone else is always around. If I didn't know better, I'd say you were avoiding me."

Raven tactfully evaded his uncharacteristic directness. "Now, Ross, you yourself know that the captain insisted that we all remain in a group. We couldn't very well have wandered off, now could we? What would the others have thought?"

"I do not care what they would have thought." He pouted boyishly. "All I know is that I have been longing to hold you and kiss you all day long. Oh, my dearest, dearest darling—" She pulled away from his embrace, and Ross was astounded by her complete turnabout in behavior. He glared at her accusingly.

"I do not understand you at all, Raven. One day you're eager to return my kisses, the next you want nothing to do with me."

She detected the scornful dejection shadowing Ross's pale face, and her mood became more compliant as she tried to pacify him. "Ross, I have told you already that I am not quite sure just how I feel about you. You know that I like you very much, and you're very dear to me, but I really cannot be pressed for more. It simply would not be fair."

"I saw you with that Captain Perez last night," he drily asserted, the insinuation made evident through his caustic voice and jaundiced expression.

"And what is that supposed to mean? How dare you spy on me Ross Fairmont!" Her haughty eyes blazed blistering ire, and her body, erect and rigid, twitched disdainfully. She stood, proud and fierce, with her hands staunchly positioned on her rounded hips as her saucy independence was asserted.

Ross retorted waspishly. "I was not spying on you!" he emphasized strongly, then acquiesced. "I am truly sorry that my jealousy flared so much just because I saw you talking to another man."

Raven scrupulously studied the downcast countenance of a man whose absorbing love for her could only be returned by platonic devotion. She was ashamed at having so guiltfully lashed out against Ross. He's such a good man, she thought. And has so much to offer a woman. I pray that he finds someone worthy of that love. I never intended to hurt him. She felt that more must be said to ease Ross's mind of that matter. "I encountered Captain Perez as he was returning to his boat. Since he is familiar with the islands, I naturally inquired if he knew either Morgan Taylor or Dr. Lightbourne, in hopes that he would know some news of my father as well. That's all, Ross."

"And what was his reply?" asked the young man, genuinely concerned.

Raven sighed wearily. "He knew both of the men and had even heard mention of my father, but he could tell me nothing more than that which I already knew." No need to tell him that Perez had promised to meet her in Nassau and had offered to escort her to Eleuthera. It would only make matters more difficult and their relationship more strained.

Ross shamefacedly rubbed his hand through his flaxen-colored hair. "I don't know what has gotten into me, Raven. Last night I went to your cabin to make sure you weren't ill, and when you didn't answer my knock I went up on deck, knowing how you love the solitude there." Relief flushed his grinning face. "I am sincerely sorry. Please accept my apology. I am so selfish that I demand all of your attentions. Thank you for your honesty. I admit that I mistakenly attributed your somewhat reserved behavior to a newly found interest in that sea captain. How foolish I must have sounded."

Raven smiled demurely and listened patiently to his discourse.

"Of course your main interest in Perez was in obtaining information pertaining to your father," he smugly deduced. "When I saw the two of you standing there, I returned to my cabin in frenzied anger. Had I only been more rational, I would have realized your motives. A romantic involvement indeed! How ridiculous for me to think such! An earl's daughter and a stray half-breed. What a preposterous thought!"

Raven could not respond to his comment, lest she betray her true emotions for Perez. She tolerated Ross's cradling her unyielding body in his arms. Last night she had been a raging inferno in Perez's embrace, but this afternoon, in the hold of a man who was her most likely choice as a lover, she could muster no more than a smouldering ember. She was relieved when Baxter yelled clamorously for the others to come quickly and view his finding. She favored Ross with an affectionate pat on his arm as they joined the others at the discovery site.

"They're turtle eggs," informed Mabry, surveying the twenty small, round eggs that Baxter had so painstakingly uncovered. "Probably ate their mother at supper last night," he added casually.

Lucy stood with her mouth agape. "That's horrible, just disgusting!"

Before she could continue her rage, Mabry interrupted. "Now, just calm down, Miss Fairmont. Why do you women have to be so sentimental? Even had we not captured the turtle, she would have had nothing else to do with her babes. You see, Lucy, female turtles always return to their own place of birth to lay their eggs. Once this is done and the eggs are deposited safely in the sand, the mother leaves. She has no interest whatsoever in watching her babies develop."

The adventurers, satisfied by Mabry's explanation to the troubled girl, took one last, long look around the island, each wishing for just a little more time to explore the unrivaled beauty of the tranquil surroundings. Mabry interrupted their thoughts of hidden treasures, sunken booty, and shipwrecked survivors with his command. "Shove off, mates!"

Raven and Lucy settled themselves comfortably in the skiff while the men pushed it into the incoming tide. Baxter and Phillips asked if they might try their hand at maneuvering the boat, to which Mabry wholeheartedly agreed. He silently decided that it was time Phillips got his eaglelike nose out of a book and Baxter started behaving like a regular fellow instead of a pompous stuffed shirt. Under the captain's mute scrutiny, the pair clumsily steered back to the ship. They goodnaturedly accepted his jabs about their lack of skill as oarsmen and blushed uncomfortably when the girls fussed over them and commended their efforts.

Upon reaching the ship Mabry meticulously inspected the progress of the repairs before joining the others in the galley for a bite to eat. There he reluctantly informed them that another day's work would be needed to complete the remaining repairs. Raven remembered Perez's threatening warning about an anchored ship being easy prey to Ames, and when she saw the harried look on Mabry's face, decided that he must also be painfully aware of their vulnerability.

After a lunch of turtle-fin soup and biscuits, Phillips rushed to his cabin to decipher his hastily scribbled descriptions of the island's flora, promising to aid Ross in his research of medicinal herbs later in the evening. Baxter, unaccustomed to the least bit of exertion, decided to retire for an undisturbed snooze in his cabin. Raven and Lucy chose to do an afternoon of cleaning and distributed their damp belongings across the railings of the deck in hopes they would air out. Raven mopped the remaining puddles of water from their cabins' floors, absently nodding in reply to her friend's endless prattling about Ross's promise to allow Jean-Claude a visit to Charleston in the winter.

## Chapter Six

The *Fancy Free* rode anchor majestically, proudly poised atop the listless waters. Her regal form swayed ever so slightly as an occasional wave lapped rhythmically against her hull. Puffy, slate gray clouds sauntered leisurely across the hueless, nocturnal skies. The waning, frosted moon emerged from behind one drifting cloud only to be shrouded by another billowy mass following closely behind. The night was breathlessly sultry; smothering heat spread throughout the ship, carrying with it hoards of plaguing mosquitoes and sand flies.

The sailors, except for the two lookouts, were stretched out in hammocks hung haphazardly from the gunnels. They dozed interminably; arms dangling over the edges of their corded beds and resting on their cutlasses, others swatting repeatedly at annoying insects. Tonight, as during many such evenings in the tropics, Mabry had joined his crew, believing the pesty bugs to be more tolerable than the torid heat in his quarters.

Mabry's usually tranquil repose was now fitful, and he tossed from one position to another. He awoke

94

suddenly from his half-dozing state, grasped the short, broad-bladed sword hanging from his plaited belt, and bolted gingerly to his feet. He alertly surveyed the deck, only to see his swarthy sailors resting as uncomfortably as he and the wary night guards methodically pacing out their watch.

Small brown pigeons cooed murmurously, nestled snugly against the wooden bars of their confines. In another cage were the cackling chickens, roosting contently on their perches. Tethered goats stood patiently chewing at their ropes and vacantly eyeing the yawning sentry positioned on the raised, narrow platform of the stern.

Satisfied that all was well, the portly skipper returned to his hammock, extended his solid frame over the edge, and after one more critical look, resolutely pulled the brim of his woolen cap over his eyes and closed his wrinkle-rimmed eye lids. He silently cursed his jitters, blaming such foolish panic on old age and Captain Perez's grim warning to be out of the shallow sound by dusk. Wind or no, this ship would pull anchor at dawn, he stoutly resolved before drifting into a troubled slumber.

Mabry had no sooner closed his eyes than the relaxing sound of the gentle flapping of the rigging was heard, heralding the approach of a genial breeze. Crew and passengers alike welcomed the languorous current and exhaustedly succumbed to its airy embrace. Even the two on watch yielded involuntarily to its tranquilizing spell.

Raven awoke with a start, feeling immediately the abrupt movement that had jarred the ship. Balancing on her knees, she raised her head even with the porthole and gasped a hoarse, muffled scream at what she saw. Stilettos gleamed sinisterly in the twilight as their ruthless owners savagely and mercilessly plunged the sharp-bladed daggers into startled victims. Mabry was on his feet in an instant, shouting hurried orders to his remaining few. The loud report of muskets sounded briefly, then Mabry, too, fell to the deck. Like his men, he lay wallowing in his own blood.

The throaty, sardonic laughter of the bloodthirsty mob resounded throughout the vessel. Raven watched speechlessly as the treacherous murderers wiped the blood off their daggers and returned them to the leather sheaths around their bare waists. They moved from one body to the next, poking each to assure none was still breathing, then searched the corpses for any valuable trinket—a coin, locket, gold timepiece—any item that could be sold or traded on New Providence to unscrupulous merchants who were unconcerned about the source of the merchandise.

After being satisfied the lifeless forms were stripped of all valuables, the soulless pirates mirthfully rolled the dead into the underlying depths.

"Below!" bellowed their dauntless commander, and the sanguine marauders greedily hastened to their plunder. Raven, upon hearing the rush of heavy footsteps in the companionway, murmured feebly. "Oh, dear God, please have mercy on us," and she tried to hide by cowering in the darkened corner beside the door. She checked to see the door was securely fastened and the oak bar latched in its lock, then she shrank even nearer to the wall in fearful dread of the horrors that would befall her and the others at the bloody hands of such fiends. She first heard Lucy's frantic screams as the girl was dragged from her cabin, then the damning curses of Ross as he leaped from his room in defense of his sister. The pirates' amused guffaws followed. Raven crouched, frozen and wide-eyed, and watched the doorknob to her refuge turn, and the lock give way to the impact of several sturdy shoulders against it. They burst into the room jeering wickedly at the young woman hiding in the shadows. They appraised her lustfully, then called to their commander. "Come see the treasure we've got in here, Capt'n!"

"Let me pass, swine!" thundered the leader as he forcefully pushed the others out of his way. He saw the crouched figure huddled by the wall and leered wantonly. "Ah, mademoiselle. Permit me to introduce myself. I am Captain Jean-Henri L'Ameur of the French corvette *Le Bordeaux.*" He bowed ceremoniously and offered her his arm. Raven ignored his gesture and elevated herself from the cramped position. He observed her mockingly, and she returned his lascivious survey with cynical indifference. "Perhaps *la belle mademoiselle* is too overwhelmed by my presence to speak," he suggested. Black beady eyes, set deep into the baleful, pock-marked face and framed by bushy, orange brows, scowled morosely at his defenseless, sullen-eyed captive. "Speak to me!" he demanded.

"I can think of no words to relate the loathsomeness I feel for you and such a horrible deed." She stood fearlessly, arms crossed at her waist and staring her captor in the eyes. The sides of her face twitched nervously, for her teeth were gritted tightly together in evident disgust.

Ames's evily contorted grimace relaxed into a wry, unholy snicker. "If you were not so beautiful, *ma petite,* I would have you thrown to the sharks. Perhaps then you would behave more cordially to a representative of the French government."

Her lofty insults added to his caustic humor. "You are not seamen from the French Navy," she challenged, "but pirates who think nothing of killing innocent people. Even the company of sharks would be preferable to the company of such degenerates as you!"

"We shall see, mademoiselle," was his cool response.

At that moment, Lucy, having eluded the pitiless grip of her captors, ran screaming into Raven's cabin. "Raven, help! Ross . . . mur . . . murdered. Tr . . . ried . . . save m . . . me." Incoherent whimperings followed as the startled girl buried her head in Raven's shoulder. "Mister Ph . . . Phillips . . . M . . . Mister Baxter! Oh, horrible, horrible things!"

"Shh, shh. Hush, hush Lucy. I am here with you. We will protect each other," consoled Raven. As she caressed the matted, auburn head on her shoulder, she glared defiantly at her hideous foe. "What do you propose to do with us?"

Ames parted his wind-cracked lips underneath his closely cropped red beard. "I have not yet decided, Raven. Ah, what a lovely name—suitable for a woman of such exquisite beauty." He motioned to Lucy, still in Raven's shielding embrace. "I see you are most capable of tender caresses, mademoiselle. Perhaps you will prove equally comforting to me."

He strode vigorously out the narrow doorway and severely addressed his crew. "Search all of the rooms. Salvage any items of use or value. Load the cargo in the hold of our ship. If I find that any of you tried to conceal anything from me, you will be quartered and hanged from the yardarm!" The motley bunch nodded solemnly. "Now, off with you. I want to sail within the hour." They began to scurry like frightened mice in all directions. "Wait!" Ames's lips turned up in a sinister grin. "Do your jobs well, mates, and you will be rewarded with an evening of celebration. I am sure these lovelies will consent to join us." He winked suggestively at his crew and motioned them away. Turning to Raven and Lucy, he sneered demonically. "You shall discover later what gallant gentlemen we all are. Put on your finest gowns and jewels, my dears, and then permit me to escort you to my ship. I shall be waiting outside, so do not try to escape." He turned to leave, then added as an afterthought. "You should be grateful my manners exceed those of my men!" He bowed low from his thick waist and left the room, the evil smirk still intact on his face.

"What are we to do, Raven?" cringed Lucy, wringing her hands in worry.

"For the moment, we must do as we are told. Let us change from our nightshifts to more conservative frocks." She pulled two, high-necked, loose-fitting gowns of twilled silk from the wardrobe and handed Lucy the gray one, keeping the black one for herself. They dressed in doomed silence. Raven pinned her cameo broach on the inside seam of her full-tailed skirt and quickly sewed the conch pearl, along with six gold sovereigns, into its hem. "These will come in handy if we are rescued, or if perhaps we escape." Lucy's tear swollen eyes implored questioningly as to the likelihood of such. And still, in a barely audible tone, Raven continued confidently.

"Captain Perez sailed north yesterday morning and

should return here later this evening en route to New Providence. When he sees the *Fancy Free* abandoned, he will realize we have encountered trouble and will pursue us. Do not worry, Lucy. It is just a matter of time before we are found!"

Ames opened the door at that moment and beckoned for Lucy and Raven to join him. "You look as though you are in mourning," he scowled. "No matter, your dull garb will but encourage us to imagine the shape of those delectable bodies beneath." He tightly gripped both girls' arms and positioned himself in the middle. "Now, *mes petites chous,*" he taunted endearingly, "it is time we go to my ship. Let me assure you of the delights that await you there." His heinous laughter echoed throughout the cramped corridor. "Do not look so forlorn, *mes amies.* I perfer happy women, not sullen ones." He pinched Raven's arm. "Please me, my beauty, and no harm shall befall you. I give you my word."

Raven winced painfully at the terrifying thought of such encounters as the ones Ames had suggestively implied, and her eyes set determinedly in a deep-furrowed frown.

"So you still find me repulsive, mademoiselle, even when I shower you with kindness?" he asked as though he could read her morbid thoughts. "My treatment of you will be much gentler than my crew's. The final choice is yours, however. I am used to taking what I want, and unless ordered otherwise, my men will do the same. Unlike me, they have no sympathy for your tears."

His cruel words stunned Raven, but her unblinking eyes were fixed straight ahead. She was staunchly resolved never to allow her fear of Ames humor the

100

ruthless pirate.

"What about my brother and the others?" ventured Lucy timidly.

Ames, feigning seriousness and concern in his answer, replied, "I shall see that they have a fitting burial."

Raven imagined the horrors implied by "burial at sea." The fresh blood would rapidly attract sharks, and the corpses would be mutilated, torn apart by razor-sharp teeth. She shuddered at such a macabre thought.

The bereaved Lucy, walking as one with no direction or purpose, appeared oblivious to the hideous gore at the top of the stairs. Raven had to close her eyes and be led lest she heave out her insides. Fetid odors assailed the trio as they walked across the deck. It reeked of fresh blood and vomit. Flies rose from their swarms atop the warm, red liquid to greet the living forms.

The haunting darkness of the night meekly surrendered to the unfolding daylight. The dawning sky, alive with purples and reds, beckoned longingly to the dead souls, outlining their intended path through the heavens with vertical streams of mauve arrays. Raven peered at the heavens and wondered why the Maker had deserted them. How could He allow his children to be unmercifully slaughtered by such vile devils? Then she shamefully reprimanded herself for such blasphemous thoughts and again pleaded for mercy on her and Lucy's souls.

Floating on top of the heavily stained surface in the narrow area between the two ships was Captain Mabry. His eyes had refused to close, and he glared accusingly at his tormentors. His right leg rested against the hull of his ship, for even in death, he refused

101

to abandon his command. Raven quickly averted her gaze, but the view off the bow offered no escape from the gruesome scene. Several bodies that had not yet drifted out to sea floated stiffly, face down, in the churning water while black fins protruding from the surges methodically encircled the lifeless seafarers.

Ames taunted Raven once again as he lifted her from the English brig, his thumbs digging into her breasts. "Do you still prefer their company to mine? Heh? My caresses would be much more tender."

She looked at the red-bearded figure in dreaded consternation, her eyebrows knitted tightly in disbelief. Her nose wrinkled contemptuously at his touch.

"I do not believe it necessary to shackle you and throw you below until we reach Gorda Cay," he prodded. "I doubt you'll try to escape. Do not look so frightened, *ma belle*. I am on my best behavior; a lover wooing his intended."

When Raven was able to recover in part her sensibility, she dared to question Ames once again about their fate. "What about us, sir? Surely two helpless females do not warrant your wrath."

Ames did not perceive the sarcastic tone in which she used the polite form of address. Instead he smiled, believing her lofty spirits to be weakening. "You are incorrect in assuming that your future is in my hands. It is you who shall determine your destiny." Her bewildered expression prompted an explanation. "I do not intend to harm you and your little friend. We Frenchmen are much too chivalrous for such. You shall both return with me to my island. If I find your presence, shall we say, soothing, you will remain there in my protective custody."

"And what if we do not prove to be assets?" she questioned challengingly.

He shrugged his shoulders. "Then perhaps I shall sell you."

Raven's temper flared. "Sell us? Dispose of us to the highest bidder, I suppose? Why, that's barbaric!"

"Of course, what did you expect from a scoundrel such as I?" He scratched his orange-whiskered chin and lecherously eyed her shapely form. "Let me see. A young and beautiful English maiden of good stock, a virgin no doubt, should bring at least ten sovereigns."

Raven glared at him with violent vexation and bitter dismay. "That is all a human life is worth to you?"

"Oh, my *chérie*. Do not get so upset. I have no intention of standing you naked on an auction block and having these dogs drool over you. Though I must admit such a picture excites me. I would prefer to sell you to a friend of mine, a Madame DuVall, who owns a most fashionable brothel in Nassau."

Crimson engulfed Raven's throat and spread rapidly upward. "We are not whores to be bought for someone's pleasure. My father is an earl, my mother a lady."

"I must make a reminder of that. Royalty always commands a much higher price," he sneered, giving her a mock salute and a sly wink. "Now you must excuse me. I have duties to attend. Please make yourselves comfortable," he concluded, motioning to a rickety bench partly shaded by the foremast. "We shall sail directly. *Au revoir.*"

"That man is Lucifer himself. Never in my worst dreams could I have imagined such a formidable, abhorrent creature. I wish I had a cutlass. I would plunge it into his heart this instant without a moment's hesitation or regret. Scum like Red Ames have no right existing." Her venomous invective was witnessed by no one, not even Lucy, for she had retired to the bench under the mast.

Even as Raven approached her friend, Lucy's expression remained unchanged, and her gaze was dull and glassy. Save for that one moment after Ross's daring attempt to save her had been thwarted by the rapier's point penetrating his stomach, Lucy offered very little display of emotion. She did not acknowledge her friend's presence, nor did she choose to seek further solace from Raven.

Perhaps she blames herself for Ross's death, reasoned Raven. Or maybe she feels guilty for having shunned her brother, intending to make him feel remorseful for forcing her to accompany him to the colonies.

Raven was powerless to release Lucy from her almost hypnotic trance. The trauma of seeing her brother heartlessly stabbed would forever be imprinted on her mind.

If only I knew what she were thinking, wished Raven, then I could help her. She must be torturing herself tremendously.

But inside Lucy's mind were no thoughts. She was as void of expression on the inside as her glass-eyed expression revealed. She had locked all of her sorrows inside, and there they would remain until that horrible impression could be erased.

By the time the sun had climbed half the distance to its noonday peak, the cages of chickens and doves, pens of goats, bales of tea, crates of gin, casks of brandy, and barrels of bully beef and salt pork had been stowed in the hold of the corvette. Lucy remained in her dazed stupor as the hours slowly passed, showing no emotion, not even when the hideous plunderers would pass in front of the bench snarling foul remarks and making obscene gestures.

Raven viewed her crude captors with shuddering disgust intermingled with shocked pity. Their murderous treachery and bloody acts were unforgivable, yet these creatures were more bestial than human. Their features were unseemly and deformed, faces grotesquely scarred. Many of the stooped bodies lacked an arm, a leg, a nose, an ear, or an eye; such disfiguration the result of drunken brawls, or a reminder of the stern discipline Ames did not hesitate administering to his crew. They reeked of sweat, of excrement, and their victims' blood. Because of their enormous intake of sweet, syrupy rum, all their teeth had rotted away, leaving only darkened yellow nubs close to their shriveled gums. They did not speak, but instead grunted low, guttural animallike sounds. Those who were not condemned murderers fleeing from British justice had been found wallowing drunkenly in the gutters of Nassau. Such outcasts willingly joined Ames's band, even though he was notoriously reknown for his insidious cruelty; even toward his own followers. The total share of their rich haul was only a small portion of that which was divided between Ames and the two French lieutenants who had previously served under him. But the mangy group was satisfied with their few coins and meager remains from the officers' table, and even with the threadbare rags covering their sore-ridden bodies, for Ames would generously reward their services with plenty of drink. After a successful raid he allowed them to devour all the rum they could consume, and for days afterward, jeer at them as they held their heads in agonizing misery while performing their servile chores.

Raven listened closely to the discussion between Ames and his lieutenants Mouliere and Dalmas as the crew prepared the sails. After mentally translating straggling words and phrases from French, she realized that Ames had no intention of leaving the *Fancy Free* in the cut. Mouliere was instructed to man the stolen vessel with half the crew and follow the lead ship to a cluster of mangrove cays west of their present location. There the English cargo vessel would remain until a deal could be negotiated for its sale. This shattered Raven's hope of Perez ever finding the abandoned vessel. By the time he would reach Nassau and discover that Mabry had never made port, she and Lucy would be stranded on Ames's stronghold with little chance of rescue. Even though she halfheartedly admitted the seeming hopelessness of her plight, she refused to admit to the chilling fear nagging inside her. Instead of depending on Juan Perez to save them, she must rely on her own resourcefulness. Even at such a critical time, the memory of Juan ignited a flame that spread quickly throughout her body as she remembered their fiery kisses and clinging embraces.

Stop it, she cautioned herself. You have no time for such romantic fantasies. There are more urgent demands that require your attention.

"I apologize for leaving your side for such a long time, *ma chérie,* but it could not be helped." Ames stood powerfully erect beside her, one hand resting on

106

the mast, the other entangling her hair. "You feel warm, my sweet," he commented, rubbing trickling drops of moisture from her neck. "Perhaps it was not such a prudent decision to wear that dress after all."

The heavy, dark material of Raven's gown retained each ray of the scorching heat. Only her face and hands were exposed to the occasional breeze that ruffled the sails. She opened her mouth to speak, but its corners cracked with parchness. "Water, please?" she murmured, trying to conceal her repulsion at his closeness.

Maybe if I pretend to be more condescending toward Ames, she thought, his treatment of us would not be so severe.

Ames yelled for one of the men to go below and fetch a gourd of water. He severely reprimanded the peglegged seaman when its delivery was not immediate.

"Here's some water, Lucy," whispered Raven, offering the discolored container to her friend. She repeated her words, but Lucy remained immersed in her own thoughts. Raven then tore part of the sleeve of her dress and saturated the cloth with water. Gently she patted Lucy's parched lips with the wet compress and then rubbed it across her vacant face. She finally allowed herself a taste, but the liquid did not offer much relief from the heat since it was stagnant and warm.

In the midafternoon, Raven spotted tall trees and shrub that appeared to be growing straight out of the water. She immediately straightened her back, wincing from remaining in her slumped position for so long a time, and rose to her feet. The vessel neared the sight, revealing that a small mass of land did indeed support the clumps of floating vegetation.

Towering casuarina pines, dense mangrove thickets and dozens of deep water channels made the tiny cay an excellent location for concealing the *Fancy Free*. Ames cautiously maneuvered the ship through one such narrow cut which extended half the width of the island. The channel forked, and the right passage gradually thinned into a narrow stream while the left one opened out into the sea.

He yelled for both ships to drop anchor and ordered the crew to the deck of the brig to assist in securing the lines.

Tightly plaited ropes were knotted at three evenly spaced points on the starboard railing. Then each of the corded lengths was thrown ashore and tied to the base of the sturdiest pine. The process was then repeated on the port side of the vessel, leaving her floating midway in the channel, but secured to land on both sides.

An hour later, the French renegade was again ready to sail. He commanded a cadaverously thin one-eyed mate to remain on board the *Fancy Free* to perform the daily task of clearing the bilge. A week's supply of food and water was thrown to him, and even though the old man did not relish the thought of being alone on the cursed vessel, his unpatched eye gleamed greedily when Ames included a case of gin in the provisions. The crew lowered the sails and manned the oars on both sides of the stout warship, for the two square sails could not be hoisted without snagging the canvas on low-hanging branches lining both banks of the left passage.

By seven o'clock that night the rowers were no longer needed to propel the ship. They wearily returned to their designated posts and, without the usual complaints and bitter resentments, ravenously devoured their evening's rations of tough strips of bully beef, molded bread crusts and maggot-laden cheese while Ames and the lieutenants gorged themselves on two-day-old turtle steak, cold yams, and cracked conch taken from the galley of the captured ship. Bawdy jokes and stuttered obscenities elicited wheezy laughter as the damnable lot ogled wantonly at the two shapely women still huddled in the shadows. They seldom engaged in such rollicking humor, preferring instead to fight among themselves, but Ames had assured them of a rum-filled celebration as soon as they were safely inside the series of jagged reefs that separated the island of Gorda Cay from the New Providence Channel.

Ames and the two other Frenchmen rejoined the crew, and the sails were once again furled. Under Ames's expert guidance and watchful eye, the ship was skillfully manuevered around the sharp obstacles dotting the watery paty.

"This is why I am invincible," he shouted ener-getically from his vantage point on the bridge. "That damned Rogers has placed a wealthy price on my head, and each of those fools in Nassau thinks he will be the one to lead me to the gallows. But I shall show them who commands these seas!" he boasted to his cheering crew. "Sometimes, we play a sort of cat and mouse game with them, don't we mates?" he revealed for Raven's benefit. "They try to follow us through these shallow cuts. Is it our fault their ships ram the rocks and break up on the reef? Am I responsible for their stupidity? Those English dogs will never have the seamanship of us Frenchmen."

Instead of balking at his cruel, egotistical vaunt,

Raven insolently challenged his treachery. "And what do you propose to do, if by chance, the pursuer's nautical skill equals yours?"

It amused Ames that the dark-haired beauty would dare question his skill or strategy. She had not attempted to humor him or to pacify his outbursts with her feminine wiles as other women had done. He could sense the loathing and contempt hidden behind her resplendent eyes and was aware of the derisory tone of her voice when she addressed him, even though her exquisite features showed only quizzical innocence.

All the more reason for my taming the vixen, he thought amusedly. He responded to her question in detail. *"Le Bordeaux* is a French warship, mademoiselle; small and quick. As you can see, she has an armament of twelve guns. If direct confrontation is necessary, those heavy tubs you British call man-of-wars have no chance of victory, or even survival. I am touched by your concern for my welfare, *ma chérie.* But there is no need for worry," his cool glaze turned to bitter frankness, "or hope that you will be rescued by Captain Perez. Do not look so shocked. I heard you speaking of him in your cabin. His fate, I swear, will be much worse than all the others I have been plagued with if he tries to take that which is mine. You belong to me, *mon amour!"* Short stubby fingers possessively fondled her statuesque shoulders.

Raven's haughty green eyes blazed with vehement hatred as she delivered a stinging slap across his formidable jaw. A surprised expression wrinkled into demonic scorn as Ames savagely grabbed the defiant woman and pulled her slender body against his flaccid flesh. One hand, pressed tightly against her back, held her in position while the other forced her face upward. His foul breath reeked of gin and pungent odors, and coarse, red bristles pierced her face as he covered her lips with his biting mouth. Raven struggled from his grasp and disgustedly wiped his slobber from her chin.

"Do you treat your gallant Captain Perez in such a manner?" he goaded.

"He is a gentleman, not an animal!" she retorted tersely. Her despite for the notorious pirate overshadowed the fear she felt.

Ames's black eyes narrowed, and his thin lips parted in a sinister grin. "Surely mademoiselle, you will retract such an accusation. How can you possibly class a French gentleman, one who has received many honors for bravery, as an animal?" He sneered evilly. "If you wish to see real animal behavior, I will allow my men, all of them at once, the tantalizing pleasure of your company. You will perhaps realize then that they lack my cultured refinement."

Raven stared at him with blatant hostility but knew better than to challenge his vile threat. Her silence appeased him, and he teasingly pinched her cheek. "I am pleased that we understand each other, mademoiselle." He wet his lips with moisture from his viperish tongue and surveyed her body wantonly, eyes resting appreciatively on the ample bosom beneath the blouse of her gown. "We shall become much better acquainted, *ma petite,* and thoughts of a real man, not Perez, will fill your beautiful head."

He grabbed a handful of curls and tightly wrapped them around his fist. He jerked back her head, and Raven, feeling the color drain from her face, bit the corner of her lower lip to hold back her cries. The evil face, reddened by gin and anger contorted misshapenly, and he morbidly warned his conquest, "I do not hesitate inflicting excruciating pain on those who refuse to submit to me."

His tense face relaxed, as did his hold on Raven, allowing her to regain her upright stance. She refused to acknowledge her torturer's beady peer, gluing her eyes instead to the ground. Ames's sun-spotted hands encircled her tapered waist and roughly pulled her into his hardening hold. His thrashing body ground against her midsection and, crushing her hips with his powerful hands, forced them to meet his stabbing movements. His hold on her delicate body was constricting.

"But for those who please me, I will see to it that they want nothing and are treated like royalty. This was but a sample, my *chérie,* of the many delights you will experience in my company." A lecherous smile creased beneath red bristles, and he raised Raven's limp, pale hand to his lips. *"Au revoir,* mademoiselle. But only *pour une moment.* I shall return."

He confidently strutted toward the bow of the ship, bellowing loudly to his impatient crew. "Lower the sails! Drop anchor! Enough work for one day! Break open the rum!" His orders were immediately carried out, and the restless bunch crowded around the wooden cask with their pewter cups outstretched greedily. "Drink up, mates. Tomorrow we sail for New Providence!" The sailors responded with a resounding cheer and began guzzling the sweet rum. Ames, Dalmas, and Mouliere stood away from the mob and regarded the scummy lot with wry superiority as they raised their square green bottles to their lips.

Finally, Raven was able to breathe a bit easier now

that she was no longer being smothered by Ames's embrace, and she returned to the bench. Lucy's dazed expression was unchanged and her body still immobile.

"Lucy, please look at me. At least try to listen to what I have to say." She tilted the auburn head toward her, but Lucy failed to show any awareness of Raven's presence. "Listen carefully, Lucy." She removed a shiny, sharp stiletto from underneath the sleeve of her dress. The blade caught a gleam of light and reflected eerily in the shadows.

Lucy blinked at the fleeting sparkle and looked confusedly at Raven, who then implored, "Nod your head if you understand what I am saying." She waited patiently for a response, and finally Lucy lowered her chin slowly, then raised it again. "Good, good girl," she encouraged.

She looked cautiously over her shoulder to make sure Ames and the others were too involved in their gaiety to be concerned with them. "I stole this from Ames. You keep it. Strap it underneath your stocking garter." When Lucy failed to do as she was instructed, Raven raised the folds of Lucy's skirt and attached the knife underneath the silk band just above her knees.

"Lucy!" she impatiently shook her friend's shoulders. "You must use this to protect yourself. I have a plan. I must leave you for a little while. Not for long, I hope. But you must use this in case one of those murderers comes near you."

Lucy's body was wracked with sobbing quivers. "Murderers? Ross?" she uttered softly. "Where's my brother? Please don't take me away from Jean-Claude. I love him."

Raven's encouraging words quieted her whimpers.

"Everything will be fine, Lucy. Just do as I ask, all right?" She patted the slender line under the skirt as if to remind Lucy of its purpose. "Later when they have all passed out, we shall try to escape to shore and hide in the bushes. That is our only chance for surviving."

Confident that Lucy comprehended the urgency of her words, Raven quickly unfastened the cameo broach from the hem of her skirt, opened it to review the contents then, checking the clasp, fastened it to the center of her high-necked ruffles.

## Chapter Seven

For the next two hours Raven sat in silence, her arm entwined in Lucy's, and waited patiently for the moment that she knew would inevitably come. She silently reviewed her plan once more, hopeful that it would work. She swallowed the fright that was knotted halfway down her throat and watched as Ames staggered toward them. She inhaled deeply, her rushing heart pounding noisily against her chest. She stood to meet her ribald foe, slowly releasing the air through her half-gaping mouth. Her folded hands clutched the indentations of her narrow waist, and her out-thrust chin jutted with firm purpose. Her velvet lips mellowed, and dark, soft lashes lowered coquettishly.

Ames was awed by the provocative form in front of him. His dilated eyeballs, inflamed with drunken desire, ravished the voluptuous quarry. His words were slurred. "I hope, mademoiselle, you have given careful consideration to my words of this afternoon."

Her response was softly passive, and she made herself coo, "Indeed I have, Captain Ames."

"And what have you decided?" he grunted.

"I have decided, Henri, that I have judged you unfairly, and I wish to make amends for my childish behavior. Only high ranking officials of the French Navy are permitted to wear that symbol of honor," she said, touching the red collar around his square neck and allowing her long-taloned fingers to linger suggestively on his corpulent body.

"Ah, it pleases me that your attitude has undergone such a drastic change." It had been some time since anyone had intimately addressed him by his given name, and his bloated jaws smacked with anticipation of the pleasure that lie ahead. "You will never regret your decision to cooperate with me, *ma petite.*"

She forced a lifeless, but nevertheless teasing sound from her throat, and she jokingly pushed Ames away, striking a sensual pose in her effort to stall for time. "Am I then to assume that I am forgiven for my horrible actions and that you have decided against sharing such bounty with the others?" Her hand stroked her thighs in a promising gesture. Her lips pouted knowingly.

Ames nodded impatiently, growing weary from their talk and most anxious to take his prize below. "Yes, yes, yes!"

Raven casually glanced to the opposite end of the deck. Satisfied that the rum-soaked crew members, outstretched beneath the cask in a drunken sleep, were in no condition to threaten Lucy's welfare, Raven winked saucily at the commander, who was more than ready to retire from the deck.

Moonlight streamed down through the creaking boards to the musky, narrow passageway. Oversized rats and roaches scampered into the shadows.

*"Après vous, mademoiselle,"* said Ames, turning the brass doorknob of his cabin.

Their shadows were projected on the dark, tobacco-scented walls by two waning candles in the middle of a bottle-cluttered desk. Parallel to it was a bunk extended from the wall, which was bare except for a soiled, down padding covering it. An ornately carved wooden chest, secured by an oversized, brass-mounted lock, occupied the opposite side of the cramped quarters. Ames barred the latch behind them, and then gestured Raven to the bed.

She sat demurely, hands folded in her lap, legs crossed at the ankles, and nervously watched as Ames swallowed another gulp from his bottle. He wiped the foam from his mouth with the back of his hand and peered suspiciously at the dignified young woman placidly positioned atop his bed. "You have mellowed considerably. Such a change of mood so suddenly baffles me," he said suspiciously.

Her lashes fluttered. "I do not intend to perplex you, Henri." She prayed that the flickering light would not reveal in her countenance the real hate and fear she had for the man beside her. "Perhaps I have softened because I realize my position as your prisoner and my duty to serve you obediently." She stared brazenly into his skeptical gaze. "And because I feel sure that since you are a gentleman of honor, you will not abuse my subserviency."

Ames scratched his chin thoughtfully, and after another swig of gin, appraised the words of his alluring beauty. French gentleman, indeed, he thought. Perhaps it would be to my advantage to continue such a charade. She obviously has no knowledge of the handsome price the French government has placed on my patriotic head. Ah, such a beautiful creature. Her body is young and ripe for the plucking. I haven't had a real woman in ages. The ones in Nassau are worn out, and trying to mount that Spanish sow on Gorda Cay is worse than wrestling a man.

Ames moved closer to his guest. "That was indeed a wise decision, for I will not abuse such a lovely as you. Unlike others who might find themselves in similar situations, I would rather delight in such joys through mutual consent, not forced submission. It has been a while since I have savored the delicacies of one as beautiful as you." His hand traced a path from her ear down her neck, and rested on her breast, fondling the mound beneath the black silk.

Raven was deathly aware of her cheekbones turning a warm crimson. Her body stiffened, and a knot formed in her stomach. She feared that at any moment her repugnance for the pirate would be revealed.

"Relax, *me chérie*. The pleasure you will experience this evening will be most memorable." He continued stroking her breast while bending down to kiss her flushed neck, and at the same time unbuttoning the pearl buttons of her gown. His breath was pungently hot, and she closed her eyes to endure the torture, a gesture Ames mistook for ecstasy. "Here, a sip of this will make you feel even better," he assured, handing her the bottle.

"Yes, th . . . that is a fine suggestion," she mumbled, grateful for the opportunity to proceed with her plan. "I shall get us each a cup. See here, the top of this is broken. Loosen your collar, and I shall pour us both a drink."

Ames was reluctant to relinquish his hold, but agreed to humor her. His lecherous eyes were fixed on the shapely contour of her well-endowed body as her hips swayed suggestively to the table.

After a seductive glance over her shoulder, Raven turned her back to Ames and nervously sucked in a deep breath, knowing that her fate would be sealed if the drunken captain were to see what she was doing. She opened the cameo broach and poured the white powdery contents in the pewter cup intended for him. Fortunately, Ames was too intent imagining the delights awaiting him between her rounded thighs to notice her actions.

"Here you are, Henri," she said, offering him the cup containing the potion Ross had given her as a cure for sleepless nights.

"Merçi, mon amour. To us," he toasted. "May this night awaken such passions as neither of us has ever experienced."

She was afraid her eyes reflected the deception, so they rested on his hand stroking her leg, not his face. After Ames began to drink from the cup, Raven turned hers to her mouth. She had intended swallowing only a small amount, but because of Ames's hawklike watch, knew a few more drops must be forced inside. The warm liquid numbed her lips and burned her mouth with its horrible taste. She lowered her cup, but Ames demanded that she drink even more, saying that a few more sips would loosen her nerves. She reluctantly raised the foul brew to her mouth again and attempted to swallow more, but she coughed, and it spewed from her mouth onto her dress.

Ames roared heartily with drunken laughter, and he

proceeded to empty his cup with one giant gulp. "This is how it is done, my pet. You will learn in good time." He roughly pushed her down onto the lumpy bed and straddled her supine body. He pounded her with violent kisses while groping savagely for her trembling breasts.

She lay wide-eyed and helpless, frozen underneath his massive weight. She gasped for breath. All she could see were red hairs hanging from his nostrils as Ames's venomous mouth engulfed her lips.

His breathing quickened, and moanings gurgled from his throat. Short, dirty-nailed fingers unfastened the remaining buttons and jerked the top of her gown off around her elbows, binding her arms by her side. He rubbed his tongue across his hungry lips, and a lusty smacking sounded from inside the rancid mouth.

Raven lay defeated, her body crushed by Ames's bulk. She could offer no more resistance than a mere toss of her head from side to side in an attempt to free her chest from his wet caresses. She squealed painfully as Ames bit the darkened point of her breast, but he growled for her to hush.

One sweaty hand raised her skirt about her waist as the other pierced the tender, inner portion of her thighs, brutishly squeezing the bare flesh until the skin turned a deep purple. He probed the inside of her struggling body with three fingers, riping against the folded skin of her maidenhood. Perspiration dripped from his odious body onto her pale, bare skin as his hand violated her flesh. He cackled at Raven's pleas for mercy. Laughingly he jerked his trousers from around his waist. The sight of his threatening manhood, hardened and poised for attack, repulsed her. Her stomach heaved nauseously, but the lewd conquerer would not be stopped. He mounted her body for the final degenerated act and humiliation. Suddenly his body collapsed onto hers.

Raven closed her eyes and bit her lip in shameful wait for the painful moment of his raping assault, but his weighty body was lifeless. Using every bit of her remaining strength, she rolled his bulging corpulence from across her weakened self. She paused only a few seconds; long enough to calm the pounding rush of her heart, then hurried from the room.

Thoughts of how she and Lucy would escape from the hellish ship raced across her mind as she bounded up the steps, taking two at a time. She peered cautiously in both directions upon reaching the top of the cramped companionway and was relieved to see the mates still entranced in their drunken slumber. After mumbling a quick prayer, she headed for Lucy.

Crying moans and ghoulish laughter caused her to stop midway. Lucy's clothes had been stripped from her body and lay in a pile under the bench. Her arms were stretched behind her head and bound to the mast with a hemp cord. A half-naked fiend straddled her body, jeering at her cries for help while he thrusted himself deeper inside of her. The stiletto Raven had given Lucy lay several yards away. In one quick motion, Raven grabbed the knife and lunged at Lucy's attacker, plunging the blade deep into his neck. His back stiffened; his paralyzed throat allowed no sounds of pain to escape. Blood gushed from the wound, and he fell to his side, face down onto the deck.

It took several moments for the complete impact of her deed to effect Raven, and she stared at the waxen

121

corpse with startled confusion and dismay at what she had done. With renewing strength she assured herself that she had had no alternative, and she eased closer and pulled the stiletto from its mark, wiped the blade clean on the railing, and tucked it securely in her garter.

No words were exchanged, only understanding glances and sympathetic nods, as Raven untied Lucy's hands and lifted the torn remains of clothing over her head onto her abused body. She eased Lucy to her feet and wrapped her arm around the battered girl's waist to support her unsteadiness. With Lucy's arm draped around Raven's neck, she carried them both as they trudged across the deck and down the stairs to Ames's room.

Once secure in the cabin, Raven lowered Lucy to the floor, propped her back upright against the chest and proceeded to rub the raw lacerations covering her body with the contents of a half-empty gin bottle in an attempt to cleanse the deep wounds. "Drink this," she whispered. "It will numb the pain."

Lucy meekly obeyed, even though the tepid liquid burned the cut on her swollen lip, for she wanted to erase from her mind all thoughts of the agonizing torture inflicted upon her by that madman. She wanted to tell Raven that he had been the one who drove the sword into Ross, but her head grew heavy with dizziness and throbbing pain.

Raven cradled Lucy's head on her shoulder, whispering soothing words of comfort to her friend until the troubled girl fell into a dreamless slumber. Raven could not rest, even though her body had been drained of all its life.

It will be dawn in a few hours, she thought dismally.

Dawn, and what will happen to us then? Ames will awaken, probably knowing that I drugged him, and when he sees Lucy in here and the dead man on deck, he'll realize that I killed one of his men. With Lucy in such a condition, there is no chance of our escaping to the island. What a ridiculous thought anyway. His men are probably familiar with every inch of that ground and would find us in no time. I wonder if he'll kill us, or throw us to his men to be ravaged like raw meat thrown to a pack of hungry wolves. Even if he spares us, we shall still be trapped on his island, always to be at the mercy of him and his men. What good is hope now? We are lost; dead to the world. Jean-Claude will never know what happened to his beloved, and my father will not know of my fate until he returns to England. No chance of escape! Perhaps even death is more welcoming than another day spent as that fiend's prisoner. Dear God, if it be your intent that we die, let us do so now in our sleep before our bodies are again violated and our souls tortured. Please, I beg of you.

Her eyelids gradually closed and sleep came, barring from her sight Ames's thrashing nakedness and closing her ears to his gasping snores and dreamful moans of pleasure. She stirred soon after the sun had risen, not to voices of angels, but to the noises on deck as the hands roused themselves from their intemperate drunkenness. Frequent loud bursts of curses and agonizing fits of discomfort sounded above her head. Finally she heard what she most dreaded; heavy footsteps plodding across the deck in the direction of the corpse.

Woeful moans sounded from within the room as Ames writhed convulsively in unendurable agony. His feet moved clumsily to the floor, but the rest of his body would not budge from the bed. He held his throbbing head between his hands as he tried to rise, complaining loudly and profanely the entire time. He raised his head, and seeing that he was not alone, jerked himself to his full height, ran his hand through his tangled hair and smoothed his matted beard. His mouth twisted into a taunting grin as he pulled his trousers up from around his ankles.

"So, I awake to find I was not fantasizing after all. I did indeed enjoy the company of two lovelies last night. I hope my men will not begrudge my pleasuring both of you, but they were in no condition to give you the proper welcome." A loud knock sounded outside. "Yes, yes what is it?"

Lieutenant Mouliere entered. "Captain, Sir, Jones has been stabbed."

Raven's heart stopped beating for a moment as she watched Ames roll back his blood-rimmed eyes and shake his head disgustedly. "It never fails. I lose more men to the blades of their greedy comrades than to our adversaries. Roll his body off deck!" he ordered indifferently.

Mouliere nodded, suspiciously eyeing the two women. "Any other orders, Sir?"

"Yes. Send some men to replenish our water supply and unload the animals. Check our provisions. We shall need enough supplies for a week or ten days. We sail to Nassau immediately to find a buyer for the cargo."

"What about them, Sir?" asked the lieutenant, nodding to the two women.

After thoughtful consideration, Ames declared, "They served me well last night, especially the darker one. It would be such a waste to sell them to others who may have no regard for true beauty or to trade them for a few kegs of brandy. Leave them on the island. Perhaps now you and I shall spend more time here than at Madame DuVall's, heh Mouliere?" he suggested, bursting into unbelted laughter. And the lieutenant, afraid not to do so, joined his commander in his riotous jest.

*Chapter Eight*

Gorda Cay, a small island eight miles west-northwest of the southern tip of Abaco and on the northern edge of the New Providence Channel, had been an impregnable stronghold for Ames since his retreat to the Bahamas ten years earlier. Undersea mountains of coral formed a natural fortification around the cay. These fringe reefs could easily crush the hardest part of a ship's bottom, and few mariners were daring enough to risk navigating such treacherous obstacles.

Dense shrub thickets and low, bushy trees outlining the perimeter of the island concealed the ten cone-shaped roofs located in the interior. Shacks built from the slender poles of the casuarina pine and thatched with palmetto fronds formed a village. In the center of the semicircular arrangement was a round fire pit where meals were prepared and where the rowdy cutthroats gathered at night to exchange drunken tales of their gruesome deeds. Beside the pit was a half-buried wooden box, that served as an oven. Across from the shelters lay a cleared plot of carefully tended ground that produced yams, corn, potatoes, and peas. Opposite the garden stood a crudely built enclosure used for housing the goats, small Yucatan deer, pigs, and hens.

Raven and Lucy, along with the animals and provisions taken from the *Fancy Free* were transported to the island by a two-masted, flat-bottomed piragua. Two cripples who guarded the island during Ames's absence manned the boat. Lucy's forehead burned with fever and violent cramps ripped her stomach, but no mercy was shown her by the pair, who insisted that both girls carry provisions from the beach to the village.

After the food was stored in one of the shacks and the animals secured in the pen, Raven and Lucy were hustled inside one of the huts. A mat woven from palmetto fronds covered its floor, another was rolled up above the inside of the doorway. Two hammocks, an earthenware jug filled with water, and a smudge pot used to ward off insects were the only furnishings. Four copper-colored, squatty women gathered around the entranceway, peering curiously inside at the two light-skinned strangers while jabbering in an unfamiliar language. Lucy's piercing screams and Raven's urgent pleas for aid summoned a fifth woman.

"Please, you must help her," begged Raven. "I don't know what to do."

The woman, taller than the others but equally as dark, nodded and motioned for Raven to undress Lucy. She did as she was instructed but whitened with fright when jellied clots of blood gushed from between Lucy's legs. The woman carefully lifted the partially limp form and laid her gently onto one of the hammocks. Then she turned to the others, impatiently shouting to them. They rushed in different directions and returned quickly with blankets, rags, and a cup filled with steaming herbal tea.

"Make her drink this," commanded the woman while she applied cooling compresses to the fevered head. She washed the streaks of blood from her legs and packed the violated area with wadded strips of cloth. The tea acted as an opiate, and soon Lucy's eyes were closed, and the sharp, jabbing pains convulsing inside her subsided.

"I am Maria," she volunteered while covering Lucy in a coarse cotton blanket.

"My name is Raven Gatewood," said the girl, almost in tears. "She is Lucy Fairmont. Our ship was attacked, and everyone was murdered, and . . . and Lucy was forced to, to—"

"Shh, shh," comforted Maria with a sympathetic nod, the hardness of her look replaced with understanding. "It would be best to not talk of such. I know well of the sorrows inflicted on you by those vile devils."

"Will Lucy be all right?" timidly questioned Raven. She was hopeful, even though she knew that the battered girl had little chance of recovery.

Maria shook her head. "I do not know. Such a large amount of blood was lost when the baby—"

"Baby?" interrupted Raven. "Are you sure? I mean, she said nothing about carrying a . . . a baby." Then she remembered how desperate Lucy had been when talking of Jean-Claude, how much they had wanted to marry even against her brother's wishes, and how enraged she had been over the incident of the abandoned turtle eggs. Now she understood the reasoning behind Lucy's frequent outbursts. "Is there

128

nothing else we can do for her?" she asked numbly. Death had taken all of those close to her. Was it necessary that Lucy, too, must die? She sat on the floor beneath the hammock and held Lucy's limp hand. She whispered over and over, "Lucy, please don't die. Please, don't die!"

Maria's eyes compassionately embraced the pitiful scene. She wished she could console the despairing girl but knew that she could offer no false hopes that her friend would survive the tragic effects of such a horrible ordeal. She decided it would be best to leave Raven alone with her grief.

When Maria returned that evening she brought with her a plate of grouper, which had been baked in the oven and seasoned with the white, odorless smoke of casuarina twigs, roasted corn, and bread made from the root of the casaba. Raven managed a half-smile of appreciation and a few mumbled words as she declined the food.

"Eat," ordered Maria sternly, placing the plate beside her. Resting her hands on her ample hips she continued. "If you do not eat, then you, too, will become sick. You are exhausted, your eyes and face show the lines of your worry and anguish. You must try to maintain your strength." Her amber-colored eyes peered sternly, and Raven meekly acquiesced. "There, you will feel much better. I do not want to have to worry over you, too." Her round, rose-tinted face relaxed the sharpened features into an approving grin. She eased her bovine body gracefully onto the matted floor beside Raven.

"It is a terrible feeling to sit helplessly by while

someone we love suffers so. Why do you not sleep for a while? Your friend is resting comfortably. There is nothing more you can do."

Raven hesitated, but at Maria's insistence she awkwardly stretched out on the other hammock.

All during the night Maria kept a vigilant watch on Lucy. When her breathing became more labored from the heat raging inside her body, Maria would splash cool water on the tormented form and force her parched lips open to drink more of the love vine brew. She dressed the ulcerated marks and scratches with soothing papaya leaves and cooed soft words of comfort to the tossing girl. Maria left Lucy's side only once, briefly, to light the smudge pot. When she had done all which could be done to bring comfort to her patient, she watched and waited, hoping the girl would survive, but knowing she would not live to see daybreak. So frequently during her years on the island had she stood helplessly by, unable to do much more than that which she had done for Lucy, while one by one the others had died from fevers, abuse, and diseases inflicted on them by the filthy heathens who forced the unwilling women into perverse acts of submission.

Early morning sunlight filtered through the cracks of the frond roof, causing Raven to abruptly open her tightly closed lids with the stabbing realization that the events of the past day had not been concoctions of a horrible dream. She rolled over, startled to see she was alone in the hut. "Lucy!" she gasped. "Maria, Maria!" She jumped from her bed, raised the woven mat curtaining the doorway, and frantically looked for some indication of life. The yard was empty, lifeless

130

except for a low-burning fire in the pit.

"I am coming," was a monotone response from around the corner of the hut. Maria came into sight, her head shaking ominously and a strained smile shaped upon her lips. Her dark eyes were swollen from unshed tears, and her words were muffled. "I am deeply grieved, Raven, but perhaps all was for the best."

Raven had read the foreboding expression even before Maria had spoken. Surges of remorse flooded her, and she sobbed until the tears would no longer fall. She admonished herself for not spending more time with Lucy on the ship and for not being more sympathetic toward her predicament. And inadvertently, she blamed herself for Lucy's death since she had left her alone on deck.

Maria sensed her troubled thoughts. "You could not have prevented what happened. Do not burden yourself with such guilt. Instead, be grateful that she is able to escape such filth and ugliness as is here." She patted Raven's shaking hand reassuringly. "I shall get you some tea."

She returned with two cups of steaming brew and a plate of assorted fruit pieces: mangoes, melons, papayas, and oranges, which she placed between them. Raven absently drank the hot liquid and nibbled bits of the fruit. Remembering the gruesome sight she had witnessed earlier, she blurted her thoughts aloud. "No, not the ocean. Don't throw her in the ocean."

Maria's words were soft and comforting. "Of course not. I dug her grave myself and marked the site with shells and stones. Perhaps I shall take you there later."

A small cross, fashioned from two limbs of a pine

and joined with a section of hemp rope designated the newly earthed site. The spot rested in a sparsely grassed clearing in the pine hammock. Raven stood solemn and dry-eyed and unable to accept that the cold waxen form beneath the firmly packed ground was her pert, vivacious friend.

"The body in there is only a shell that clothed her soul," lamented Raven. "The real Lucy, my Lucy, is somewhere else. Her soul has already lifted to the skies. God would not allow her to suffer any more than what she had already." A faint smile crossed her face. "She's probably smiling down on us this very moment." She then knelt beside the grave and somberly hung a wreath of bouganvilleas braided with hybiscus and other wild flowers on the cross. Her hand lingered down to its base, and she endearingly caressed the soil.

"I shall miss you, Lucy, and always love you. You were dearer to me than any sister could have ever been." She closed her eyes and recited the twenty-third psalm, the words suitably affirming human faith and divine reassurance for both the living and the dead.

During the days that followed, Raven easily adjusted to the wearisome work routine that dominated island existence for the female workers. Their chores commenced at dawn with the gathering of driftwood from along the rock-lined beach and ended at dusk with the preparation of the evening meal. Most of the time the women were left unsupervised. The lazy pair Ames had left on the island descended from their watch tower only when they were hungry or needed to replenish their supply of rum. The two had learned some time ago to stay a safe distance away from the stocky, bronze women, whose strength equaled that of many men. Raven toiled strenuously at the tasks she shared with the others, believing that such incessant labor would prove to be an escape from the self-torturing thoughts that plagued her idle moments. Her hands became blistered and hardened with callouses, and her body ached each evening from lifting, carrying, bending and straining. She would fall exhaustively into her hammock at night, but the same recurring visions of purple-faced, bloated corpses beckoning to her from their watery graves haunted her sleep each night. Night after night she would twist frantically, violently thrashing against the tormenting demons that refused to be exorcised from her mind, while Maria would sit quietly on the mat until the pathetic turbulence gave way to weakened prostration.

On one such evening those convulsing spasms continued wrenching throughout Raven until well after midnight, and she began to scream and shout as one possessed. All attempts to awaken her were futile until Maria finally jerked the quivering girl half out of bed and delivered a half dozen stinging smacks across her ashen cheeks. She looked up dazedly and mumbled, "Bad dream! Bad dream!"

Maria hugged the whimpering girl close against her chest, stroking her head the way a mother does a child's. "Everything is fine, now. Nothing will escape from your dreams and harm you. I won't let it." She gently lay Raven back down onto the corded bed and covered her with a coarse blanket. "This is the eighth night I have watched as you tossed in your sleep, crying out names unfamiliar to me. Your soul is much troubled and until you can find the inner peace that you seek, I fear such nightmares will continue. If you can, please tell me of the thoughts that haunt your mind. Perhaps speaking of them will make them disappear."

Raven spoke unsteadily. "I dream the same dream night after night. Those same images float above my head. I know that what I am experiencing cannot possibly be real, and I try to awaken myself, but I cannot." Maria urged her to continue, and Raven vividly described the dead sailors as they were being thrown to the sharks while the merciless pirate wagered which one of the bloodied corpses would be the first devoured. She gravely recounted how Ross had been murdered while the cutthroats roared with laughter at his pain, and of how Captain Mabry lay face down, wallowing in a puddle of his own blood while the beastly rogues kicked and jeered at the fallen commander.

"They are no better than animals," hissed Maria spitting at the ground to emphasize the contempt she felt. "Cowards who will not fight as men, but sneak up and stab their unsuspecting victims in the back when they have no hope of defending themselves. Such brave men that three must hold down one woman while a fourth rapes her. What you have described is what I am well familiar with. But how is it that you were unharmed?"

After a determined sigh, Raven was able to tell Maria of her encounter with Ames. Her teeth gritted with disgust as she recounted the ghastly details of how she flaunted herself in front of him to get him down below, of how she pretended to succumb to his drunken pawings and finally how she was able to drug him. "Then I ran to get Lucy. I had this foolish notion that while Ames and the others were asleep, we could swim to the island and hide here. Oh, I should never have left Lucy. None of that would ever have happened." Her hands quickly covered her eyes as she remembered Lucy lying helplessly, hands tied to the mast and unable to defend herself against the degrading assaults of that insatiable demon straddling her. "I grabbed the knife and plunged it into his neck. Then I helped Lucy to Ames's cabin, and when he awoke the next morning he boasted to his lieutenant of a night of debauchery with the two of us. Oh, why could I not have stayed on deck with her? Why?"

"You did what you thought was right," encouraged Maria. "Your intentions were to save both of you. Do not blame yourself for that which you have no control."

Once Maria was able to convince Raven that her horrible nightmares were caused by such an overpowering shadow of guilt as the one she just revealed and of being the only one aboard the *Fancy Free* to escape death, her hellish dreams ceased.

Even though the Indian women found Raven's foreign speech and mannerisms peculiar, they behaved most congenially toward her. Her awkward attempts at conversing with them would be met with giggles and incoherent chatterings, thus limiting communication to basic gestures and motions. Nevertheless they were aware of her amiable intentions and from time to time gave her presents they had made: a wide-brimmed straw hat woven from the palmetto fronds, tortoise shell combs, sandals of braided strands of hemp, shell necklaces, and a shapeless shift spun from wild cotton to replace her tattered black dress.

Nature had provided all that was necessary for

sustaining life on the tiny island. Turtles, fish, land crabs, crawfish, wild yams and an assortment of fruit were plentiful. If the fresh water wells ran low, rainfall replenished them. Cotton for clothes could be spun from the cotton plants, shelters constructed from palm leaves, and medicines derived from herbs and plants.

Had it not been for the dread of Ames's return always nagging inside her, she could easily have accepted her fate. Her learning was not impeded by the lack of books or the absence of a tutor, for Maria and the others patiently taught her the lessons of survival. By the end of the month she was able to construct farming implements from tree limbs and flat stones, spin the wild cotton into a coarse material using a crude Indian loom, weave baskets, mats and rugs from the palm fronds, and extract medicines and dyes from the many plants and trees.

By mid-June her practical studies became increasingly difficult and her teachers more demanding. She quickly mastered the art of building a fish trap using only palm fronds and palmetto stalks. The women showed her how to burn wood and crushed conch shells for the lye residue, which could be mixed with pig fat to make soap. They gave her detailed instruction for making the fiberish cord used in fashioning ropes and hammocks, insisting that she repeat the process until they were satisfied that she was skilled in cutting the long green pods of the sisal plant, beating them against trees, and soaking them in salt water until all fibers had separated from the flesh and could be hung in the sun to dry. Later, Raven learned how to preserve fish and meats with the salt crystals that formed on the salt water ponds when the wind and sun caused the water to evaporate and left only the salt.

By the last of June, it became much more difficult to work for extended periods of time without frequently seeking a shaded refuge from the scorching heat. Raven's creamy complexion darkened to nearly the copperish color of her companions, and she had to coat her body each morning and night with cedar sap to repel the hoardes of mosquitoes and flies that were abundant on the island. Roving breezes would occasionally ruffle the palms, but more than often they would die down before the soothing effects could be felt and enjoyed. Some cooling relief would come in the form of afternoon downpours, but the rains quickly passed over, and the torid humidness would return. The nights were even more unbearable than the sultriness of the late afternoons. Maria kept the smudge pot burning continuously, and the smoke would linger all night in the already stuffy hut. As the haze lingered out the top of the cone-shaped roof, roaches hidden in the palmetto would fall on top of the hammocks, forcing Raven to pull the coarse covers even tighter around her sweating body.

The only way of comfortably escaping the sweltering heat and annoying bugs was by relaxing in refreshing, open air baths in the ocean. They would all go together to the white, crescent-shaped beach of the lagoon, each woman carrying with her a container filled with fresh water to pour over her after the salty bath. Upon reaching the brackish lake which was partially hidden by bending coco palms, the cottony shifts would be quickly discarded, and in they would plunge, like sea nymphs, into the welcoming relief of the alluring waters. Sometimes the women would float on top of the shoulder deep water, splashing playfully at their friends. Other times they were content to sit in the shallows while the tepid waters rippled over their skin and they scrubbed their hair, clothes, and bodies with lye soap.

During one of these relaxing frolics in the blue green pool, Maria talked openly of her life prior to being captured by Ames eight years earlier, revealing to her one spellbound listener—for the two were usually ostracized by the others—answers to many of the questions Raven had hesitated asking. "When I was your age, my family arranged my marriage to a man whose own wife had died the year before. Hernando was much older than me, and my father profited greatly from our union. He was a kind and gentle husband, as well as an important government official. He was a scholar and well versed in the language and customs of your people."

"I was wondering how you were able to speak such beautiful English," complimented Raven.

Maria blushed at such praise. "Our king appointed him governor of a province called Hispanole, and we left Spain a year after our marriage. During our fourth year there, a French warship tried to sink one of our armada, and its commander was imprisoned."

"Red Ames?" guessed Raven.

Maria nodded sadly. "Yes. He strangled a guard and escaped from the jail, stole into our home and kidnapped me. He sent a message to my husband offering to exchange me for his impounded vessel and crew and a guaranteed safe passage north. Hernando agreed, but Ames did not keep his word after the demands were met."

"Eight years," sighed Raven, shaking her head in disbelief that someone could exist so long in such primitive surroundings and under such barbaric conditions. "I am certain I will never be able to endure this place for a year, much less eight."

"You are wrong!" she disagreed stoutly. "If need be, you will survive just as I have survived. At the beginning I wanted to die. I prayed to die, for I did not believe I could endure another day of their degrading assaults and abuse. The humiliation I felt each day is indescribable. But now," her words were harsh and emphatic, "now I want to live; live to see all of those dogs punished. I hope Red Ames's flesh is ripped from his bones and the meat thrown to wild animals. The sound of his voice pleading for mercy while all of the onlookers jeer and poke sticks at his half-dead body would be sweeter than music to my ears."

"I know well that feeling," concurred Raven. "I suppose that makes us no better than him."

The wild-eyed, frenzied look vanished from the older woman's face as she dwelt upon Raven's statement. "You are right, I suppose, but some way he must be made to pay for his horrible sins and the suffering he has inflicted on innocent people. His insatiable lust for power and wealth will never be satisfied until there is no one left for him to rob or kill."

"He will be made to account for his deed," replied Raven firmly. "His own country has an attractive price on his head, and the governor of the Bahamas has just sent a crew in search of Ames determined to bring him to the gallows."

"Ames has often made jokes of such men," warned Maria. "I have seen him purposely lure boats onto these reefs and applaud when they crack up on the rocks. I do not foresee much hope of his capture," she concluded pessimistically. "He is far smarter in eluding his followers than anyone suspects.

"I have a feeling that his pirating days are about to come to an abrupt halt," she disagreed, telling the woman about Juan Perez and his mission. "I am confident it is only a matter of time before Perez reaches Gorda Cay," she concluded.

Maria remained obstinate. "I have watched countless others try and fail. He will be no different."

"But Juan is no ordinary seaman. Rogers commissioned him for this task because he is well acquainted with these waters. His crew is not what one might expect; they are all former pirates who had signed Rogers's Acts of Pardon. Having been rogues themselves at one time, they can anticipate Ames's moves far better than a trained military officer."

Maria relented. Raven's zeal and optimism caused her to be more objective. "Perhaps your Captain Perez has already succeeded in his mission."

"What do you mean?" asked the girl confusedly.

"When Ames left the island, he took with him supplies for only a short period of time. Two months have passed, and still he has not returned. He may be rotting away in prison now, or better yet, hanging from the gallows this very day," she said gleefully. "By any chance, did you overhear Ames discussing his plans for this voyage?"

"He did mention something about a buyer for the *Fancy Free,* and I think he intended to sail to New Providence to dispose of the stolen booty."

"If he is in Nassau, he is being well cared for. He

hides on an uninhabited cay northwest of there and has easy access to food and provisions. From there he disperses the stolen cargo to a merchant in Nassau who readily deals in that sort of good without asking too many questions." She smiled encouragingly. "Let us just be thankful that he has not returned here, whatever the reason!"

Raven remained silent, staring forlornly at the translucent water as a school of tiny fish frantically swam past her. Fleeing memories of that brief encounter with Perez rushed through her mind, and her body yearned for his caress. Surely I am not destined to remain here forever, she reasoned. Juan must find me!

"Hurry along, Raven. The others have already gone back to the village. If we do not follow soon, there will be no chowder left for our supper," insisted Maria, already on shore. When this failed to elicit a response from her daydreaming companion, she tried again. "Raven, it is almost dark. If I were you, I would not be in this pool when the sharks decide to come for their evening swim."

This deliberate mention of the deadly predators of the deep prompted an immediate response from Raven, and she scampered to shore. Maria showered her with fresh water, waited while she dressed, then led the way back to the village.

The guards had already eaten and returned to their watch towers camouflaged high among the casuarinas. Maria and Raven filled their bowls with the aromatic conch chowder that had been cooking all day in the caldron hanging above the pit. No sooner were they seated around the fire with the other women than the

Indians retired to one of the huts. Soon, strains of humming music and monosyllabic chants sounded from within.

"I wonder why they are so insistent upon keeping to themselves. Do I offend them?" asked Raven, soaking her bread in the thick, rich soup.

"It is not you they distrust. I am the one whose presence they wish to avoid. You see, my people explored the New World and discovered the existence of a civilization far more advanced than their own. The people who lived there were called Mayans. They were eager to please the fair-skinned conquistadors who visited them because they thought the soldiers to be gods. Unfortunately, the Spaniards found gold and enslaved the Indians for work in their mines. Their culture crumbled under Spanish domination. Those four," she explained wearily, "are descendants of those Mayans. They hate the Spanish, with good reason I suppose, for they know their whole civilization was destroyed by them. Those women were on their way to Spain to be used as servants when Ames attacked their vessel."

"But surely they realize you were not to blame for such historical events," reasoned Raven.

"Perhaps so, but I am still a Spaniard, and they believe I think myself to be superior to them. I have long given up trying to convince them otherwise." Maria shrugged her shoulders, a gesture that could easily have been mistaken for indifference had Raven not seen the noble woman blinking fiercely to hold back her tears.

Raven studied the dejected countenance of her friend. "It seems that they would at least realize that all

142

of us, regardless of our birth, are bound together merely by our situation as prisoners. That should be enough to encourage friendship. Has it always been just the five of you here?"

"No, at one time there was as many as twenty of us."

"What happened to all of them?"

Maria shuddered nervously as she reminisced. "Most of the women were too weak from island fevers or diseases carried by those dogs to survive here for very long. Many lost their will to live after being raped at knife point night after night. Some of the ones who could endure were taken to Nassau and sold as whores or exchanged for weapons and supplies." She dared not mention the desperate woman who drowned her twelve-year-old daughter rather than have the child subjected to further sexual abuse, and who then killed herself. Nor could she talk of how the drunken, deranged pirates continued the mass rape of a beautiful duenna long after the Spanish lady-in-waiting had died from such physical violation.

Raven, appaled at the horrors that she instinctively knew had not all been revealed to her, shivered inwardly, knowing that when *Le Bordeaux* returned to the protective, reef-filled waters of their haven, hers could easily be a similar fate.

"So," continued Maria, sensing a need to speak to the visibly shaken girl, "those four have survived because they are strong people. They are good workers, and Ames needs their endurance to build huts and watch-towers, and to farm this rocky soil. They have learned to offer no resistance to their captors and even believe that life is no worse here than it would have been under Spanish dominance. And I . . . I have been able to live because Ames has great visions of my kinsmen offering a handsome reward if I am found. I am certain that by now my husband has forgotten about me and has already taken another young bride."

They both stared vacantly into the smouldering fire. The sing-song chanting from the Mayans' hut ceased, and the only other noticeable interruption to the stillness was the incoming tide bashing against the weed-covered rocks.

"I know we shall be rescued, Maria. I know that will happen," said Raven.

Maria's lips shaped a negative response, but she hesitated. "I used to dream, too, Raven, but even then I could not believe strongly enough in my fantasy. I would plot for days devising some type of plan for escape, but all were foiled." She stroked Raven's shoulder protectively. "Once when Ames was away on one of his many raids, I saw a ship's sails in the distance, and I ran down to the point shouting and waving my arms, but the ship continued on its course. I returned crying to the village and was greeted by the toothless laughter of the old men who had witnessed my desperate attempt."

Raven pensively studied the situation, her eyes squinted in deep concentration. "But there are ships that pass by here?" Maria nodded. "Frequently?" Again the puzzled woman shook her head.

Not understanding Raven's point, Maria shrugged. "Of course there are ships that pass by here once or twice a month. One of the main reasons Ames chose this site is because of its location relative to the Channel. Ships laden with gold and silver from Cuba and South and Central America go through this cut on their way to Europe. I have even watched them pass. Ames would rush to his ship and raise the tricolored flag of France and pretend that he is in distress. As soon as the other vessel ventured closer in, he fired on them."

But Raven was not listening. Instead she was formulating her own plan of salvation. "Each day, Maria, we can drag loads of driftwood down to the point. Then when we see an approaching ship, we can light the fire. Perhaps the blaze will attract their attention."

Maria did not wish to dampen Raven's enthusiasm, for she suspected that without hope, the girl could easily lose her desire to live. But she did not want her to believe that her scheme was without problems. "First, if we are spotted from the tower, you know what our punishment will be. Secondly, suppose it is the *Bordeaux* that we are so blatantly signaling. What then?" Seeing Raven's distraughtness made her feel guilty at shattering the young girl's hopes, but still, she felt a need to continue. "Even if a friendly ship were to spot our fire, its captain would not want to risk his ship going through that maze of rocks for fear it was another pirate trick. I am sorry to be so blunt. You do understand that my words are not intended to bring you grief?"

Raven nodded and rose to leave.

Maria watched as she walked cheerlessly to the hut. Her head was lowered, and her arms were folded tightly under her bosom. Her steps were short and slow. The sudden, harsh realization that she was trapped on the island until her death gave her the appearance of a stooped, dejected old woman.

Maria sighed a long, exasperated sigh. How can I prepare her for the chilling horrors that await her when Ames returns to claim his spoils? How can I tell her of the excruciating torment that will rip through her as she is maimed by those bastards while their friends cheer them on and await their own turn? Will she understand that no matter how hard she tries to scrub their filth from her body the taint of their indecency will scar her flesh forever? Should I tell her of that urgency to destroy oneself once one has been subjected to such carnal wantonness by those creatures whose desires and lewdness are unnatural? Her heart grew heavy, and her eyes cried for the unmitigated pain and rankling misery to which Raven must soon become accustomed.

## Chapter Nine

Summer downpours became more frequent during the earlier part of July. They halted the work during the early morning hours so that the women were forced to spend the extended daylight laboring diligently to complete their chores. The two sentries continued their impatient wait in their pine-covered lookout, their spyglasses constantly raised to their puffy eyes for the first sign of their long overdue leader.

But the French warship failed to appear on the horizon. Even the disfigured corsairs soon felt some horrendous evil had befallen their fierce-visaged commander. They could not envision him being apprehended by those government forces who were always stalking him because their captain's skill at avoiding such men was widely known. Instead, they attributed his tardiness to the cursed luck imposed on a vessel when women, even as prisoners, were permitted aboard. Fires, disputes among the mates, mutiny, or even cyclonic storms were not uncommon events when an unspoken law of the piratical code was so blatantly violated. They dismally concluded in one of their soberer moments that the abysmal sea was responsible for his misfortune. After all, the bottomless depths had mysteriously been the downfall of many able mariners; more than one crew had left port never to be heard from again.

With crates of the captain's own brandy they had discovered underneath the barrels of salt pork and bully beef in the supply hut, they reconciled themselves to a doomed existence of being marooned on the tiny cay. While they gorged themselves with expensive drink, the Mayans and Maria continued their farming, fishing, and salting, for they knew that even if by some blessed stroke of luck they would not be plagued with the pirates' presence ever again, they must still survive in their island prison. Despite Maria's persistent cautioning against false hope, which could do no more than cause further grief, a determined Raven watched eagerly for the approaching sails of a friendly vessel, spending long hours at the rock-lined point waiting and praying for such a ship to arrive.

"Maria! Maria! Come quickly!" she yelled, racing one day from the point to the settlement. The hut was empty, and she stopped briefly to rummage underneath a pile of cotton to find a drawstring pouch containing all of her personal valuables before running down to the animal lot where her friend was milking the goats. "A ship!" she exclaimed joyfully. "I saw a ship! And it was flying the Union Jack!"

Maria's look was one of pitiful doubt, for she felt sure Raven's ship was a result of the hopeful anticipation she had warned her against combined with the severity of the sun's rays on an uncovered head.

Sensing Maria's skepticism, she wailed desperately. "Please, Maria. Come with me. There really is a ship

ailing toward us. Go with me to the rock. You'll see
'm telling you the truth."

"All right," she relented hesitantly, "but only to
prove to you that you cannot continue wasting your
days hoping for a miracle."

Raven shouted defiantly. She shouted loudly to
attract the vessel, waving her hands frantically and
dancing around her stunned friend. "Here we are!
Here we are!"

"Let us just pray that it is not another black ship
belonging to other vicious sea mongrels." But for once
Maria's dismal warnings could not hamper Raven's
zest, and she continued motioning and yelling until it
was apparent that the ship was deliberately being
maneuvered closer to the treacherous shoreline.

"It is an English ship!" proclaimed Raven. "I know it
is. Look, it seems that they are going to anchor outside
the reef. They're lowering a skiff over its side. They're
coming for us, Maria. They're here!"

Maria's bland expression slowly transformed into a
perplexed smile. She should have been happy, but her
feeling was ambivalence. Even with the thought of
finally being free after an eight year captivity, she could
allow herself very little happiness, for she knew she
would still be imprisoned by the events she had been
forced to endure. "For years I have longed for such a
time. Now I am numb. I am happy for you, Raven," she
said tensely. "You can go home to your people. I have
no one." She turned to leave.

Raven grabbed her wrist and jerked the sobbing
body around. "What are you talking about, Maria?
You yourself said that you used to dream of escaping.
Well, now's our chance."

"I will be all alone if I leave, Raven. My husband, if he is alive, has probably built a new life for himself. My parents were old when I last saw them. I doubt they still live. Besides, if I go to them they will know of my shame and humiliation, and my burden will become theirs. will be looked upon as an outcast, one who has brought dishonor to the Valdez name."

"But you can start your life over in Nassau," suggested Raven pleadingly. "I am sure my father will help you. If you do not go, then I will not go," she threatened.

"Do not be foolish," she said harshly. The eight years of mental and physical abuse had convinced her that she had no place in a normal society. Faded bruises and scars that covered her body would always be there as a reminder of her dishonor. The English would treat her no better than had the Mayans, and her own people would never accept her. "There is no place for me among your people, Raven."

"And you think your place is here?" asked Raven annoyedly. "Here on this cursed island with women who refuse to associate with you, and filthy, depraved men despoiling your soul as though you were a vessel to be stripped of its cargo? This is where you feel you belong?"

Her harshness penetrated Maria's struggling uncertainty. "I suppose you are right. It can be no worse in Nassau than it is here."

"I will take care of you," promised Raven, locking her arm into Maria's. "After all, without you, I would have never been able to face a new morning."

They turned to face the skiff and prayerfully watched as it was piloted over the surging maze. They did not breathe easily until it had conquered the final jagged outline. Raven blinked in disbelief as the boat glided closer to shore. She could utter no words of relief or acknowledgement, and her feet refused to be uplifted from the ground beneath her. She was oblivious to the men's appraising whistles or their gleeful shouts of "Women! Women!" while they slapped each other across the shoulders.

As the boat neared shallower waters, all but one of the men jumped overboard to pull the craft to shore. The solitary figure rose slowly from his seat and stretched himself to his full height, his eyes fixed to the beach. "Raven?" he asked himself softly. "Can this really be her? Is it too much to hope?"

He leaped from the boat with a single, agile bound, lifted her up from the glittering sand, protectively enfolded her thinned waist with his outstretched arms, and drew her close to his massive, unshirted chest.

She clung to him desperately, fearful that he would disappear the same as he had done night after night in her dreams. Her tear-streamed face buried itself deep into his lofty shoulders. "I knew you would come for me, Juan," she whimpered. "I knew you would!"

Perez lowered her quaking legs back to the ground so that his arms were free to endearingly caress her the way he had three months earlier on the deck of the *Fancy Free*. He reassuringly quieted her soft whines and gently hushed her words when she tried to tell him of the horrors she had witnessed. "Shh, my darling. There will be time enough for that later." He brushed his lips across her wind-tangled hair. "All that matters is that we have found each other again."

Perez's crew shuffled their bare feet impatiently into

the warming sands. Embarrassed looks of dumbfounded awe covered their unkempt faces. Finally, a young blond lad, with an innocent, boyish face and wavy shoulder-length curls tied away from his face with a brightly colored handkerchief dared to speak "Beggin' yer pard'n Sir, but will ye have us search out the rest of the island?"

Maria spoke before the handsome captain had a chance to reply. "There is no need for that," she said dully. "All you will find are a pair of drunken guards and four Mayan Indians who will run into the thicket the instant they see you."

"And Red Ames?" asked Perez. "Where is he?"

"He left the same day he brought Lucy and me here and has not been back since," answered Raven shakily

"There were no other survivors?" he gently prodded not wanting the memories of that dreadful experience to upset her again.

"No, no others." Then she recounted the details of the deaths of the passengers and crew. Perez tried to silence her recollection of the macabre occurrence, but she was insistent upon continuing. It seemed she wanted to put herself through such torture as punishment for having lived. She tearfully confessed of having left Lucy alone in her despondent state and explained her ludicrous plans for their escape. "Oh, Juan, I will never forget that horrible sight if I live a hundred years: that madman on top of her, laughing and baying at the moon like a lunatic while she was helpless beneath him. I had to stop him. At first I didn't think I had the courage to kill another living creature, but I did and felt nothing afterward. I enjoyed it, Juan; I enjoyed it because I knew that he was sure to be punished and that he would never again rape another helpless woman!"

"That is enough, Raven. You are safe now. I am here to see to that. And to see that all of their deaths will be avenged. Now I am more determined than ever to see to it that those depraved animals are hanged." His catlike eyes scorched with vindictiveness as he silently cursed the pock-scarred French pirate. "See what information you can obtain from the guard," he ordered to his crew. They were anxious to begin their search, eager for battle, for it had been such a long time since they had enjoyed a good fight. "Try to find the other women as well. Explain to them that we are all enemies of Ames and that we shall take them to safety."

The group, led by Ben Horningold, dispersed quickly and made their way cautiously through the clumps of bushes and shrubs that hid the primitive village from view from the beach.

Perez turned to address Raven's stone-faced companion. "I assume you will be sailing with us to New Providence, señora. Permit me to introduce myself: Captain Juan Roberto Perez of the *Falcon.*" He bowed low and the taut muscles of his bronze chest flexed with sleek ripples. He nodded curtly then tossed the glossy, black strands of hair from his face as he waited for a reply.

Maria eyed him suspiciously. "I am Maria."

"What's wrong, Maria. Your face looks troubled. Surely you are not still worried about leaving this place?"

Maria's dark eyes remained intent on the tall stranger while she addressed Raven. "I do not trust him. We would be safer to remain here and take our chances that Ames will not return."

"You don't trust him? Why that's ridiculous, Maria. You are just tired and confused. Why, Captain Perez is the man I told you so much about. His intentions are perfectly honorable. We will be safe aboard his ship."

Perez's pensive expression was replaced with an amused realization. "Several of my mates look familiar to you, do they not, Señora Valdez?"

She nodded. Her undaunted look of scorn was unaltered.

"Lucky for you Cockram used to sail with Ames. I would never have found this cay without him. And without Mr. Horningold, I would surely have rammed the boat against the first reef in our path."

"Ye be much too mod'st, Capt'n," chuckled the wizened rogue who had once sailed with Ames. "Ye would haf fount this place 'ventually." The others returned as he explained to Perez, "Just as Señora Valdez said, the rest went scamperin' off into the bushes. Wouldn't e'en listen to whut I had to say."

"And what of the guards?" asked Perez. "Were you able to obtain any information from them?"

"Those drunken stiffs can't even crawl away from their own filth," answered Horningold. "And I thought Cockram was the only fellow who couldn't hold his share of rum," he joked, poking the flaccid stomach of the paunchy mate beside him.

"What will ye have us do now, Capt'n?" asked one of the crew.

"Hang those drunken fools by their feet and slice their bodies in half?" came one suggestion from the crowd.

"Wouldn't that be some sight to greet the ol' dog

when he returns, eh men?" offered another.

All of the men readily agreed, for they were all anxious to see a little bloody excitement, even at someone else's expense. They were rapidly growing weary of their life as law-abiding citizens.

"I do not believe such flagrancy is necessary, gentlemen," answered their skipper coolly. "It will serve our purpose equally well if we hang our flag from the poles of his tower. Perhaps then he will resign himself to the fact that his lawless days are quickly drawing to a halt."

Perez untied the *Falcon*'s flag from the single mast of their tiny sloop, and handing it to Cockram urged him expediency in the task. Perez then lifted the two women into the skiff, and when they were rejoined by Cockram, gave the order to shove off.

"Good-bye Lucy!" whispered Raven, overtaken by sudden guilt-ridden remorse at abandoning her friend yet another time.

Seeing the girl's gloom Maria gently urged, "Remember, you yourself said that those bones are not the real friend with whom you spent hours laughing and sharing secrets. They have no soul, no emotion. You are not deserting her, for the memories you have of her will always keep her close." She looked pleadingly to Perez when Raven did not respond.

"I did not tell you how I acquired the *Falcon* did I, Raven?" he asked, hoping to divert her thoughts to more pleasant things.

She shook her head.

"Just a few years ago it belonged to Bart Roberts, a loathsome pirate who had taken over four hundred vessels during his three-year rampage throughout the

Atlantic. It was seized by the governor shortly after he arrived in the Bahamas. Since the governor's ships were needed to guard Nassau Harbor against avenging pirates and Spanish patrol groups, it became necessary to make use of this impounded vessel. She was christened the *Falcon,* named for the bird of prey that is trained specifically to hunt. Under Mr. Horningold's close scrutiny she was transformed into a sea-worthy privateer. Her sails were meticulously mended, chipped paint was replaced with fresh, even coats and cannons and guns were mounted on both her sides."

"I don't know what took longer, Sir," piped Horningold. "Gettin' the ship in shape or cleanin' up these ol' rum guzzlers."

The throaty chuckles jolted Raven away from her dismal thoughts. Her eyes were blank from numbness; blurred from unshed tears and unforgetable memories. She blinked in rapid succession until her sight was clearly focused, then looked eagerly ahead to the ship that would carry her away from the wretchedness of Ames and his cohorts.

The former pillagers took turns rowing the sloop back to the mother ship, which was nodding listlessly atop the aquamarine stillness. While six of them manned the oars, the other four laughed and joked, their mirth attributed to the knowledge that they had so far been successful in keeping Ames on the run. They riotously applauded each other's efforts for such an accomplishment.

"Ye know, Sir," said George, "hangin' a man by his feet and cuttin' out his entrails while he still breathes is punishment that ye frown upon, but by God—oops, sorry ladies for that slip—that would be a more fittin' reward than just the gallows when we do catch Ames."

"Aye, Sir," concurred Cockram. "Ames has done worse than that to his own men."

Perez sternly disagreed. "If we are to succeed in making Nassau a civilized colony, we must adhere to the laws of our country. You're right though, mate, the gallows do seem too noble for the likes of him."

"Aye, Sir. Maybe if we do capture the ol' dog, you'll permit me a moment alone with him. I'd like to show him just what it feels like to have his nose split right down the middle," said Cockram, holding his shapeless nose, the skin of which had long since mended. But its form was forever maimed by a crooked scar that began between shaggy, mismated brows and ended right above a funnel-shaped mouth.

"Ames did that to you?" questioned Raven.

"Sure did," answered George. "And I was right there when he did it."

"But why?" she asked.

"Stumbled against him and spilt a little brandy on that fancy red collar of his," answered Cockram.

"Spoiled yer handsome face, didn't it, friend?" ribbed Horningold unmercifully as the sloop glided alongside the deep bow of the *Falcon*. The affectionate tone of his voice assured them all that his words were not words of ridicule but remarks of devoted friendship.

Maria scaled the corded ladder first, followed by Raven, who could have done so just as effortlessly had it not been for Perez's steadying hands on her thighs, burning through her thin shift as he steered her up the thirty, tightly braided steps.

On deck they were met by the rest of the crew, who

157

demanded to know of any activity on the shoreline. Disappointed that no bloody activity had ensued, they restlessly awaited Perez's next order.

Raven curiously appraised the line of men that had formed in front of them. While their general appearances were very similar to those of criminals, their linen breeches were clean and they behaved in a rather orderly fashion. She suspected their haggard features had been softened considerably by a forced abstinence from days of plundering and wreckless living. Their faces, some badly scarred, were neither threatening nor demented. Most had scraggly beards and shoulder-length hair that hung as a single strand down their backs. Several had gold hoops dangling from their ears. Not one of the men reeked of aged sweat, filth or rum. Instead of ogling her and Maria with lusty, brazen stares, their beady eyes refused any contact whatsoever.

After the skiff had been secured to the port side of the *Falcon*, the anchor was lifted and the sails were hoisted and unfurled. A southwestern course was charted for New Providence. Once underway, the women were momentarily abandoned mid-deck while Perez left to discuss the proper cleaning and oiling of the artillery with the gunner, Mr. Phipps.

"Now ladies," summoned Perez upon his return. "I shall show you to your quarters. Mr. Garner has cleared two of the cabins for you and has removed a trunkful of clothes from storage." He offered each woman an arm, and they attached themselves on either side.

"Clothes?" asked a surprised Raven as the trio

158

descended the narrow stairway. "Clothes for us?"

"Yes," he explained. "We discovered a chest filled with women's apparel in the ship's store. Apparently Captain Bart was not above having his men dress as ladies in order to snare a reluctant ship. Señora Valdez," said Perez, opening the door of the cabin. "This will be your room. I shall send one of the cook's helpers around later to check and see if you need anything."

Maria nodded her appreciation then closed her door, snapping the lock behind her. Perez's hand clasped Raven's, and they lingered for a moment in the passageway. "Had I not pressing duties awaiting me, I would be content to stand here and hold you in my arms for the remainder of the day. But for now, I must leave you." He bent down and brushed his lips across her forehead. "Try and get some rest. I shall see you this evening, my sweet."

Raven stood in the doorway and watched as her gallant hero climbed the stairs and was out of sight. She sighed contentedly, closed the door to her room, and leaned slumberously against it.

How fortunate I was to have met such a man! she told herself. Her eyes fluttered dreamily, and a smile flickered across her lips. So courageous! So handsome! And so very wonderful! I don't care if I do act like a giddy twit. I love him. I'm dizzy with his touch, his smell, his look. Just the feel of his fingers on my lips or his hand reaching for mine makes my stomach flutter with nervous excitement. I know Papa will approve of him. He must! I want to spend the rest of my life with that man. If Papa refuses to accept him, I will just— No, I mustn't even think of such.

To Raven's surprise, the tiny quarters had been carefully prepared to allow her as much comfort as possible. A faded blue chenille spread covered the cot. Beside it was a dressing table, and on top of it a red and white porcelain bathing bowl and pitcher. A dainty, white wicker chair had been placed in the corner, giving the room an aura of femininity. Beside it, alongside the wall, was a nail-studded oak sea chest.

Raven knelt beside the trunk, unlatched its lock, and raised its creaking lid. It was packed with over a dozen dresses of assorted colors, designs, and materials.

I will get some sleep, she resolved, and then I shall dress myself in the most beautiful gown there; one deserving of Juan's undivided attention. She untied the braided strand of her pouch, which encircled her waist, removed her few precious belongings, and reflectively separating each one, laid them on the table.

Thank heavens I had the good sense to carry this broach with me aboard Ames's ship. I shudder to think what may have happened had I not had it. And my sovereigns. They will surely come in handy when I try to find my father. Ah, and my sweet little conch pearl. You are my only link with my father, for you are something the both of us cherished.

Her eyes caught the light of a reflection in the wavering mirror above the table. An unkempt face glared at her. Oh, surely that cannot be me, she moaned, touching her tangled, disheveled black strands that fell limply around her dirt-streaked face. How vain you are! she reprimanded. You should be grateful at having been saved from such a perilous situation instead of fretting about your appearance. A little soap and water, a stroke with a comb, and you'll be your same old self. No, I shall never be myself again. My days of innocence and naiveté are over. I was forced into complete maturity by the traumatic events I witnessed and the torturous hardships that confronted me. Never again will I be that disillusioned young girl who departed Plymouth for a world unseen.

## Chapter Ten

It seemed only moments after Raven closed her eyes that a faint tapping roused her from the bed. She awoke instantly, panicking, for she did not remember where she was. After realizing she was safe aboard the *Falcon* she laughed at her unwarranted fright. She hurriedly slipped the soiled cottony shift over her head and called out, "Who is it?"

"It be Wally, mum. Ship's cook," came the reluctant reply.

Raven unbarred the sturdy latch from its wooden catch and opened the door to a squab-plump, russet-haired young man whose left eye was twitching nervously.

"Oh, how thoughtful of you!" she said, eyeing hungrily a plate of assorted breads, cakes, and cheeses.

"Yes, mum," he answered, thrusting the plate in her hands, then putting his fists into the deep pockets of his blood-stained apron. "Captain Perez thought ye'd be gettin' a mite hungry." His cheeks turned redder than the color of his hair as he stammered under his breath. "I was also told to tell ye that a tub of water has been drawn for ye in the Captain's quarters. No one will bother you there, mum." He retreated hastily, without waiting for a reply, and stumbled up the steps.

He certainly is timid, thought Raven. How could he possibly have been a pirate?

She stretched herself out on the bed, propped up the worn, down pillow, and was content for the next half hour to leisurely indulge herself with the rich tasting snack, smacking her lips and licking her fingers until the last crumb was consumed.

By four o'clock she grew discontent with her own company, and when she heard no sounds from the room next to hers, decided to rummage through the chest for suitable apparel. The trunk not only contained clothes, but bath salts, jasmine fragrances, hair ribbons, combs and several pairs of soft, kid leather slippers. A pink, full-bodiced gown with short, puffed sleeves, and a pearled waistband immediately caught her fancy. She draped it over her arm and, carrying the mint green jar of bath powders and the cloisonne vase of jasmine scents, tiptoed across the hall.

The captain's quarters was as large as a half a dozen of the other rooms combined. None of the furnishings had been built to extend from the wall, a practice commonly adhered to by shipbuilders. Instead, they were secured to the floor in an effort to prevent them from being tossed about during inclement weather.

Apparently this Bart Roberts was a man whose elaborate means could readily afford such exquisite taste, she surmised delightfully, appraising a mahogany, roll-top desk, two over-stuffed tipped-back chairs, an ornately gilded coffer, and a tall cedar wardrobe. A conspicuously large, four-posted brass bed enclosed in red and black velvet draperies occupied the center of the spacious room, and just above it swung a chandelier of glass-enclosed candles. A barrel-shaped tub sat in one corner of the room, and stacked beside it were thick, huge towels. Raven sighed longingly. At last, a real bath with fresh water! She peeled off her dress, dropped it to the floor, and with much oohing and aahing, eased herself into the steaming lather.

After blissfully soaking in the luxurious bath for almost an hour, she vigorously scrubbed her hair and body, purging from both the grimy reminders of her captivity. She stayed in the cleansing suds until her hands began to draw and wrinkle from the self-indulgent luxury, then began toweling herself dry. The door opened, and Maria appeared.

"I thought you might be in here," said Maria to a startled Raven, who had modestly wrapped the towel around her body. "I decided to take advantage of the captain's kind offer as well." She began removing the dirty clothes and looked wistfully at the suds. "I have forgotten what it feels like to lounge in a real bath, and to soak in fresh, scented, perfumed waters instead of brine."

Raven laughingly agreed, splashing the jasmine oil over her body.

"Ah, in eight years, the comfort I most longed for was this very thing," she said, slipping into the tub. "Did I ever tell you that I once went for nearly a year without bathing?"

Raven's face wrinkled in distasteful scorn.

"You see, I decided that if I made myself totally revolting to Ames he would be too repulsed by my sight and smell to want to bed me. He called me a Spanish sow. It mattered little to him how I smelled, though, for his own smells were far more rank than mine."

Raven dressed with deliberate slowness, stroking the soft texture of her gown and admiring the fine, quality workmanship of the seamstress, before slipping it over her damp curls. "I wonder what ever happened to the woman who once wore this?"

Maria grinned mischievously. "I would imagine that she found herself a handsome sea captain who attires her in much finer silks now.

Raven blushed and turned her attentions to a faded, brown parchment that was tacked above the desk. "Listen to this, Maria. 'The Articles of Piracy: Proposed by Captain William Bartholomew Roberts.' Why, it looks like a code of behavior for pirates." She read it aloud while Maria bathed.

"Article One: Every man shall have an equal vote in the affairs of this ship. Every man shall have an equal title to fresh provisions and drink, unless a scarcity of either deems rationing.

"Article Two: If any man robs from his fellow seamen, the ears and nose of the guilty are to be slit and he will be put ashore at a place where he is sure to encounter hardship.

"Article Three: The captain of the vessel shall have two full shares of the total haul, the quartermaster one and a half, the doctor, gunner, boatswain and sailing master one and a quarter. The rest will be distributed equally among the crew. He that first sights a prize shall have his choice of weapons aboard her, and he who boards her first shall have double his share of the booty.

"Article Four: None shall game at cards or dice for money.

"Article Five: Lights and candles shall be put out at eight each night. Any drinking done after that hour shall be done on the open deck to avoid fire.

"Article Six: Each man shall keep his piece, cutlass, and pistol at all times clean and ready for action.

"Article Seven: No boys or women are to be allowed on the ship. If any man carries a woman to sea, he shall suffer death. Likewise, if he chooses to ravage a female prisoner.

"Article Eight: He that shall desert the ship in time of battle shall be punished by death or marooning.

"Article Nine: Every man's quarrels must be resolved on shore. Fighting on ship will not be tolerated!

"Article Ten: He that shall have the misfortunes of losing a limb during battle shall be given a sum of eight hundred pieces from the common store: six hundred for an arm, five hundred for an eye, four for a hand, and furthermore shall retain some post on the ship.

"It is quite apparent that Captain Roberts did not tutor Ames in the finer points of piracy," murmured Raven, intrigued that the previous owner of the *Falcon* would foresee the necessity of keeping order and fairness aboard his vessel.

By this time, Maria had finished dressing and had begun braiding her knee-length hair in a single plait. "That devil certainly twisted the original code to fit his own wanton greed," she said. "And to think, Ames prided himself on being such an admired corsair."

Raven gasped at her friend in startled awe. "I had no idea you were so lovely, Maria!"

Her bronzed complexion was smooth and flawless.

The deep haggard wrinkles of worry and abuse had disappeared. The stooped posture from many months of unaccustomed menial labor had vanished as well. "Thank you, Raven. What a kind thing to say!" Her lively eyes gleamed, and a pinkish glow tinged her high, regal cheeks.

"I have a wonderful idea," revealed Raven. "Let's go topside for a stroll. It will be so invigorating to feel the burning spray of salt water upon our faces and smell that sea wind."

"Are you mad?" balked her friend. "Those men will throw you overboard the moment they spot you on your little walk."

Raven frowned. "Throw me overboard? But they have no reason to hate me."

"Sailors are all a superstitious lot. Did you not notice them squirming and exchanging doleful looks of doom when Perez told them we would be sailing with them to Nassau? If we encounter any bad weather tonight, or if even one sailor trips over his own feet, you and I will be blamed for it. Heed my word!"

Neither had heard the creaking of the timbers as the door was pushed ajar, nor did they sense the presence of a third person until the intruder spoke. "I will admit, my crew is a bit skittish by your presence, but I doubt very much their doing anything quite so drastic. You both look exquisite," praised the lean, solid skipper as he bowed to greet them. "I am certain that had Captain Roberts known that two women as beautiful as you would grace his galley this evening, he would have tried harder to dodge those cannons."

"Thank you, Captain," Maria graciously acknowledged. "Your words are most appreciated. Thank you for all the trouble you have gone to for our sakes. Our gratitude is exceeded only by your kindness!"

Perez, embarrassed to be the subject of such elegant thanks, quickly offered them his arm. "Permit me to escort you to dinner. Wally has prepared a meal that will please even the most finicky of palates: fried grouper, buttered yams, and stewed cabbage."

"I did not think pirates were nourished so well," joked Raven.

"Ah, but mine are," he answered, leading them down the lengthy companionway. "If I expect my men to do a good day's work, their bellies must be satisfied. I'll wager that before they signed on with me that many of them had never had a complete meal. Good food will soothe even the wildest of beasts, and they soon learn to appreciate the hand that feeds them," he reasoned.

The dining room consisted of a long, oak table, which gleamed lustrously from a recent polishing, two benches of equal length and shine, and a straight-backed chair situated at the head. Perez seated Maria first, on his left, then Raven opposite her. He leaned forward to push the bench up the table after she had been seated and mumbled in her ear. "You are even more stunning than you were the last time I had the pleasure of dining with you."

Raven felt her cheeks redden at the feel of his warm breath so close to her neck. When Perez had taken his place at the head of the table, she glowed radiantly, her look of joy penetrating deep into his green eyes.

"My men will eat with us tonight, the same as usual, except of course for those on watch. If I wish to maintain order on my vessel and be successful in that which I have been commissioned to do, I must treat my crew with equality and respect," he explained. "They are all aware that by my position, I am superior to them, but as men, we are all equally banded together in the hope of achieving a very difficult, dangerous task."

"Well said, Sir!" applauded Horningold, entering the room with his comrade, Cockram. They seated themselves beside Maria. "Ladies!" they saluted respectfully. It was obvious from their appearance that they had both made a special effort. They were attired in clean shirts and pants. Cockram had shaved the bristly growth of the morning from his face, and Horningold had trimmed his full whiskers.

"Why you run this ship just as fairly as I did me own," he complimented, for he genuinely admired his superior.

Horningold was basically good-natured, even if he was taken, from time to time, by an urgency to discuss his pirating days. And he found in Raven and Maria a curious attentiveness for such a monologue.

"Aye, those were the days," he began, a distant, faraway glow shimmering in his eyes. "My *Golden Nymph* sailed from Hispanole to Boston. We plundered every ship that chanced our path. That is, only the rich merchant ones. I'll swear on my dead mama's grave that I ne'er stole from a poor ship. Didn't take prisoners nor cause a drop of blood to fall if the weapons and goods were surrendered peacefully. No swearin' or drunkin' on my ship neither! Women were treated with respect. We were true buccaneers!"

"Why did you give it up, Mr. Horningold?" questioned Raven. "I mean, if you didn't kill anyone and you—"

"Aye," he interrupted, shaking his head disgustedly.

"No honor existed even 'mongst those of us who prowled the high seas. Capt'ns was also squabblin' and fightin' o'er boundaries. Ye couldn't find a crew without going to the taverns or jails. Jest wasn't worth the effort no more!"

"Tell her the truth, ye old fool!" piped his companion. "Tell her how the gov'nor sailed up to the harbor, fired his guns, and told you your piratin' days were over!"

Horningold grinned mischievously. "Well, that was the second reason I gave up me good life! After he chased away Capt'n Vane, he strolled right up to me and Cockram and Burgess and Westman, offered us a pardon for our sea crimes, and said if we didn't sign it, he'd hang us. I knowed when I was beaten so there was nothin' left to do but salute the ol' fellow."

"Didn't you say you used to sail under Ames, Mr. Cockram?" inquired Raven.

"That I did, Missy. And not a more loathsome man will e'er be found! I was the boatswain; sail mender. He treated his own as poorly as he did prisoners. Kept us dressed in rags, fed us barely enough to keep us livin', and gave us a share of the hauls only large enough to buy a night's supply of women and grog."

"I've been meaning to ask you, Cockram. How did you manage to get away from him? Very few have done so and lived to tell about it," entreated Perez.

Cockram's face scowled fiercely as he remembered. "After the old cuss split my nose wide open, I mustered all the strength I could find and kicked him; right between the legs I did. Striking an officer, if ye could have called him such, usually led to bein' hung from the

170

yardarm, but after he'd recovered—and been shamed by feelin' pain the same as ev'rybody else—he decided to make sport of my execution and maroon me on an island with not a drop of fresh water."

Horningold interrupted. "And if'n there's one thing a sailor fears more than death itself, it's bein' left like that. Why, I've seen many a men drink salt water and become crazier than a caged animal in a matter of seconds."

"So," Cockram continued. "The old crow sets me out and gives me a pistol and a single bullet. Then he takes bets from the men 'bout whether I'd die from thirst or by my own doin'. He laughed and told me they'd return afore the month's end and settle up. Had it not been for my good friend Horningold a'rescuin' me, I would probably have gone mad from the heat and used that bullet. I would have given my soul to have seen his face when he found me gone." He slapped his friend on the shoulder. "When this one decided to accept the pardon, I did, too. After all, somebody's gotta watch over the old goat."

"It'll take more than you to keep this old devil outa trouble!" exclaimed George, seating himself beside Raven. "The rest will be here shortly, Sir. Trying to get their courage up to dine with ladies, I s'pose."

"I hope our presence here isn't causing you too much trouble," said Raven, turning to Perez.

"Nonsense," assured Perez. "You're welcomed sights."

The other three nodded in enthusiastic approval.

A dozen or so of the men shuffled in slowly, careful to keep their eyes lowered to the floor. Those leading

171

the way began seating themselves at the far end of the table. Wally appeared from the arched doorway leading from the cooking area with steaming platters piled to the top with fish, potatoes, and vegetables, and placed them along the shiny tabletop.

"This is delicious!" exclaimed Raven, sampling the grouper.

Instead of eagerly diving into their food with both hands, the men patiently waited their turns. Odd, unfamiliar requests sounded the length of the table: "Pass the potatoes . . . please. . . . A little salt, if you don't mind. . . . A bit more fish, please?"

An uncomfortable stillness enveloped the room after the last fork was placed on the plate. The mates mumbled among themselves, but did not venture to address the women.

Horningold broke the awkward silence. "Miss Gatewood, Señora Valdez, me and Cockram was just talkin' and we both think it was mighty brave the way you two held out at Gorda Cay. I know a lot of sailors who couldn't have lasted there. Anyways," he grinned toothily, "we're mighty proud to have you sailin' with us."

"That's right!" concurred Cockram. "Why, you're ready to join them pirates in petticoats!"

"There aren't really women pirates, are there?" questioned Raven, quite taken back by such a suggestion.

"Aye, lassie," piped a shrivel-faced man at the end of the table. "Why, not more 'en two months ago, I was a sailin' with Calico Jack Rackam. We called him 'Calico' cause of them striped pants he was always

172

awearin'. He had two women with him; Annie Bonny and Mary Read. Them gals is so crazy they'd make Bedlam look like a refined tea party."

"Tell them what happened," egged on a hook-armed mate beside him.

"Ol' Calico Jack was as fine a seaman who e'er sailed these islands, but that Bonny woman was the death of him. Always a screamin' and a cussin' at him she was. Orderin' him about the ship lik'n she's the capt'n. No matter now." He sighed reminiscently. "Can't change history. We's anchored right off the harbor when all of a sudden a man-o'-war charged us, firing all her guns and cannons. Why we's just a sitting target. The whole crew, e'en Calico Jack, had had a wee bit too much grog that night and was in no shape to lift our guns, much less use 'em. So we tucked our tail between our legs and ran down into the hold to hide." The entire group burst into rollicking laughter, and teasing insults were hurled unmercifully at the storyteller.

"Please continue, sir!" implored Raven earnestly. "I find it all to be most fascinating!"

The wise sailor beamed and inflated his chest proudly, for he had never been addressed as such, nor had anyone ever said that what he had to say was fascinating. "All right, lass, for you, I'll finish." Giving his mates a superior "Humph," he continued. "We waited down in the hold for the longest time while those two crazy loons on deck tried to defend the ship. When they realized they'd been beat, Bonny raised the hatch and they commenced firing on us, callin' us cowards and yellow-bellied dogs and yellin' such curses that e'en some of you men would blush at. Well, sure 'nough, we were taken and hauled to Jamaica to stand trial. Annie was pardoned 'cause she was expectin' a lit'le un, and Reed died of a fever in her cell. When the judge sentenced us all to hangin', Annie let out this God-awful laugh and told us that had we fought like men, we wouldn't have to die like dogs. She was a tough one, that Bonny gal!"

Raven was amused by the pirate's humorous account of his antics. "Were you pardoned as well, sir?"

"No, not 'xactly," he sneered. "I 'scaped. Don't ask me to tell you the details fer your gut would turn inside out, 'specially since you just ate. I will tell you this much. I got back to Nassau and signed those papers the moment I hit shore. Signed on as the sailing master for the *Falcon.*"

"You were lucky to have escaped!" cried George, remembering his own narrow escape. "Just feelin' that noose around my neck made me decide that if I cherished livin', I'd stay on the right side of the law for a while."

"What happened to them other five that wuz with you?" asked Phipps, the gunner.

George shook his head sorrowfully. "That was a sad lot. All of them had been pardoned once by the gov'nor, but they went back to their old ways. John Auger did die like a man. I'd have to admit to that. On the way to the gallows, he asked for a glass of wine and proceeded to drink to the success of the Bahamas and to the good health of Rogers. MacKarthy joked about not wantin' to die with his shoes on so he took them off and tossed them into the crowd. Ol' Will Lewis repented at the end and began recitin' the Psalms while

174

Tommy Morris screamed at the top of his lungs 'bout how he wished he had been an even bigger plague to the Bahamas. And little William Dowling laughed like a madman, saying how he hoped he didn't see his dear old mama in hell cause he had stabbed her in the back before leaving Ireland."

"Sorry bunch! All of 'em. Just as well they're all gone," concluded Cockram. "They'd all just as soon stab a friend in the back as they would an enemy." He snickered. "Can't imagine old Lewis repentin' though. He was the worst of 'em all. Once slit an old priest's throat because the padre offered to pray for his soul." He shook his tonsured head remorsefully. "Aye and because of the likes of them and Vane and Spriggs, all of us Brethren of the Coast were given a bad name and filthy reputation to match."

"Vane," repeated Phipps. "He was a real scoundrel. He captured Ed North's *Lucky Lady,* and when the mates wouldn't reveal the hiding place of the ship's money, he tied the captain to the bowsprit and propped his eyes open with slow burning matches. When he still refused to tell, Vane pointed a pistol at his head and pulled the trigger. Then he complained about the bloody mess on deck."

"I used to sail with Cap Spriggs," offered Wally, bringing out a large bowl of rice pudding and eager to be included in the conversation. "He was as mean as any of 'em. Once when we plundered a Frenchy ship, the haul was so bad that he had all the captives hoisted aloft to the main top, then gave the order to let go the ropes and giggled like a crazy man when the people bounced upon the deck."

"He did have some redeemin' qualities though," interrupted George. "Those who survived the fall were freed."

"I don't care what any of you say, we all know the worst of the whole lot was Ed Teach," flared a cherubic-faced, blue-eyed lad beside Cockram. "Compared to him, Ames is a saint."

Horningold readily agreed. "You're right, lad. We seem to have forgotten about him. Why, he used to sail under me when he was first gettin' started in the business. Even his looks would make the bravest man shake in his tracks." He elaborated with contorted faces and humorous gestures.

"Fierce lookin' ol' devil! Braided hair, braided beard, and he'd stick matches all through that frizzy black mane and light them. Made his eyes glow red. Yellow teeth, sharper and more pointed than e'en a wolf's fangs, and a drooping, loose-lipped mouth. He wore a tall robber's hat made of black felt and a purple silk coat with huge velvet cuffs rolled up to his elbows. Green knee breeches and dark stockings. Ne'er saw him with less 'en four cutlasses and two pistols stuck in his belt and three holsters full of pistols strapped 'round his chest." He chuckled softly to himself. "But he was sure appealin' to the ladies for I heard he had fifteen wives and sired at least forty brats!"

"How long did you sail with Blackbeard?" directed Perez to the boy.

"Too long," was his quick reply. "I deserted right before he sailed to the Carolinas. I hear he met his match off the coast of 'Ginia. Killed in a duel and his

176

head was chopped off at the neck and mounted on a stick for all the folks to poke at."

"Why did ye desert, lad?" questioned Phipps, knowing that even the attempt to do so was punishable by the worst kind of torturous death.

"I ain't a coward, if'n that's what you mean," replied Blackwell indignantly. "I'll stand and fight with the best of you but that man was a fool, a mean, crazy fool. His motto was that if you don't shoot one or two of your own every day, they'll forget who's running the ship. One evenin', after we'd gone for weeks without spottin' a ship, Blackbeard decided that since we were all on our way to hell anyways, he'd make a hell on the ship and see who among his men could last the longest. He ordered us all into the hold, pulled the hatch and told us to sit on the ballast. Then he set fire to four kegs of brimstone. Pretty soon the hold was filled with smoke, and choking men began to stagger around coughin' and wheezin' like they were dying. Everybody climbed out except Teach, and we all thought he had died in his own joke. A couplé o' hours later, the hatch swings open and he climbs out, laughing at us all because he had proven just who was closest kin to Lucifer." The crew laughingly agreed that even Satan must have his hands full with Ed Teach.

Horningold interrupted the festivities. "Sorry mates, but if we're to see Nassau before noon, we must be on about our chores." Then signaling to a specific group said, "Jaminson, Greaves, Hessie, Richards, Blackwell, relieve the men on deck. Ever'one else rest up for the next watch. Anything else, Capt'n?" Perez shook his head. The crew ambled out the door, shyly nodding

177

to Maria and Raven. Cockram and Horningold followed closely behind.

Raven deliberately allowed her hand to brush against Perez's folded ones resting on the table. "I cannot remember ever having enjoyed dinner more. Why, those stories they told of Blackbeard and Vane and all the rest were most exciting."

"I was wrong about you and your crew, Captain. I apologize for my misgivings earlier," remarked Maria graciously. "Now if you both will excuse me, I am very tired. Good night!"

"I do not know how I would have been able to live with the deaths of all my friends," said Raven after her friend had departed, "had it not been for her. I owe her my very life." Then blushing, she added, "And to you, too. Had it not been for the faith I had in you eventually finding that cay, I would have lost all will to live."

Perez gently cupped her face in his calloused hands and gazed longingly into the emerald depths of her eyes. "You have been in my thoughts every waking moment. An image of your soft loveliness filled my sleep each night. I was afraid that you had been but a trick played on me by the moonlight, a vision of beauty that would never appear to me again. I was so terrified to think that you had been murdered, but Cockram assured me that Ames spares females and takes them to his island. I was even more determined to search out every island until I found you and you were safe in my arms again." He eased her head forward to his own and firmly kissed her rose-petaled lips. His tongue explored her mouth, savoring its warmth.

178

Raven's pulsating heart surged rapidly, and she feared that at any moment it would burst from within her breast.

"You are mine!" he whispered fiercely, opening her mouth again and covering its fullness with his own. "I must have you!"

Raven nodded in acquiescence, fully aware of the meaning of such words. "Yes, oh yes, my sweet. I want to be yours, all yours."

With that unabashed encouragement, Perez lifted her from the bench. She wrapped her arms around his neck and buried her head in his dark hair, cooing softly words of love in his ear. Without speaking, he carried her to his cabin and laid her down on the oversized bed. He stared at her for the longest while, curiously looking at her as though she were a goddess to be held in awe by mere mortals, but never to be touched. She regarded him with solemn reserve, much like that of a timid bride anxiously anticipating that culminating moment of intimacy that would truly join the pair together as one. He knelt beside her, ardent desire flaming from his eyes. She opened her arms wide. A sensually pursed mouth pleaded wordlessly for his embrace, and Perez fell hungrily into her hold.

"Ah, my dearest, dearest darling," he murmured. "If the ship were to sink this very moment, I fear that I would be powerless to tear myself from you." He began covering each inch of her upturned face with frenzied kisses. "I have dreamed of this moment ever since the hour I first set eyes on you, my sweet."

Raven returned his inflamed embrace with equally fiery ardor, praying that time would stand still so that

179

she might linger in such passion forever. His lips drifted down to her quavering chest, and she clung desperately to his shoulders, digging her fingertips into their broadness as his hands stroked the material covering her breasts. Her breathing quickened at his exploring touch. "Are you certain, Raven, that this is what you want? I want you to have no doubts whatsoever."

"Oh, need you even ask, Juan?" She trembled, shamelessly moving his hand once again to her silkened bodice. "Never have I desired any man. I want you to be the first, the only one to ever—"

He questioned her hesitantly. "Then Ames did not dishonor you?"

"No, no, no!" she softly exclaimed. "Oh, he tried, but I would not permit it. I knew even then that such was intended only for the man I love, only for you." She proceeded to explain how she drugged the gin so that his already drunken body would soon succumb to a heavy sleep.

"I will be gentle, my darling," he promised. "God, how my very soul has ached for you. The agony of suspecting you were lost from me forever was unbearable." He eased her gown from her shoulders and gaped at the lush roundness revealed to him. He caressed his voluptuous, ivory treasures. "How beautiful you are," he muttered, sinking his head between the two perfectly formed mounds. "How beautiful indeed!" His tongue encircled the darkened nipples, teasing them into a firm erectness.

A tempestuous craving surged through Raven, awakening in her an intense vigor never before felt, and she closed her eyes in sensual enjoyment. Moans of pleasure escaped from her lips as her lover's fingers began searching for forbidden territory. "Oh, Juan. Darling, darling Juan."

Perez slipped her gown over her tapered waist, down her slender, long legs and off her well-turned ankles. "Venus herself must be envious of such a lovely form," he remarked, surveying her invitingly contoured body. "If only you knew how the sight of such lusciousness moves me—your angelic face with black tresses fanning against the pillow arouses me with a longing such that I have never known before. I would kill Ames with my bare hands had he defiled such beauty. I want to please you, Raven, to have your body swell with an abundance of love for me." With that, he stripped the linen shirt from his body, revealing a hard, muscled chest covered with dark, curly hair.

Her eyes followed his every movement as he rose from the cushioned bed and unfastened the corded rope around his waist. She watched as his breeches fell around his feet. The sight of his stiffly, upright manhood neither frightened nor repulsed her, for she knew that it would soon be the very core of her being and from it her womanhood would be truly fulfilled by the man she loved.

He slipped down beside her and drew her body close against his own. "How I love you!" he whispered.

"And how I love you!" she answered with soft boldness, nestled into his protective embrace. "From that first meeting I have loved you with all of my heart, all of my self."

He rolled her over so that she lay flat on the bed, tenderly parted her legs with a light touch, then lowered his head to kiss the source of ecstasy between her smooth thighs. He eased himself over her and gazed into her eyes, fondling her rounded breasts the entire time. His inflamed member readily found her quivering being and gently forced its way inside. The sudden twinge of sharp pain was short-lived, and Raven rose to meet the probing surges of her lover. Their bodies rocked together in a slow, undulating motion.

"Oh, my dearest." Her breath rustled, her pulse raced. "Surely there exists no sweeter bliss than this!"

And their bodies exploded with climactic currents.

They were content to lay in each other's arms for a long while, drained by the frenzied cravings of their lovemaking.

"Did . . . did I please you?" stammered Raven awkwardly as she curled his chest hairs around her finger.

"Need you even ask?" he mimicked a curt reply.

They drifted into an exhausted slumber. When she awakened, still wrapped in a clinging hold, Perez's eyes were feasting on the delicate features of her face.

"What are you thinking, Juan?"

"Only of you, my love, and how I have waited so long for that perfect creature I have found in you," he answered, finding her lips once more.

"Have . . . have you had many women?" she questioned timidly.

"I will never lie to you, darling Raven," he assured her. "For I am a man whose desires for those of the fairer sex has not gone unfulfilled. But no woman has ever caused such sensations within me as you have done. You are the only one, I swear, who has ever had my heart. My very soul is yours. I am unable to put into words that which I feel for you. To merely say I love you does not seem enough."

"Oh, Juan, you have made me so happy!"

"You, too, my dove."

And once again he eased his body across hers, filling the eager passageway between her silky legs with a love-aroused hardness.

"Such heavenly ecstasy!" she moaned, rising to meet his throbbing thrusts with an equaled rhythmic steadiness.

They collapsed, this time completely emptied of all life, powerless to move. They lay wordlessly, legs entwined, arms clasping each other. They did not awaken until the dawn when the sunlight streamed in through the porthole. Perez was the first to stir. His eyes glowed with a yearning desire to return to the pleasures of last evening, but his words were desolate and harsh, almost cold. "We will arrive in New Providence soon. We must dress quickly."

His cold words burned her ears. Tears swelled as Raven watched him put on his clothes that had been so carelessly tossed aside in the darkness. "What is wrong, Juan?" she pleaded. "Can it be that the person you spoke such elegant words of love to last night offends your sight in the morning?"

"No, no Raven. Please, you mustn't think such a dreadful thing," he hurried to soothe her worries. "If my words sound distant, it is because I know that duty demands that I leave you in Nassau while I resume my search. That is all. That is why I seem so despondent this morning."

"Can I not stay on the *Falcon* with you?" she asked, assuring him that she would cause no trouble and would not at any time venture from the confines of the cabin.

He laughed, eyes twinkling amusedly. "While that is most tempting, my love, I fear it would be far too dangerous. You will stay with Henry Lightbourne, the doctor who treated your father. A week from today, on Sunday, on every Sunday, a provisions ship sails to Eleuthera to deliver supplies and mail. Arrangements will be made for you aboard her. Captain Jack is the skipper and he'll take care of you and see that you reach your father safely."

"And then?" she questioned boldly. "What about us?"

"By then, Ames will be in prison, and I shall be free to come to you. I am confident I can convince your father of the advantages of your being married to an old sea captain such as me."

Her face brightened, sparkling with enthusiastic approval as he teased. "But let me warn you, my girl, not a moment's rest will you have once our marriage bed is made!"

"Oh, Juan! Juan!" was all she could mumble before pulling him down to her.

Once again they became lost in the fury of their love, and she became his for a third time with the assurance that she would remain such for the duration of their lives.

"As much as I would like to stay and dally with my favorite wench," joked Perez, forcing himself from her grasp, "I must go topside before my men all mutiny." Shaking his finger playfully, he warned, "Don't try and detain me, woman, or it's forty lashes for you on your bare backside. Get dressed and join me on deck!"

After a quick kiss on her cheek and an airy slap on her exposed thigh, he left, leaving her alone to relive in her mind every detail of their lusty night of unharnessed love and desire.

## Chapter Eleven

Raven lounged contentedly in the cushiony softness of the huge, brass four-poster. Sighing dreamily, she snuggled closer to the pillow and buried her head in its billowy warmth. The faint smell of her lover lingered there, giving her a satisfying solace. The heavy covers embraced her supine nakedness, and she tingled warmly at the remembrance of the previous night's passion.

"Get out of bed! Lazy girl!" she scolded herself. Her words were light and cheery. "No point in your lollygagging around here all morning when you could be on deck with your betrothed!"

Her lissome body sprang nimbly from the bed. She hurriedly dressed and smoothed her tousled mane. "You certainly do look like a woman in love." She giggled aloud, staring at her crimson-cheeked image in the mirror. Holding the sides of her skirt high above her ankles, she skipped out of the memory-filled room and bounded up the steps, girlishly taking two at a time.

She paused for a moment beside the railing, her hands folded on the wooden barrier. Fresh, salty air nipped against her face, and she inhaled its invigorating crispness. Her eyes were mesmerized by the aqua-crested waves that parted as the bow of the *Falcon* glided across the churning swells.

"Good morning, Miss Gatewood!" came a greeting from behind her.

"And a good morning to you, Mr. Rounsivell," she replied heartily, turning to face the grinning lad. "This is all just too marvelous for words, isn't it?" Without awaiting a reply, she added, "I think that if I were a young man I would become a sailor. This briny air invigorates the soul as well as the body. One can almost become intoxicated breathing its freshness. And oh, the sea itself! It is by far God's greatest creation. A true masterpiece!"

George leaned his stout frame against the railing. "You've put into words 'xactly the way I feel. I don't think I'd ever be happy any place else. I wish I could explain that to my folks. They want me to come home, you know, to till the soil like my Pops, and his before him. They just don't understand that once the salt mixes in your blood, you'll ne'er be content any place else."

"Where is home?" inquired Raven.

"Weymouth in Dorsetshire," he answered, grinning. "Thank God for that. It be the only thing that saved me from danglin' at the end of a noose."

"How so?"

"Lucky for me, that's where the gov'nor's parents live. I guess remembering how he, too, had left a white-haired mama and stoop-shouldered father to go to sea made him decide to give me a second chance," revealed George. A hint of a tear glistened in his eye at the recollection of his humble parents standing beside their vine-covered cottage begging him not to leave. "Well, at least they'll never know about my piratin' adventures. When I go home, they'll be proud of me."

"And what parents wouldn't be?" she encouraged. "After all, it takes a very brave men to aid in the campaign to rid this area of such a pestilence as Ames and to try and establish a civilized colony in Nassau. Why, I know if you told them that, they'd forgive you for leaving them and be ever so proud of you!"

"Rounsivell, Mr. Rounsivell!" impatiently blared Horningold. "To your post, man! This is not a bloody tea party! You'd do well to remember that!"

"Aye Sir," replied George, then turning to Raven he mumbled his appreciation. "Thanks ever so much. I shall post a letter to England this very afternoon. It's the least I can do. Let 'em know I'm alive. Maybe they'll even want their prodigal son to return home."

"Rounsivell!"

"Aye, Sir. Coming!"

"I fear that I am the one to blame for his tardiness," apologized Raven when the first officer joined her. "I was asking him of his family, and well, one comment led to another. It really was my fault," she entreated.

"No need for makin' amends, gal," Horningold assured her. Then leaning closer as if to tell her a secret, he said, "You see I was only pretendin' to be angry. I have to cuss and yell at all of 'em from time to time so's they'll give me a little respect." His corded chest inflated boastfully. "Now that I am an honorary officer in his Majesty George's Royal Navy instead of a stinkin' rum guzzler, I deserve a little courtesy." He nodded in George's direction. "That lad has the makin's of a fine seaman, and I aim to see that that gift ain't wasted. He needs a stern hand in back of him, pushin' and proddin' him along until he learns some sense!"

Raven's understanding somberness eased into a beaming smile as she realized that the main reason she felt such an affectionate attachment to the reformed sea rogue was because his genial nature reminded her of Captain Mabry's. "I would venture to say, sir, that Mr. Rounsivell, as well as the rest of the crew, holds you in the highest esteem," she assured him.

A sheepish grin flushed his face, and he stared at his bare feet as her praise continued.

"It is a very admirable task that you have chosen to undertake, Mr. Horningold. I understand that you single-handedly captured Phineas Bunch, even after his pistol had fired into your chest. The Bahamas will forever be indebted to you for such courageous efforts."

"You flatter him to much, Miss Gatewood," said Cockram, coming upon them. "Why he'll gloat over those words for weeks!"

Perez, climbing down from the bridge, joined the group. "Ah, good morning, Miss Gatewood." He bowed politely. "I trust you had a restful night." Luckily, no one caught his sly wink.

"Yes," she answered calmly. "Very well, thank you. Everything you provided was most comfortable and accommodating!"

"Come along, Cockram. Let's see if Wally has any more of those biscuits left," said Horningold.

"But you just ate a dozen of them," protested Cockram. "How can you be hungry again?"

189

"That may be true," he answered, nudging his companion, "but this salty air makes me all the hungrier."

After his two best crewmen ambled off, Perez tenderly lifted her slender hand to his lips and grinned cunningly. "I am so relieved that all was to your liking, miss." Holding her elbow, he led her over to the bridge and lifted her onto the platform. "Ah, when I saw you standing on deck, my love, your hair streaming out and your skirts billowing around your legs, I knew those feelings I had last evening were not imaginings."

"And," she prodded playfully, "just what do you intend to do about it?"

"After giving that very question ample consideration, I decided I could choose but one of two options."

"And what are they, if I may ask?"

"Well, the first is to gather you in my arms and take you back to our bed and spend the entire day ravaging your luscious body."

She feigned disappointment, sticking out her lower lip sullenly. "And you decided against that? I do not understand." She struck a provocative pose. "Could it be that dallying with a fallen maiden is not quite to your liking?"

"If I were not in full view of my crew, I would guide your hand to the appropriate place and show you just how much a certain fallen maiden excites me," he threatened. "The reason I cannot submit to such urges, however, is because it would be most difficult to explain my absence from the deck," he declared, planting a light kiss on her forehead. "So that leaves us to my alternative plan."

"Well, get on with it, Captain. I am confident it will prove more exciting and tempting than the first."

He cleared his throat and, with mock dignity, began. "Plan number two is to point out certain points of interest to you as we draw closer to port." He sighed dully. "Not quite as stimulating as the first plan, mind you, but interesting never the less!"

She applauded his idea. "Why, that's a marvelous idea!" She turned away haughtily and faced the oval-shaped landfall outlining the horizon. "Well, I'm waiting!"

"If that is the case, my love, then I shall be more than happy to accommodate you!" His arms encircled her waist, and he pulled her tight against his sturdiness. "We shall begin with geography," he said, nuzzling her ear. "Please note, Miss Gatewood, how natural barriers surround the island. Those cays, reefs, and shallow channels make entry most difficult. I would imagine that is why the pirates fought so to retain control of New Providence. The southern and eastern sides of the island have no harbors at all. The land is flat and low with many shoals. Now this western side has an excellent harbor and is protected from both the north and south. Are you paying attention, miss, for if you're not, I shall be forced to turn you over my knee this instant and spank you!"

"Uhmmm!" she cooed.

"Raven!" he admonished, pretending to be stern. "Are you listening to anything I'm saying?"

"I certainly am! I was just thinking of something."

"Oh, and that is?"

"Maria mentioned something about Ames having a

retreat on one if the islands around New Providence. It seems he has friends in town who look after him and supply him with food."

"That could very well be," agreed Perez. "I hope she will be willing to discuss more of his activities with me. Why, her knowledge of that man will help us tremendously!"

Raven relaxed once again in his protective embrace; her head rested comfortably on his shoulder, and she urged him to continue.

"All right. Do you see that rock tower over there?" he asked, pointing to the eastern tip of the island. She nodded. "That was built by our shortly departed friend Blackbeard so he could keep an eye out for any British ship that tried to surprise him. He fancied himself as being the governor of all of these islands. Even formed a fraternity for all of the pirates; the Brethren of the Coast, he called them. They would all meet at the tower's base to hold their council meetings and plan their next plunder."

"Quite a pirate's paradise!" mumbled Raven.

"I regret so. Every good-for-nothing sailor in this part of the world decided to make the island his home. They would all band together and pillage ships that were misfortunate enough to sail their way. In retaliation the French and the Spanish both began burning and plundering Nassau. I'm surprised there's more to the island than a few ash heaps."

"But what about the British government?" inquired Raven. "Had they ever attempted settlement here before now?"

"Their meager efforts could hardly be called attempts. Everyone wanted the Bahamas, but no one quite knew what to do with them once they had them. King Charles granted this land to his attorney general, Sir Robert Heath, in 1629, but no one tried to settle it. Do you remember me telling you about my father's endeavors with the Adventurers? Well, William Sayle shipwrecked here once. He gave it the name of New Providence, in fact, because he was so grateful he was not killed."

"The foreseeing guidance of God. Providence," remarked Raven. "Sayle chose the name well."

Perez continued. "In the mid sixteen hundreds, Charles II granted the territory to the eight Lord Proprietors of the Carolinas. The port city was called Charles Town. It was destroyed by the Spanish in 1684. A fort was built and the city constructed ten years later, and its name was changed to Nassau."

"Ah, in honor of William III, Prince of Orange-Nassau," she smugly told him, not mentioning that her father had given her that bit of information during his last Christmas at home.

"Right you are, my little vixen!" he complimented, chin resting atop her head. "It delights me to know that such beauty is matched by a fair amount of wisdom. Nothing is duller than a woman with infinite beauty who lacks wit!"

"Yes, yes, yes. When you tire of my beauty," she joked brazenly, "my wit can serve to captivate you once again. Now please, on with my lesson, sire."

"What an apt pupil I have in my charge. Well now, oh, yes, the Proprietors continued sending governors over to oversee the development of their holdings, but

193

the men they assigned to the position were more often than not greedy, sniveling fools who saw their jobs as the perfect opportunity to increase their wealth. They would stop at nothing in order to accumulate a sack of gold. Many even bargained with the pirates. They would allow them the freedom to plunder and pilfer in their waters in return for an attractive share of the haul. The Proprietors finally admitted failure, and the Crown offered to retain the islands. Rather than allow New Providence to fall to Spain or to be overrun with pirates again, the king approved of a plan of settlement, assured the investing group funding for the project, and appointed the leader, who was Rogers, as Governor. Being a privateer himself once, Rogers was able to assert his authority the moment he blasted through the harbor."

"But even if you are successful in eliminating the pirates, New Providence is still as vulnerable as ever to an attack by Spanish forces," observed Raven.

Perez shook his head sadly. "With Havana so close, that is always a possibility. Governor Rogers certainly has his share of problems. He's worried himself into old age since he's been here trying to solve them all. Sometimes it seems that his efforts were all doomed from the start."

He explained that within three months after Rogers had assumed control of the island, an epidemic broke out, taking the lives of ninety of his men. Later on, Mr. Whitney, the captain of the *Rose* deliberately refused an order, and the governor, enraged by the officer's impudence, planted the butt of his pistol on Whitney's skull. Humiliated, the captain deserted his ship and returned to England and spread vicious rumors about Roger's lack of organization and competence. Since then, the Lord Commissioners have been deaf to Roger's plea for a man-of-war to be stationed in the harbor to protect the island. "I remember when Woodes first came here. His hopes were so high! Such optimism! He saw fields of sugarcane and cotton on barren land, had thoughts of a whaling industry and devised a method of exporting salt to the cod fishermen of Newfoundland. What magnificent aspirations! He is even convinced, and rightly so, that if England can fortify this island stronghold, she will be able to maintain her dominance of the sea. Too bad George does not recognize its strategic importance."

"Strategic for what?" asked Raven, wondering how a small clump of islands situated in the middle of the Atlantic could hold any significance to a country as powerful as England.

"If the Spanish take over the Bahamas, they are one step closer to the American colonies. Already they have advanced well into Florida."

"Then surely there must be others in England, learned men who are well aware of the problems of the nation, who realize the necessity of establishing a viable defense here. I know my father used to discuss that very thing during his afternoon meetings at the coffee houses. Does Rogers know of anyone at home who can plead his case for more funding?"

"Do the names Richard Steele and Joseph Addison hold any importance to you?" questioned Perez.

"I should say so," she replied, impressed by the mention of two of the most prominent literary figures of the day. "Their periodicals, the *Tattler* and the *Spectator* are both widely read and very influential."

"Indeed?" asked Perez, pleased with this information. "Both men are close associates of the governor. From what I understand, they have been attempting to raise the capital necessary to finance a large undertaking such as the one Rogers has set out to do. He has friends in Parliament who have sought special audiences with Walpole to discuss the same thing, but the man never has time to listen to their demands. Too busy running the country for King George, I suppose!"

"It appears to me that King George is knowingly neglecting his duty," deduced Raven gravely. "The cost of financing Rogers's colony with money, provisions, a man-of-war, and skilled soldiers is a mere fraction of what will be spent if England's empire in the New World crumbles."

"Rogers, as well as England, will suffer severe losses if this situation persists for much longer. Well! Enough politics for one day," he decided, swinging her off the bridge.

Will my heart always skip so many beats when he touches me, and my legs turn to jelly when he is near? mused Raven silently as they walked arm in arm across the deck toward Maria and Horningold who were engrossed in a discussion about Ames. ". . . . So that explains him not returning to Gorda Cay," concluded Horningold, reflectively scratching his densely whiskered chin.

"What explains it?" questioned Perez anxiously.

"Señora Valdez has been tellin' me some very int'resting things; such as Ames's recent dealings with

196

Henry Jennings."

"Henry Jennings?" repeated Perez thoughtfully. "Ah, I have it now!" he exclaimed, snapping his fingers. "He lifted the Spanish Plate."

"He did what?" asked Raven.

"The Spanish Plate Fleet," explained Maria, "was a flotilla of ships which brought supplies to Spain's New World holdings. On its return trip home, it was usually laden with treasures from the colonies."

Perez continued. "Henry Jennings and his crew had their base on New Providence for many years, but when he refused to join Blackbeard's elite group, he was encouraged to plunder elsewhere. It just so happened that he was within viewing distance when one of the ships of the flotilla wrecked near Florida several months later. He plundered the sinking ship and became a very wealthy man. I still can't understand his relationship with Ames, though."

Horningold motioned for Maria to give her account of the relationship. "Several weeks before Ames raided Raven's ship," disclosed Maria, her eyes narrowing with pensive recollection, "Ames met with Jennings in Nassau and brought him back to Gorda Cay. From what I was able to overhear, it seemed that Jennings wanted Ames to procure a vessel for him and outfit it with a hundred of the meanest, blood thirstiest men he could find. In return for his service, Jennings promised to reward Ames with a vast fortune in gold and silver and the opportunity to combine forces with him to sack Nassau and divide the spoils equally."

"Of course, why else would Ames have bothered attackin' a cargo ship. He had more in mind than a few

197

bales of tea," cleverly surmised Horningold. "And that is why he secured it on Mangrove Cay instead of settin' it adrift. Now if'n I's Ames, I would have gone back home just long enough to stock up on food and water and get rid of the prisoners. No offense, ladies. Then I'd most likely leave a few mates hidden on New Providence to get rid of the stolen goods little by little. In the meantime, I'd be goin' to the other islands findin' some men. Then go to Mangrove Cay and pick up the ship and sail to Jamaica and meet Jennings. Of course, I'm not so sure Ames is as smart as me, but that's what I'd do if'n I's in his shoes."

"But if Jennings salvaged so much wealth from the Spanish ship, why would he even want to risk the gallows again?" wondered Raven aloud.

"Revenge," answered Perez. "That and greed. You see when Blackbeard was stationed at New Providence, Jennings had no hopes of ever commanding the city. Teach was too strong of a rival. Poor Henry always wanted to be governor and fancied himself becoming one after Blackbeard left for the Carolinas. But Rogers's arrival spoiled his plans."

"Ames seems far too greedy to become involved in a partnership with anyone, especially someone whose reputation for evil matches his own," observed Raven aloud.

"Exactly!" agreed Perez. "Why settle for a portion of the profit when you can have the full amount? That is exactly what we must rely on; the lust for total power and complete, undivided wealth. Ames has the advantage, though, for I am sure that the good life Jennings has grown accustomed to has spoiled and pampered him. It will only be a matter of time before Henry's plan of dominance is thwarted by his conniving partner. Of that I am certain!"

The wind shifted, bringing with its abrupt turn a most offensive odor. The pungent smell wafted onto the deck. The sailors as well as the two women, grabbed their noses in repulsion as the noxious fumes attacked their nostrils.

"That smell's better 'en a compass to guide us into the harbor," shouted Cockram, scaling down the mast from the crow's nest. "If'n ye can believe it, the smell used to be ten times worse."

"Aye," concurred his friend. "I remember sailin' into the harbor more 'en once when them vapors wuz so strong many a good man turned green."

The wind once again changed its course, and with the returning of fresh, salted air, breathing resumed to normal, the chores completed, and conversations continued.

Perez offered an explanation of the repugnant smell. "Some years back wild cattle roamed the islands, and the inhabitants would roast the cows over an open pit. The pit was called a *bouccan,* hence the origin of buccaneer. After they had gorged themselves on the meal, they would leave the carcasses to dry and rot. As a result of such filth, periodic epidemics would rage across the island. After that last bout of fever last year, efforts were made to combat it and prevent its occurrence once and for all. To achieve this, Rogers has appointed a group to scour every bit of the area and burn any remaining carcasses. I suspect that burning is what we just got the whiff of."

"Hogg Island ahead!" sounded the helmsman.

The *Falcon* rounded the sandy point of the long, narrow island that shelters Nassau's harbor from the furies of the ocean. She then effortlessly glided across the brownish waters of the shallow bar into the deeper, shimmering turquoise of the harbor.

## Chapter Twelve

Fort Nassau, constructed atop a peaked ridge that jutted out into the channel, lie dead ahead. Perez explained that its walls were made of tabby, a substance of crushed shells cohered with sand and lime. Throughout the years it had braved invasions by the Spanish, sackings by the French and burnings by numerous cutthroats who vied for its control. Four towers rose from each of its corners, such that an incoming vessel, regardless of its direction, could be immediately sighted. Twenty-eight nine-pound cannons were mounted on her walls, making an attack from the sea virtually impossible. This caused most of the nine hundred inhabitants to view their coastal fort as being impregnable, but Rogers was not as confident. He insisted that all of the three hundred able-bodied males age sixteen or older, including pardoned pirates, spend three hours at the fort each morning, alongside his own regiment of a hundred and fifty soldiers, practicing drills with Lieutenant Turnley. The demanding governor's reasoning behind such extensive training was to ensure protection against an invasion by land as well as by sea.

"Since we are commissioned on government business, we are permitted to tie up at the fort's wharf," said Perez. Pointing to the east at two brigatines, he explained. "Trade ships like the *Martha* and the *Eastern Star* make regular trips back and forth from England." He shouted a hearty greeting across the way to two mates on the commercial pier who were scrubbing the deck of the *Island Lady*. "That sloop carries provisions to the outer islands and returns with fresh fruit and produce that is sold here. The schooner tied up next to her is the *Tempest,* a whaling ship. Eventually Rogers hopes to have an entire fleet of them."

Two naval frigates, the *Rose* and the *Milford,* two sloops, *Buck* and *Shark,* and a thirty-four gun vessel that brought Rogers to the island, the *Delcia,* were already secured at the fort's pier. A sixth ship, the largest of them all, bore the name of *H.M.S. Flamborough.*

"She sure is a beaut," admired Horningold. "Must be eighty feet long, at least thirty in the beam. Aye, nobler vessel I've yet to see—full sided, and deep, too. I'd give my soul to sail on her."

"Who'd want it? It's blacker than Satan's," ribbed Cockram. "I pity the Spanish galleon or the pirate sloop foolish enough to challenge her. She'll blow them to pieces."

"Tie up alongside her, Mr. Cockram. Grab the lines!" ordered Perez.

"Aye, Sir," he replied, throwing the heavy, plaited rope onto the pier. Then he agilely leaped from the vessel to secure her lines on the pine piling.

"Juan, look!" squealed Raven excitedly, pointing to a large-billed bird with a drooping pouch beneath its beak. "See it? Over there sitting on that pole. What is it?"

"You've never seen a pelican before? No, I suppose you haven't," answered Perez, grinning.

"Pelican," she repeated. "Pel-i-can. What a funny looking bird."

"What a fascinatin' bird the pelican! His beak can hold more than his bel-i-can. And I'll be damned if I see how the hel-i-can!" chanted Horningold in a sing-song manner. "Watch him closely. See what happens when he spots a fish."

As if on cue, the pelican folded back his white wings, dove into the water with a sounding splash, and emerged with a frantically flapping speckled fish hanging out of his mouth.

"But he's just sitting on the water. Do you think he's hurt?" she asked.

"They all do that," Perez assured her. "The dive into the water stuns them for a moment. See? Now he's returning to his perch to enjoy his catch."

The bird tilted his head, and the fish slid down his throat. His pouch vibrated until his squirming meal was digested.

"Lines secured, Sir!" shouted Cockram from the recently constructed dock.

"Welcome to Nassau, ladies," declared Perez. "Mr. Horningold, have the crew make a thorough inspection of the ship, from the nest to the keel. Any repairs that need to be made, order them so. Check with Phipps to assure that all artillery has been cleaned and oiled.

Every man's musket, piece, or pistol must be in excellent condition. Have Cockram examine the sails and the riggings. The least tear must be mended. And have Cookie order more provisions for the ship's store and see to it that a careful inventory is made of all purchases. If there are any problems, I can be found at Henry Lightbourne's residence."

"Sir," said Horningold. "What about the crew? After a month at sea with no rum and no women, they'll be itchin' to get into town. It'll result in nothin' but trouble if their shore leave's denied."

"You're right," agreed Perez. "After the chores are completed, give them the wages due them, but," he cautioned sternly, "warn them that if they are not back on board the ship by daylight and in a sober condition, we sail without them, and they will be considered deserters."

"They're decent men," defended Horningold. "Not one of 'em 'll risk disappointin' you. You have their respect as well as their loyalty. They give very few men that."

"I'm proud of them, Ben. They've all developed into able mariners. And I am especially pleased with you. I could not have gotten a better first mate had I been given my choice of all of His Majesty's sailors."

Horningold smiled and mumbled incoherent modesties.

"And one other thing, Mr. Horningold."

"Yes, Sir?"

"I shall check with the captain of the Flamborough and see if he would mind your visiting his vessel later."

The first mate beamed at such a prospect. "Why,

thank you, Sir. I'd certainly be grateful."

Perez lifted Maria first, then Raven, onto the dock. "Now for the grand tour of Nassau, ladies."

They walked past the fort and onto the commercial wharf. It was bustling with its usual mid-morning activity as the trio sauntered across. Bare-chested, tow-headed youngsters dived off the tabby wall, which separated the pier from the water. They yelled their challenges to each other to see who could go the deepest or stay down the longest. Shriveled, weather-worn seafarers slumped on the wall's edge, lazily dangling their fishing lines into the water while one tried to outdo the next with exaggerated tales of when they had once sailed the ocean. These wizened old men would occasionally pause from their fantasies long enough to chew on bits of conch they were using as bait, to slurp from their rum bottle, or to yell obscenities at the rambunctuous divers who were scaring away their fish.

Aggressive vendors were positioned along the pier, hawking their wares and shoving their merchandise out to passersby for inspection. Baskets heaped with oranges, limes, peas, coconuts, and yams lined the way. Piles of loose salt were stacked on straw mats alongside stalks of green bananas. Fresh grouper, snapper, and crawfish, as well as an upside-down turtle struggling frantically to right itself, were on display. Sponges strung on cords stretched the length of the dock. Enough conch shells had been discarded throughout the years to form a wall at the end, their bright pink coloring having long been bleached white. And beyond it lay gleaming, white-sanded beaches.

A coffee-colored woman, garbed in a batiked dress, sat at the end of the dock singing. The chanting words of the song were in her African tongue, but the quick, rhythmic beat of the verse indicated that it was a joy-filled one.

"Watch how she takes the meat from the shell," instructed Perez, pausing beside a basket of fresh conch.

She flashed her audience a wide, square-toothed smile and performed her tedious chore with elaborate motions. Carefully holding the shell in one hand and a hatchet in the other, she tapped a tiny hole in its ringed, right front. Then she jabbed a knife into its flared lips, pulling out a clump of white meat. Then in a single motion, she skillfully stripped the outer skin away from the tender white meat and tossed it over her shoulder. Placing the meat on a cutting block, she scored it with her sharp knife and sprinkled it with lime and hot peppers. She held it up for Perez who took the package of meat and tossed her a tuppence. He then tore the spicy treat into three strips and gave portions to Raven and Maria.

They made their way along the sand-packed clearing separating the wharf from the settlement's center of activity, Front Street. Five flourishing businesses were housed in unpretentious buildings constructed from timber, tabby, and cut coral rock. The first of the group was the Mercantile Store.

Its proprietor, Paul Ingraham, supplied the townsfolk with a vast assortment of imported merchandise: teas, spices, tobaccos, grains, meal, flour, hardwares, ropes, whale oil, lanterns, pewter dishes, crockery, skillets, and yard goods. Beside it stood Pinder's Cobblery and a haberdashery whose owner, Newt Albury, was a nailmaker as well as a tailor. Next was an establishment owned by three industrious brothers whose skills were much in demand in the thriving community: a gunsmith, a blacksmith, and a cutler. Their services included the making and repairing of guns, cutlasses and pistols, and the fashioning of locks, hinges, grates, axeheads, farming implements, and eating utensils. The fourth business was "Malone's Carpentry Shop: Builders of Fine Furniture, Doors and Windows." At the end of the line was Pratt's Bakery where tantalizing smells of freshly baked breads, pies, puffs, and tarts seduced even the thriftiest passersby.

A rectangular plot of ground containing charred remains of structures burned by the Spanish in 1684 conveniently separated the business district from the Jolly Roger Tavern. Only a few years earlier its name had been the Hawknest, and rascals such as Calico Jack and his women looters, Bart Roberts, Blackbeard, and Red Legs Greaves were regular customers. Its present clientele consisted of a rather dull and ordinary group: seamen, shopkeepers, council members, farmers, craftsmen and pirates-turned-upright-citizens.

Farther down the street, they paused in front of a stone well. It was completely shaded from the summer sun by a spreading fig tree. Perez told them that Blackbeard had his men dig the well so he could be sure his ship would always have access to fresh water. "Incidentally, legend has it that once you drink from

207

this well, you'll never want to leave the island. Being on friendly terms with the islanders, Blackbeard would always leave a barrel filled with rum under the tree. If someone passed by and refused his hospitality, he had them tied in chains and rolled off the wharf."

"Captain Perez! Captain Perez!" shouted a voice from across the clearing.

Perez returned the greeting and led his companions over to the tall, thin figure. The right side of the man's face drooped noticeably, the result of his taking a musket ball in his jaw. "Governor Rogers," he acknowledged, extending his hand to the settlement's leader. "I was just on my way to see you."

"The sentry of the fort just advised me of your arrival," he revealed, eyeing the two women curiously. "Well, let's go over to the tavern. I am most anxious to hear of your progress."

The sallow-complected, graying governor limped up the street into a building marked by a skull and cross-bones banner bearing the words "Jolly Roger." Its dimly lit interior was smoky and stuffy. Thatched mats were lowered midway over each of the four windows permitting some light but little air into the room. The walls were covered with braided, wicker rugs and decorated with flags bearing the colors and insignias of the tavern's most ruthless patrons. Conch shells, pieces of coral, an upright starfish, and green turtle shells now rested atop the shelves that had once exhibited jeweled goblets, silver platters and other elaborate mementos from a lucrative haul.

Rogers nodded indifferently to three unshaven men seated on rum kegs playing cards. He chose a

208

driftwood table in the corner of the room where their conversation could not be overheard. "There's a lazy lot; all of them. Most of the islanders would rather game and guzzle rum than earn a full day's wage," he mumbled disgustedly. "There's timber to cut and fields to plow, but see how their time is spent?"

A long, narrow serving bar stood to one side of the room and was attended by a burly, black-bearded sea-farer whose eyeless hole was covered by a soiled red patch. A weighty silver cross adorned with emeralds, diamonds, and rubies hung down from his neck. His one good eye squinted drolly as he plopped two foaming ales in front of Rogers and Perez. He acknowledged their appreciative words with a fierce scowl and a throaty grunt.

"My new informant," confided Rogers softly as he lit a long-stem clay pipe. "Simon's ears have been invaluable." He retained his upright posture, and a faint smile crossed his thin lips. "I am curious to know how two such lovely ladies happened into your company."

He listened spellbound, frequently shaking his head in wonder that two women were able to survive such a perilous ordeal, as Perez recounted the events leading up to Raven's imprisonment. After the explanation was completed, Rogers pounded a clenched fist on the table. "Those degenerates must be eliminated. Will we never rid ourselves of them?" he asked despairingly.

"Ames will not elude us much longer," Perez assured him. "My men are familiar with his movements. We are certain that he has equipped the English brig with men and provisions for Jennings and taken it to Jamaica.

We think they will meet on Gorda Cay later to plan their strategy for attacking Nassau."

"If the Spanish don't beat them to it," said Rogers drily. "Soon after you left, a Captain Dennis sailed into the harbor and requested to see me. He was returning home after a mission to Havana to see if the Spanish would exchange English prisoners for Spanish ones. While there, he discovered they were outfitting four large ships and ten sloops and galleons with over two thousand men for an invasion of New Providence. Frankly, I doubt our being able to offer much resistance."

"But I saw the *Flamborough* in the harbor. She certainly looks powerful enough to thwart any attempt," interrupted Perez.

"Regretfully, King George did not send her to us. Captain Hildersly came into port only to bring us some sorely needed provisions. He was en route to the Carolinas where the ship has been permanently stationed."

"But what about our man-of-war? He did promise us one," argued Perez angrily. "The threat of an invasion is greater here than in the Carolinas."

"I fear that we shall never see a stationed man-of-war in our harbor. I have written request upon request to the Lord Commissioners of Trade urging—no— begging them to commission one into our port. It seems they ignore my letters as well as our danger." He slumped dishearteningly in his chair. "In addition to that worry, if it alone were not enough, there is talk among these insolent islanders of a conspiracy to seize me and hand the fort back over to the pirates."

"Surely such a rumor is ill-founded, Woodes," said Perez.

"I think not. The inhabitants lack ambition. They are unconcerned about a better life for themselves and their children. Why toil and sweat planting crops when enough food grows wild? What is the point in rebuilding a town if you're content with a ramshackle shanty on the beach? The men seldom present themselves for drill anymore. No one is willing to cut timber or haul rocks, even though we desperately need to fortify. The plantations of cotton and sugarcane that I envisioned will never materialize, for over two-thirds of the Huguenot immigrants I brought with me for such purposes have died. Sometimes, old friend, I think I would be much better off to take my family and return to England."

"You must not allow yourself to become so distraught," cautioned Perez. "Already you have invested over eleven thousand pounds of your own funds into this settlement. If you give up now, that investment is lost. You expect miracles to happen, progress to appear overnight. Do not dwell on all of the settlement's problems. Look instead to all of your accomplishments here. When you first arrived, the fort was in shambles. Only one small cannon was mounted. Garbage was piled high throughout the town, emitting a stench so noxious that no one was free from disease. The streets were infested with pirates."

"I know, Juan, but you don't un—"

"And now, look at the town. The streets are clean, and businesses flourish. Ever since you made an example of the Flemings fellow and hanged him for looting and burning the Walker's home, there has been a low incidence of crime. And only a small minority of pirates are left who have not agreed to surrender peacefully. Once Ames is in chains, the others will rush in hoardes to make their mark. All of the settlers you brought with you from England are hard working, industrious people who will see to it that farms are established as well as a salt and whaling industry. You mustn't underestimate your accomplishments!"

"You certainly are long-winded, Captain," joked the governor. "Almost as bad as my wife." His tension-creased face relaxed. "Without your optimism and abundant confidence, dear friend, I feel my days here would be limited." Suddenly he realized that Raven and Maria had been completely ignored, and turned to them to apologize. "I hope you will excuse an old man's rudeness, but Captain Perez is a gracious sounding board for my troubles."

"There is no reason to apologize, Governor Rogers," said Raven graciously. "I have been most intrigued by your discussion. Such an undertaking is quite admirable."

"Thank you, my dear. Your words are welcome to my ears." Such a lovely lady, he thought. No wonder my friend is in such high spirits today. "Perhaps Captain Perez has told you already that I have had the pleasure of meeting your father."

"No, he didn't. But please tell me, Sir. How was my father when you last spoke with him? You see, I have not seen him for nearly four years. The only news I received of him was a letter earlier this year from a Mr. Morgan Taylor, who informed me of my father's illness

212

and of his plans of going to Eleuthera once his health permitted travel."

"When I last saw your father, Raven . . . hmm, back several months ago I do believe, he was recovering rather nicely. He was most anxious to return to England, but we feared his strength had not been sufficiently regained and a sea voyage would only prove to complicate the illness. I must say, if I were him, I don't know whether I would hug you or spank you for attempting such a dangerous voyage."

"I know now that it was a very foolish undertaking on my part, but I felt a responsibility to help my father," retaliated Raven. "Tell me more of him, Sir. I long to hear any news about him. Did you see him frequently?"

"Yes, we visited together quite often. Mostly we talked about our families and of the future of the Bahamas. He assured me that when he was fit to sail to England, he intended to go to London and personally plead my cause to King George, and tell him that it is imperative that he grant us the protection and funding we were promised."

"I am confident that he will do your cause justice. I so wish he were still here and that I did not have to wait an entire week before seeing him."

"I've told Miss Gatewood that she will be able to sail with Captain Jack on his next supply run to the Taylor Plantation," explained Perez, noting the governor's puzzled expression.

"What about you, Perez?" asked the governor. "I mean, how do you plan to proceed with your mission?"

"I intend to stay on the open sea in full view of our

honorable French friend until he locates me," he said simply.

"Are you insane, man?" asked Rogers incredulously. "You are the hunter, not the hunted. Why such a risky plan."

"I fear that is the only way I will ever come face to face with that dog. There are hundreds of small cays on which he can take refuge. We have already wasted too much time in pursuit of him. What I plan is to let him come after me. His cunning will be weakened considerably by his wrath."

"Talk sense, Perez. I've hardly been able to follow a word you've said," implored the confused governor.

"When we were at Gorda Cay, I purposely hung my banner from Ames's tower so he would know exactly who had invaded his territory and stolen his prisoners. I want him to know that it is Juan Perez who is in pursuit of him."

"Ah, now I am beginning to understand. Do you think it will work?"

"Outsmarting him is dangerous enough, but to humiliate him by flaunting my success in his face will enrage him. Of course it will work. He is most anxious, no doubt, to confront me now. As a matter of fact, I am relying totally on his thirst for vengeance to occupy his mind. If my suppositions prove correct, he will become so twisted by his obsession to find me that he will become careless. At this point, he will once again become the quarry," revealed Perez confidently. "And in the meantime you will be given much-needed time to fortify the city against an attack by forces from Havana."

214

"Those damned Spaniards!" cursed Rogers spitefully. "I do not know who is the worse enemy. Both Ames and Cornego would kill our inhabitants, ravage our women, and burn our town to the ground in a matter of minutes. Perhaps I should schedule a mock battle between those two and to the victor, New Providence!" He added sarcastically, "Perhaps then some of our people would be spared and all our efforts would not have been in vain. Oh, I am sorry Señora Valdez. I seem to have forgotten that—"

"Do not apologize, Sir," answered Maria quietly. "How I hope my people have not resorted to such animal behavior, but I know in my heart that the words you speak are true." She wiped her eye with the sleeve of her blouse. "Don Cornego is even more vile than Ames. Many times I listened to him boast to my husband of how he dealt with the spoils of war. It made him such a big man! Even innocent little children were shown no mercy. His brutality is barbarian, and yet my people worship the man as a hero. I feel such shame for my country. With such men as Cornego, she will soon fall. Her time as the greatest nation in the world is coming to an end."

She paused deliberately and looked Rogers squarely in the eyes. "I want to remain on your island, Sir. I have no home to go to. Knowledge of my imprisonment will only bring shame and humiliation to my family. I assure you that I shall be no threat to your town. I am tired of hatred and injustice. I have seen enough bloodshed over lust for power and greed to last the rest of my life." She lowered her head and awaited a reply.

After careful deliberation Rogers answered, knowing that most of the townsfolk were sure to question his decision. "You will be welcomed here, Señora Valdez. I do not believe you pose any threat to the security of our island."

"I am most grateful, Sir," was her meek reply.

"When do you intend to weigh anchor, Captain Perez?" inquired Rogers. "Even though they have agreed to our terms of amnesty, your crew makes me nervous."

"Not until dawn, Sir."

"But why wait until then? Is she in need of some repairs?"

"Aside from our completing a few routine chores, the *Falcon* is fit to sail on command."

"Then why the delay? Nassau is in enough danger without permitting your troublesome crew to run wild through the streets. Oh, I don't know why I ever let you talk me into such a fool notion as having pirates as your crew."

"Don't be so easily riled, Woodes. I owe the men some time for pleasure. They have all upheld their part of the pledge and have been as devoted to their mission as your best officer would have been. I have confidence that the fellows will not be a menace to society tonight. If I am wrong, I shall have no choice but take full responsibility for their actions."

"I suppose you are right," Rogers grudgingly admitted. "But warn them, I will not tolerate any drunken brawls or mischief of any sort, no matter how small the infraction!"

"I understand completely, Sir. A night on the town is just what their spirits need to drive them on. Besides,

Ben will see to it that their night of freedom does not get out of control."

"And how is that old rogue? Causing you any problems?" asked Rogers, remembering Horningold's welcoming when he first arrived in the Bahamas.

"I like the old chap," said Perez. "He's proven a most valuable asset. I've given him complete authority on the vessel."

"How about Cockram and Rounsivell?"

"They are performing admirably as well."

"Good! Perhaps your theory of catching a thief with a thief warrants more praise than I've given. Perhaps with the right guidance, young George could make something of himself."

"You do have a weak spot in your heart for that youngster, Woodes. And I know he thinks just as well of you."

"You know, I will never forget the day I sailed into the harbor. After Vane had escaped our fire and fled out to sea, Horningold realized that he had no other alternative but to give me a royal welcome to New Providence. He fired a round of salutes and stood at attention when my men disembarked. No one jeered him for it, either. When I read my offer aloud, he was the first in line to make his mark. Made such a grand showing of it that the others soon followed suit."

"What of Stede Bonnet? Heard anything of him lately?"

Rogers nodded wearily and rolled back his eyes. "Lord, yes. Rumor has it that he sneaks onto the island by way of the western channel from time to time. He never causes the least bit of trouble though. He probably just does it to taunt me with his insidious cunning. I am certain that he is given refuge by that damnable Madame DuVall."

"You could just deport her back to France. Of course, then you would have to face the consequences," teased Perez. "I understand several of our illustrious council members frequent her establishment."

And what of you, Juan Perez, wondered Raven. Are you equally as familiar with her favors?

"She is a wicked woman!" interjected Maria, almost violently. "Ames spoke of her often. Those women who were too weak to labor were sold to her to be used in that . . . that bordello!"

"The whole lot is incorrigible," agreed Rogers. "Something must be done about that woman. I know her establishment is the gathering place for many of the pirates. I have warned her on numerous occasions that if she persists in harboring those demons, I shall have the militia come and drag her to jail, regardless of the consensus of my councillors. I fear, Juan, that because of one of their loose tongues, Ames has been able to evade you."

"But I thought you trusted your council members," remarked Perez.

"At one time I thought I could, since half were my own men and half elected by the townspeople. But it appears that there are those among us who are anxious to aid those scavengers and contribute to the downfall of my settlement."

"Then in the future, our plans are to be discussed with no one. Absolute secrecy is to be maintained if I am to achieve my goal. And furthermore," instructed

Perez, "no one is to know of my trip to Gorda Cay or that Raven and Maria were hostages there. I do not intend to put their lives in danger."

"I agree wholeheartedly," said the governor, pulling his watch from the pocket of his damask waistcoat. "I have a meeting with our trusted friends in a quarter of an hour. Problems with Commander Hildersly. Did I tell you?"

"No, you didn't. Problems with the *Flamborough?*"

"I have managed to detain that ship as long as I can because I have feared an attack. Now I wish to somehow force it to remain in port."

"And what if Hildersly offers resistance?"

"Would you believe that that abominable man has threatened to put me in irons if I make any attempt to prevent his departure? I suppose that, too, is one of the risks of this job," added Rogers, smiling. "The pirates want me in chains, as do the Spanish and many of my own people. And I am so far in debt that my creditors will no doubt toss me in debtor's prison if I ever show my face in England again. Come up to my home later this afternoon, Captain. We can solve all of our problems over a bottle of port. Sarah and Melinda will be away at a church social then, so do come."

"Very well, Governor. I have several more things to attend to after chatting with Henry, then I shall meet you around five o'clock."

"Good. Ladies," he said, bidding them good-bye. Then he left the tavern and proceeded up the street to Government House for his conference.

"A most interesting man," commented Raven. "You can't help but admire someone like that. So determined, even though his is quite a troublesome task with many unsurmountable problems."

"A most determined fellow, indeed," agreed Perez. "But if anyone can civilize the islands, he's the man to do it. Now, ladies, on to Henry Lightbourne's. You'll find him even more fascinating!"

## Chapter Thirteen

Raven, Maria, and Captain Perez walked arm in arm up the lane joining Front Street with George Street. Perez pointed out Christ Church and its coral-walled cemetery, already too crowded for a developing colony due to the last epidemic that swept the island. They passed the modest residences of the more prosperous settlers and the driftwood shacks of the less industrious ones. Situated on a ridge at the top of George Street stood Rogers's home. On past it was a two story, box-shaped house that was enclosed by a white-washed fence. They entered the gate and walked up the shell-lined walkway. A weather-beaten board was tacked beside the arched doorway reading: "H. Lightbourne: Physic and Apothecary.

"Henry!" yelled Perez as he pounded on the door. "Dr. Lightbourne. Are you in there?"

"Just a minute! Just a minute, damn you!" growled an angry voice from inside. "I'll be damned if I'll mend another of you lazy bastards! You can bleed to death for all I care. Nothing better to do, I suppose, than beating yourselves over the heads with rum bottles." His close-set, bespeckled eyes glared furiously as he opened the door, then danced with surprised astonishment. "My good friend Captain Perez!" he shouted happily as muscle-corded arms powerfully embraced Juan. His mountainous belly, bulging from behind a blood-spotted smock, oscillated with laughter as he released his herculean grip. "I thought for sure you'd be dead by now. Fully expected to see your puny body washed up onto the shore with Red Ames's initials carved into your gut." He stroked his blond, sun-bleached whiskers and eyed Perez's two companions. "Hey, what have we here, man? Which of these lovelies did you bring for me?" he jested good-naturedly.

It was obvious that Maria and Raven did not appreciate his comment; they scowled at their host with obvious distaste.

"Watch your manners, Henry!" reprimanded Perez, trying to sound sharp. "Miss Gatewood and Señora Valdez are not as well acquainted with your wry humor as I."

"My brashness is unforgivable. I do apologize," he said genially, assuming an upright, gentlemanly stance. Then, delivering a hard blow between Perez's shoulders, he boomed, "Well, don't just stand out in the street all day. Come in! Come in!" He led them up a narrow stairway directly in front of the door. "The room off the right is the treatment room and apothecary shop. My living quarters are upstairs."

The cheery doctor opened an ornately carved door, explaining to the women that he had salvaged it from a Dutch cargo ship that had wrecked off Hogg Island some years before.

The large living room was elaborately furnished, also with items that had at one time belonged to the

Dutch ship. Two cushiony sofas of gold velvet faced each other, and in between, on a deep-piled, ruby-colored fringe rug, was a low, marble table. Bookshelves filled with worn, leather-bound volumes lined the walls, and the walls were covered with paintings of ships and seascapes. "Sit. Make yourselves comfortable," he encouraged. "I'll brew us a pot of tea."

"He'll take some getting used to," whispered Perez. "But once you do, you'll find he's a quite likeable chap."

"Is he one of the settlers the governor brought from home?" asked Raven.

"No one is quite sure where he came from, actually. He was already here when Rogers arrived. I'm as close to him as anyone, and I know very little about him. There are a lot of suspicions concerning him, but he's too well-liked to be the subject of idle town gossip. He has a small skiff and sails around to the other inhabited islands every few months to treat the sick."

"What a lonely life for a man like that," mused Maria.

"No, not at all, señora. Just the way I like it," said Lightbourne as he placed a silver serving tray containing a porcelain teapot, cups of the same cornflower design, and a plate of sweet cakes on the shiny, white-topped table. He seated himself next to Perez on the sofa, facing the two women, and graciously poured the tea. "No offense is intended, ladies, but women have proven to be more trouble than they're worth. Always complaining about the lack of social events, always conniving for more clothes. Nope, I'm most content as a bachelor." He sipped his tea, and his eyes narrowed in recollection. "Gatewood . . .

223

hmmm, Gatewood. Surely you cannot be Robert's daughter."

"Yes, I am. Captain Perez told me that you treated my father. I am most grateful for all that you did for him."

Lightbourne was reluctant to accept praise. "Ah, nature's more responsible for healing than I. I just tied him to the bed and threatened to beat him within an inch of his life if he got out. I suspect he's recuperating nicely by now?" he asked, looking questioningly at Perez.

"I'm sure he is," conceded Juan, "although I have not spoken to Taylor in quite a while. Raven is going to Eleuthera on Sunday to see her father, and I was hoping I could impose on your kindness and permit her to stay here with you."

"That may be a bit difficult, my boy," said Lightbourne, his round rubicund cheeks jiggling with amusement. "You see, my housekeeper, ol' Molly, left me this past week. Said she had enough of my cantankerousness, and no pay in the world was worth putting up with such a sordid fool. She'd rather work for those old maids at the rooming house than for me. Imagine that! Of course, if there happened to be another lady in the house, tongues wouldn't wag nearly so much." He arched his eyebrows questioningly at Maria. "What of your plans, Señora Valdez? Will you be in Nassau for long?"

Maria stiffened. "My only plan was to escape from my captor. I did not think to make any plans for my future, Dr. Lightbourne."

The tone of the middle-aged surgeon softened. "So that is how you met up with this scoundrel. You also, young lady?" he addressed Raven.

"Yes," she replied, telling him of the events that followed after she left England in search of her father. "But I was much more fortunate than Maria. Three months on that island was unbearable. I could never have withstood such anguish for eight years."

"Eight years," he echoed, glancing at Maria. "Incredible." No wonder her features are so harsh, he thought. No wonder she scowls so at me. "Well, friends, I have a solution to everyone's dilemma," he resolved gaily. "That is if Señora Valdez accepts my proposition."

Maria glared at him with cold suspicion. All men are the same calculating creatures, only out for their own gain, regardless of the hurt it may cause others, she thought. My own father was no better than the rest; even sold his daughter to the highest bidder. Power in exchange for a woman of marriageable age. I thought Hernando was different, but he was the same. He made no secret that he was only concerned for me because I was young and could produce sons for him. No better than a cow! A producer of fine animals!

The Lorenzos had been a family of substance and respect, but years of mismanagement and bad investments left them penniless. The only solution the old Don had was to bargain with his only child; his daughter, whose beauty was sought after by all. A most suitable trade!

Sons, she thought, is that all a man ever thinks of? The Don's first wife had died in childbirth, and the old man was obsessed with the idea of producing an heir. And Red Ames? He was worse than all of them, more base than a viper. Every night he tied her wrists and

225

ankles with heavy cord that cut her skin, and pounded his blubbery belly against her body as his men rolled with laughter. He stripped her of every bit of pride and self-respect she possessed. Hernando was not totally dissimilar after all, except the agony he inflicted was just to the mind, not the body. She remembered the way he used to look at her when, after a year of marriage, she still had not conceived. His eyes were full of pity and disgust, damning and scorning her barrenness. And now this unruly bastard. He looked to be no different than the others. Animals, all of them! His intelligence is in his breeches, not his head.

"I said that you can remain here, Señora Valdez, in my employment of course, and be my housekeeper and assistant. All I ask is that my quarters be kept in reasonably good order and deliciously appetizing food be placed before me three times a day." Patting his stomach, he joked, "Mustn't go hungry, you know! I'm a rather hefty eater, in spite of my minute size. And of course," he continued with the list of responsibilities, "you would tend to the patients, wrap bandages, feed them tea and broth, things like that. I shall supply you with food and lodging and, in addition, I shall pay you a pound a week and give you every Sabbath free. Are you interested?"

She deliberated carefully before answering. I have no other place to go, she thought. Who would want to employ a woman from a country that is preparing to attack them. It seems I have no other choice. "Thank you, Doctor. Your offer is most generous." Her face remained expressionless, for her apprehension about the man persisted.

"Fine!" exclaimed Perez. "Then it's all settled. I knew I could depend on you to solve this problem, Henry. I shall make arrangements with Captain Jack, just as I promised I would do."

"But what of Mr. Taylor?" she asked. "Do you think my presence at his home will annoy him. After all, I am an uninvited guest."

"Not in the least. Of that I am certain," answered Lightbourne. "I have known Morgan for many years. Besides, he's away so frequently that he will welcome the company for your father."

"He's right," offered Perez. "I doubt his being there long enough for a proper introduction to be made."

"And what of his wife, his family? Will they mind?"

"Just like a female to think that every man's got to have a wife before his life is complete," grumbled Henry.

"Mr. Taylor is not married, but even if he were, I am confident that you would certainly not be a burden," assured Perez.

"That certainly relieves me," sighed Raven. "He has done so much to help my father already, I would certainly not want to impose on his good will."

"No chance of that, Raven, my gal," said Henry. "A face as pretty as yours is just what the old goat needs to welcome him home from his voyages."

Perez rose hurriedly from his seat. "If you will excuse me, I have several errands to complete before evening. So Henry, if you permit me, I shall entrust you with these two."

"You do intend to be back in time for supper, don't you, Captain?" asked Henry. "I might even be persuaded to do my specialty tonight in your honor: fresh lobster, peas and rice, maybe even some guava duff."

"With an offer like that, how can I stay away? I shall return by seven," he told Raven. "That should give you and Maria adequate time to get settled in. One of the mates will bring your trunk around later."

Raven listened as the creaking steps sounded Juan's departure. I had best get used to being without him again, she thought. Four hours is not as bad as the indefinite period I will face once he leaves to resume his search. In a week, I shall be with Papa. When Juan comes for me—if he comes for me— I wonder if he will? I wonder if he'll even remember his proposal of marriage once I am out of his care.

Such thoughts nagged her long after Henry showed her to her room. She sat on the bed, despondent, and in concerned meditation of her relationship with the handsome captain.

He will come for me on Eleuthera. I know he will, she resolved determinedly. Just as he promised to do. And he will ask Papa for my hand, and I will convince him to give his consent. I would imagine that Papa already knows of Juan's heroics. Even if Juan's English blood is mixed with that of his mother's homeland, he is loyal to England and to the Bahamas and would never betray them.

Knowing that this night was to be the last she would spend in the arms of her love for quite some time, she dressed with deliberation. The ruffled, green satin gown she chose to wear for their final encounter accentuated boldly the darkness of her well-defined features, as well as the womanly attributes shaping her curvaceous form. The off-shouldered sleeves, gathered mid-arm with bands of black velvet, served to emphasize her perfectly formed shoulders. The tight lacings of her corest drew her narrow waist even tighter and proudly uplifted her firm, rounded breasts, leaving very little but the tips to one's imagination. She brushed her hair until its thickness shone with a rich shiny luster and wore it in loose ringlets about her face, just the way Juan had told her he liked it.

True to Lightbourne's word, by seven o'clock, he and his guests were feasting on a succulent lobster, which had been speared that afternoon, and peas and rice in a thick tomato sauce. Perez could not concentrate on the savory repast, nor could he be engaged in lengthy discussions with his friend without his eyes drifting longingly to the luscious beauty beside him. He squirmed uncomfortably throughout dinner, aching to kiss her and bury his head into the well-defined cleavage between her taunting breasts.

Lightbourne robustly entertained the women with humorous tales of his and Juan's first turtling adventure off Little Cay, their many fishing expeditions off the coast of Bimini, and of their days of diving deep into the ocean to explore wrecks of Spanish galleons. He told them of their futile search for the buried chests of gold coins that were said to be hidden deep in the caves underneath a steep bluff on the northern coast of Andros Island, and of the legendary "checkarnies" who were reported to dwell in nearby trees and would cause horrendous misfortune to anyone who dared venture into their forest after dark.

"Indians who had paddled across the ocean in dugout canoes from Florida lived in the interior of the island," revealed Lightbourne, "and were petrified of going into the trees at night. Creatures whose eyes shone in the dark and hooted threatening sounds would be sure to cast an eerie spell on any trespasser."

After an hour of such rollicking reminiscences, the conversation steadily turned to talk of Ames and of the five ship-loads of sailors who had lost their lives in pursuit of the orange-haired demon.

"You cannot be too careful in Nassau," Perez told Maria and Raven. "I fear that some of Ames's men may be disguised as townspeople in order to spy on the activities here. For that reason, I think it best if you remain inside the house and keep your presence unknown to anyone on the outside. Ames will be only too eager to reclaim you, and some of the islanders will be anxious to help him in exchange for a couple of gold coins.

"It seems those bloody fools would know by now that dealing with the likes of that motley lot will bring nothing but destruction to our settlement. Why Ames would just as soon slash the throat of his own mother if she crossed him—and then pour salt in her wound to make himself feel more mighty," said Lightbourne, disgusted by the recent behavior of the islanders.

"The governor and Henry are the only ones in Nassau who know that you were imprisoned on Gorda Cay, and I would prefer that for your own safety, it remain that way," emphasized Perez.

"But your men know," said Raven. "Is there any chance they would reveal the events leading to our being in Nassau?"

"Not at all," answered Perez with stern confidence. "They have already been warned against saying anything about that matter."

"As long as Raven and Maria are in my care, Captain, you can rest assured that no harm will befall them."

"I know that, Henry. Aside from Woodes, there is no one else on the island I can trust so implicitly."

"Well ladies, how did you enjoy your supper?" questioned Henry, pushing his emptied plate away to make room for his massive arms.

"Never have I ever tasted anything so delightful. Of all the Bahamian delicacies I have sampled, this is certainly my favorite," complimented Raven.

"You'd best not tell Wally that," chuckled Perez. "He went to great pains preparing your supper on the ship; even caught the grouper himself. Regardless of his shyness, I'm afraid he was quite taken with you. Good thing I'm not a jealous man!"

"And you, Señora Valdez? Did you like the meal as well?" entreated Henry, eager to make even the lightest conversation with the stone-faced woman who listened politely to his stories but remained quite aloof throughout the meal.

"I do not see why you have need of a cook. Your culinary talents are quite adequate," was her haughty reply.

Lightbourne cleared his throat nervously, thinking of the proper words that would make her feel more at ease. His voice was brittle, but only because of his uncertainty.

"Señora Valdez, if you and I are to have an amiable relationship, we must be perfectly honest and direct with each other. I offered you a job in my household for one reason, and that was because I knew that you had

231

no place to go, or no hope of making a life for yourself here unless someone is willing to give you that opportunity."

He felt like pounding his fist on the table to emphasize his point, but he controlled his actions and lowered his voice instead. "And that was my only reason for offering you this job. No ulterior motive whatsoever! I will admit that at times I am a difficult man to get along with. I do rant and rave like a madman when I've nipped too much at the sherry, but other than that I am very likable."

He looked at Maria for a reply, any reply. When she uttered no sounds, he continued. "It will be difficult for you to adjust to your newly found freedom and to view any man as a friend. I understand that. But you cannot continue suspecting the motives of everyone who tries to help you." He snorted impatiently, sensing that his monologue had not affected the woman in the least. "Well, enough of my sermonizing. Excuse me. I believe I promised the good captain some guava duff for dessert."

"He's right, Maria," said Raven, reaching over the table to squeeze Maria's arm reassuringly. "You cannot begrudge someone for showing kindness toward you."

"You don't have anything to fear from Henry," added Perez. "He's as gentle natured as a child."

When Henry reentered the room, Maria looked up at him and smiled. "I was wrong to judge you so unfairly, Doctor, before giving myself a chance to know you. I hope you will forgive me."

Lightbourne nodded in acceptance and distributed the dessert. After everyone had finished, he rose to clear the table.

"No, no," insisted Maria. "You stay seated. It is my responsibility to clear the table. You entertain your guests."

Henry watched admiringly as Maria assumed her chores. "Ah, a rare woman, indeed," he said absently.

Polite conversation was exchanged for the next half hour, and Henry, sensing that Perez wished to be alone with Raven, stifled a feigned yawn and pushed back his chair. "Good night Juan, Raven. I seem to be overly fatigued this evening. Your usual room downstairs has already been readied for you, Juan. I'm always up before the roosters so we'll have more time to talk over breakfast." He waved good night to the pair and ambled down the lantern-lit hallway to his room.

"Alone at last, my sweet," sighed Perez, brushing his lips against Raven's cheeks.

"Oh, Juan." She panicked, throwing her sylphlike arms around his neck. "I would give anything if you did not have to leave in the morning."

"There, there my darling," he comforted, patting her head as though she were a frightened child. "You know of my obligation. I could not rest peacefully knowing that I had shirked my duty."

"I just fear so for your life, Juan. Ames is a wicked, immoral man. I would die if anything were to happen to you. Life would not be of any value at all if you were not here to share it with me."

He cupped her worried face in the palms of his hands. "There is no need for you to worry so, my stunning little wench. You must not concern yourself with my safety. I would match my crew against Ames's any day. And I am as well versed in the use of swords

233

and pistols as he. My determination to apprehend him far exceeds his cunning. I swore to you that I would make Ames pay for his vile treatment of you and for the murders of all of your friends. You do want the deaths of Captain Mabry and Ross and Lucy to be avenged, do you not?"

"Of course I do, Juan," she answered. "I just don't want anything to happen to you in the process."

"Just knowing how Ames tried to rape you is reason enough for me to run my sword through his fat belly and tear out his insides while he still breathes." Perez's catlike eyes gleamed sinisterly. "How he will pay! He'll rue the day he ever heard the name of Juan Perez, and he will regret a thousand times over ever having caused a single tear to fall from your eyes!"

"I cannot help but fear for your life, Juan. While you were gone this afternoon, I had such horrible dreams. They were like a warning, an ominous warning of what would happen to you." She swallowed hard, but knew she must continue. "Remember my telling you of those horrible nightmares I used to have? The bodies of all my friends floating away in a bloody mass surrounded by sharks? I envisioned that same gruesome scene this afternoon when I lay down for a nap. Except this time, Juan, your face appeared on *all* the bodies."

"I promise, my beloved, that I shall be more than cautious in my dealings with him. I know that Ames is capable of any horrible deed; the man is totally irrational. He behaves like a mad dog. You must remember, though, sweet Raven, that instead of my chasing him halfway across the sea, he will be in pursuit of me. It will make my task so much easier, for as I explained earlier, I actually have the advantage, while he thinks himself to be in control."

"Just remember, please," she begged, "that he is no better than a wild animal, crazed by the smell of blood."

"Exactly, pet. Just like a shark in a feeding frenzy. That is what I must rely on if I expect to snare him in my trap. He will be so occupied with thoughts of my capture and will gloat on the hideous punishment he has planned for me that he will completely lose all perspective. I shall patiently lie in wait for that precise moment," divulged Perez confidently.

The waning candle light flickered and illuminated the strong, determined countenance of Raven's courageous lover. She stared into his daring eyes and stroked the bristly fullness enveloping the lower portions of his face. She traced the coarse outline of growth shading his lips then pulled his head down even with her own and covered his lips with fevered kisses. "Let me go with you. That way I would know you were safe, and I wouldn't have to worry so much. Please. I want to make sure you're going to return to me."

"No, Raven. I do not want to risk losing you a second time to Ames. There is little doubt in my mind that we will not be successful in our mission. But, just in case our plans are foiled, I want to be certain that you are far, far away from danger." Seeing the dejected shadow cross her face, he admitted cheerily, "Besides, how could I explain to my men my wanting to stay in my room hour after hour? You must understand that just knowing you are in Henry's protective custody will ease my worries and give me the determination to pursue that monster."

Raven reluctantly relented. "But you must promise

me that the moment you deliver Ames to Governor Rogers, you will come to Eleuthera so I can see with my own eyes that you are alive and well. Promise me?"

He nodded. "It will be just as difficult for me to be separated from you again. But let us not talk of separation now, my sweetest," he implored, pulling her from her seat onto his lap. "We have the rest of the night to spend in each other's embrace before daylight awakens us."

"You sound just like Juliet's Romeo."

"Perhaps, but ours is not a star-struck romance destined for tragedy," he corrected. "Come."

They walked arm in arm down the narrow corridor.

"Shh," he cautioned, raising his finger to his lips. "Henry Lightbourne would mark my back with fifty stripes if he suspected me of dishonoring an innocent maiden in his home."

They tiptoed past the closed door of Henry's room and proceeded to the far end of the hallway. Raven quietly turned the brass knob to her room, and the floor creaked stridently as they entered. "Do you think he heard that?" whispered Raven.

"The way Henry snores, a cannon exploding at his feet would not rouse him."

The room was for the most part bare, except for a small cot and the trunk containing Raven's clothes. A straw woven mat covered the shuttered window, and shimmers of moonlight streamed in through the loose braidings.

They tumbled onto the bed, fully clothed, and intoxicated by the volcanic surgings of desire that flowed through their bodies. They rolled playfully atop the lumpy mattress. Raven pulled her lover's face against her own, covering his mouth with hers while nimble fingers unbuttoned his shirt and entwined the black, curly hairs covering his chest.

"What have I created?" he joked, pretending to gasp for air.

"A wanton wench," she declared smugly. "One whose fire for love matches your own."

With little difficulty, he slid her arms from the binds of the satin gown and pulled it off her burning body, slithering his tongue across each portion of her exposed flesh as he undressed her. He tossed her dress on the floor and buried his face between her round thighs, gently petting and teasing her with his darting tongue and exploring the forbidden regions until she was on the verge of erupting in satisfaction.

"Please, my darling," she pleaded. "I can stand such torment no longer. I am raging inside like an uncontrollable fire," she moaned. "Please, I must have you."

"Not so rapidly," said Perez. "I want you to enjoy this night and to remember it for those long nights to come."

Finally, after what seemed to be hours of his teasing and caressing, he fell into her wide embrace, smothering her with frantic kisses while caressing her swollen breasts. He filled his mouth with her voluptuousness and taunted her with his craving. She felt sure she would soon burst from the longings that mounted inside her. He savagely tugged his woolen shirt off his back and jerked away his breeches with the same quick movement. "Always be so eager for my love, my darling."

"Oh, I shall, I shall, ahhh!" Her legs spread wide in

anticipation, and her yielding eagerness was crushed beneath his weight. "I am yours. Always!" she cried. "Take me, Juan. Possess me anyway you wish, unlike anyone else you've ever had," she begged, fondling his rigid manhood and guiding it into her passion fevered self. "I want you! No one else, just you!"

Perez fiercely clutched her derriere and drove himself deeper and deeper in answer to her pleas. Their bodies blended together in a single motion, lost in the consuming craving they felt for each other. Her back arched, and she rose to meet each penetrating thrust of his ardor with a raging intensity that well matched her lover's. She squealed with satisfying delight, and at that same instant his body exploded the fullness of his bounty. Exhausted and drained, he collapsed.

"Juan, are you all right?" she asked, after some time had elapsed and still he had not moved. No answer. "Juan, speak to me," she demanded, shaking his shoulders. "Is something the matter with you?"

Unable to hold his breath any longer, he released the air held inside and shook with laughter.

She slapped him, pretending to be miffed by his trick and, using all of her remaining strength, she rolled him aside. Then Raven straddled his chest, pinning his arms back on the bed, and began teasing his body with her roving lips. First the ears, then the eyes, and then his startled mouth. Her tongue moved languidly across his muscled chest, biting lightly each of his brown nipples. She moved stealthily down his stomach and into his navel with provocative licks. His fatigued form could not help but undulate underneath her wet caresses as her mouth beckoned his limpness inside, coaxing it into ripe maturity. She gazed at him saucily and

238

lowered herself beside him, striking a seductive pose; her hair streamed sensually over her breasts, legs arched with alluring invitation.

He rolled over on top of his seductress and effortlessly slid himself inside. Their bodies pounded together in convulsing flurries, their midsections grinding together in unabashed gyrations.

She spoke brazenly. "You have made me insatiable. I cannot get enough of your love."

"What a bold hussy you are," he teased. "And all of you is mine!" He marked his territory with incessant thrusts and molded his form even tighter into her own. "All mine! No one else's!"

After an hour of such zealous activity, they submitted reluctantly to their bodies' limitations and lay side by side, wrapped in the warmth of each other's embrace and content to listen to the rapid pounding of the other's heart. Perez's whispered goodnight was met with a sighing moan of satisfaction, and smiling dreamily, Raven snuggled cozily into his arms.

Later, she reached out for her lover, and finding his side of the bed cold and unoccupied, she awoke with a start. "Juan, Juan," she cried out softly, fearful that he had left while she had slept.

"I am here, dearest," came a voice from beside the window.

"Come back to bed," she urged. "I cannot sleep without your arms around me."

"Shhh. It's almost dawn. See how the sun is creeping up over the ocean," he said, lifting the shade and pointing to the orange-rayed sky.

The light revealed that he was fully dressed and ready to return to his ship.

"Surely it cannot be," she said, scrambling from her bed. But the orange flame on the cloudless horizon showed otherwise. "Why did you not awaken me sooner?"

"What? And wipe that satisfied smile from your lips. I want to remember you lying there like that when I stand watch on the bridge tonight. That will make me try all the harder to return to you as quickly as possible." He picked her up and laid her gently on the bed, drawing the covers close beneath her chin. "Sleep, my love. A week from today you will be at Eleuthera and soon afterward I shall sail into the harbor and into your arms forever." He kissed her lightly and brushed stray wisps of hair from her face, and he gazed longingly into her half-closed eyes once again. Perez tiptoed to the door and quietly pulled it open. After looking back at the peaceful form cuddled atop the bed, he had to force himself to close the door and be on his way.

## Chapter Fourteen

In her drowsiness, Raven would reach out yearningly to caress the sinewy sensuousness of her lover, only to discover that that which had seemed so real during the moon-mad night—the sound of Juan's steady breathing in her ear and the comforting feel of his body lying next to hers—had been but a well-disguised dream, a cruel fantasy of her copious imagination.

Three days had passed since their last love filled encounter in her bed, the very bed where she now cried herself to sleep each evening remembering the gentle warmth of his touch. The days were lonely and uneventful, the nights torturously empty.

Each new day's dawning filled her soul with hope, but once the sun had risen out over the harbor and its hazy brightness cast no illumination on the blue- and gold-striped banner flying from the towering mast of the *Falcon,* she slumped once again into despondency and here, beset by such solitary brooding, she would dwell the remainder of the day. Neither Maria nor Henry possessed the right words to snap her from this sinking depression.

By the fourth morning, July the tenth, Raven did manage to goad herself into higher spirits. Knowing that her customary trip to the window would prove to be but another disappointment, she stayed in bed until she heard Maria stirring in the sitting room. She threw back the covers, dressed hastily, and pulled back her hair in a bright red ribbon. She rolled up the straw mat and leaned out of the window, resting her hands on the inside sill and peered curiously down onto the alleyway separating George Street from the backs of the merchants' shops.

I simply cannot allow myself to continue moping about this room a day longer! she resolved stoutly. What I need is to stir around in the sunshine, allow the salty sea air to fill my lungs, amble down the street with everyone else. I feel like a caged animal confined all day and night in my room.

"Be you entirely insane, gal?" questioned Henry over breakfast when Raven proposed her plan to him. "I promised Captain Perez that I would keep a careful watch over you, not let you go out wandering into trouble."

"What kind of trouble can I possibly get into?" she persisted. "Just a short walk. I promise I will be ever so cautious."

Henry sat stubbornly sipping on his tea and indulging himself with a fifth croissant.

"I won't stay out over ten minutes," she urged.

"In five minutes," he argued, "one of Ames's boys could spot you out on your leisurely stroll, grab and gag you, and drag you off into the brush." He paused for a second, then added with a sarcastic grin. "How could I ever explain that to my friend? 'Oh, but Captain Perez, she blinked those big green eyes at me and swore she wouldn't stay gone long.'"

Raven shrugged her shoulders defeatedly, knowing there was a certain amount of truth in Henry's statement. "Oh, I don't mean to cause you any trouble, Henry. Really I don't. It's just that—"

"I know, Raven. I understand how you must feel. Your man's gone to sea after a lunatic, and you're naturally worried about his safety. Don't think I haven't heard you pacing back and forth across your room during all hours of the night. I gave my word, Raven, that I would not let you out of my sight, and I intend to keep it."

"You could accompany me," she suggested timidly.

"That still doesn't solve our problem. Even with me by your side, telling curious passersby that you are my niece from Bermuda, if one of Ames's spies about town were to recognize you, I could not offer much toward your salvation," he protested, patting the thick roll around his middle. "I am certainly in no shape to defend my own honor, much less yours."

A sheepish grin crossed Raven's face, and her eyes twinkled craftily. "But suppose you were to introduce me as your young nephew from Bermuda?"

"I think you have been out in the sun much too long already, Raven Gatewood!" scolded Henry.

Raven did not hear his snide remark. "I have it!" she exclaimed, snapping her fingers. "Raymond Lightbourne can be my name."

"All right, Raven," said Henry, throwing up his hands. "I implore you to reveal to me this preposterous

243

scheme of yours. I know that until you do, you won't allow me a minute's solitude. Well, what are you waiting for? Out with it!"

"Well, I do agree with you completely, Henry, that as myself, I would be putting my own life, as well as yours and Maria's, in grave danger. But if I am disguised as a young man, and if you introduce me as . . ." she lowered her voice to a convincingly masculine tone, ". . . your brother Edward's son who's staying with you until a ship sails for England . . . I do not see what difficulties we could possibly encounter."

"But to try and pass yourself off as a boy? Dear girl, there are some things that just cannot be concealed." He pushed himself away from the table and removed the crumb-filled napkin from underneath his doubled chin. "Now, I have work to do downstairs. Try to entertain yourself as best you can, and this afternoon I shall teach you to play a most remarkable board game called backgammon. A most fascinating game! As I understand, it's one of the oldest games of mankind. Egyptian pharoahs used to wile away the hours trying to figure out its strategy. Cheer up! Today won't be so bad. You'll see."

With her hands clasped behind her back, a trait Raven had acquired from Sir Robert, she paced restlessly across the room. She would pause in front of one window long enough to look down at the humming activity below, then walk over to the next as though she half expected the scenery to change. Taking a volume of poetry from the shelf, she blew the dust from its cover and flipped through it, but the verses that filled each page could not even capture her attention. She returned the book to its place and lifted an unsheathed, lightweight sword from its wall mountings and ran her hand carefully over the dull side of the broad blade. Holding it at arm's length, she bowed to an imaginary opponent and challenged him to a duel. With one hand on her hip, she danced around the room, cutting into the air with several impressive slashes. But soon she bored of her game and drove the shiny point deep into her rival's stomach, thus ending the match.

I do wish Juan would have allowed me to go with him, she thought from time to time. After all, Mary Read and Anne Bonny accompanied their men to sea. They dressed in men's clothing, and no one ever caught on to their deception.

She called out for Maria, but no response came from the cooking room. Probably downstairs, she decided. No matter, though for I do believe I've found a solution for my dilemma.

She ran to her room, locked the brass bolt behind her, threw open the lid to her trunk and began rummaging through its contents. I know I saw a . . . ah, here it is. She smiled, casting aside the lace ruffled silks and satins.

She gazed at her reflection and could not help but chuckle at the disarrayed figure staring back. The rumpled, many times patched breeches had been several lengths too long so she cuffed them up to her knees. She tucked a navy linen shirt inside her trousers and knotted a rope cord around her waist, lest her pants fall down around her ankles. She frowned,

245

removed the shirt, and binded her breasts tightly with some material. Smugly, she turned sideways and looked for any hint that would give her away. With her breasts secured and her hair pinned up inside the woolen cap pulled down to her eyebrows, she had to admit that she did indeed make a rather suitable boy. Something is still missing, though, she decided, staring pensively into the mirror. Of course! She ran down the corridor to the sitting room, scooped some loose dirt from one of Maria's flowerpots and smudged the grime over her face.

Now my attire is complete, she mused, hurrying back to her room to take another look. Yes, I can pass for a boy! she decided cheerfully, critically surveying her body from head to toe.

Maria and Henry were busy at work downstairs in the treatment room; Maria tearing bandages from worn bed clothes and Henry extracting citrus juice for a cough tonic he had concocted by mixing the juice with whiskey and syrup.

"Yes, yes, what is it, lad?" asked Henry, glancing up briefly, then returning to his work. "Young man, I haven't got all day. So tell me what your problem is instead of standing there gawking at us," he demanded when the visitor failed to speak.

The boy cleared his throat. "I don't feel so good, sir," came a low, muffled reply.

"What ails you, lad?" gruffly asked Henry. "You look perfectly fit to me. A bit too skinny perhaps. Well, speak up! Cat got your tongue? Bellyache? Been in a fight? What is the matter? How do you expect me to help you if I'm not even told your problem?"

246

"I . . . I feel a bit woozy, sir. Reckon I've been out to sea too long," finally offered the boy.

"All you need, son, is a little sunshine to liven up those seaweed bones of yours," said Henry. "Maybe even a glass of ale to settle your nerves."

"That's exactly what I had hoped you would say, Dr. Lightbourne," she said, her voice returning to normal. She tugged at her cap and her long black tresses tumbled out of confinement.

Henry stared angrily at the girl but could not maintain his sullen frown for long. His stern face began to twitch and soon his entire body jiggled with laughter. "I see the joke's on me, right? Damned if you didn't fool me, but good, too. A rather presentable lad, I must say, Raymond my boy."

"Then you will permit me outside for a few minutes?"

"Yes," relented Henry. "But only if I accompany you. And only if you keep your mouth closed, your eyes fixed to the ground, and let me do all the talking. Agreed?"

"Oh, yes, yes, anything," she promised, throwing her arms around him.

"And we'll have none of that in public, either. Men simply do not hug those of their own kind." He pulled off his starched smock and hung it on a peg. "Come along now!"

Raven could hardly keep step with Henry's long strides as they walked down George Street past the rooming house operated by the Spence widows and the residences of council members Robert Beauchamp, William Fairfax, and Wingate Gale. They paused for a moment in front of the church, and the minister rose from his stooped position in the cemetery long enough to rub his aching back and wave a cheery good-morning to the pair before resuming his weeding.

"Reverend Maynard," acknowledged Lightbourne. "Pleasant day to you!" He turned to his nephew. "A very devout man, that Mathew Maynard. Rather courageous as well."

"How so?" asked Raven softly as they resumed their pace.

"Several years back, a pirate captain forced him at gunpoint to accompany him to his vessel. It seems that this fellow Daniels wanted the reverend to bless his ship and to lead his crew in a psalm before embarking for Bermuda. Of course the poor fellow had no choice but do as he was told."

"I certainly had no idea that reverence and piety were among the pirates' virtues," joked Raven, careful to keep her head low and eyes to the ground when someone passed.

"Apparently so," he replied. "At least when they're hoping for a good haul. Anyway, one of the mates snickered during the sermon, so Captain Daniels shot him in the back and begged the reverend's pardon for the man's actions."

"What happened after the minister led them all in prayer?"

"According to Mathew, the captain thanked him, escorted him back to the church, and offered to make a sizeable donation to the church if his voyage proved to be lucrative."

"What about the street behind this one?" she asked, motioning in the opposite direction. "There are several buildings back there and a rather stately house as well," she said, standing on tiptoe. "Who lives there?"

"No one that would concern you," he replied, pulling her along. "Perhaps, nephew, when you are a bit older, you will receive a proper introduction to such places, but I do not think that now is the time. Come along, now. Mustn't tarry."

As they neared the fort, they heard the robust voice of Captain Turnly shouting loud commands to his troops. The men responded in unison with equal enthusiasm. The high tabby and rock wall prevented Raven from viewing the training action inside.

"Can we go in?"

"No, only those who have qualified for training are permitted beyond the gate. Tight security is to be maintained at all times."

Activity in the town had commenced several hours earlier at daybreak. Already the wharf was occupied with the usual group loudly hawking their fruits, vegetables and fish. The ancient, shrivel-gummed seamen were shuffling to the wall for their daily gathering and unproductive fishing. The town's housewives had begun their morning haggling with the shopkeepers over the exorbitant prices charged for the staples of their daily diet. Dirty-faced, thumb-sucking children clung bashfully to their mother's skirts. Older boys roamed through the streets like unruly urchins, followed by yelping yellow mongrels nipping at their heels. With a strip of discarded cloth tied in a sash around the waists of their torn, baggy trousers, these noisy mischief seekers pretended to be swaggering swordsmen whose days were spent slaying dragons and hacking off the heads of treacherous adversaries.

As a result of the governor's proclamation the day before emphatically recommending that the men of the settlement report for drill and marksmanship practice—lest their hands and legs be cuffed in iron manacles for seventy-two hours—nearly all of the male inhabitants of military age had taken their assigned places inside the fort for three grueling hours of regimented marching and training.

A familiar figure limped toward them carrying a large bundle. "Henry!" He waved. "Out for your morning exercise, I suppose."

"No, not at all. Just indulging in a pleasant absence from knife wounds and baby's colic."

"Raven Gatewood!" exclaimed Rogers. "What are you doing dressed in that ridiculous garb?"

"Well, I . . . I," stammered the embarrassed girl as she fidgeted uncomfortably. "How did you know it was me?"

"Your outfit certainly does not flatter you, my girl," said Rogers. "I must admit that it does, however, conceal that which nature so graciously endowed you. For a moment even my keen vision was fooled. In spite of your hair hidden and dirt smeared on your nose, such startling green eyes could only belong to a woman. What nonsense ever possessed you to try and pass yourself off as a lad?"

Feeling rather foolish at being recognized in her deception and trying to avoid Henry's scowl that said, "I told you so," Raven reluctantly told the governor of her restlessness and the feeling that if she did not get outside she would go mad. "I thought time would pass all the more quickly if I could mingle with other people instead of sitting upstairs twiddling my fingers and wearing out the floor pacing across it."

She half expected him to scold her, instead he advised, "Just don't allow anyone to get close enough to discover you've no hair on your face."

"What do you have there?" questioned Henry curiously. "A package full of money from King George, no doubt."

"Would that we were so lucky," said Rogers dismally. "Captain Emerson of the *Eastern Star* realized this morning that he had failed to give me all of my correspondence. I can hardly wait to get home and devote the rest of the day to reading it."

"Ah, a book. It's been such a long while since I have had the good fortune to read something I have not already read and twice," hinted Henry.

"Then by all means, I shall loan it to you when I've finished. This is one of the few copies already in circulation. I must admit that I am particularly proud of this book since my friend Dan Defoe used as its basis one of my own personal experiences. The title is *Robinson Crusoe*."

"What experience was that, Woodes?" asked Henry. "You have had so many exciting times one should devote a book entirely to your life."

"When I was privateering during the war, I rescued a fellow named Alexander Selkirk from a Spanish held island. He was a ship's surgeon and the sole survivor of a shipwreck. I was at a party with Dan one evening shortly afterward and recounted my story to him. He had been so enthralled by my account of Selkirk's captivity and of his rescue that it inspired him to write about it. From what Dick Steele tells me, Daniel changed the story quite a bit. His main character, also a surgeon and shipwrecked, is stranded on a deserted island. How he manages to survive under such adverse conditions is the gist of the novel."

"You must indeed be pleased that such a well-known author would be inspired by one of your adventures," complimented Raven. "I would imagine a strong disadvantage of living here would be the lack of reading material and the absence of formal education for the children."

"Very true," agreed the governor. "But very soon, if our settlement prospers, I hope to build a school here. Education is the only means through which man can ever succeed in advancing his culture. I even hope to be able to bring a well-qualified instructor from England."

"Seeing as how most young men are out for a bit of excitement, that shouldn't be hard to do. Many would jump at such an opportunity," agreed Henry. "After all, if Boston and Charles Town can import wives for their bachelors, surely we should be able to attract a teacher for our children."

"Import wives?" asked Raven, shocked by the mere suggestion of such a practice. "You don't mean that unattached young women are taken to the colony specifically for that purpose, do you?"

"Yes," said Lightbourne. "Many marriage-aged girls go to the colonies after a husband."

"What a strange practice," she murmured. She certainly would not want to be any part of such a convention.

"Not really," reasoned Rogers. "If a girl is very homely with no hope of a suitor, or if she has no dowry to offer her perspective mate, answering an advertisement in the gazette may be her only way out of remaining an old maid."

"Then there are also those women who are given the choice of spending time in prison for assorted crimes they've committed or of settling in Virginia with a decent landowner and raising tobacco and children," added Henry.

Raven shook her head in disagreement. "I don't care how ugly or how poor a girl is. To leave your family and country to go to a foreign place and marry a man you've never even seen. . . . Surely spinsterhood is not nearly as bad a fate!"

"A woman's viewpoint," joked Woodes. "It takes all of the romance right away, doesn't it Raven?"

"Not to mention the courtship and the wedding," remarked Henry sarcastically. "Why, from what I understand, the instant the bride-ship reaches port, the farmers are already fighting over the best of the group. Once all of the women have been distributed to everyone's satisfaction, the captain of the vessel conducts a mass wedding ceremony."

Raven wrinkled her nose in revulsion of such an idea. "Surely those poor girls have other options available to them. The idea that they would allow themselves to be treated like animals at an auction is just deplorable!"

"It seems as though I may have to resort to such drastic means to get Henry married off," vowed

253

Woodes. "Well, with that, I suppose I must be on my way, or Sarah will be getting overly concerned about my absence." He excused himself and hobbled on down the street. "Good day to you both. And don't forget my advice, Master Lightbourne."

"It's a bloody shame," mumbled Henry under his breath. "And a nicer fellow couldn't be found anywhere."

"What are you talking about, Henry?"

"Oh, just thinking about Woodes. He's plagued with such a quarrelsome nag for a wife," answered Henry disgustedly.

"Oh, Henry, the way you carry on about women I'd be surprised if there's even one on the island who speaks to you. Don't you ever have anything nice to say about females?"

"Now that is not at all fair, and you know it," he chided. "I have lots of nice things to say about you and Maria." Then, taking a second look at Raven in her outlandish garb, corrected himself, "Well, about Maria at least."

"All right, Henry. You've made your point. Tell me, what is it about Mrs. Rogers that offends you so."

Henry frowned disdainfully. "All right, but just remember that you asked. Subtlety has never been a virtue of mine, as you should know by now. Without my mincing words, that woman is quite incorrigible; extremely domineering. She sulks and groans, threatens and complains about all that Woodes is trying to achieve here. Mark my word, she'll end up making his life so miserable here that he will just throw up his hands in disgust and let her have her way. He'll have no other choice but to return to England so she can live the sort of life she fancies herself as deserving."

"Even *you* must admit that this is a lonely place for a woman," ventured Raven.

"Just like a female to make excuses for one of her own," he said sharply.

"Well then, since you're such an authority on the matter, what do you perceive her problem to be?"

"She's spoiled to the core," answered Henry, quite matter-of-factly. "Sarah's been pampered all of her life, being the daughter of Admiral Whetstone, that she expects everyone to pay her homage. She's always fretting about the lack of social events here. *Social events,* mind you. I can think of at least a hundred other things she could be worrying about. I would imagine that after spending day after day listening to her tell him how much better off she would be married to someone more deserving, fighting the Spanish or the pirates would be a welcomed diversion for Woodes," said Henry sourly. "Maybe with her niece being here for a while, Woodes will have all the time he needs to properly devote to his project, and Sarah can concentrate her precious efforts on the latest fashions or gala events of the entertaining sect in London this season."

"I certainly hope so," agreed Raven. "Poor Mr. Rogers always looks as though he's in constant worry over something. Too many problems and not enough solutions can make a man grow old over night, or so my father used to say. Why is their niece visiting here? This hardly seems an appropriate place for a family holiday."

"Melinda's here alone. Seems like I heard something about her being involved in some sort of scandal. Broken engagement or being left at the altar. Something like that."

"Why, I didn't know you were one to listen to gossip," she teased as Henry's pudgy cheeks flushed crimson.

"Well, Raymond, my boy, after we see the sights of Front Street," he said, eager to change the subject, "why don't we go home and sample some of Maria's coconut custard. You bothered me so much this morning with your incessant chattering that I hardly had a chance to enjoy my breakfast." They lingered for a moment in front of Ingraham's General Goods and Mercantile, skimming the notices advertising bargain prices posted just outside the door. "That man's prices are outrageous!"

Raven read aloud the listings, the intonation of her voice reflecting her surprise at such high costs. "Mutton, veal, pork, and beef nine pence per pound. Butter; one shilling sixpence a pound, milk; sixpence per quart. Eggs; a penny ha'penny each. These prices are not outrageous, they're abominable!" she exclaimed, turning to Henry. "How can the proprietor sleep at night knowing he's exploited his customers so?"

"'Tis apparent that Mr. Ingraham cares little about this settlement's wretched state of affairs. He probably excuses his greed by considering himself to be a shrewd businessman. Unfortunately he has a monopoly on the sale of imported goods, so if the townspeople want their tea, coffee, flour, or tobacco, they are forced to do business with him."

"Surely not all of the merchants take such advantage of their own countrymen?" she asked. "It appears that the settlement would have a far better chance of survival if they would all try to help each other along as best they can."

"Luckily, there are only a few such avaricious souls here. Most do adhere to the notion of 'you help me and I'll help you,'" he said pleasantly as they resumed their stroll. "Many of the tradesmen even perform their services in exchange for fresh produce or fish. No doubt bartering has been the economic formation of many struggling settlements."

"Good morning to you, Mrs. Pratt!" he greeted as they passed the bakery. Inside a rosy-faced, white-haired matron was displaying the morning's yield of pies and tarts on a table underneath the window. She returned their waves with a toothless smile and continued the arrangement of her freshly baked sweets. "Just don't know how the old dear can manage the shop by herself. She's up baking before dawn and never closes the door until well after dark. I thought for sure she'd leave last year after the fever took her husband, but she stayed on. She does quite well for herself, though I'd wager she gives more of the cakes away to the children than she sells to their mothers."

"What do you suppose would make a person leave the sort of life he's accustomed to and come to a place like this and start all over?" wondered Raven aloud.

"The quest for adventure and excitement," he replied knowingly. "I am certain many of them dreamed of leading a simple existence on an island, walking along the beach or fishing during the morning, snoozing under the palms in the afternoon. A lot of the settlers wanted to make a better life for themselves and their families and saw this as their chance of accomplishing it. They were given one main incentive to make them risk their lives crossing the Atlantic; the promise of ownership of land, which would be passed on to the next generation. The Swiss and French Huguenots agreed to come here and farm because of religious persecution they had to endure in their own countries. Here they can worship in any manner they choose without the fear of being punished or murdered for their beliefs."

"I do not mean to pry, Henry, for it is really none of my business, but why—"

"Why did I come here?" he completed the question. They stopped at the top of George Street so Henry could catch his breath. "I suppose I, too, longed for the adventure of a different sort of life. I thought I had a full existence in London; drinking, gambling, socializing with the best of them—a good medical practice as well. Then one day my wife left me after what I thought had been ten good years of marriage. She ran off with a barrister friend of mine. So I locked my house, closed my office, and signed on as a ship's surgeon."

"Just like Robinson Crusoe, huh?"

"Not quite. I sailed across Europe, explored primitive civilizations in South America, even stayed on in Boston for a couple of years. But once I came to this island, I fell in love with her white-sanded beaches, her purple and gold sunsets, and got to where I liked falling asleep listening to the palms rustle and the waves bash against the rocks. Yep, I decided this was the place for me. That was fifteen years ago, and I have no intention of ever leaving."

"Fifteen years. How it all must have changed during those years."

"Aye. Right after I arrived in 1703, the settlement was burned to the ground. Wasn't much here those days anyway—a fort, a tavern and a few shacks and shanties scattered in the pines. And a lot of half-naked fools running around roasting cows. Three years later the Spanish came again, and what they hadn't destroyed the first time, they made sure they did then. Afterward, the population began to grow. Some settlers in Bermuda became discontent there and began farming here, but that, too, was short-lived, for it was about that time that pirating began to flourish."

"But with all those dangers here, how did you ever manage to survive?"

"Just good luck, I suppose. Both times New Providence was attacked, I was island hopping on my skiff."

"And what of the pirates? Weren't you the least bit afraid of them. I hear some infamous characters had this island as their home base."

"Had any of those scoundrels lifted a hand to harm me they would have had to answer to Ed Teach," he said laughingly.

"You were friends with Blackbeard. Henry, I'm surprised at you!"

"Before you start reprimanding my choice of acquaintances, you should give me a chance to defend myself. You see, one of his wives slipped some poison into his rum bottle when she found out she shared him with at least ten other women on the island. He thought for sure he was going to die. I'll never forget the look of that man when he stumbled up my walk, holding his stomach, moaning, those big black eyes rolled so far back in his head that you just could see the whites. I practically had to gag myself to keep from laughing."

"And did you cure him?"

"I made him drink a whole jug of the bitterest tasting potion. I told him it was an herbal brew that would counteract the poison. Anyway, he spent the rest of the night throwing up his guts, swearing with one breath, praying the next. By morning he had recovered and swore his indebtedness to me." A distant gleam glowed behind Lightbourne's sea-colored eyes. "He even invited me to join him on one of his forays to the Carolinas, but I told him I was getting too old for such foolishness."

"Are you satisfied with the kind of life you've chosen here, Henry? What I mean is, don't you miss England?"

"My life here has been totally fulfilled," he replied. "I have been able to do that which I do best, make people feel better. But equally as important, I had a lot of time for myself, which I had quite neglected in England. Time to do all those things I never had time to do: painting, reading, walking through the woods, fishing, sailing, and just getting to know Henry Lightbourne better. Yes, I am extremely satisfied with the way my life has turned out." He stooped down to pick up a basket containing four fat red snapper someone had left on his doorstep. "Payment for extracting a rotten tooth," he explained. "Mmm, just thinking about having fresh snapper tonight, baked in a rich sauce and covered with potatoes and onions, makes my mouth water. Let's go in, nephew," he said, giving Raven's dirt-smeared cheeks an affectionate pinch, "and see if Maria can spare a couple of bowls of her custard."

## Chapter Fifteen

Raven's remaining time on New Providence passed fairly quickly. During the days she would don her disguise as Lightbourne's nephew and go with him into town for a short while or down to the beach, or into the woods to gather roots and herbs for his various healing brews and elixers.

"Nature provides her own remedies for ailments," Henry had told her one afternoon.

His words saddened her for the moment, for they were almost the same ones Captain Mabry had used on Abaco.

They would gather the leaves of the white elder, jackamado, gale of wind, and bitter root that would be brewed into teas or made into poultices for reducing high fevers. They searched for breadfruit and guinea hen plants for curing headaches, and the shepherd's needle for relief of stomach pain. Henry made an extra effort to search for an abundant supply of catnip and old lady mangrove since he was presently tending to eight expectant mothers.

Raven also tried to spend as much time as she could with Maria, knowing that she would always be indebted to the Spanish noblewoman who had made her life bearable on Gorda Cay. Unlike Raven, Maria found a comforting security in staying inside the house. She had not once offered the slightest desire to venture outside, saying that she still feared being discovered by one of Ames's men, who would drag her back to her island hell.

"But Maria," reasoned Raven on one occasion. "I have been into town several times, and I did not see anyone bearing the slightest resemblance to one of his men. I'm confident that not one of his slimy crewmen have been skulking about in the shadows following me. I could have easily spotted him."

"Those dogs would not dare show themselves during the daylight hours," spoke Maria, her entire body shaking with an encompassing hatred that swept through her upon remembering the hideous appearances of her captors. "No, they are far too sneaking to do that. It is best that they conduct their sordid dealings during late night hours when darkness can shroud their evil intents."

"I'm sure that's true, but why won't you at least go out for a breath of fresh air in the afternoon?"

"Because I know how Ames operates. For eight years I listened to his scheming and overheard his talks with his men. You must believe me when I say that he maintains constant contact with several of the high-ranking officials here. In exchange for valuable information concerning the government's plots to capture him, Ames keeps their pockets filled with gold. Do you remember when Captain Perez was talking with the governor in the tavern right after we arrived? They decided then that at least one of the councillors had divulged information to Ames, and because of this breech Perez's search had revealed very little up until that time."

Raven nodded, beginning to see Maria's point. "He could easily be the most respected member of the council, couldn't he? The one man who is thought to be beyond reproach."

"Until I am positive that Ames and all of his men have been captured and hanged," resolved Maria bitterly, "I will stay in here where I am safe!"

Raven's tanned face turned ashen. "But Maria, we could be threatened this very moment, without ever having gone outside."

"Yes, I'm aware of that. If any word has gotten around town that Perez returned with two women, or if by chance this traitor took notice of us leaving the *Falcon,* Ames could easily know of our being here already. But do not worry, for soon you will be safe with your father."

"What about you, Maria? How can I be sure you will be just as safe as I?" asked the troubled young woman.

"Henry will take care of me," she answered proudly.

Raven had been pleasantly surprised with Maria's sudden change of attitude toward their protector. It was evident by her look when her eyes sought his over dinner and by the melodious tone of her voice when she spoke to him. Her wide, brown eyes would sparkle and her cheeks would glow proudly when Henry complimented her cooking skills or the expert mending she did on a tattered shirt.

And even the brash, sometimes rough, Henry had undergone a rather apparent change. His customary harshness became quite subdued in Maria's presence.

Gone were his gruff smirkings about women being a bothersome nuisance, replaced with compliments and adoring glances.

"I have spoken to Captain Jack," remarked Henry Saturday night after dinner. The three of them were seated in the sitting room discussing the week's events over a glass of port. "He's leaving shortly after daybreak. I'll get you up early and walk down to the dock with you myself."

Raven clasped her hands in joyful delight. "So it has happened at last. By tomorrow this time, I shall be rejoined with my father, and we shall be talking and laughing just the way we used to do." She looked first to Maria and then to Henry. "I do not know how I will ever be able to repay the kindness you both have shown me. Words can never express my gratitude. I love you both! You're as dear as my family to me!"

"Nonsense," scoffed Henry. "It is I who is indebted to you." He smiled at Maria and patted her shoulder affectionately. "Had it not been for you needing a place to stay, I'd still be cooking my own dinner, scrubbing my shirts, and boring myself to sleep each night with my dull stories. Come now, let's propose a toast," he suggested warmly, filling their goblets with more of the sweet, red wine. "May all our lives be filled with a joy we've never before dreamed possible."

Sleep did not come easily to Raven that night, despite the five glasses of wine, for she was filled with anxious anticipation of being reunited with her father. She felt a bit guilty as well, knowing that she was equally excited about the prospect of seeing Perez once she was on Eleuthera.

Before the first sign of daylight Raven was dressed,

packed, and seated at the dinner table, her fingers thumping impatiently against its mahogany luster. "Oh, Maria. I'm glad you're up. Wherever can Henry be? He insisted upon walking me to the boat, and yet he's no where to be found."

Maria held up a piece of paper. "Here. He must have left you a note. Read it," she said, handing Raven the hastily scribbled message. "What does it say?"

"Claude Jackson came for me shortly after three o'clock. Wife's having a hard time birthing. Back soon. Wait for me! Oh, Maria, if he doesn't come soon, I'll miss my passage. What should I do? It's almost light now."

Maria eased her portly form into the chair. "I don't know what to say Raven, for fear that anything I suggest may be wrong."

Raven tried to evaluate her situation as objectively as possible. "If I go to the wharf, he'll be angry, but if I stay here, Captain Jack will sail without me. Heaven only knows when another boat will sail to Eleuthera. Besides it is growing lighter outside, so I won't be walking alone in the dark. If I wish to see my father, I have no other alternative," she resolved stoutly, rising from her seat and taking the straw bag in her hand. She bent over and hugged her dark-skinned friend. They both had tears of farewell streaming down their cheeks.

"I do not think it is wise for you to go alone; I will go with you," she insisted.

"No. You stay here, Maria. I'll be fine, really. In case Henry does return soon, send him on down to the dock, and I'll blow him a kiss from the deck. Good-bye, Maria. Thank you so much for everything."

"Be careful!" called Maria.

"I shall run the entire distance and stop for no one," promised Raven.

Maria listened as Raven bolted down the steps and slammed the door behind her. Then she went over to the window, and her eyes followed Raven down the hill and across the street until she finally disappeared between the shops of Front Street.

Having once reached the main street, Raven stopped to allow herself to catch her breath. She looked around curiously, for none of the usual morning activity had begun. The only other people she saw were the Spence widows in their rockers dressed in the same mourning outfit they had worn every Sunday since their husbands, who were brothers, had left on a sea voyage and not returned. They rocked peacefully on their porch.

Of course, realized Raven, it's Sunday. That's why the town is so deserted. She made her way on across the clearing separating the street from the harbor.

"Be ye waitin' fer Capt'n Jack, mum?" mumbled a voice from behind her.

She turned, startled, for she had not heard the approaching footsteps. "Yes . . . yes I am," she replied suspiciously.

The man's face was hidden; his chin drooped low onto his neck, and his back was bent.

"Did Captain Jack send you?" she asked timidly.

"Yes, mum. Seys I's to row ye oot to our boat, mum." His forehead wrinkled, and his one partially visible eyebrow arched high waiting for an answer.

"Row me out to the boat?" she asked. "I thought his vessel was to be tied up at the dock."

"Ain't my place to question anythin' he does or tells

267

me to do." His feet shuffled as he waited for a reply. "If'n ye don't believe me, there's always next week. If'n ye don't want to go with us to 'Luthera, tell me now so's I kin git back to the ship."

Why so apprehensive? she asked herself, frowning. Don't be such a silly goose. After all, he did know I was to meet Captain Jack here and sail with him to Eleuthera. All of that talk about evil men lurking in the shadows has made me much too jittery. "All right. Thank you," she told him.

He took her bag from her hand and shuffled in front. "Follow me. The skiff's o'er yonder on the beach." He pointed to a small dingy turned on its side in the incoming tide. "Better hurry afore they go without us." His feet moved faster, past the end of the dock, past the fig tree and on into a pine thicket.

Her heart raced frantically, and her ears perked up at the sound of footsteps behind them. She stopped abruptly, whirling around to see who was following her. She gasped as her eyes rested unbelievingly on the leering grimace of Lieutenant Dalmas. "No, no. It cannot be," she shrieked. "Stay away from me, you murderer!"

Her panic was met by shrill, incidious laughter as Dalmas slowly walked toward the stunned girl. "Ah, yes, *ma petite*. It seems you are not pleased to see me."

Raven bit her lip, determined not to be overcome with fright and left powerless against her foe. "What do you want with me?" she demanded, trying to think of an escape.

"I understand you were going to Eleuthera this morning. I beg your indulgence, mademoiselle, but there seems to be a slight change of plans."

"How . . . how did you know I would be here?" she stammered, trying to stall for more time.

"One of our friends saw you and that woman Maria shortly after that bastard Perez brought you here. I knew you would soon be going in search of your father—information supplied to me by another friend—and the only access to Eleuthera is Captain Jack. What a shame! Poor mademoiselle. Where is your gallant rescuer now, heh?" He fumbled at the sword hanging by his side. "I am disappointed your fat friend did not come down with you. I was all ready for Dr. Lightbourne." He reached out and grabbed her shoulders.

At that exact moment, her foot found its way deep into the shin of his leg. Dalmas fell back, cursing and in excruciating pain. Raven leaped past him. "Help! Help! Someone help me!" she screamed at the top of her lungs.

"Get the bitch, you fool!" ordered Dalmas to his accomplice.

The mate straightened his body, for there was no longer any reason to carry on his charade as a crippled seaman. He jumped across the sprawled body of his superior and bounded into the clump of trees in pursuit of Raven.

His agility was no match for Raven, and soon he overtook her. He lunged at her, jerked her arm savagely, and threw her over his back.

"Let me go, you beast!" she yelled, kicking, clawing and sinking her teeth into her assailant's shoulder. "Put me down this instant!"

Dalmas limped toward them, his fanglike teeth gleaming with the wickedness of his laughter. One hand held a bottle of clear liquid and a soiled rag he had taken from the pocket of his coat. The other hand massaged his swollen leg.

"Don't you come near me, you God-cursed demon," she cried. "Don't you dar—"

The liquid saturated rag was thrust against her nose and held tightly there until her cries turned to gurgles and her fighting body collapsed across her captor's shoulder.

## Chapter Sixteen

Francesca DuVall reclined pensively on the red velvet chaise lounge underneath the barred window of her third floor suite. Bare feet stretched out in front of the svelte ashen-haired woman. Her elbows rested on the sleek pine finish of the chaise's sides, and carefully manicured hands folded demurely in front of her. If her oval face possessed a single flaw it was that her nose was a bit too long. There were no freckles or wrinkles or unsightly moles to challenge her vanity. Her coloring was that of smooth ivory, for in all of her thirty-five years she had taken precautions against exposure to the sun. The only exception to her pale features was a pair of deep set, violet eyes, framed by thick, dark lashes. Eyes that now were hardened cold and expressionless. They used to not be so frigid, but after years of dealing with all sorts of men, she taught herself to control that one feature of herself that would betray her innermost emotion.

She had never known a father; he could have been one of hundreds of men who visited her mother. Smiling to herself she remembered how she would wander across town, seeking a man whose hair was the silvery color of her own. She had secretly imagined him to be a dashing military hero, but her mother would give no clue to his identity. Her mother, a plump, buxom red head, had been a whore in Paris, driven by poverty to dispense her body's pleasures for a few coins. Many nights they had spent outside, huddled in cracks and crevices of back alley shops. She shuddered now thinking of how she had been initiated into her mother's trade at a very early age. She was sold one morning to a fat, slobbering merchant who had a perverted penchant for young girls who had not quite reached puberty. He had locked the door to his market, pulled the shade and led her into the back storage room. He told her to take off her tattered skirt, and then had her sit on his lap while he rubbed her tiny breasts with one hand and poked inside her with the other. Her reward for being a good girl had been a bag of chocolates.

It was in this sort of sordid atmosphere that the young child reached adolescence. One December morning a crowd had gathered on the left bank of the Seine, and Francesca had curiously joined them. She shed no tears as the frozen, purple form of her mother was dragged from the water, nor did she come forward to claim the body. Instead, she walked calmly away, without taking a second look behind her, and skipped up the street to a seamstress shop and apprenticed herself to its owner.

She had learned this trade quickly and tried hard to please her elderly employer. Madame Pascall allowed her to sleep on a cot in the rear of the shop, fed her a noonday meal and occasionally would permit her to choose a particular material of her liking so she could ew herself a new dress after the shop closed its doors at night. From time to time prominent men of the city, hearing of the violet-eyed, silver-haired beauty who worked there, would venture into the shop on the pretense of selecting a gown for their wives. More than one had begged for a clandestine rendezvous with her, but she refused to pay them even the slightest attention.

While her mother had lived, Francesca had no alternative but to obey her command and perform such demeaning servitude with any man capable of paying for his wantonness. But now she was on her own, the controller of her destiny, and she swore to herself that she would never again have to resort to such drastic means to survive.

Little did she know that she was also doomed to a similar existence. Madame Pascall passed away, leaving her business to her son and his wife. The young seamstress was no longer needed, for the two of them intended to manage the dressmaking shop themselves. She was given a week's wages and sent on her way. Stunned by the sudden change of events in her life, she walked aimlessly around the square for the remainder of the day, her suitcase in hand.

As fate would have it, one of the gentlemen who had propositioned her earlier, a captain in the Navy, happened upon her. Distraught, she told him of her plight, and he extended his offer once again. This time she had no other choice than to accept. The next afternoon, he had procured a fine apartment for her on the edge of town, and she became his mistress, to be visited by her benefactor two evenings a week. He was a soft-spoken, well-educated man married to a hopeless cripple, and in no time Francesca had developed a strong attachment to the man who had rescued her. She cried until her eyes were red and puffy when his orders arrived transferring him to a foreign assignment for an indefinite period. On the morning of his departure he left on the pillow beside her an envelope containing enough money to support her until his return. A year passed, then two years, but her protector did not return. Several of his friends approached her, knowing of her previous arrangement with Emile Richard, and she found herself in an unsolicitous involvement with all three. If I am to be a whore, she bitterly resolved, I will not be satisfied with a few meager tokens. If a man really desires my charms, he will pay dearly for his weakness.

And pay dearly they all did, for she made exorbitant demands of money, elegant gowns and furs, and expensive jewelry in exchange for her sensual generosity. She moved into a larger home and established herself in a profitable business. More than one voluptuous serving maiden or bosomy country girl was willing to come to work for her in exchange for the opportunity to wear silk finery and lead a life of relative ease.

Madame DuVall's, as her establishment became known, catered only to the affluent, the elite few, for they were the only ones wealthy enough to pay the fees she so brazenly charged. In return, she made certain her girls were all well-versed in all aspects of boudoir entertainment and in fulfilling even the most bizarre fantasies.

Unfortunately, Francesca's insatiable greed overcame her better senses. One of her regulars was a prosperous inspector of the gendarme whose perverse

274

pleasures would only be gratified by abusing his partner with a leather whip. During one of his afternoon visits he lost control, and his macabre affinity resulted in a young woman's death. Knowing that the inspector feared scandal, she tried to extort a large sum of money from him in exchange for her silence. He laughed at her, and the next day, two of her best girls were found in the cellar with their throats slashed. That night an unexplainable fire erupted in her house. Fearing she would be the next victim, she and four of her girls boarded a vessel that would take them to Port-au-Prince, Haiti, a French inhabited island city that boasted of vast wealth. The French foreign legion was stationed there, as well as men of substance who had come to that mountainous island knowing that a fortune was to be made producing sugarcane, sisal, and coffee.

Francesca never reached her destination, for she chose instead to unload all of her possessions on the island of New Providence rather than endure another night on the rat-infested boat or risk her life in one more ocean storm. She moved into the abandoned home of a governor who had fled the island some years before and again started her business. She and her girls were frequented by notorious sea renegades as well as French and Spanish naval commanders who took turns calling truces from their battles in order to visit the bordello.

The exterior of the tabby and rock residence was plain and unpretentious, but the interior had been transformed into a home as elegant as the one she had had in Paris. The first floor housed a large tavern and gaming room for those who had enough money to drink and gamble but could not afford any of the other services offered. Exquisite furnishings of regal velvets, bright brocades, and fine-grained mahoganies adorned the lavishly furnished salon on the second floor. Artfully woven tapestries, detailed charcoal sketches, and colorful canvases depicting couples engaged in the most intimate of carnal pleasures decorated the walls. Here sea captains, pirates, and officers of substantial worth could be entertained by enticing, scantily clad women. Living quarters for Francesca and her protégées, as well as a private sitting room and dining room were on the third level.

It had never been difficult to maintain discipline among her workers, for Francesca treated them all well, and they felt loyalty and gratitude toward her. As far as the clientelle were concerned, if anyone gave the management any trouble, whether it be jealous rage over one of the girls or a drunken brawl, he was escorted outside by one of the black-skinned giants who were always stationed at the door.

*"La jeune fille est tout triste. Elle demande avoir une audience avec madame."*

Francesca's meditative solitude was interrupted by Anna, a flaxen-haired servant girl whose face had been disfigured by small pox. Francesca had found her in Paris, orphaned and roaming through the streets, surviving by pillaging garbage. Taking pity on the girl, she had taken her into her service as her maid.

*"Merci,* Anna."

The room was dark, even in the mid-afternoon, for the heavy curtains barred any sunlight from entering the room. When Francesca entered, Raven was sitting up rigidly atop the bed, her eyes ablaze with anger. *"Je ne Savais pas je suis ici, Madame DuVall!"* she said, demanding to know why she was there.

Her visitor smiled knowingly. "It is not necessary that we converse in French, mademoiselle, for I am quite fluent in the language of your country. I see you know already who I am."

"Yes!" retorted Raven crisply. "And I have heard of how you buy and sell women as though they were chattel."

"And who spoke of me in that manner?"

"Your *bon ami,* Red Ames. Or perhaps you know him better as Henri L'Ameur."

Francesca sat down on the bed at Raven's feet. "Between the two of us, Red Ames is a pompous ass."

"If you hold him in such low esteem, why was I brought here to you?"

The pale woman smiled. "Many years ago, when I was still a young girl in Paris, he saved my life. I will not bore you with the details of our encounter, but when he discovered that I, too, had sought New Providence as a refuge against our common French adversaries, he proved useful once again by procuring for me much of the decor for my home. In return for the debts I owe to him, I am asked to do certain favors for him from time to time."

"And I am one of those favors?"

Francesca sighed heavily. "I am afraid so. This morning I was awakened by Lieutenant Dalmas pounding on my door. Another man accompanied him, and a bag was slung across his shoulders. You were in that bag. All I was told was that I was to keep you here until Ames returned."

"And when will that be?" asked Raven, already

dreading the orange-haired demon.

"I have no idea."

"So I am to be his prisoner once again," she said indignantly. "It was not enough that I had to endure that cursed island of his for three months."

"Ah, so that is it." She nodded solemnly. "The last time Henry visited us he was in such a tirade because his refuge had been discovered and you had been taken from him. He left Dalmas here to try and locate you because he was positive that this Captain Perez had brought you to Nassau. Do not consider me your captor, mademoiselle, for I am only doing that which I was told."

"It certainly does not appear that I am your guest," remarked Raven bitterly. "The door is locked from the outside. There are bars on the windows. Such does not constitute gracious hospitality, madame."

"You must understand my position, Raven. Is that not the name Dalmas called you?" she asked, but Raven stubbornly refused to answer. "How lovely! *Tres belle.*"

"And just what is your position," challenged Raven.

"I must do that which is required of me, even though it may not always be in my best interest or what I feel is right. The governor has warned me time and time again that I am not to harbor men like Ames, but if I refuse to do otherwise, my life, as well as the lives of my girls, is in jeopardy."

Raven curiously studied the petite woman. Her words were gentle, her manners very ladylike, and she seemed most sincere in her reasoning. She is certainly not at all as I imagined Madame DuVall to be, mused Raven. She doesn't seem at all threatening. Perhaps she, too, is a victim of Ames.

"I hold no malice toward you, mademoiselle. And whether you believe me or not, I pity you for the situation you are in. As long as you are in my home, I will see to it that you are as comfortable as possible. You will be free to wander about my home, but I warn you that any attempt to escape will meet with opposition. As you have already noticed, the windows are barred, and Dalmas has placed his own man outside my home to ensure that you do not leave."

"And what do you expect from me in return for such hospitality?" inquired Raven suspiciously.

"You will not be expected to earn your keep, if that is what you mean. I do not intend to make any demands of you, mademoiselle. Now, I am sure you must be hungry. Perhaps you would like to join me for a bit of supper?" she suggested graciously.

"I am not hungry," said Raven dully.

Francesca shrugged indifferently. "As you wish, but your obstinance hurts no one but yourself. Denying your body nourishment is no solution to your dilemma. Besides, if you do intend to plan an escape, you do not want to collapse from hunger once you have evaded the guards."

"In that case, madame, thank you for your offer," replied Raven coolly.

"Have the others already dined, Pierre?" she asked as they entered the tiny dining room.

*"Oui, madame."* He placed two bowls of bouillabaisse and a loaf of hot bread on the table.

Francesca raised a spoonful of the thick fish and vegetable stew to her mouth, blowing lightly on the steaming soup. *"Très, très bon,* Pierre," she praised as the peg-legged cook flashed a smile and hobbled back to the cook room, his wooden appendage thumping loudly on the tile floor. "I was indeed very fortunate to obtain Pierre's culinary talents," she said, trying to make light conversation with her stubbornly quiet dinner companion. "He had served as a cook with Philip Moureau, another of my country's infamous scoundrels. "One night a meal he had prepared for his Moureau was not to his liking so the drunken fool had him keelhauled, and a shark bit off the lower part of his limb."

Raven winced at the thought of the pain the poor Frenchman must have endured. When a man's punishment is to be keelhauled, according to Mr. Horningold, a rope was tied to his waist and he was lowered into the water while the ship was under full sail and dragged alongside the vessel until he was almost dead. That in itself was unbearable enough, for few seamen were able to survive such an ordeal, but to have a limb mutilated by a shark was even more excruciating.

"I hope I have not spoiled your appetite," apologized the madam as Raven pushed aside her unfinished stew. "Conversation, as well as good food, should be shared during a meal. It is rather apparent that you feel a tête-à-tête with me is too demeaning." She, too, pushed aside her bowl.

Raven refused to raise her downcast eyes, for she knew that Madame DuVall was not to be held responsible for her being there and that her sentiment of not wishing to inflict further injury on her was sincere. "Madame DuVall, I . . . I," she began clumsily.

"What I mean to . . . to say is that I realize that you are not at fault for my predicament. I am sorry I placed all of the blame on you. No doubt you fear Red Ames as much as I. I am most sorry for my rudeness."

"You owe me no apology. I understand what pain you must be going through. That man is completely despicable. He has changed so much since our days together in Paris. I thought it was such good fortune that my old friend was here, but my association with him has brought me nothing but trouble. You are right, I do fear him. He will resort to any means to collect any unpaid debts owed him." She shook her head gloomily. "It grieves me that I am powerless to aid you, but Dalmas maintains constant surveillance on my house. If he were to even suspect that I betrayed him, it would mean instant death to all who live here."

Raven reached across the table and touched Francesca's trembling hand. "I am aware of that Madame DuVall."

"My name is Francesca. If we are to become friends, I expect you to address me as such."

"I have no desire to see you or anyone else harmed because of me, but if there is any chance at all that I may be able to flee from here, I shall take the chance. I would rather die than become Ames's victim again."

"If you do not mind my inquisitiveness, what misfortune drew you into the path of Ames to begin with?"

She listened with avid concern as Raven recounted the seizure of the *Fancy Free* and of the gruesome deaths of all of her friends. Her eyes even clouded with sympathetic compassion when Raven choked on her words and could not continue telling her of Lucy's horrid ordeal. Francesca placed her arm around the young woman's shoulders and drew her into her lilac-perfumed bosom, patting her head as one would a frightened child's. When her sobbing subsided, the older woman pulled a lace-embroidered handkerchief from the sleeve of her gown and wiped the tears from Raven's resplendent eyes. "Hush, hush, *ma petite,* I can well imagine what must have happened to your friend. Do not punish yourself by allowing the image of her to dwell in your mind."

Sniffing, Raven quickly ended her story. "Captain Perez rescued me and brought me to Nassau. I was to sail to Eleuthera this morning when I was kidnapped by Dalmas. Oh, how could I ever have been so foolish to have trusted that other man who told me that Captain Jack had sent him to escort me to the boat. I knew better than to follow him," she wailed, "but I did anyway."

"Do not be so distraught. Perhaps there is a way to solve your problem. Talking of death will only depress you more. It is getting late now. I must go downstairs and greet my evening's guests. It will make you feel better if you join us in the salon. I will see to it that everyone understands that you are not one of my workers. You have my assurance that no one will bother you."

Raven declined the invitation, but after careful deliberation, reconsidered. Perhaps, she pondered wisely, I might see a familiar face who can be convinced to relay word of my whereabouts to Henry.

Raven was awed by the splendor of the rich decor of the salon as she descended the circular staircase three hours later. Never had she seen such magnificence.

Thick, plush rugs from the Orient carpeted the floor. Heavy, ornate Spanish chairs were arranged alongside festal embroidered satin and damask sofas from France. A high oaken serving bar with a copper enameled top curved in front of the mirrored wall. Cloisonné vases containing pink and purple sprays of hybiscus and bougainvillia adorned each table.

"Sing me a tune, Colette," urged a burly seaman seated on a sofa between two of the house lovelies, his arms draped over their shoulders.

The frail, waifish one lifted a scarred Spanish guitar from the stool beside her. In one complete motion, she positioned it on her lap, tossed back her long side-braid and began strumming the chords lightly, tenderly, as though she were coaxing the sound from its strings. Her tiny body swayed suggestively from side to side as she kept in time with the music. Her voice was low and seductively soothing as she crooned a lusty sea melody about the humorous antics of a virile sailor and a reluctant wench. All eyes were upon her as she breathlessly concluded her song. The audience applauded her with thunderous cheering and clapping.

"Come along, both of you," said the big Swede. "Since I can't decide between you, I'll take both of ye to bed!"

The girls wrapped their arms around his thick middle and attempted to support his drunken bulk. He stumbled between them, dragging them with him. He exchanged full-mouthed kisses with each in turn while groping underneath their sheer coverings, squeezing Nicole's ample buttocks with one hand while the other tweaked the pointed tips of Colette's boyish chest.

Two couples were too engrossed in their own frolic

to give much notice to the drunken display of Hans and his consorts on the opposite side of the room. One was involved in their own rendition of the French gambling game of baccarat. Instead of wagering money, the players cast in articles of clothing for each round they lost. The second pair was seated on the rug, a hazy smoke surrounding them as they took turns puffing on a pipe filled with hashish.

Two girls, who looked even younger than Raven's nineteen years, sat cross-legged on one couch, bored, pouting expressions on their faces. Creamy breasts swayed provocatively underneath their short, satin camisoles. Their smooth-skinned faces reminded Raven of a meticulously painted porcelain doll's she had as a child.

Footsteps clamoured up the stairs, and the pair's sullen, empty-eyed features were erased, replaced with low murmured whisperings and teasing giggles. The two men who had just entered continued their conversation at a corner table and were unconcerned with the performance of the girls. Their sensual glances faded once more into scowls.

Raven squinted at the two figures seated in the shadows, then realizing who they were, immediately turned her back on them; she was not eager for any further confrontation with Dalmas.

But the other man, who is he? she asked herself. Oh yes, now I remember, she realized after several glances over her shoulder at the two figures. Wingate Gale! That's who he is. I wonder why he's conferring with a man of Dalmas's reputation. Undoubtedly he is the council member who does not know where his loyalty lays. She watched surreptitiously as Dalmas withdrew an envelope from his jacket and handed it to his overstuffed companion. Just as she suspected he would do, Gale cautiously surveyed the room. Satisfied that his actions were unobserved, he jerked the envelope from Dalmas's hand and shoved it into his pocket. Exchanging no further words, Gale hurried from the room, and Dalmas walked across to the serving bar.

He motioned for Francesca to join him. Raven was able to listen unnoticed as pleasantries were exchanged.

"Ah, madame. How lovely you look tonight."

"*Merci,* Lieutenant. I trust your meeting with Monsieur Gale was satisfactory."

Dalmas reached for his drink. "He gave me the information that I had hoped for. It seems that Captain Hildersly refuses to be detained any longer, and that he has given notice that he intends to leave on Wednesday. What a pity!" he said, a wicked smile on his smug face. "The harbor will be left unguarded." His narrow lips parted in a sinister grin. "And I suspect that by midnight Wednesday, you shall be relieved of your house guest."

Of course, thought Raven, the perfect opportunity for an invasion. I have only three days to caution the governor or else Nassau will be overrun with Ames's and Jennings's men. Three days and I, too, shall be just as unfortunate! She grimaced, watching Dalmas leave.

"You heard?" asked Francesca, who waited until Dalmas was down the stairs to join Raven. "I was so afraid he would see you sitting down here."

"I kept my back to him. It's frightening, isn't it. To think that Nassau is once again going to fall to those rascals! Something must be done to stop them, and I haven't got much time."

"We haven't much time," corrected her companion, her face drawn with worry.

"We?"

"Come, let's sit for a moment over there." She motioned to two high-backed, velvet cushioned chairs. "I am as concerned as you, whether you believe that or not. If Ames and Jennings follow through with their plan to combine forces for a joint invasion, the entire island will be in a state of mass confusion. One group will attack from the ocean, and while the troops and militia are trying to defend the fort, the second group will enter unnoticed from the east."

"You are certain that is the strategy they intend to proceed with?"

"I heard Ames and Jennings plan the seizure. I am positive that is their plan."

For a moment Raven was suspicious of the woman's motives in telling her these things. "But why should this even concern you?" she asked, pointing out that as their ally, she should have nothing to fear.

"Perhaps not, but if the pirates do succeed in their coup d'etat, a bloody power struggle between them is sure to follow. I have worked hard to establish my business here and am not anxious for those drunken fools to destroy in one night all that has taken me ten years to accumulate."

Raven smiled. "I think, Francesca, that you are not so selfish. That is just a pretense to conceal your true concerns."

"What is so unusual about my wanting to protect my business? I certainly do not want those bastards coming in here and demanding for free what I provide

286

for a price. Why, I would be destitute within the week."

"You know as well as I that when New Providence is taken, nothing can stop the pirates' insatiable appetites for looting, burning, murdering and raping. Innocent children and helpless women will be the ones who suffer the most."

"Enough discussion of my virtues, even whores have compassionate sides to their natures," she said, ending their conversation.

"All right, but one other thing about you still concerns me."

"Oh?"

"As I told you earlier, Ames threatened to sell me to you if I did not behave toward him in an appropriate manner."

"Yes, go on."

"And when I was on Gorda Cay, one of the women there told me that several of the others had been sent to work for you. What happened to them?"

Francesca nodded in sad remembrance. "Ames did bring three of those poor women here. Such scrawny, pitiful creatures. But why should I buy women to work for me when healthy ones do so of their own accord. *Mon Dieu;* festering sores the size of coins inflamed their thighs and chests. They were so weak they could not raise their hand to brush away the flies that swarmed around their blisters."

"So what became of them?"

"I had no alternative but to pay Ames for them. Otherwise they would have been auctioned away on the docks." Her face clouded with grief. "One of them did die. I could do nothing to save her, but I did see to it that the other two found their way to a Spanish supply boat that was anchored off of East End."

"Found their way?" asked Raven, feeling a sudden warmth for the woman.

"With a little assistance, of course. Several of the flotilla's commanders come here from time to time, and in return for this favor, I provided them with free entertainment for an entire week. But my good heartedness is not our immediate concern, as well you know. The lieutenant's grim prediction worries me, and I fear we are helpless to alter those plans."

"If we could somehow manage to get word to the governor and warn him of the attack," suggested Raven. "He would know what to do."

"But do you think Rogers would believe anything I had to say on such a matter? Of course not. He would assume that it was a ploy, another of Ames's schemes to outwit him. I had already thought of doing that, but they would never heed my warning of impending doom. Besides, he would undoubtedly discuss my sudden change of loyalties with the council, and then Monsieur Gale would betray me to Dalmas."

"Governor Rogers knows that I have no reason to lie to him, for my contempt for Ames is ten times greater than all the townspeople's combined. You must help me escape, Francesca. You must!"

"Think of me what you will Raven, but I cannot permit you to endanger yourself so. One of the lieutenant's own men is stationed outside the only exit onto the streets. He would apprehend you the moment you stepped outside the door. As long as you are in my custody, I can see to it that you are safe, but if I assist in your escape, Dalmas would see to it that both of us are punished severely. I have seen him do such often enough. Our clothes would be stripped away, and we would be flogged within an inch of our lives."

Raven trembled at the thought of such ugly brutality. "But we cannot sit placidly by and watch as the island is ravaged by those fiends."

Even as she spoke, Raven knew there was very little likelihood that Rogers's army could defend New Providence against the intruders. Hildersly could never be convinced to stay in the harbor, even though many lives depended on it. Aside from several cargo vessels and a few impounded pirates' sloops there were no ships in the harbor that could be used in the settlement's defense. And Juan was probably still out at sea waiting for Ames to discover him. By now, Ames could be anywhere, since that which had been stolen from him on Gorda Cay was once again in his possession.

"If we do not at least make some effort to save Nassau from those ruthless scavengers," she pleaded frantically with her friend, "the deaths of all of those innocent people will weigh on our consciences the rest of our lives."

"I am aware of that. And I will do my best to resolve this dilemma, but I need time to think. You must trust me to find a simpler solution than what you propose, and to do the right thing. You see, it must be I who will bear the consequences of such an act."

"But—" argued Raven.

Francesca interrupted. "That is the only way."

Raven nodded in reluctant acquiescence, for she had no other choice but do as she was told.

"Good," said Francesca, then nodded to the entranceway. "Ah, I see Major Bonnet has decided to again risk the gallows for an evening with us," she said, rising to meet her guest. "Excuse me for one moment, Raven. Stede, Monsieur Bonnet!" she called out gaily. *"Je suis très joyeux tu voir cette nuit."* Her crinolines swished around her ankles as she hurried to greet him.

## *Chapter Seventeen*

The overbearing figure standing alongside the bar aroused Raven's interest. So that is the Major Bonnet I have heard so much about, she thought.

"You are as lovely as always, Francesca," he praised, bowing low, then kissing her extended hand.

"We have all missed your company," she replied. "So seldom do we have the opportunity to entertain such a gallant guest.

Raven smiled to herself at the thick exchange of pleasantries between the well-mannered rogue and the ladylike madam.

Stede Bonnet was a powerfully built man. His tall, sturdy frame dominated the room, for his very presence demanded everyone's attention. Dressed in a fashionable red damask waist coat, snug fitting breeches of the same texture and color, and a silk, ruffled, cuffed white shirt, he gave one the impression of a wealthy, highly respected English gentleman. Large brass buckles on the sides of his knee boots were shined to perfection and reflected the lustrous black sheen on his shoes. The wavy, shoulder-length hair the tawny color of a lion's mane, was smoothed straight back from his forehead. A sword hung from his side, encased by a leather sheath. Around his neck were three gold chains, and upon his fingers he wore large rings of ruby, emerald, and onyx stones. A wide band of braided gold was clasped around his wrist.

"I am afraid that Nicole is occupied for the evening, Stede. Had I known to expect you, I would have had one of the other girls attend to her duties," apologized Madame DuVall, knowing of the Major's preference for the plump young woman whose warm, soft touch could calm even the rowdiest of customers.

"No matter." He casually brushed aside her remark. "I see Daphine is still in your employment," he remarked, nodding in the direction of the buxomy, creamy-skinned girl sprawled on the sofa.

"Ah, yes, Daphine," she answered wearily. I should have rid myself of that one a long time ago, thought Francesca. She has brought me nothing but trouble. A month ago the girl had deliberately provoked two of her suitors into a duel, and earlier there had been that incident with Anne Bonny. All of the girls had been warned against flaunting their wares in front of Jack Rackam, but Daphine had refused to heed the warning. One afternoon, Anne found her cowardly lover with Daphine on his lap, his face buried beneath her milky globes, and his hands underneath her dress stroking her silky thighs. Anne shook her pistol and threatened the lives of everyone there, then proceeded to shoot at everything in her sight: mirrors, chandeliers, bottles, chairs, surprised men, and frightened women. In the end, Calico Jack had meekly followed her outside.

Casually puffing on his ivory-stemmed pipe, Bonnet surveyed the room with detached interest, though somewhat amused at the scenery—voluptuous women whose pouting faces showed boredom, and squat, balding men, their foreheads red with perspiration, who panted like animals for the slightest attention shown them. Bonnet had little interest in their tedious sordidness. Then his cold, gray eyes rested on a corner chair, hidden in an arrangement of hanging plants, for there, seated demurely atop the velvet plushness, was the most striking female he had ever encountered. "Who is she?" he asked with avid concern, never for a moment taking his eyes from her soft loveliness for fear she would disappear.

Francesca chuckled softly. "She is not one of mine, dear Stede."

"I beg you to introduce me to her," he implored. "In all my travels I have yet to meet a female who could hold a candle to such beauty."

Before Francesca could stop him, he had moved across the room in quick, long strides. He clicked his heels together ceremoniously and bowed low to the bewildered young woman.

"Forgive my impudence, but for some reason unknown even to me, the stuffy formalities of proper behavior must be cast aside. I throw myself at your feet, oh, beautiful creature!" he stated eloquently, eyes piercing Raven's startled countenance.

Francesca came to her defense, and Raven frantically eyed her in a mute appeal for help. "Come along with me, Stede, *ma chèr ami*. We shall find someone else who will better suit your tastes," she urged, tugging at his sleeve.

He apologized profusely to Raven. "Most likely you think me a madman or a drunk, but I assure you that I am intoxicated not with strong drink but with your beauty. And the only thing that maddens me is you."

"Shh," said Raven, motioning for him to hush. "Must you be so loud? We are the center of everyone's attention. I assure you, sir," she hissed between her teeth, "I do not wish to either madden or intoxicate you. Will you please direct your attentions elsewhere?"

Without invitation and much to Raven's ire, he slid a chair over to hers and sat down beside her, their knees almost touching. Raven fidgeted uncomfortably in her seat and turned to Francesca, but the confused expression on her face revealed that she was powerless to do anything.

"It is I who am confused," began Bonnet. "If you are not in Madame DuVall's employ, then why are you in the salon on display for all the others?"

Francesca seated herself on the arm of Raven's chair. She explained Raven's unfortunate situation to Bonnet, her voice barely rising above a whisper. "You see," she confided, "Ames sees her as his property, something rightfully his that was snatched from his possession, and now he intends to regain that object regardless of the consequences."

Bonnet looked to Raven for verification. "It is all true," she confided. "Everything."

"It was just as well you didn't sail with Captain Jack," he told her.

"Why? What do you mean?" she flared indignantly.

"No offense intended, Miss Gatewood. Just let me explain myself. You see, a Spanish supply ship sunk the boat this morning. To the best of my knowledge, there were no survivors."

Raven looked as though she were in a trance, her

body motionless. Her face held an empty look. "Providence," she uttered to herself.

"Providence?" repeated the French courtesan. "What are you talking about?"

"Ah yes, Providence!" exclaimed Bonnet knowingly as he rubbed his close-shaven chin. "Providence; the foreseeing guidance of God."

"You're both speaking in riddles," declared Francesca.

"My being kidnapped and brought here was ironically the only thing that saved me from being on Captain Jack's boat this morning. Otherwise, I, too, would have died en route to Eleuthera. Poor Captain Jack! Why could *Le Bordeaux* not have been the one hit?"

Bonnet answered her question. "For the same reason, dear girl. Providence! We have no control of our fate. Speaking of which, I understand that Ames and Jennings have resolved past differences long enough to attempt a raid on the island. They asked that I join them in their little escapade."

"And do you intend to do so?" asked Raven candidly.

"Merciful God, no!" he exclaimed. "I have no desire to be anywhere near here when their bloody power struggle begins. Besides, I am far too civilized to cast my lot with those barbarians."

One of the shiny black bare-chested Negroes who maintained a threatening stance at the doorway approached them. He leaned down and whispered in Francesca's ear. She nodded and hurriedly excused herself, mumbling something about a drunken brawl between Hans and his two friends.

Raven felt awkward in Bonnet's presence. Her eyes

remained fixed on the rug, for she felt the heated stare of Bonnet's piercing eyes fixed to her face and did not wish to meet his glance.

Finally, after motioning to the hefty barkeeper to bring him a glass of port, he broke the icy silence. "I do wish you would not be so uneasy. The way you keep twisting around in that chair, one would think I had a cutlass at your throat." A teasing smile turned up his thin lips. "Needless to say, I would not hesitate filling your purse with gold sovereigns for an evening of your company."

"Major Bonnet, as Madame DuVall has already informed you, I am not a member of her . . . her group. It is not by my choice that I am here, so believe me when I say your promise of gold coins does not entice me the least bit."

"A woman with spirit! I like that. Such dynamic vigor only enhances your unequaled beauty," he flattered. "Ah, if you would but permit me, I should like nothing better than to hang precious jewels from those ears, drape your exquisite neck with emeralds and rubies and attire you in the finest of silks from the Far East."

"If you find that you must persist in this mode of conversation, sir, I must excuse myself," she said, haughtily rising from her seat.

"Oh no, no, no," he pleaded with an almost childlike persistence. "I have really blundered this horribly! Please, I beg of you, sit down. All I desire is to converse with another human of equaled intelligence. I promise I shall make no more offensive remarks to you."

She eyed him suspiciously. "As you say, Major, but only as long as it is perfectly understood that polite conversation will be the limit of our acquaintance."

"You have my word, gracious lady. I truly did not mean to be so impetuous," he remarked, reaching for her hand. But the anger that reddened her face cautioned him against such an overture. "Yes, well ... I am truly sorry that my intentions were misinterpreted. Surely you realize that had I wanted a wench for the night ... what I mean to say is—" he stammered so uncomfortably that Raven could not help but smile. "Well now, there are those who would have been honored to have me grace— Oh, you know what I'm trying to say. Anyway, my attraction to you is so consuming that I would settle for even a platonic relationship if that is what you would prefer."

The nervous solemnity of his chatter amused Raven, and she found it quite difficult to maintain her aloofness. The more sincere his countenance, the harder it became for her to control the twitching of her lips. Finally, she could endure it no longer and burst into uncontrollable mirth. The sight of Bonnet's dejected embarrassment quieted her, and sensing his wounded pride, she struggled to apologize. "I fear that it is I who owe you an apology, sir. Truly, I was not laughing at you. It is just that I never expected such eloquence from one of your profession."

He cheerfully joined in with her sudden mood change. "I admit that men like Jennings or Ames would take you by the hair and forcefully drag you out onto the streets if they were so moved, but no, dear girl, give me credit for being a different sort. I'll not deny I've had my share of plunders and raids, but where affairs of the heart are concerned, I assure you I am as docile as a lap pup."

297

With an elaborate gesture, he was bending down on one knee, kneeling at her feet, reciting, "Come live with me and be my love."

Raven shook with glee, almost tumbling from her chair. "Come now, Major, I am not a nymph, and you are certainly not a shepherd."

"Perhaps not, but Marlow did seem appropriate for the moment. I am at least relieved I was able to make you smile. Please, call me Stede. I insist!"

Raven agreed to do so. "Please now, get up. You look most ridiculous!"

He obliged her request. "Contrary to what has been said of me, I do lead a rather dull existence." She gave him a doubting grin, and he requested, "Suppose you tell me what dreadful tales you've heard about me, and we shall see how they correspond with my true nature."

Raven deliberated carefully before answering. "Hmm, actually nothing. I've only heard your name being mentioned in conjunction with Blackbeard, Greaves, and Daniels. Though I must admit, you hardly seem to fit in with such a slimey lot."

"Of course, I would be a liar of the worst kind if I tried to convince you that my reputation is above reproach, but I do not belong in the same category as those vultures. I prefer to think of myself more in terms of a gentleman scoundrel."

"And are not gentleman scoundrels subject to the gallows as well?" she asked mischievously.

"I'm afraid they are."

"If you don't mind the inquiry, why did you ever become involved in such a perilous profession?"

"Well, Raven. You don't mind if I call you that do you? Good." He relaxed in his chair with his legs stretched out in front of him and began his loquacious explanation. "I can honestly say that until several years ago, I had not intended to pursue my present course. My father was a military genius, and it was assumed that I would carry on the family tradition in His Majesty's service. I did as was expected and devoted most of my life to a military career. For my loyalty and devotion to the Crown, I was granted extensive acreage in Barbados, and I retired to the life of a sugarcane plantation owner. Unfortunately the solitude I felt would accompany such a transition was nonexistent. My wife nagged me incessantly day after day, badgering me about the least incident. Not one moment's peace existed with her, so I was forced to turn to a life of piracy."

"That's a poor excuse, Major. How can you blame your own shortcomings on your poor wife?"

"But it's true," he said convincingly. "That woman is an offspring of Medusa herself. I'd swear to it. Had I stayed around her for another week, God forgive me for my actions." He drew slowly on his pipe before resuming his story. "Anyway, being an infantry man, I knew nothing of the sea or of sailing so I became quite preoccupied with learning about both. I read as much as was available on the subject, but book knowledge is not nearly as comprehensive as that gained from experience.

"Finally I found someone who could teach me what I needed to know, an old fellow who had been Henry Morgan's first mate. Without his guidance, I would still not be able to distinguish the bow from the stern. He taught me how to read the water, direct my course according to the stars, and to draw my own navigational maps and charts. Am I boring you?" he asked, pausing to relight his pipe. "You're not just listening out of politeness to humor a long-winded sailor, are you?"

She assured him she was not. "Please continue."

"All right, but if I see you stifling a yawn, I will be most perturbed at you. Where was I? Oh, yes. Soon after my lessons ended, I made arrangements to purchase a seaworthy vessel. I scrubbed, scoured, and painted her myself until my hands were raw with blood and sweat. I found a decent crew. We christened her the *Revenge* and began our raids."

"Why the *Revenge?*" asked Raven, curious he had chosen such a name.

"It seemed appropriate at the time. A sort of reprisal against my wife. I'm certainly not condoning my actions, mind you, but I never inflicted any serious injury to anyone. It was customary procedure to fire three warning shots into the air before opening fire on another vessel. If the ship didn't surrender, I'd run up the red."

"Run up the red?"

"I'd raise our red flag. It was a warning that if they did not voluntarily surrender no lives would be spared."

"And did you ever have the occasion to carry out that threat?"

"No, everyone suddenly became very cooperative. After we had taken from her cargo what we wanted, we'd maroon the crew and set the vessel on fire."

"That's horrible!" she said, making no effort to conceal her distaste for such actions. "Just leave those poor men to die, would you?"

"Don't make me sound so barbaric. Of course I didn't just leave them there to die. I allowed them a sufficient supply of food and fresh water to sustain them until another ship came along. Actually, the way I see it, they were quite fortunate."

Raven was stunned. "Fortunate?"

"Well, I reason that had I not been the one to raid their ship, someone who lacked my charitable clemency would have, and along with losing their cargo, the poor fools would have lost their lives."

"I suppose every pirate has his own mode of operation," she admitted. "There's no reason why all of you have to be as despicable as Ames or Blackbeard."

"Please do not equate me with the likes of those rascals. At one time, I held Ed Teach in high esteem. Except for his Satan-like cruelness, he was the epitome of what I wanted to be."

"And what happened to change your mind?"

"Both our ships were anchored off New Providence a while back. He sent a message to me, an invitation for me to join his piratical fraternity. The Brethren of the Coast! How much I wanted to be a member! I returned his note with one of my own, which said I would be honored to join the group and asked if he would come aboard my ship for dinner that evening. I fell right into his snare. I must have looked more like a dandy than a ship's captain that night, for I had dressed in my most elegant finery in order to impress him. We feasted on an elaborate seven-course meal, and while we sipped our brandy afterward he calmly informed me that at that very moment his men were taking control of my ship. Quite a way to return my hospitality, don't you agree?"

301

"But why would he have wanted your ship when he had one of his own?"

"Oh, he guilelessly informed me that mine was in far better shape than his own, and a master seaman, not a bumbling idiot, deserved to be in command of such a fine vessel. He even forced me to remain on as a common deck hand. Eventually we did capture a ship of superior size and speed, and my command was returned."

"Have you ever thought of retiring from this sort of life. Your fate is inevitable if you persist in plundering, no matter how compassionate you are toward your victims," scolded Raven with serious concern.

"I suppose that eventually I will have to return to the dull life on a plantation, but for the time being, the spirit of adventure compels me to continue." He removed a silver, jewel-encased timepiece from his breast pocket. "It is almost midnight," he said with a remorseful sigh. "As much as I have enjoyed our evening, I regret to say I must return to my ship."

Raven stood with him. "Be careful, Stede. The militia keeps a close watch on the house in hopes of capturing you," she revealed, a bit guiltily, for she felt as though she were betraying the governor's confidence."

"I've been aware of that for some time," he replied, easing her guilt. "But thank you for the warning just the same. Before I depart, I should like to request a small favor of you if I may."

"And what is that?"

"I have a proposition that I would like you to consider. No, no! Nothing wicked, I assure you," he said in reply to her enraged look. "A proposition that is perfectly innocent. Just listen to my proposal before you make any rash judgment about my intentions."

"I'm listening."

"You and I both know that even if Ames decides not to cancel plans for the attack, he will nevertheless come here eventually and claim you."

"I know that, Stede. I live in constant dread of such a time."

"The way I view your situation," he continued, "you have no other alternative but allow me to help you escape. I can see to it that you reach my ship safely and then deliver you to your father on Eleuthera. I give you my word that no harm will befall you as long as you are in my care."

"I don't know what to say, Stede," she said with uncertainty.

"I am not asking that you make such a decision this very instant, only that you consider my offer. I shall return on Tuesday evening for your answer." He felt an urge to lean down and kiss her piquant face, but instead reached for her hand and squeezed it reassuringly. "Just promise me that you will devote careful thought to what I have said."

"I will do that," she promised, walking with him to the stairs.

"Before I envisioned myself as a swashbuckler, I frequently fantasized of delivering a beautiful, virtuous maiden from the evil clutches of a lustful ogre. Don't deny my being able to live my dream. Good night, dear girl. Until Tuesday!" With a gallant bow and a slight brush of his lips across her hand, Major Bonnet turned and descended the stairs, glancing back several times before he reached the bottom.

Raven paused for a moment beside the ornately carved serving bar and skimmed the writing on a wooden plaque that had been tacked to the wall. She smiled to herself, for at the top of the list was the school-boyish scrawl of B. Horningold, followed by the flaired, cursive letters of Henry Jennings. Many of the etched signatures were illegible, but most of the names she could distinguish: Ed Teach, Johnny Martell, James Fife, Chris Winter, Nicky Brown, Major Penner, and Charles Vane. Most likely, she decided, all were frequent visitors to Madame DuVall's during the days when pirating flourished.

## Chapter Eighteen

Raven spent the following day in her room. Her only companion the entire day was a volume that had been left outside her door earlier that morning; a popular collection of plays written by the seventeenth century French dramatist Molière. Even though she found the antics of the pseudopious Tartuffe most entertaining, she could not become completely absorbed in the satirical comedy for her mind wandered from concentrating on the plot of the play to her own indecisiveness concerning Bonnet's generous proposal.

True, he is a gentleman, she reasoned upon completion of the first act. And as such, he must be honorable and trustworthy. But he is still a pirate! He himself admitted that his reputation was not without blemish. I suppose I would be a simpleton if I believed he would keep his word and deliver me to Eleuthera. Perhaps like Tartuffe, his show of goodness is but a guise to hide his true nature. He was most charming during our encounter last evening, but was such suaveness just a facade? Would he forget the pledge he made to me once we were at sea and force me to submit to him or be tossed to the sharks? You silly girl! Of course he would do nothing of the sort. Or would he?

Such nagging thoughts persisted until Raven felt as though her head would burst from the mounting turmoil within.

"Oh, where are you, Juan Perez?" she asked, staring dismally at the cedar chest at the foot of her bed. Oh, what should I do? If only you were here with me. It would have been so much simpler had you allowed me to sail with you. But then you had no way of knowing that my carelessness would get me into such a mess. Providence, Chance, Fortune spinning their wheels to plot the course of our lives. Had I gone to the wharf without Dalmas and his man who kidnapped me, I would be dead by now. If I had not been brought here, I would never have known of the bloody disaster that will befall Nassau the day after tomorrow. Remember what Papa used to say: "Everything, be it good or bad, happens for a reason, and it is not our place to question its intent."

She returned to her reading, still torn by the decision she must make. Should I trust my intuition concerning Bonnet's character? In my heart, I am confident that he would take me to the Taylor Plantation, and there, I would be free of Ames. But what would happen to Francesca once Ames learned of his prisoner's escape? Would he avenge my disappearance by subjecting Francesca to punishment too horrible to even think about? she wondered wearily. If I agree to Bonnet's proposal, how can I ever get word of the impending attack to Rogers? Without some advanced warning of the raid, the present system of defense would surely crumble. The soldiers would never suspect they must defend the inland route as well as the harbor. Perhaps

Francesca can advise me on what I should do. I do want to do the right thing! I will just have to explain my dilemma to her, and maybe she will have a feasible solution.

Raven opened the door to her room and peered outside into the hallway. Anna was leaving her mistress's suite, and Raven summoned her.

*"Oui mademoiselle,"* she answered, lowering her head.

*"Où est la madame?"*

*"Je ne sais pas, mademoiselle,"* replied Anna, telling Raven that she did not know where Madame DuVall was.

*"J'aimerais parler avec la madame quand elle retourne. Merci, Anna."*

*"Oui, mademoiselle."* She cursied and went on about her chores.

"Where were you all day yesterday, Francesca?" demanded Raven in an annoyed tone when she entered the dining room for breakfast the next morning. "Did Anna not tell you that I needed to see you?"

The older woman looked tired; worried lines creased her forehead as she sipped her coffee. "Yes, she did, but when I returned home, I was detained by Lieutenant Dalmas. He stayed until after eleven o'clock, and by then I assumed you were already in bed."

"Oh, Francesca. We have so little time left before tomorrow evening. How are we ever going to get word to the governor?"

"I have already seen to that matter, Raven."

"But how? When? Did he believe you?"

*"Mon Dieu,* if I did not convince him of my sincerity,

the blood of hundreds of innocent people will be on his hands, not mine."

Raven was relieved. "Good. Perhaps now he can prepare a viable plan for the settlement's defense. But what about Dalmas? Did he suspect your betraying Ames?"

"No, not at all. He only wanted to gloat on his accomplishments."

"Accomplishments? What do you mean?"

"Do you remember Major Bonnet telling us of the sinking of the boat that was to take you to Eleuthera?"

"Of course I remember. Had I been on that boat I would have perished with the rest of them. But what does this have to do with Dalmas?"

"The Spanish were not responsible for its sinking. Dalmas was."

"But . . . but why?" questioned Raven, disturbed by such news.

"Because had the ship been allowed to reach its destination and then return to Nassau, it would soon have been revealed that you were not on board."

Raven was slowly beginning to understand. "And those who knew I was to be aboard her would know that I had most likely been kidnapped by Ames and his men."

"That is correct. And Dalmas could not risk that chance with the invasion so close at hand."

"Then Bonnet lied to us about the Spanish being responsible."

"No, I am sure Stede is no part of their scheme. He only repeated what he and everyone else heard. Apparently, Dalmas bribed a fisherman into circulating the story that his skiff had been nearby when it happened, and he saw the Spanish attack Captain Jack." Francesca's hands began to tremble, and she was unable to raise the cup of coffee to her mouth without spilling some of its contents on the table covering.

"Francesca, what is it?" urged Raven. "Are you all right? Here, let me take that," she insisted, taking the coffee from her hand.

"If it becomes known that it was I who divulged Ames's scheme, nothing or no one will be able to save me from his vengeful wrath. It will be a horrible death, slow and painful, a punishment Ames takes pleasure in for those who betray him."

"You mustn't even think such thoughts," comforted Raven. "Governor Rogers can be trusted to keep your identity secret. And you told him about Mr. Gale, did you not? Well, see now, he certainly won't mention you at the council meetings. I pray that he will be able to halt the invasion."

Francesca shook her head doubtingly. "The only men who are trained for such matters are those troops he brought from England. The inhabitants here are farmers and merchants; they are not trained soldiers."

"But the militia. Surely they will be of some assistance."

Francesca wearily disagreed. "Over one half the militia is comprised of surrendered pirates. Do you think they will uphold their vow of allegiance when weapons are put in their hands? Of course not. Ames is one of their own kind. They'd much rather be killing and pilfering than burning rotting carcasses or cleaning up the town."

Raven tried to convince her friend that she was

309

wrong, but even she herself doubted the settlement's ability to hold off the attack. "The governor is a shrewd man, Francesca. Why, at this very moment, I'll wager he already has a plan to defeat Ames and Jennings's forces."

"But strategy does not win battles," she reminded the girl sorrowfully. "It takes much more than words and plans on paper."

I cannot abandon Francesca now, decided Raven later in the day. It was at my insistence that she risked her life to save the town, and now it is my duty to remain with her.

That evening, as the sun was being rendered powerless in the purple and amber sky, Raven was seated at the writing table in her room composing a letter to Stede Bonnet. Frustrated because her words did not convey adequately what she wished to say, she crumpled the paper and started over again. After the fifth attempt, she was satisfied that even though her explanation was not detailed, it did relay the proper sentiment, for if Major Bonnet's offer was indeed a sincere one, she did not wish to offend him. She read it aloud before sealing it with the drippings from her candle. "Dear Major Bonnet: I have spent many hours in careful contemplation of your generous offer. For reasons that I choose not to discuss, I cannot accept your proposition. I sincerely hope that you do not view my refusal as a personal insult, for I feel certain that your intentions were most honorable."

At half past seven, Anna tapped on her door. *"Monsieur Bonnet est dans la salon. Il demande vous voir."*

Raven opened the door, handed Anna the letter, and

310

requested that she tell the Major she was indisposed and could not meet with him.

Raven then waited by the window until she recognized the richly attired Bonnet moving stealthily in the shadows, and she hoped that he had understood her decision to remain behind had nothing to do with him.

She was awakened much later that night by a rough hand jerking her from her bed. "Come along, wench. I've orders to take ye to the stockade!"

"What? What are you talking about? I don't understand. Remove your hand from my shoulder this instant," she blared, half-awake. The light from her bedside candle outlined vaguely a red-uniformed figure. "But you're one of the Governor's regiment."

"That's right, honey. Now get dressed!" he ordered roughly, leering at her muslin night dress.

She was confused. What did he want with her? Fearing that his actions would become brutal if she refused, she did as she was told, but only after demanding that he turn his back while she dressed.

Had his orders not emphatically stated that severe measures would be taken if any of the soldiers were unduly rough with the women, he would not have submitted so easily to her demand.

She dressed quickly, perplexed by such unexplainable actions. How can the governor do this, she wondered, especially since Francesca risked her life to warn him to prepare for the attack. Oh, no! Surely Francesca did not lie to me about her conference with the governor.

Then Raven remembered Rogers's threat to close the brothel if Madame DuVall did not heed his warning concerning giving pirates refuge. Raven scrambled into the first dress she could find. Suppose Stede had been seen entering the house, and now the troops were there to arrest them all for harboring a criminal.

That must be the answer, she thought. Had Francesca indeed spoken with Rogers he would not be raiding her home, nor would they be carried off to the jail. Now it is apparent to me, Raven decided, that Francesca deliberately deceived me. She's still in an alliance with Ames and Jennings.

Francesca and her girls, along with Anna, Pierre, Jack the barkeeper, the two Negro guards, and a man Raven had never seen but suspected of being allied with Dalmas clustered around one of the gaming tables on the lower floor. A dozen troops stood at full attention around them.

"Is she the last?" demanded a small-statured lieutenant who was obviously in charge of the silent group.

"Yes, Sir," replied the sour-faced soldier as he shoved Raven into the center of the silent group.

"I demand to know the meaning of such madness!" stormed Francesca. "You break down my door, barge into our rooms as though we were criminals and herd us into a group like cows. Why? What did you expect to find? If you have finished with your childish games, I shall return to bed."

The lieutenant grabbed her wrists as she whirled past him. "I'm afraid I cannot permit you to do that."

"Oh, and why not?" she demanded indignantly. "We've done nothing wrong. You have no authority whatsoever to hold us."

"My orders, madame, are to take the inhabitants of this house to the stockade."

312

"And what are the charges, sir?" she asked, a hint of sarcasm in her tone.

"Conspiracy with the enemy."

She scowled at him with fierce ire.

"All right men, march them to the stockade," he ordered.

The soldiers herded the prisoners outside, encircling them to prevent escape. The mid-July night was shrouded in an ominous stillness. The stars were all lost behind the hazy thickness of the formless, gray cloud layer that veiled the sky.

I've got to get away from them, thought Raven desperately. They think I am one of Madame DuVall's whores. They would jeer at my attempts to prove the contrary. If I pleaded with them to send for Henry so that he could identify me, would they listen to me then? Aside from Henry, Maria, Juan, and the governor, no one knows I stayed at Henry's home last week. Everyone who saw us together was fooled by my disguise as a boy. I cannot depend on the lieutenant allowing me to see Henry, so my only chance of proving my innocence is to try and break away from the rest. Perhaps if I were to cry out that I have twisted my ankle, I might be permitted to linger for a moment in the rear. Then, when they're farther ahead, I will run as fast as I can to Henry's. Surely the lieutenant won't risk more than one man in pursuing me for fear someone else will escape.

"Ohhh!" she cried, stumbling to the ground.

The rear guard stood over her and she looked up imploringly at him as she rubbed her foot. "Get up, gal. What's the matter?"

"It's my ankle. I think I may have turned it."

313

"Well, what do you expect me to do about it. Shoot ye?" he grumbled.

"It is so painful," she moaned convincingly. "If I may be permitted to sit here for a moment."

He jerked her to her feet and tossed her left arm around his shoulder, grasping it with such force she knew she could never break his hold. "Lean most of your weight on me. There that's better, isn't it?" She limped as convincingly as she could. "Just a few more steps, and we'll be at the fort," he comforted, almost sympathetically.

The sentry swung open the double gate and saluted the lieutenant. "No sign of any disturbance, Sir," he told his superior.

A rectangular parade field comprised the central interior of the rock fortress. Three of the boundaries were bordered with a row of identically proportioned, frond-roofed, driftwood huts that housed the company of soldiers. Along the fourth wall were three square-shaped mortared structures: the cook shack, artillery magazine, and stockade. The guard outside the jail unhinged the triple-barred lock, and the prisoners were ushered inside.

The low flame of the whale-oil lantern hanging on the front wall of the prison shed an eerie illumination on the sparse surroundings. The barred enclosures looked like animal cages. The floor was hard packed sand and dirt, and the walls were windowless, not even the smallest opening to allow a condemned man a glimpse of the outside world or brighten his dull existence. Nauseating stenches of human waste and sickness hovered in the musty stuffiness of the room.

"Ah, Madame DuVall," came a half-awake voice

from the end cell. "And your entourage. Did you overcharge one of the officers? Perhaps you refused credit to one of the council members, heh?" His tone was unusually pleasant, and he sounded almost relieved to see her there.

"Quiet, Dalmas, or I shall have to chain you to the wall in the back," threatened the guard as he locked Raven, Francesca and Nicole in a cell on the opposite side. The other women were secured beside them, and the men in the cell beside Dalmas.

Dalmas's sinister countenance appeared even more foreboding, more malevolent, in the half-lit haze. He sneered demonically at Raven before returning to the uniform jacket he had spread on the floor as his pallet. "Do not worry, *ma belle*. Captain Ames will soon release us from our prison."

"I demand to know why you deliberately lied to me!" demanded Raven, whirling around to face the adversary she had mistaken as a friend.

"You are in no position to demand anything, Miss Gatewood," replied Francesca scornfully.

"But, how could you?"

"Hush!" snapped the woman, delivering a stinging slap across Raven's cheek. "I am in no mood to listen to your whimpering!"

Raven brought her hand to her face and rubbed her cheek. "But I thought—"

"I am not the least bit interested in what you thought," she retorted sharply. "Do not bother me with your ignorant babbling or I will have the guard put you in with your friend," she threatened, motioning to Dalmas.

Raven retreated to the back of the tiny cell, wanting

to get as far away from that despicable creature as she could. She eased herself down onto the floor and sat down in the dirt. She leaned her back against the damp tabby wall, raised her knees tight against her chest and cupped her face in her hands and sobbed.

What a fool I was to trust her. How could I be so gullible? She only wanted to obtain information from me for Dalmas to give to Ames. And I fell right into her trap. She made me think she wanted to help me, wanted to help save Nassau, and all she really wanted was to gain my confidence so she could use me. And I allowed her to do just that! Oh, how she pretended to be so compassionate and sympathetic to my situation How she feigned such concern for the poor little children of Nassau! "Even whores have compassionate hearts." Ha! Yours, Francesca DuVall, is harder and colder than the rock of this cell!

At daybreak the guard announced his presence by clanging a tin cup across the metal bars. He distributed the morning rations to each prisoner; chunks of maggot-infested cheese, a slice of molded bread, and a cup of stale water that smelled and tasted as though it had stagnated in a wooden barrel for days.

Dalmas tossed the food back at him. "Keep this in your pocket, old man. You'll be needing it soon enough."

The guard calmly picked up the food and moved to the next cell, ignoring Dalmas's comment. "The strangest thing happened last night," he mumbled underneath his breath, but loud enough for all to hear.

"Just keep it to yourself!" shouted the agitated French lieutenant.

"Jes' talkin' to myself. It sure is hard to believe that

316

such a strong ship like that could be tossed on its side by a spout," casually revealed the guard as he went about his morning chores.

He must be talking about a water spout, thought Raven. Juan had told her how even the most powerful vessel could be rendered helpless if the funnel-shaped portion of a cloud touched the water's surface near a ship, for it sprayed water in all directions.

"I guess even ol' Jennings got swallowed up in it."

At the mention of that name, Dalmas's ears perked up with sudden interest. The color seemed to drain from his fearsome face. "You're a liar!" he snarled viciously.

"Sergeant Rumley told me all about it," said the old man. "I'd like to hear you call him a liar. He could flatten you with his little finger."

"And how does your Sergeant Rumley know of such an occurrence?" ventured Francesca. "Did he see it happen?"

"No, but one of Jennings's mates that washed up on shore did. The sarge found him up against the rocks, clinging to a board he must have floated on. Kept mumbling about a mountain of water that appeared from nowhere."

"Where is that man now?" asked Dalmas dully.

"Dead. Thrown back into the water." He paused in front of the lieutenant's cell on his way out. "By the way, I almost forgot to tell you, sir. Your trial is to be this afternoon. Most likely you'll pay a visit to the hanging tree by dusk."

Dalmas paced his cell, cursing vilely and wringing his hands despairingly. Raven glanced to see Francesca's reaction, but she appeared neither frightened nor upset about the news. She had even thought the woman had sighed a breath of relief when the news was revealed.

I wonder what she's scheming now? she thought bitterly. Surely she realizes that without Jennings, Ames stands no chance of succeeding in his mission.

The guard reappeared unexpectedly a half hour later, unlocked the cell and pointed to Raven. "You with the black hair. Come with me. The lieutenant has some questions for you."

She hurried from her cage without question, brushing past Francesca who had touched her shoulder and mumbled something softly as she passed. Her eyes, having adjusted to the lack of light on the inside, squinted and winced painfully as the main door of the jail opened. She shielded her eyes from the blinding glare as a familiar voice called out her name.

"Henry? Oh, Henry, is that really you," she squealed joyfully. She ran to his open arms and flung herself upon his massive bulk. "Oh, you can't ever know how glad I am to see you!" she exclaimed, tears intermingled with laughter. "How did you know where to fine me? I was so afraid you had given me up as dead!"

"I'll answer all of your questions in good time. I see all my concern over your health was useless. Such talkativeness is a sure sign of a well woman."

"I know you're angry with me for not waiting on you the other morning," she remarked, ignoring his last comment. "But I didn't know what else to do. I wanted to get to Eleuthera so bad!"

"I tried to hurry back, Raven, but I couldn't leave Marriah Jackson. I thought I had lost her. Her baby was a healthy little thing, screaming his head off the

318

whole time, but its mama couldn't pass the afterbirth."

"Did she die, Henry?"

"No, luckily I remembered a treatment one of the Indians had shown me a long time ago for that same exact thing. Boil mud dauber nests, larvae and all, and force the tea down the patient's throat. I felt awful about not coming home, but I couldn't leave the poor woman."

"I know that, Henry," she said sympathetically. "Did you know that it was Dalmas and not the Spanish who sunk Captain Jack?"

He nodded and linked his arm in hers as they made their way to his home.

Maria greeted her at the door. "Thank God you are unharmed," she said, drawing the young woman close against her. "Oh, poor, poor child. Is there no end to your suffering? Are you certain you are not injured?"

"I am fine, Maria," she assured her as they climbed the stairs. "Really I am. Oh, it is so wonderful to be among friends once again."

Despite Raven's insistence that she was not abused in any way, Maria hovered about her like a mother, petting her and fretting about her comfort.

"What I would like to know," she began, having had three generous portions of bandana bread and a tall glass of coconut milk, "is how you knew where to find me. Now, Henry, you promised you'd answer my questions, so don't give me that annoyed look."

"All right." He laughed, then in a more serious tone he explained that she had Madame DuVall to thank for her safety.

"Francesca? You are certain?" she asked in stunned disbelief.

"Surely she told you she had spoken to Woodes and me. Why, according to her, you gave her the courage to defy those villains."

"But when her house was raided, I assumed she had lied to me and pretended to be my friend only so she could gain information for Ames. I was so mean to her in jail," she admitted, ashamed she had shunned the woman so.

"That poor woman had an impossible time trying to convince Woodes of her sincerity. Knowing of our friendship, she came here and told me that Dalmas abducted you and forced her to hide you. I was rather skeptical at first, but finally I had the good sense to believe her. After she revealed Ames's plans for seizing Nassau, I went back to the governor's with her and urged Woodes to consider the possibility of such an attack and to make the necessary preparations. Merciful Jesus, it frightens me to think what may have happened had Jennings not encountered his misfortune."

Raven was confused. Her mind was jumbled with all sorts of incoherent thoughts. "I . . . I still do not understand why we were imprisoned in the stockade."

"When Francesca told us of their plans, she placed her life in grave danger, for her punishment would have surely been death had Dalmas suspected her of the breech."

"So she had to continue her performance even inside the jail for fear Dalmas would realize she was the informant and send word to one of his men to kill her."

"Precisely," agreed Henry. "I don't think we'll have to worry about Dalmas anymore. Or Ames for that matter, for he does not possess the manpower to continue with the original strategy. Just in case, though, both the harbor and the eastern entranceway are heavily guarded."

"What of Francesca? How long must she remain in the stockade?"

Henry smiled. "No doubt she and her girls are already back at home plying their trade as dilligently as before."

"Now that Ames's plans have been foiled by a well-planned trick of nature, what do you think he'll do, Henry?"

"When he realizes that Jennings had encountered some type of trouble and is not able to meet him at their designated meeting spot, no doubt he will retreat as far from Nassau as possible."

"Perhaps he will sail right into Juan's direction," hopefully concluded Raven. "Oh, Henry." She sighed wistfully. "Do you think I shall ever reach Eleuthera? My poor papa does not even suspect that I left England four months ago in search of him. And what of Juan? Suppose he has already heard of the sinking of Captain Jack's boat and thinks me dead. How will he know there's no reason to mourn my death if I am not at Governor's Harbor to greet him when he returns? I wish I knew when I'll finally reach my destination."

"Tomorrow," replied Henry matter-of-factly.

"Oh, I'm sorry Henry. My babbling again. What was that you said?"

"You asked me when you'd get to Eleuthera, and I told you that maybe tomorrow."

"Tomorrow? What do you mean? Are you teasing me again Henry Lightbourne, because if you are, it isn't very funny!"

"Tomorrow, my dear Raven, if the winds are favorable and the skies are clear, I promise you that I'll take you myself to Morgan Taylor's plantation."

"Oh, Henry. Thank you, thank you so very much," she said, on the verge of tears.

"Why thank me?" he scoffed uncomfortably. "My reasons are purely selfish. Since you've proven that you can't be left on your own without attracting the worst possible company, Maria and I have decided that since our consciences will not permit you out of our sights again we must personally escort you to Sir Robert."

## Chapter Nineteen

As the opalescent dawning ripened into golden rayed splendor, the *Island Wanderer* was well on its way, scudding across the sixty miles from Nassau to Eleuthera. The horizon and sea merged together in a singular sapphirine color, making it difficult to distinguish one line from the other. The unveiled sun shimmered on the listless waters, dancing across the glassy smoothness like dazzling brightness upon a multifaceted diamond. Tiny, sea-girdled cays, inhabited only by dense, swampy mangroves, dotted their watery path.

At the onset of the four-hour trip, only the jib of the single-masted sloop was raised in order to allow Henry complete control as he competently steered the boat across the shallow bars and honeycomb coral outlining the eastern shore of New Providence. But now, in open waters, both the jib and the mainsail billowed softly in the wafting breeze.

Henry sat on the cockpit's gunnel, barechested and white trousers rolled up to his knees, whistling tunelessly as he held the tiller. His passengers sat on pallets underneath the shade of a worn canvas that had been extended from the tiny cab at mid-deck. Maria's eyes were closed in contented solitude, her head rested against the wooden frame, and Raven was lazily fanning herself with a letter.

The letter, written in Francesca's elaborate script and on satin-textured, lilac-scented stationery, had been delivered to Lightbourne's shortly past eight the previous evening. In her note, she pleaded with Raven to understand why it had been necessary for her to maintain a cold, almost hostile attitude toward her in Dalmas's presence. She closed by telling Raven that it had indeed been Providence that brought her to her home, for without Raven's strength and conviction, she herself would never have had the courage to betray Ames and do what had to be done in order to prevent blood from flowing freely throughout Nassau's streets.

Along with her letter, Francesca's burly African had brought a straw braided bag into which Raven's half dozen dresses had been placed, along with several outfits she had included as gifts to her friend. On top of the pile was an ivory jewel box carved in the shape of a heart, and in it were her cameo broach, conch pearl pendant, and the six gold sovereigns that had been left behind the night of the militia's raid.

The air was sultry, even the steady breeze that blew from the west could do little to relieve the stickiness of the torrid heat. Raven rose from her seat underneath the canvas and moved between the boxes of lard, tins of tea, coffee and nails, barrels of grain and bully beef that were all secured to the starboard railing. Because Captain Jack's boat had been sunk, Henry decided to carry a sufficient supply of provisions with him in case those at the Taylor Plantation were running low on supplies.

"How much longer will it take, Henry?" asked Raven, seating herself beside him.

"We shall be there directly," he assured her as beads of sweat trickled down his cheeks. "Should have already been there, but the wind died down."

"I know. I think I could blow and do a better job of puffing out the sails."

"Your restlessness won't get us there any sooner. I had better lash those barrels tighter. They're moving around too much. Here you take the tiller while I tend to that."

Raven laughed nervously. "You must be joking, Henry. I have no idea how one goes about maneuvering one of these. Suppose I turn us over."

"You won't do that. Just follow my instructions. See that one lonely cloud forming on the horizon?"

"Well, yes, I think so."

"Just steer toward it. If you find you're getting away from it, pull the tiller toward you to go to the port . . . to the left side. Push it away to go to the right. All right?"

"Pull left, push right," she repeated. "It sounds simple enough. Are you sure you trust me?"

"I will make a sailor out of you yet. It won't take long to tie down the cargo. Hold her steady now. There, that's fine."

Raven adjusted to her task with relative ease. The feel of maneuvering the sloop along its course gave her a confident feeling of control.

Juan would certainly be pleased to know that I have taken an interest in sailing, she decided. Perhaps he will even let me try my newly developed skill aboard the

*Falcon* once he comes for me on Eleuthera, she thought, remembering the morning they stood on the bridge and watched as Nassau came into view.

Had that only been a few weeks ago? It seemed more like a year. Oh, I can almost feel the touch of his lips, she mused.

The noise of the wind flapping the tailing edge of the sail jolted her back to reality.

"Take more wind in the sails!" yelled Henry from mid-deck.

"All right! But how do I do that?"

"Push the tiller away from you. There, that's better. See how easy it was to pull her into the wind," he said, finishing his task and taking control of the tiller. "You did rather well for a novice, first mate Gatewood. Keep up the good work, and I shall see to it that you get your admiral stripes in no time."

"Aye, aye, Sir," she returned with equaled zest. Then in a somber tone asked, "Henry, do you think my father's changed a great deal since I last saw him?"

"Keep in mind, lass, that your father's been a very ill man. He was fortunate that Morgan found him and even luckier to have survived that fever and all the complications. He has undergone tremendous pressures, both physical and mental. There was a period of time when he did not even know who he was or where he came from. And when his memory did gradually return, he had to face the news of his wife's death and a troubled daughter who most likely thought him dead as well. He would probably have recovered so much faster had it not been for that guilt nagging away at him day after day."

"I just hope I will be able to convince him that there

is no reason for such guilt. He certainly could not have helped what happened to him. Had he even suspected that Mother was ill, I know he never would have returned to the Bahamas."

"Just don't expect too much from him, Raven. At least not right away." Henry saw Raven's face tense in troubled thought, and he tried to ease her worry. "Take old Henry Lightbourne for instance," he said, glancing at mid-deck to the snoozing Maria. "Before your friend entered my life, I always had the strangest notion about women, as well you know! Anyway after being cuckold by my wife, I decided that all women were that way, and I wanted nothing to do with any of them."

"And Maria proved your theory wrong, didn't she, Henry?"

"One would never guess she's of royal stock. Never fusses or frets and there's never a cross word spoken between us. She's always so eager to please me. Quite a woman!" he said dreamily.

"Anyway, when we thought you had drowned on Captain Jack's boat, I suddenly realized that one should never take advantage of life, for it can be snatched away when you least expect it." He shrugged his shoulders uncomfortably. "What I guess all of this is leading up to is that I've decided I love that woman, and without her I'd be the most miserable man on the face of this earth. And I mean to take some drastic steps soon to see to it that I don't have to live without her."

"Henry, do you mean you're going to propose to her?" asked Raven, finding it hard to believe what Henry was implying.

"Of course that's what I mean," he replied, trying to

sound like his gruff self. "The, uh, the only problem is, well . . . I'm not so sure she'll have me."

"Even with all of your faults, Henry Lightbourne, you are still the most wonderful man I have ever known," answered Maria without opening her eyes or moving her head from its resting place. "Of course I will marry you. Just allow me a few more moments of this idle repose."

Henry beamed with unconcealed delight. His bulky chest swelled proudly, and he began humming a rollicking sea-going ditty, totally immersed in his own exhilarated thoughts while leaving Raven to her own pensive reverie.

Once again her thoughts were guiltily divided between her father and Juan, wanting so desperately to see the both of them. Ah Papa, what will your reaction be when I tell you that I am in love with a sailor, a sea captain whose blood is mixed with that of England's bitterest rival? Will it matter to you that he is performing a brave, dangerous mission for the Bahamas; will you be able to look beyond his Spanish heritage? Will you forbid me to ever again see the man to whom I have given my love and my complete self?

Oh, why is my heart split in half? Am I selfish to be so completely in love with him when all of my thoughts should be devoted to you? Poor, dear Papa! I am all you have left. Of course, I must be a dutiful daughter, and yet I cannot pretend that I am that same naive child you left four years ago.

Will you understand that I am a woman; a woman whose passions and love have been given to a man without the sanctity of marriage? Please do not force me to choose between the two of you, for such a

328

decision would surely kill me. How I pray that you will understand and not cast me aside once I bare my feelings to you. I know that Juan Perez will come to Eleuthera for me. I am certain he will not desert me.

Ah, Papa, I beg of you, do not abandon me either. I need both of you; love you both equally but in totally different ways. Will you be able to understand that without feeling that I am forsaking you. Am I really so insensitive? How can I think of my own selfish desires when you have had to endure so much?

She closed her eyes to alleviate the tense pain mounting within her head. Henry's booming voice awakened her shortly afterward. "There it is! Segatoo! Eleuthera."

Her eyes strained across the motionless waters to a long, narrow landmass undulating atop the devouring Atlantic. As the sloop steadily plied closer to the distant shoreline, rolling hills of lush, verdant vegetation came into view.

"Ah, at last Henry. How beautiful it all is," she said, taking a closer look with the aid of Henry's spyglass.

"That it is, lassie, a Garden of Eden set right out in the middle of the ocean."

His words caused Raven to wince with painful remembrance, for those were the exact words Captain Mabry had chosen to describe Abaco.

"So many of the islands are barren except for a few low shrubs and twisted vines," continued Henry. "But Eleuthera is indeed a tropical paradise. God's finest exhibit of his craft! The most beautiful of all Bahamian jewels is this island, Raven. Her soil is so rich and fertile that an abundance of plants thrive here. High cliffs that jut out over the water leave you speechless, and the

329

fresh water ponds are so rich a blue you'd swear they had been dyed with indigo. All of her geography is magnificent! That tiny cay just off our starboard side is called Cupid's Cay, the original site of our Eleutheran Adventurers," he informed her as they rounded its point. "You've heard of them, I suppose?"

"Oh, yes," she said eagerly. "Juan—I mean Captain Perez," she blushed, knowing that such a blunder need not be corrected, for Henry had certainly noticed the obvious show of affection between her and his friend, "told me about their settlement. It's a shame that after so much work and hardship they became discouraged and returned to England." She wondered if one of those ruins was the house where her beloved was born. The thought of being so close to a part of his past made her feel warm and peaceful all over.

"And did Captain Perez also tell you that because of these hardworking souls, a university was established in Boston, Massachusetts?" She shook her head, so he continued.

"Captain Sayle was forced to venture to the colonies to plead for enough food and supplies to get his settlers through the winter. He was given all that he needed. To repay such kindness, he sent them a shipload of brazilwood. The people in Boston sold the shipment and with the funds erected Harvard University."

He lowered the mainsail and adeptly steered his sloop into the narrow, sun-splashed area known as Governor's Harbor. He secured the line on one of the pilings that supported the weight of the dock and lifted Raven and Maria onto the crudely built wharf. Recognizing two of the young men idly standing on the dock as being the sons of Ezra Tarlton, Morgan

Taylor's overseer, he instructed the pair to unload the cargo and deliver it to the main house.

"Come along now ladies," he said holding an arm out for each of them. "The house is just a ways up on the beach."

The beach on Eleuthera was unlike any Raven had ever seen. Even Abaco, where the sands were a glittering white, could not compare. The sand of this verdant island was powdery soft and its coloring more of a pale pink. According to Henry, this was the result of many years' accumulation of wave-worn bits and pieces of conch shells and pink coral.

A solitary figure stood farther up on the beach watching the waves as they frantically broke against a partially emerged reef, only to grovel meekly to shore. The loner paced sluggishly up the beach, his hands clasped tightly together behind him and his head lowered in intent contemplation.

"Papa!" she exclaimed, her voice barely above a whisper. Raven felt as though her heart had sunk to the pits of her stomach, her eyes brimmed with tears, and an uneasy nervousness numbed her. She lifted her skirt and tried to run, but her feet would only sink deeper into the powdery surface. Obstinately she plowed on in the direction of the man. How she longed to call out his name, to tell him that he was no longer alone in his suffering, but the words froze in her throat, and she could utter no sounds.

The man turned abruptly, sensing the presence of someone behind him, and viewed his follower with irritation.

The instant he stopped, Raven, too, ceased her awkward gait, and she moved slowly toward him.

The man was stunned by the woman's sudden appearance. As she neared him, he blinked his eyes disbelievingly, calling out, "Elizabeth?"

"No, no Papa," she answered with soft meekness. "It's your daughter. Raven."

"Raven? My daughter?" his words were uncertain. He rubbed his eyes fiercely. "Surely the sun is merely playing a trick on me. My eyes are deceiving me," he assured himself. But when he looked up for the third time, expecting the mirage to have disappeared, he faltered, for the ebony-haired woman remained.

"Yes, Papa. I am here." Her vision was blurred by her streaming tears. As she cleared her eyes and moved even closer, she was shocked at what was revealed to her. The well-proportioned vigorously energetic man she had known was not standing opposite her. Instead, there stood a stranger; a thin, haggard man whose dark hair was streaked with an abundance of gray strands and whose face was drawn and exhausted. This man looked much older than her father's forty years. His aristocratic poise had been replaced with a dull, defeated look of hesitation.

They stood there staring at each other; the father whose age had increased by twenty years instead of four, and the daughter who possessed an uncanny resemblance to her dead mother.

The gaunt figure stepped toward her. He stroked the smoothness of her face and brushed a wisp of her wind-blown hair from her cheek. He touched her face, her nose, the lids of her eyes, half expecting the form to vanish or be hauntingly cold and transparent.

"I am real, Papa, not a vision of your imagination. Truly I am," she pleaded, trying to soothe his worries.

She caressed his skeletal arm. The sallow skin hung loosely from his bones. "I am your daughter, your only child. And I have come from England to care for you." Still, he issued no response, and Raven turned pleadingly to Henry. "Please, you tell him."

"Raven! My baby!" said her father, gathering her quaking body in his arms and drawing her into his thin chest.

His jabbing bones protruded against his daughter, and the tears that flowed freely from Raven's eyes were shed at finding her father in such a deplorable condition.

"You must forgive my shock, Raven dearest, but for one brief moment, I thought you were Lizzy coming back to reprimand me for abandoning the both of you," he apologized tearfully when they finally separated. "The likeness you have to your mother is rather eerie."

"I know, Father." She sniffed, trying to smile and erase his fears.

"Henry!" Sir Robert greeted the doctor, trying to make his voice sound healthy and robust. "It is good to see you, again." Turning to Raven, he said, "Had it not been for the good doctor here and my friend Morgan, I would not be standing here now." A look of confusion crossed his face. "But how did you meet Henry? How did you get to New Providence? I don't understand."

"All in good time, Robert. You and your daughter have plenty of time for discussion later on. Now, let's get out of this sun," suggested Henry, clasping Sir Robert's outstretched hand. It was clammy and lacked the strength to return Henry's grip. "I could do quite well with a shady spot and something nice and cold to drink," he remarked, sensing that Sir Robert was overly fatigued and needed a rest.

He quickly introduced Maria to his waning patient, and the four of them trudged up the beach to the main house, with Raven and Henry supporting most of Sir Robert's slight weight.

The Taylor home was constructed from sun-mellowed lumber and was set back from the beach on a verdured hill shaded from the intense heat by palms and casuarinas. Weather-worn louvre doors led out onto broad, lofty verandas on both floors, and on sultry nights all of them would be opened to permit cooling ocean breezes entrance into the spacious rooms. Flowering bushes of bouganvillea and hibiscus lined either side of the stone walkway.

The four of them sat on the veranda; Henry and Maria in a wooden swing suspended from the ceiling, and Raven and her father in chairs made from sturdy bamboo. Sir Robert reached up beside the door and rang a brass ship's bell. Almost immediately, a woman whose skin was the dark, rich coloring of chocolate waddled out onto the porch, her flabby flesh rippling beneath a tight-fitting dress of red batik. Coarse, frizzy hair was kept away from her sweat dampened forehead by a bandanna of the same color and print. Her round face was a friendly one, and her cheeks puffed to the size of apples when she flashed her pearly, square-toothed smile at her guests.

"Why, Missuh Henry. Ah's didn't know you's s a'comin' to visit us." Her jowls jiggled as she spoke.

"Mama Bella. It's always good to see you," greeted Henry heartily as he clasped her pudgy hand in his and introduced Maria as his future wife.

334

The Negro housekeeper covered his back with congratulatory pats. Then she turned to Sir Robert. "You don' haf'ta tell me who dis chile is." Then with mock anger, she questioned him, "Wha's da matta'? You don' like how Mammy Bella's nursin' you?"

Sir Robert tried to appease her. "You've done an outstanding job, Bella. It certainly isn't your fault I haven't any meat on these bones. You've been trying to fatten me up ever since I arrived.

"Dat's right, suh. Not 'nough ah cooks big meals fer you. No suh! Looks like ah'm gonna haf' to start pushin' it in your mouf."

"Please, Bella. I am quite certain our guests must be famished from this heat and would prefer a tall, cold citronade to your mindless chatter."

The sharp words brought a sudden halt to their jesting merriment. Bella glared defiantly at the scowling young woman standing in the entranceway, then lumbered lackadaisically into the house.

"Dr. Lightbourne, how very nice to see you. I had no idea Morgan was expecting you." Her voice was in the tone of demure sweetness.

Melinda Nelson had been described by many of her suitors as a celestial goddess, but after having become better acquainted with her they decided that her angelic features did not match her moody temperament.

Raven, however, was quite taken with her beauty, for the two of them were striking contrasts. Melinda's honey-colored hair fell in loose ringlets around her shoulders. Her eyes were a hazy, smoky blue. Her face reminded Raven of the austere white portrait on her cameo broach, for the pale colorings were very much alike.

"I did not know I was coming myself until yesterday," he replied curtly, almost rudely.

"We have not been introduced," remarked Melinda, turning to Raven and deliberately snubbing Maria.

"This is my daughter, Raven," said Sir Robert. Then turning to his daughter he told her that Melinda was Governor Rogers's niece.

"I'm very pleased to meet you. I had the occasion to speak with your uncle several times while I was in Nassau. He's a very fine man. You must be terribly proud of him."

"So, will you be staying here for long?"

"Only until Father is able to make the voyage back home."

"Well, isn't that just grand? What I mean of course is that it will be wonderful having another girl around for a while. I have been here only a few days, and already I am so bored!" Inside she was seething with a jealous rage for she already viewed Raven as her rival for Morgan's affections.

Melinda had met the wealthy Taylor at her uncle's home shortly after her arrival from London. Her mother had written to sister Sarah asking her to please allow her daughter to visit their tropical home for a short while. Sunshine and relaxation were what her poor darling needed to help her recover from a broken engagement. That good-for-nothing son of Admiral Marlton had jilted her only two weeks before their wedding date, but not for another woman as Melinda so maliciously led every one to believe, but because William had learned that his intended had already bestowed her sexual favors on several of the other young men in his company.

Perhaps if Melinda could visit with relatives for a while, they had decided, the vicious tongues would cease their wagging, and her scandalous behavior would be forgotten. She could return to London in time for the next season's flurry of activity. Maybe then Melinda could become betrothed, perhaps to an older man, a widower would be even better; a man of comparable status and substantial wealth.

Melinda immediately had other intentions the moment she laid her eyes on Morgan Taylor that afternoon in her uncle's library. A more handsome man she had never seen. And the discovery that he had accumulated vast acreage throughout the Caribbean and considerable wealth as well served to enhance his appeal.

How those gossipy old hags would gloat if I were to return home married to such a man, she thought. It mattered little to her that he only paid her the politest attentions, for she reasoned that he could do little else with her uncle seated in the same room.

Several weeks later, her aunt had give a party in Melinda's honor, and she managed to stay by Morgan's side most of the evening. She coerced him into escorting her out onto the veranda, telling him that if she did not get some fresh air soon, she would collapse from the stuffiness of the smoke-filled room.

Being a gentleman, he had politely obliged her, and once on the porch and out of anyone's view, she had flung her arms around his neck and pressed herself tight against him. She was convinced he would have kissed her, she had after all felt a hardening against her thigh, had it not been for that obese Mrs. Livingston stumbling out onto the porch noisily complaining of an attack of the vapors.

The week after the party Melinda had innocently inquired of her uncle where Mr. Taylor had been keeping himself. Uncle Woodes had explained that Taylor was a very busy man who traveled extensively in search of land suitable for the production of sea cotton. To her chagrin, he told her that sometimes Taylor was gone for as much as six months before returning to Nassau.

When the governor had recieved warning of the impending pirate attack, he had urged that Sarah take Melinda and go to Eleuthera and stay at the Taylor plantation until the Jennings-Ames threat was squelched. Sarah refused to leave, not necessarily due to any allegiance to Woodes or concern for his well-being, but because she had no intention of risking her home and possessions to those loathsome pillagers. She did insist that Melinda be taken there immediately, and her niece was overjoyed at the prospect of being unchaperoned in Mr. Taylor's company.

To her disappointment, Taylor was not on the island. Instead, she found Mama Bella and Sir Robert, both of whom she anticipated as being formidable obstacles in her plan to snare the unsuspecting plantation owner in her matrimonial trap. But now, with the ill-timed arrival of Gatewood's daughter, she feared her well-plotted scheme would prove even more difficult.

No doubt Sir Robert recognized the potential of having Taylor as a son-in-law and would do all he could to initiate such a romance. But that can be dealt with later, decided Melinda. Morgan Taylor impresses me as being a man who would prefer the company of an older, more mature woman. I am nearly twenty-two, and I doubt Miss Gatewood having celebrated her twentieth birthday yet.

"That servant is undoubtedly the most trifling creature I have ever had to deal with," remarked Melinda indignantly. She turned to the guests and flashed a gracious smile. "I do apologize for such insolence. I know you must be famished. This weather is so dreadfully hot, so if you will excuse me. No, no, gentlemen, do not bother to rise. If you will all excuse me, I shall go and see why your refreshments have not yet been served."

That damnable Mama Bella, she cursed, storming in past the sitting room and into the cooking room. Once I am the mistress here, I will send that impudent black bitch back to Africa where she belongs!

Returning shortly afterward with an exasperated frown on her face and carrying a silver tray that held five crystal glasses, a pitcher of citronade, and a plate of petit fours, she awkwardly explained that since Mama Bella was feeling a bit faint, she had offered to serve the guests in her place.

"Do tell me, Dr. Lightbourne. How are my dear relatives?" she implored, handing him a glass full of the sweetened refreshment. "It was so difficult for me to leave without them, but they insisted I would be much safer here. I miss Aunt Sarah dreadfully. We had become so very close."

How I detest that fat idiot, thought Melinda while trying to maintain her gracious hostess charm, but I suppose I have no other choice than to resign myself to his abhorrent presence until Morgan and I are married and I can convince my husband to return to civilization with me.

Henry sighed boorishly. How he loathed making pleasant conversation while he ate, especially with such a pampered female. Still, she is Woodes's niece, and for no other reason I must at least be affable, he decided.

"Both your aunt and uncle are well. I regret to say that I left so hastily this morning I did not have a chance to see if they wished to send you a message." His eyes twinkled devilishly. "Since there is no longer any concern for your safety in Nassau because Ames and Jennings's plan was foiled, I am certain you are most eager to return there to your relatives. You are more than welcome to join Señora Valdez and me on our return trip."

To his hidden delight, she fidgited uncomfortably and said that had she not promised her aunt she would stay on Eleuthera until Uncle Woodes came and personally escorted her home, she would be all too willing to escape the loneliness of the island.

Henry unquestioningly accepted her excuse, even though he suspected that her motive for remaining on Eleuthera was quite different. He had observed, unnoticed of course, the way she had brazenly sidled up next to Morgan at the party that evening and how she had cajoled him into taking her outside.

Even now he had to strain to keep from laughing at the startled look of sheer contempt on Melinda's face after he had convinced a slightly tipsy Sylvia Livingston that all the smoke in the parlor would irritate her condition and bring on another coughing attack if she

340

did not seek fresh air immediately. He had watched the amusing scene from behind the curtain of the front window and was almost certain that Melinda had heard him choke with laughter as Sylvia interrupted her little tête-à-tête. Even now, he chuckled to himself.

*What I wouldn't give to see the look on Morgan's face when he returns to find that he has two lovely ladies in his household.*

"I . . . I am sorry, dear," he apologized. "I'm afraid that I was so engrossed in this delicious tea cake that I did not hear your last question. Would you mind terribly repeating it?"

Melinda was clearly flustered, but she tried to regain her composure. "I was simply asking, Henry, if you had the opportunity to see Mr. Taylor." She tried to sound only politely interested.

Henry finished his petit four and reached for a sixth. "The last time I saw Morgan was quite a while back. He was in remarkably good health and spirits, though. What a life! Always galavanting off to Jamaica or Barbados on those trips of his."

"I have not seen Morgan since mid-January," remarked Sir Robert. "We were in Nassau, shortly before I came here. It was then when I asked that he write to you, Raven. I feared so much that my little girl would despise her papa for abandoning her."

"Don't be silly, Father. Despise you? Of course not! What a ridiculous thought indeed! I knew there had to be a good reason you had not contacted me!" She put his bony hand to her face. "And now that I am here to care for you, we shall have a marvelous opportunity to make up for those four years."

341

Melinda found the poignant family reunion unbear
ably dull. Satisfied that Lightbourne could give her no
further news about Morgan, and since there was no
other reason to subject herself to such trivia, she left on
the pretense of checking on Mama Bella.

"I would wager that that spoiled snipe has finally met
her match with Mama Bella," noted Henry in sudden
good spirits. "She's been in charge of this plantation
and of Morgan, for as long as I can remember, and I
doubt her willingness to relinquish her position to such
an indulgent young woman."

"I certainly hope Bella is able to protect Morgan
from that young lady," remarked Sir Robert. "She has
hinted on several occasions that they are soon to
become engaged."

"I wonder if Morgan is aware of his upcoming
nuptials?" asked Henry sarcastically.

"That Miss Nelson would do well to keep her
distance from that old Negress. It would not be wise to
oppose that woman," observed Maria.

"Whatever do you mean, Maria?" questioned Raven.
"Why, Mama Bella seems extremely kind."

"There was an African Negress who worked in the
household of one of Hernando's advisors. This advisor
was a very irrational man who beat her for leaving a
fingerprint on a wine goblet. Within the next week,
both his wife and son had died of a fever that was
unknown to any of our physicians."

"And the African was held responsible?" asked
Raven.

Maria nodded. "Yes, but everyone was so frightened
of her powers no one would dare accuse her for fear

342

they would be her next victim. Those people have strange religious rites. Obeah is the name of their belief. They can invoke dead spirits and cause evil to befall their enemies. They have control over the dead and can even make them do their evil bidding for them."

"I am sure that what you say is accurate," commented Sir Robert, not wanting to offend the Spanish woman, "but what makes you think Bella practices this obeah. The idea of that sweet, old woman causing any danger to anyone is a bit farfetched."

"The coiled band of gold she is wearing around her neck is identical to the amulet worn by the slave in Hispanole to ward off evil."

"The true symbol of a mambo," remarked Henry knowingly.

"What is a mambo?" asked Raven.

"The high priestess of a tribe. Maria is right, Mama Bella is a mambo. It is a position of honor, which she is no doubt proud of, for all the people in her village look to her as their spiritual leader. Do not misunderstand me. She is by no means dangerous, although I would much rather have her as my friend than foe."

He walked over to the edge of the porch and gazed up into the sky. "It's nearly four o'clock. We should be leaving, Maria."

"Must you leave so soon?" pleaded Raven.

"Do spend the night, Henry," encouraged Sir Robert. "Why it's mad to start out for Nassau this time of evening."

Henry returned to the swing and squeezed Maria's shoulder with obvious affection, and she gazed up at him with unhidden adoration. "We have no intention

343

of returning home tonight," he said. He enjoyed their puzzled looks, then after a moment, explained. "I have a friend up at Hatchet Bay that I'd like to visit with. And it just so happens that he's a minister, and since Maria's consented to marry me, I had best get her to a preacher before she's had a chance to change her mind. And then I thought we would stay there for a couple of days before going home. Maybe do a little fishing, some diving and even go spelunking. Maria would enjoy that."

"Spelunking? I have never heard of such a word. How can you expect me to do that on my honeymoon, Henry Lightbourne, when I don't even know what it means?" demanded Maria with mock sternness.

"Exploring caves," answered Henry. "Oh, it's great fun. You will enjoy looking for buried treasures of pirates and ancient Indian artifacts."

"You will stop here on your way back to Nassau," Sir Robert said, his tone more a command than a question.

"That we will, Robert," promised Henry. "Expect us early Sunday morning. And make sure Mama Bella knows I'm coming so she can boil some fish and bake me a lot of her johnny cakes."

"Good-bye!" called out Raven. "Congratulations! Have a wonderful time!" As soon as they were out of her sight, she returned to her father. "They have been so good to me, Papa. Better friends could not be found anywhere."

He reached for her hand and patted it. Then he motioned for her to sit down. "I am glad that you had the good fortune to find friends like them when you arrived in Nassau. Four years," he said softly, shaking his head in sorrowful disbelief. "Four years. What a

344

long time for a daughter to be without a Mama and a Papa. The one thing that comforted me all that while was knowing that George and Mattie would take good care of you. They had been with us long before you were born. I cannot believe they would allow you to leave home and undertake such a dangerous task!"

## Chapter Twenty

She did not wish to upset her father, but Raven knew that he must be made aware that the fate of his beloved estate lay not with his faithful servants but with his hateful sister-in-law and her squandering mate. She proceeded with caution. "Papa, there are some things that I feel I must make known to you, but I do not wish to do so at the risk of endangering your health."

Sir Robert interrupted. "I do not wish to be treated like a weakling, Raven. No doubt there are things I must be made aware of, and I insist that you do so."

"All right, Papa. Right after Mama died," she gently began, then taking a deep breath continued, "the magistrate was emphatic that I should not live at Ravenwood without the supervision of parents or kin. Since you were away, he . . . he notified Aunt Martha and suggested that she and her husband take charge until—"

Sir Robert exploded, not giving her a chance to finish. "Of all the fool things for that cursed Mr. Bently to do!"

"Now calm down, Papa. You know such outbursts are of no good whatsoever to your condition."

"How long did they stay?"

Raven hesitated. "Well, father, as I said they moved in upon Mr. Bently's notification, and . . . and they've been there ever since."

"They've what?" he shouted. "Oh, good God!"

"That's right, Papa. They're still there. Martha took command as though she were the mistress of the house."

"Why, that's preposterous!" he ranted. "I will post a letter to Mr. Bently this very afternoon informing him that I want that insidious pair evicted from my property immediately."

"Please, Papa," scolded Raven. "If you persist in such a tirade we can most certainly not continue with our discussion."

"Oh, all right!" he huffed defeatedly. "But I do intend to do something about them. How did she and her pompous husband treat you?"

"They kept their distance, as I did mine."

Sir Robert lowered his head sadly. "It galls me to think that they have been living in my home. Martha never kept secret her hatred for Lizzie, and now that insufferable shrew has her paws all over her finery. It just makes me furious that for the time being I am helpless to do anything about that situation."

"Oh, cheer up, Father. I have been just as worried, but after careful consideration I realized that John and Martha will still be there when we return. I'm sure they think me dead by now and you too weak to even care. Without your authorization, they will never be able to collect any of your funds. If you send word to Mr. Bently to prosecute them for trespassing, I fear the house will be stripped of all but its walls when we do return home."

"Yes, yes of course you're right, dear daughter. We shall just have to wait until we arrive home to take care of them. Now I insist you tell me whatever prompted you to make such a perilous sea voyage to the Bahamas."

"After I received Mr. Taylor's letter, I began worrying that your health may again fail you before you had recuperated sufficiently enough to make the trip home. I . . . I was so afraid that you would die here, all alone, and I would never see you again."

"No doubt your concerned aunt and uncle did all they could to encourage such an attitude," he remarked with caustic bitterness.

"But it was I who made the final decision to come here," admitted Raven.

"But you had no idea where to find me. You had never before been away from home. My, my, how cosmopolitan my little girl has become."

"I did not know exactly where to find you, but Mr. Taylor did say that you were being treated by a Dr. Lightbourne in Nassau. And I knew that if I could find him, he could direct me to you."

"I commend you for such foresight. Now, tell me, how did you like your first sailing experience? I remember my first voyage. I spent most of my time heaving over the railings."

"I was fine until the land disappeared from sight, then I got a bit woozy. Captain Mabry assured me that I would have my sea legs in no time, and that made me feel a little better. And, oh, Papa, I met some of the most wonderful people on board—a girl named Lucy and her brother Ross who were going to Charleston so

348

he could practice medicine, and—"

Raven tried to hide her sorrow by making her words appear light and cheerful. No sense in worrying Papa any more tonight, the shock of finding out that John and Martha are living in his home was enough of a surprise for one evening.

"And a botanist named Mr. Phillips who knew of your studies of the Lucayan culture, and umm, let me see, who else? Oh yes, one of the king's advisors, Mr. Baxter, who boasted of being a connoisseur of fine wines and rich foods. He looked it, too, Papa, for he was so heavy he could barely fit—"

"Horatio Mabry?" interrupted Sir Robert.

"What Papa?"

"Horatio Mabry?" he repeated. "Did you say he was the captain of your ship?"

"Why yes, Papa. The *Fancy Free* was the name of the vessel."

"Surely you must be mistaken Raven. That ship left Plymouth last March. To my knowledge she never reached New Providence. From what I've been told, there's been quite a bit of speculation as to what happened to her. Most say she was probably swallowed up by the sea. Strange things do happen in these waters."

Try as hard as she could, Raven could not erase from her mind the waxen, bloated images afloat in a sea of blood. "No, Papa, the sea was not at fault for what happened," she said ominously.

Sir Robert was speechless. His drawn face became even paler than the unhealthy white pallor his illness caused. He looked at her in stunned amazement. "You were not mistaken about the captain's name, were you?

You were a passenger aboard Mabry's vessel?"

"Yes, Papa. We had had a fairly smooth voyage from Plymouth until a storm blew us quite a way off course. When it subsided, Captain Mabry said we were on Abaco and would have to stay there for a few days to make some necessary repairs. Before we were able to get underway, our ship was seized by a group of pirates led by Red Ames."

Sir Robert could not believe his ears. "Pirates? Red Ames?"

"I did not mean to upset you so again, Papa. Please forgive me," she said softly, resting her head on his shoulder.

"I had considered letting you assume I had arrived from England only last week, but I—"

"No, no. I would have been even more angry had you kept that from me. Were . . . were you the only survivor?" he ventured, stroking her curls.

"No, my friend Lucy was spared as well. The two of us were taken to Gorda Cay, Ames's hide-out. She died of a fever there." Raven decided there was no point in recounting the horrible details of Lucy's death for her father would only conclude that she had been ravaged as well. "It was while I was there that I met Maria. She had been a prisoner there for eight years."

"How long were you there, Raven?"

"Three months," she answered, then hurried to rid his dismal fears. "But Ames and his men were away the entire time. He left shortly after Lucy and I were delivered there."

"Thank God for that," he said, letting out a heavy sigh. "At least you were not . . . were not forced to . . . to—" he groped for the proper words to complete his thought.

"No, Papa. Rest assured that I was not harmed in any manner," she quickly assured him. "It was our good fortune that a ship sent by the governor to capture Red Ames found us, and its captain, Juan Perez, took us to Nassau and entrusted us to Henry." Just the casual mention of his name made Raven's heart flutter, and she hoped her father had not noticed the slight quiver of her voice.

"I have heard of this Captain Perez. The Bahamas will forever be indebted to him. So shall I for that matter. Had he not rescued you— no, I can't even bear the thought of it!"

Raven was pleased that her father felt gratitude concerning the efforts of her gallant lover, but she could not help but wonder why he had not recognized the name as belonging to Mr. Taylor's ship's captain. Surely he had the occasion to meet Juan.

He eyed his daughter suspiciously. "I fear there is more that you are keeping from me. Otherwise you would have been brought here several weeks ago. What caused your delay in Nassau?"

"Transportation to Eleuthera was arranged by Captain Perez aboard a provisions ship that makes, which did make, weekly trips here. I was to stay at Henry's until the following Sunday when Captain Jack sailed. I was on my way to the wharf that morning when Ames's lieutenant, a man named Dalmas, kidnapped me. You see, he had been sent to Nassau to find me."

"Merciful Jesus! Is there no end to this?"

"It does appear that I am leading a cursed existence," she agreed dismally, then resumed her story, telling her father of the friendship that developed between her and Madame DuVall and of the French woman's courageous effort to thwart the success of Ames and Jennings's raid by divulging their scheme to the governor.

"But all worked out well, Papa. There is certainly no reason for you to worry yourself with my misfortunes. I am here with you now, that is all that matters," she said, reaching up to kiss his hollowed cheek. "Do not be angry with me for leaving England, but I needed to let you know that I was close beside you and would nurse you back to health."

"You are a good daughter, Raven. Thank God you were not injured or killed in search of me. I could never have forgiven myself for that. Now tell me, how is my good friend Woodes? Was he able to successfully combat the pirates' invasion?"

"All considered, I suppose everything worked out quite well for the governor, probably even better than he thought. Luckily, Jennings's ship was caught in a waterspout, and Ames was forced to retreat out to sea. Lieutenant Dalmas was hanged, and the governor discovered that one of his council members, Wingate Gale, had been responsible for supplying Ames with valuable information."

"At least you are here with me, Raven. Safe from any more danger." He shook his finger sternly at her. "Mind you, I am not condoning that fool idea of yours to try and find me," his face lit up in a smile, "but now that you are here, I am thankful that you loved me enough to make the voyage."

"We are both very fortunate, Papa; I, for having finally reached you, and you for having been found by

Mr. Taylor. We truly do have so much for which we should be grateful."

"I am most anxious for you to meet Mr. Taylor, Raven. I am certain you will think as highly of him as I." He gave his daughter a sly wink. "And as a matter of fact, he's a bachelor."

"Oh, Papa!" She blushed. "No one seems to know very much about your friend, do they?"

"Morgan cherishes his privacy. I think he enjoys having that air of mystery surrounding him. He's a very private individual. Why, I couldn't even begin to estimate how much he is worth. All I know is that he is a gentleman, in the truest sense of the word. Quite a Good Samaritan!"

"I take it you've seen very little of your host since he rescued you."

"Very little indeed. I saw more of him in Nassau. He would visit there quite frequently and the four of us— Henry, Morgan, the governor and I—would meet most evenings after supper for conversation and brandy. And then, when my health began to improve, he brought me here to recuperate in these lovely surroundings."

How odd, thought Raven, that neither Henry nor the governor had much to say about their friend, Mr. Taylor.

"Mmm, strange indeed," she mumbled.

"What was that you said, Raven?"

"Only that it is strange that Mr. Taylor would be away so frequently. It seems he would want to spend more time here caring for his plantation."

"He has a fine overseer, Ezra Tarlton, who supervises the plantation as though it were his own, and of course there's Bella who runs the household for him. I suspect Morgan of being somewhat of a loner, perhaps even a bit eccentric. A bit like myself in my younger days. How I loved to travel, to explore new cultures, and discover things never before known by man. It was only when it was too late that I realized the necessity of having a stable home life. You and your mother never complained, but I remembered how overjoyed she had been with the prospect of my putting an end to my travels. I will never forgive myself for waiting so long to retire from that sort of life. Perhaps had I done so earlier, your mother would be alive today."

"Hush, Papa. There is no point in torturing yourself. You know as well as I that your presence at Ravenwood would not have prolonged mother's life."

"I intend to make amends with you, dearest daughter. Never again will I allow anything to separate us," he vowed. "I will make up for all those hours of suffering and loneliness you have had to endure. You will be just as pampered and spoiled as our Miss Nelson."

"And then I couldn't stand myself, and neither could you! There are no amends to be made, Papa. We are together, and that is what's important." How can I tell Papa now of my love for Juan Perez, and that we wish to marry? To think his daughter intends to desert him so soon after she has been reunited with him would undoubtedly cause too much sorrow for a man of his condition. Why do I even think of marrying Juan? Papa would never consent to it. If he did overlook Juan's heritage, he would surely oppose my living here. I could certainly not expect Juan to return to England with us. It would be most unfair of me to even suggest

354

such a thing to him and to much to hope that he would consider leaving his land of crystal-clear water and white-sanded beaches.

Mama Bella served their supper on the veranda that night. She had prepared a platter of bits of seafood delicacies: cracked conch, crawfish, and grouper morsels along with peas and rice, an avocado salad and guava duff even finer than Henry's.

"Will Miss Nelson not be joining us?" inquired Raven.

"Lawd no, child. She wans to eat in dat big dinin' hall, right thar in Massah Morgan's place. Sed she doan' wanna loose dat del'cate skin o' hern ta skitters. No Miz Rav'n. You makes sho' yo' daddy gits in dat bed right aftah he eats. What wid all dis 'citment, he plum fergots ta takes his nap. When you gets ready fo' bed, ah'll haf my gal Ullah draw you a nice, hot bath."

"Thank you, Mama Bella. I will see to it that Father retires right after he finishes this delicious meal. Good night!" She gazed out over the trees. "The sunset, Papa," she marveled. "Such spectacular scenery is rather awesome, isn't it?"

Both of them were mesmerized by the golden splendor out beyond the beach. The sands rolled out from the woods like an amber carpet. The soaring coco palms were regally erect, and the waters, reflecting the same saffron color of the sinking sun, were motionless as well.

"In all my time here," remarked her father, "I have yet to see two sunsets that are alike. While none are as beautiful as this, there exists a certain uniqueness about each one."

"Will you be sad when the time comes for us to

return to England?" she asked softly.

"The life here is truly idyllic, Raven. While part of me longs to remain in this paradise forever, I realize I have important obligations at home that have already been neglected too long. Perhaps one day we shall return here, if only for a holiday. Eleuthera is by far my favorite island of them all. While the setting is definitely tropical, there are things about it that remind me of Scotland; tranquil lakes and serene woodlands. Yes, I will miss it here."

"So will I," she mused aloud. "I have been here for such a short time, and yet I feel as though I belong, almost as though I have become a part of these islands myself. Come now, Papa, it is getting late, and I do not want Mama Bella putting a curse on me for disobeying her orders," she joked, helping her father from his chair.

Several wall lanterns shed an inviting light on the bleached pine interior of the house. What Raven was able to see of the downstairs reflected a surprisingly simple, but definitely masculine, taste. A large room, which she assumed served as both a sitting room and a library, had both a tropical and nautical atmosphere. A sofa and several fan-backed chairs made of bamboo cane and padded with fluffy cushions of bright blues, yellows, and greens sat on one side. A square, sisal mat covered the center of the lustrous floor. A large writing desk was situated in the corner and cabinets carved from that same sturdy Madeira wood held at least a hundred, leather-bound volumes with English, French, and Spanish titles. Displayed in smaller cases were smoothly polished, finely shaped ax heads, spear heads, and white clay pottery pieces, all artifacts

356

belonging to the Arawak, Taino, and Carib Indians who were once the only inhabitants of the island.

On an oak sea chest, its top closed and latched with a shiny brass lock, rested an ivory chess set and a brass sextant. The walls of the spacious room were covered with etched drawings of various British sailing vessels, hull models of ships, and charts of England as well as islands of the Atlantic and Caribbean. Raven noticed that several seascapes on the wall were similar to the ones that hung at Henry's home, and she wondered if they possessed the same "HL" signature.

Raven and her father ascended the steep staircase cautiously, her father relying for support on both her and the lignum vitae cane Mama Bella's son Jacob had carved for him. Raven kissed him good night and opened the door to the room Mama Bella had designated as hers.

A perfumy scent wafted through the room. The source of the sweet, aromatic scent was a piece of bark, that when burned, created a flowery incense. Her pale blue chemise had already been laid out for her, and her dresses hung on quilted hangers. The brass four-poster was shrouded by a pavilion, a tentlike netting made from thinnest gauze, and was suspended from the ceiling in order to protect the person sleeping from annoying insects. The oval, copper tub had already been filled with hot water and soothing, fragrant powders. A movement from beside the dressing screen frightened her the moment she was getting ready to step into the alluring water.

"Ah be Ullah, ma'am. Ma mammy toles me ah's ta he'p you git ready fo' bed." Her skin was the same smooth chocolate color as Mama Bella's, and her brown eyes were just as full. The only contrast between mother and daughter was that no fat hung from Ullah's tiny bones. She moved across the room toward her mistress with that same graceful ease as Mama Bella.

"Ah don puts dem purty dresses in de closet fo' yo'. Dey shore be purty dresses," she said longingly, her voice caressing each syllable.

"Thank you very much, Ullah. You may go now. I think I'll be able to manage myself." Raven draped her dress over the top of the scallop-topped screen.

"Ahs'll warsh dis up real nice fo' you, ma'am," offered Ullah, anxious to please, for Raven's words were kind and gentle, not mean and sharp like the other woman's. Just that morning, Miss Nelson threatened to box her ears if she ever caught her winding the key to her music box again.

"Thank you very much, Ullah. If I need anything else I will be sure to ring for you," she said, dismissing the gawking girl.

How uncomfortable it makes me feel having someone so young assigned to wait on me. She remembered Mattie brushing her tangled hair, bathing and dressing her and singing her songs when she woke up frightened in the middle of the night, but Mattie was like a second mother to her, not a complete stranger.

When Raven stepped out of the refreshing warmth of her jasmine scented bath almost an hour later, Ullah appeared unnoticed and thrust a large, thick towel into her hand. "Mammy toles me nots ta leave till ah's sho' you's tucked in bed."

Raven slipped the chemise over her head, braided her damp hair in a single plait and hopped into bed.

Ullah fluffed her pillow, then pulled the coverings up

around Raven's chin. Then she opened the shuttered doors and propped a heavy piece of coral in front. She blew out the candle and, satisfied that her charge was comfortable, tiptoed out of the room. Within moments, the genial southerly breeze, combined with the sound of the ocean as it caressed the beach, lulled Raven to sleep.

No sooner had Raven stirred from her repose than Ullah appeared, carrying a tray containing a pot of herbal chamomile tea, a papaya half, a basket of hot bread and a dish of orange marmalade. After indulging herself in a leisurely breakfast in bed, Raven decided to wear a white muslin skirt and puff-sleeved blouse that had been embroidered with flowers of all colors and shapes. She flipped her braid on top of her head and fastened it with a tortoise shell comb, then raced down the creaking stairs to bid her father good morning.

"Ah, my dear. I cannot tell you how good it feels to have my daughter begin my day with a kiss."

"How do you feel this morning, Papa?" she asked.

The morning light revealed much too clearly the roundness of his shoulders and the tired lines surrounding his eyes.

"Hale and hearty. Almost as spry as I used to be." He chuckled, running his hand through his hair. Four years ago, his hair had lain in shiny black waves, but now it was dull and straight and was covered with far more gray than black. "Shall I have Bella prepare a tray for you?"

"No, thanks. Ullah served me in my room earlier."

"Good. Then you're ready to accompany me on my morning stroll through the gardens!"

"Do you think you're up to such activity. You were a

bit peaked last night."

"Don't be silly. A little walk is just what these rusty bones need to get them back into action." He tucked his arm into hers.

The garden stretched out before them in lush splendor. It was enclosed by thick stone walls that were bordered by an impenetrable hedge of bayonet grass, a plant Raven noticed was surprisingly similar to the aloe except its leaves were sharper and thicker and pointed up.

Whiffs of orange blossom drifted through the air, as did the honeyed fragrances yielded by the arovia and mignonette trees. Tamarind, almond, pomegranate, limes, and citrons enhanced the garden's verdancy and shaded the low-hanging flowering foliage of the colorfully arrayed bushes and plants.

"Oh, Papa. Listen. Why it's like music tinkling in the wind."

"Nature's own orchestra," he replied. "Bella calls that her own singing tree."

"A tree that actually sings? Come now Papa, don't tease me."

"Seriously. Do you see the large one over there in the corner, the one that's spread out like an umbrella? After it has flowered, the leaves all drop off and it's covered with those pods like you see on it now. Notice how the pods rustle against each other. That's what produces that musical sound. Come, let's venture on into the cotton fields."

During the one-mile walk from the house to the fields, Sir Robert never faltered, for he felt a surge of renewed strength at having his daughter with him. He brushed aside all of her insistences that they pause to rest.

"Don't fuss over me so. If you want me well," he scolded jokingly, "then humor my little wishes."

They came to a native village of a dozen thatched, frond-roofed huts and paused to watch the activity there. Naked, round-bellied children each took their turns throwing four shell chips onto the ground. One side was white, the other blue. Sir Robert explained that the name of the game was *mayamba,* and that the object was to roll an even numbered color combination. An older girl had been left to tend to the youngsters and to keep the fire burning underneath the iron caldron filled with the evening's supper, while the women of the village hoed the individual garden plot of vegetables located behind each hut.

On past the village was the native cemetery. The graves had been marked with stones or large shells. Bowls of food had been placed on each mound. Sir Robert explained the Africans belief that when a person dies, only his body is buried for his soul still wanders about. If the Negroes wanted the souls of their departed to be content, they had to provide the spirits with food. Otherwise, they would come into the village and cause some tremendous misfortune to their negligent kin.

A little way past the cemetery was the cotton field. As they neared the long rows of cotton, a low, monosyllabic chant was heard. There were at least twenty-five black males who were rhythmically chopping the puffy balls of sea cotton from the tall, gnarled vines. Soiled loincloths covered their midsections, and their lean, angular bodies glistened with sweat. The overseer, Ezra Tarlton, worked alongside them.

"Ezra's a good man," remarked Raven's father. "Morgan is certainly lucky to have him. He doesn't expect the darkies to do anything he himself won't do. It's a shame those good-for-nothing sons of his are off somewhere else when there's so much work to be done."

"Are all of those Negroes Mr. Taylor's slaves?" asked Raven, her disapproval obvious in her tone. She had heard tales of how these humble blacks would be herded up like animals far away from their homes in the jungles of Africa and sold to slave buyers on the coast. The name of the island meant "freedom," and yet it was ironic that the slaves should be subjected to forced labor.

"I had envisioned Mr. Taylor as being a bit different from this. A Good Samaritan? Why he's no better than the men who capture these poor people. I have read of those pitiful creatures dying in resistance. Others die during that long sea voyage when their cruel captors cram dozens into a space barely large enough for five grown men and toss them an occasional bread crust to keep them alive. Just disgusting!"

Sir Robert laughed at his daughter's display of temper. "I certainly do not condone slave labor either Raven, but I feel that you have jumped to the wrong conclusions about Morgan. He pays his workers a decent salary, and they are free to come and go as they choose without the fear of being tied to a tree and lashed with a whip. You see, these people's ancestors were brought in chains from Africa and forced to do this sort of work, but most of the plantations were in Bermuda. The blacks there rebelled against their tyrant masters because they were unaccustomed to such cruel

362

treatment and back-breaking toil. After that uprising, the settlers there banished the troublesome ones to this island. They were here long before Morgan."

It was nearly noon when they completed their morning outing and returned to the main house for a mid-day snack. After they had eaten, Mama Bella threatened that if "Missuh Robert" didn't go upstairs and take a nap, she would throw him over her shoulders and tote him up to bed herself!

## Chapter Twenty-One

The next several days continued in much the same fashion. Raven relished their morning outings and looked forward to their time together. Sometimes they would walk the entire distance from the garden to the village and on to the fields in complete silence, for just being in each other's company was enough.

The time during the afternoon when Sir Robert had to submit to Mama Bella's insistence that he rest were lonely hours for Raven. She had strived to maintain at least a civil relationship with Melinda, but the brooding young woman made even that most difficult. She spent most of her time up in her room, relaxing on the bed while Ullah fanned her with a palm frond. During the evening meal was the only real opportunity Raven had to attempt any conversation with her. And then she returned Raven's polite inquiries with brief, mildly cordial answers. At most she would complain about the way the food had been prepared or criticize one of the six house-servants.

One day Raven did invite Melinda to walk down to the fish pond, a small salt water pool cut into the inlet and separated from the ocean with an underwater bamboo-stalk gate. Here fish of varying sizes and species and a lobster and a turtle that had been caught in Jacob's fish pots were kept alive until Mama Bella decided which would grace the huge mahogany dinner table that evening. Raven could sit there for hours watching as the iridescent, aquatic creatures darted through the waters, but Melinda wanted no part of that.

"You should do well to guard your skin from so much exposure to the sun," she smugly told her before dismissing her as curtly as she did Ullah. "Why, already your face is as ruddy as a fish wife's, and I do believe I see a spray of freckles popping out on your nose!"

Despite her desire to retaliate against Melinda's sharpness with some equally lashing words of her own, Raven chose simply to ignore her impotent comments and not give her the satisfaction of knowing that she had demeaned one more person during the course of the day. Once outside the room, however, the subtle smile vanished, and Raven bounded down the stairs, her fists clenched in anger and her jaw set in formidable determination.

"Oh, that wretched woman!" she raged, bumping right into the corpulent folds of Mama Bella's stomach. "Oh, dear me. I'm so sorry. Are you all right?"

"Shore ah iz. Dis belly's sol'd as a rock. Wha's dah matta wid yo'? Yo' looks like a cert'n Miz Nelson's done gone an' made youh boilin' mad. Whut did deh lady do ta yo'?"

"She's no lady, Mama Bella," said Raven, still fuming. "That woman is a spoiled, sniveling, arrogant, heartless—" Her list of unpleasant adjectives was interrupted by the Negress's rollicking laughter, and Raven, realizing how utterly ridiculous she must look standing in the middle of the hallway ranting and raving, joined her.

"Deys jes one thang dat gal needs, an' das a good raz'r strap taken ta her backside."

"I agree wholeheartedly!"

"Nah, Missy Rav'n, why don' yo' come keeps Mammy Bella comp'ny and ah'll let youh taste mah coc'nut patties."

Raven gave the old woman an affectionate grin, for her offer of sweets sounded like an attempt to bribe an implacable child into better humor.

She nibbled on the patties and watched Mama Bella knead the thick bread dough with her quick, massive fingers.

"Do you miss your homeland?" asked Raven, believing Mama Bella to have been victimized by a greedy chief or a cruel slave trader.

"Dis heah's mah home," she answered without looking up from her work. "Ah's been on dis heah island fo' sixty yeahs. Ma chiluns; fifteen of 'em is all heah, an' mah man and first born babe buried on dat hill o'er yonder."

"Were you born on Eleuthera?"

"Nah, ah's born on a ship a'comin' ovah from Afr'ka. My mammy died a birthin' me, an' one of dem otha' gals dat had a li'l 'un suckled me. We lived on 'nother island afore comin' heah, but ah doan member much 'bout it. My pappy wuz a big man in his village," she said proudly. "A houngan. Da chief wuz so jel'us of his pow'rs he sold mah pappy to some white men."

"Is that how you became a mambo? I mean, because your father was a . . . a houngan?" No sooner had her question been asked did Raven immediately regret doing so. She feared Mama Bella would be angry, or even worse, insulted by her curiosity.

"How youh know dat, gal?" she asked, pausing from her work to eye Raven sternly. "Wha's wrong? Cat got your tongue?"

"Your necklace. Maria said that the coiled symbol of a snake around your neck signifies your position as an obeah priestess." She gulped uncomfortably, for the woman was still staring at her with a sharply critical look. In a much softer tone, and hoping to appease the old Negress if she were indeed offended she added, "And Dr. Lightbourne said that it was a position of honor bestowed on only a select few and almost never on a woman. He also said that your people look to you for guidance."

Finally Mama Bella's full red lips broke into a wide grin. "Yo' means youh ain't afeared o' mah pow'rs?"

Raven breathed easier now. "It's hard to fear that which I know so little about."

"Yo' wans dat Mammy Bella puts a spell on dat gal up stairs?" she laughed with mock seriousness.

"No, while it is tempting, I will have to deal with her my own way. But one day I would like to learn more about your beliefs. My father used to tell me of the religious practices of the Indians and how all of their myths and legends were an attempt to help explain something in nature they knew existed but did not understand."

When Mama Bella had completed her morning

chores, she sat down on the bench beside Raven and explained as simply as she could the basics of her religion. Raven sat spellbound listening to every word of Mama Bella's drawling accent.

That night, after she had retired to her room, she reviewed all that Mama Bella had told her. She realized that the beliefs of the old Negress and her people were surprisingly similar to the religions of the civilized world. The word obeah meant "spirit," and the religion concerned itself with attempting to relate man to his ancestors and to the natural and supernatural occurrences of his universe. It connected the living to the dead and to those not yet born, and tried to account for those things in life that were not understood.

The following morning Raven was up early and anxiously awaiting the arrival of her good friends. She heard Henry's heavy footsteps on the veranda and ran down the stairs to greet him and his bride. The chubby doctor was even more jocular than usual, laughing with Sir Robert, teasing Mama Bella unmercifully and captivating them all with his tales of spelunking at Hatchet Bay. An air of serene bliss surrounded Maria, and Raven knew at first glance that the dear Spanish woman was jubilant with her newly acquired status as Mrs. Lightbourne. Just as he had requested the day of his departure, the breakfast table held large platters of boiled fish and four over-sized johnny cakes, along with plates stacked high with early morning sweets.

"You have most definitely outdone yourself!" Henry told the pleasant housekeeper when she came to clear away the dishes. "I do not think anyone else in all these islands has your culinary talents. Delicious!" he exclaimed, wiping the last morsel from his chin, then popping it in his mouth. "Nothing goes to waste when I'm around!"

He turned to Sir Robert nodding. "I must say, Robert, I do not believe I have ever seen you looking so fit!" he remarked, pleased that the man's hollowed cheeks had attained a healthy, rose-tinged hue. "I would wager that daughter of yours had quite a bit to do with that."

The time passed far too quickly, for soon it was ten o'clock and Henry was anxious to begin his trip home. "I wish we had the time to sail on down to the Exumas," he told his bride as the four of them stood chatting on the veranda. "I remember once, not too long ago, when Morgan and I were there on Conch Cay. We went there with the drunken notion of digging up the mound of gold."

"The mound," explained Sir Robert to his questioning daughter, "is an extraordinarily large grave that is in the shape of a cone. Quite a bit of mystery surrounds it. From what I understand the natives swear that underneath the rock and shell exterior is buried the wealth from all of Blackbeard's plunders, along with the bodies of his prisoners!"

"His reasoning, of course, was that no one would dare face the wrath of the dead and risk being haunted with curses the rest of their lives by excavating the mound," added Henry.

"What happened to you and Mr. Taylor? Were you haunted when you attempted this feat?" inquired Raven.

Henry blushed and a mischievous grin crossed his rubicund face. "We did not stay there long enough to find out. Eerie noises began the moment we put our shovels in the ground. Of course, I'm sure it was nothing more than the wind or an owl, but to us drunks, it sounded like a group of dead people moaning in their grave. Needless to say, we grabbed our bottles and spades and ran the entire two mile distance back to the settlement."

"Don' yo' go a messin' wid dem daid folks no mo', Doker. Yo' heah me?" reprimanded Mama Bella sternly, shaking her finger at him as though he were a naughty child. "Dey could come right up outta der hole an' snatch yo' back down wid 'em." She handed Maria a wicker basket filled with food for their voyage home.

Maria smilingly thanked her; her apprehensions about the African mambo had clearly vanished.

"You didn't have to go to any trouble on our account," said Henry. "But I'm glad you did. Don't know if I can wait until we're out to sea to eat that chicken. It smells awfully tempting."

"Dats whut Mama Bella heah fo', ta makes yo' bellies fat and happy," she teased.

"We will walk you as far as the beach," offered Sir Robert.

"Yo' be shore ta takes dat cane, suh. Jest cause you's feelin' a bit betta is no reason ta ova' do you'self." She turned to Maria. "An yo' makes sho' yo' takes good care of our Doker."

"And you take good care of Mr. Morgan," returned Henry, giving her solid shoulders an affectionate squeeze. "I have a feeling our Miss Nelson is more dangerous than a baracuda."

"Humph!" replied Mama Bella, hands defiantly on her wide, fleshy hips. "Ah may jes' haf'ta let dat gal know jes who be de big'st fish in dis heah oshun!"

Henry and Maria walked arm in arm down the path, followed by Raven and her father. The men shook hands while Maria and Raven said their teary good-byes.

"I'm so happy for you, Maria," she said, hugging her friend. "Thank you, thank you both so much for everything that you've done for me. I will never forget your kindness."

"We shall see you soon in Nassau," called out Sir Robert as the pair strolled up the beach to their sloop. "As soon as Morgan returns, we shall be sailing with him to England. I am sure we will spend several days in Nassau readying for our voyage. Good-bye! And good luck to you both!"

Raven's heart sank as she and her father walked back up the hill. "When do you think that will be, Papa? When will we be leaving?" Would it be before she had a chance to see Juan once again? To feel the tautness of his muscled chest as he held her close against him? Would she ever be able again to smell the sea and salt aroma of his body as they embraced?

"I suspect that it will not be long now," he answered with renewed energy. "What's wrong? You look so distraught."

"Oh, no . . . no Papa," she quickly assured him. "I'm not at all upset. Well, a little, perhaps. Henry and Maria have been so kind to me, it will seem strange not

371

seeing them any more. I guess I really did not know how much I would miss them."

"I know how you must feel," he said, placing his arm comfortingly around his daughter's shoulders. "As Mama Bella would say, a rock in the water does not comprehend the suffering of the rock in the sun."

"What?" she asked, trying to keep from laughing at such a ridiculous proverb.

"If you'll think about it, it does make sense. If you haven't suffered, you cannot understand the suffering of others. Come along. I shall race you the rest of the way to the house." He walked quickly in front of her.

"Papa! Slow down. You know you shouldn't be racing. Stop! Papa!" Then realizing that he had no intention of heeding her, she kicked off her sandals and ran to catch up.

The following morning, she was awakened by a faint thump at her door. Thinking it was Ullah, she sleepily called out for her to enter. "Why, Melinda," she said, sitting up in bed. "What a lovely surprise. Do come on in."

The fair-haired visitor was dressed in a brown- and gold-striped riding habit and seemed in an unusually chummy mood, instead of her usual volitile self. "I hope I am not disturbing you, but it is such a lovely day, and I decided to make use of such a pleasant morning. Your father tells me that you are quite an accomplished equestrienne, so I thought you might care to join me for a ride."

"Oh, I didn't know Mr. Taylor kept horses." Her dislike for the haughty young woman was forgotten for the moment, and she told her of her own horse. "I haven't been on a horse in quite some time now," she remarked longingly. "I have quite forgotten how wonderfully free it makes one feel to gallop for miles and miles without stopping."

"Mmm," echoed Melinda, disinterested in her rival's reminiscences. "If you would care to accompany me, I shall wait in the dining hall. Do try and be dressed in quarter of an hour," she said, more in the tone of a command than a request. "I don't like being kept waiting."

Raven finished with her morning toiletries in less than ten minutes, but stubbornly refused to budge from her room until sixteen past the hour of seven. When she did venture into the dining room, Melinda was completing her tea and fruit. A place had already been set for her, and she had barely situated herself in the chair when Mama Bella entered with her breakfast and a probing look that warned her to be leery of Melinda's sudden change of temperament.

The two girls walked briskly to the stables, which were a half mile east of the main house—Melinda in her fashionable riding garb and Raven in a white muslin dress tied at the waist with a trailing red sash. They both sensed the other's dislike, and yet neither of them made the slightest attempt to reconcile their differences.

Raven was puzzled by Melinda's abrupt gesture of friendship, for she believed her incapable of such kind consideration. She probably asked me along, she decided bitterly, so she would have someone to praise her own adept riding skills. But I will show her. Her ladyship doesn't know that I was riding a pony long before I had taken my first step.

When they reached the stables, Melinda's temper flared up discovering the horses were still in stalls. "Jacob! Jacob!" she yelled impatiently. With a frown she turned to Raven. "I told Mama Bella to make sure that lazy son of hers had our horses ready for mount. Morgan will be sure to hear of their insubordination when he returns. Well, it's about time you were here," she screamed to the lanky, grinning boy who strolled into the enclosure making no effort to hasten his pace. "Well, don't just stand there. Saddle the horses!"

His wide grin slowly faded. "Bof of 'em?"

"Of course, Jacob. Surely you cannot expect us to ride the same horse," she replied cynically.

"But, ah done tole yo'. Massah Morgan's ho'se won' let nobody but de massah—"

Melinda interrupted indignantly. "You are certainly in no position to question me. Now, saddle them!"

He humbly meandered toward the tack room.

"Insolent darkies. Morgan needs to take that young buck and his mammy and whip some respect and obedience into them. Hurry along, Jacob. We haven't all day!"

Prancer was saddled first. She was a pleasant dispositioned mare so named because she held her head regally alert and lifted her legs high as though she were marching. Melinda had her mount outside while the boy began his struggle to saddle Storm. One glance at the ebony stallion assured Raven that this one was just as appropriately named. Despite the lad's attempt to calm him with quiet whispers and gentle scratches behind his ears, the horse staunchly refused to stand still. His nostrils flared, and he snorted threateningly while his hoofs pawed the ground.

"Let me try, Jacob," suggested Raven. She removed from her pocket some sugar she had taken from the china sugar bowl on the table and held it in her hand for the skittish stallion to inspect. Brown, long-lashed eyes started quizzically at her before Storm decided to lick her outstretched palm.

"There," cooed Raven into his velvety soft ear as she stroked his neck. "I'm not going to hurt you. I want us to become friends, very good friends. You and I are going for a little ride along the beach. All right?" She turned to Jacob. "Saddle him now," she instructed without changing the soft, moderate tone of her voice. "And make sure the girth is pulled as tightly as you can. This is a very bright horse, and I do not want to begin my ride by falling out of the saddle."

Storm stood surprisingly still, neighing gentle whinnies as he nuzzled closer to Raven in search of more sugar.

"A'right, Missy. Nah youse be ca'ful," he cautioned, handing her the bridle.

Raven pulled herself up and straddled one leg over his glossy back. Storm lowered his head obstinately and once more began pawing the ground. Raven jerked the bridle with all her strength, and Storm was forced to raise his head. "I will not tolerate any more of this nonsense. Now, behave yourself. You are I are going to show Miss Melinda that with the right horsewoman, you are as docile as a pup." She spurred him lightly, and the spirited stallion walked obediently outside.

Melinda's astounded look gave herself away immediately. Instead of throwing his rider as she had hoped the horse would do, he trotted and cantered to his rider's command.

"Let's race to the water," challenged Raven, tossing aside her long hair.

Without replying, Melinda angrily dug her heels into Prancer's sides and began lashing her rump with a leather riding crop. As she had so often done with her own horse, Raven confidently gave the sprightly steed its head. He immediately shot past Melinda, kicking up the sand behind him.

How good it feels to have my hair streaming out behind me! thought Raven as the air whipped against her cheeks. She pulled him to an abrupt halt when she noticed puddles of sweat beading up on his neck. "Good boy!" she praised, patting his head. "That was a splendid run!"

"What's the matter?" demanded Melinda when she finally caught up. "You didn't have to wait for me. A little more, and we would have gained on you." She was as out of breath as her horse. "This broken down old mare would hardly move!"

"Is that why you so generously insisted that I ride Storm?" she asked with wide-eyed innocence.

For once, Melinda was at a loss for a curt retort.

"You really should try riding him yourself, Melinda. That is, if you like a horse with as devilish a temperament as your own!" With that she whirled Storm around and cantered him back up the beach, leaving Melinda to stew in her own speechless rage.

That evening as she and her father sat down to a game of backgammon after supper, he urged her to try and be a bit more friendly toward Melinda. "We both know she is little more than a spoiled, selfish child, but she is the niece of a good friend, and I would sincerely appreciate your effort at being friendly with her. Who knows? Perhaps her aloofness is a facade to keep us from knowing how unhappy and lonely she really is. You and I have each other, but Melinda has no one."

"All right, Papa. I promise I will try much harder to make friends with her." Raven sighed and nodded acquiescently. She decided against complaining to her father of Melinda's hateful prank for fear that Sir Robert would think her a child as well.

"Good. I would certainly appreciate it. Now, I think I shall retire for the evening. Are you aware, dear daughter, that you have not allowed your ailing father to win a single game?" he joked, kissing her good night.

"I promise I shall let you win tomorrow night, Papa," replied Raven as they ascended the stairs to their rooms.

During the next days, Melinda's attitude toward her younger rival began a slow change, once she realized that Raven had no intention of either being bullied or pleading that they resolve their differences. She was surprisingly cordial, and at times even friendly, but she knew that once Morgan returned to his plantation, she would allow no one to interfere with her scheme.

After the incident with Storm, Raven found herself even more skeptical of Melinda's seemingly cheerful prating, and she could not help but wonder what else she would try to do to annoy her. But she had promised Sir Robert that she would make every conciliatory effort.

"How can you sit there hour after hour fiddling with those old palm leaves?" said Melinda during one of the frequent mid-summer rain squalls.

Raven looked up from her half-finished basket. "These are not old leaves, Melinda. They are palm fronds, and I am not fiddling with them, I'm making a basket. Besides we can't go outside, and I'm tired of backgammon and chess and darts. Why don't you let me show you how this is done? Your constant complaining is getting a bit much!"

"I have no desire to make those silly little baskets," she said sullenly. "Oh, God! How I hate this place. I cannot wait until I am back in London!"

"It rains there, too, Melinda."

"But at least I'm not bored there. There are so many things to do. I can go visiting or out for tea, shopping for new clothes, go to parties. . . . Oh, the parties," she squealed. "How I miss those parties. During the season there are at least four a week. And to think, I'm having to miss all of that now. I could just cry!"

"Don't do that, Melinda," said Raven with mocking concern. "Your eyes will get so red and puffy." She put aside her work, knowing that until Melinda was appeased, her basket could never be finished. "Once you and Mr. Taylor are married, you will have to adjust to life here, so you might as well get used to it now."

Melinda plopped down on the couch beside her. "Oh, no I don't! I expect we shall have to come back here from time to time, but I have no intention of residing on this desolate island for the rest of my life. Morgan and I shall live in London, right in the center

378

of all the social activity."

"And what does your fiancé have to say about that?" asked Raven, doubtful that Taylor would give up his tropical paradise to appease his spoiled bride.

Melinda smiled connivingly. "We really haven't discussed that little matter yet, but I feel certain that when the time comes, I can convince him that I would be a much better wife in London." Her smug look changed to suspicion and malice. "Why are you so concerned with Morgan's feelings anyway?"

"Do not be absurd, Melinda. I know what you're implying, and you can rest assured that I have no intention of snatching your precious Morgan from your sharp talons!" she scolded. Then with a mischievous grin she could not help but threaten, "But if I really and truly wanted to—"

Melinda jumped from her seat, her nostrils flared like Storm's. "Just what do you mean by that? How dare you insinuate—"

"Oh, hush up, Melinda. I had forgotten that you are not one to be teased. Such violent outbursts must cease if you expect to catch a husband. I swear, the way you erupt at such little things would make one wonder if that blood of yours is mixed with hot volcanic lava."

"And just what do you know of waylaying a husband?"

"Lesson number two, Miss Nelson. Do not meddle in affairs that do not concern you." Raven knew she was being extremely wicked, but somehow Melinda's past behavior seemed to justify her cruelty.

Melinda returned to her seat and drew her feet up under her. "How could you have a sweetheart?" she asked curiously. "Was it someone you met on the ship, perhaps?"

"Remember lesson number two," reminded Raven good naturedly.

"Of course you are lying!" accused Melinda in an annoyed tone. "You're must making up having a beau because you're so jealous of my association with Morgan."

"I could care less about your 'association,'" she replied calmly.

"Then who is he? What does he look like? Is it one of the Tarlton boys?" she persisted, frustrated with Raven's silence. "Perhaps it's someone you met in Nassau?"

Raven realized that she would have no peace until Melinda was confident that there was no reason for her to be afraid that she would be a rival for Morgan's attentions, and yet she was hesitant to confide in her since she suspected that keeping a trust would be far down on Melinda's list of redeeming qualities.

"Do tell me about this Prince Charming of yours," she pleaded childishly. "I swear your secret is safe with me. What's his name? Oh, please, Raven!"

She sighed defeatedly. "Oh all right, but if you mention a word of this to anyone, I will steal your precious Morgan the moment he arrives. His name is Juan Perez, Captain Juan Perez."

Melinda swooned. "Oh, you lucky girl!"

"What? Do you know him?"

"By reputation only. Uncle Woodes told me all about his exploits. I meant to ask Aunt Sarah more about this mysterious hero, but I had to leave. How did you meet him? I thought he was off chasing pirates."

Raven patiently disclosed all of the events of the past four months to Melinda. "Had it not been for Juan rescuing me, I would probably have rotted on that hellish island."

"How romantic! Not about your rotting, of course, but to have such a gallant fellow save you. And are you truly in love with him?"

Raven nodded. "So you see, there really is no reason for us to continue our bitterness. We are not rivals for one man's love. Now tell me all about Morgan Taylor. From what Father says, no one knows very much at all about him."

"Oh, I know all there is to know. He's tall and dark and deliciously handsome. When he holds me, I melt in his arms like butter in the noonday sun. And his kisses. Such delicious kisses would make even a naughty girl blush."

"And has he indeed proposed to you?" challenged Raven.

"No, not exactly. But I feel that it is only a matter of time before he does. I did overhear him whispering to Uncle Woodes that he needed to discuss a very private matter with him, one that could not be discussed at the party."

"So you think that you are that very private matter?"

"Oh, I know it," answered Melinda with unabashed vanity. "That was just after he had kissed me on the veranda. Besides, my Aunt Sarah thinks so as well. She told me that Morgan's attitude of being a confirmed bachelor would change the instant he returned home and found me waiting for him."

"Quite a domestic scene you've planned," remarked Raven. "But what if—just suppose for a moment without jumping to any conclusions—that he has no desire to marry. How do you hope to overcome that obstacle?"

Melinda gave Raven her most seductive pose as she answered. "I do have ways of convincing him. Any man, even one who is obstinately opposed to wedlock, is no problem once he is caught in a web of feminine charm."

"That description sounds more like the spider and the fly."

"I prefer to think of myself more in terms of a siren, not a spider. Of course, a clever woman will manipulate her lover by allowing him to believe that any romantic overtures are at his suggestion, not hers."

"And once this is accomplished, he has fallen right into your web, correct?" questioned Raven with a deliberate show of distaste.

"Exactly," answered Melinda with complete innocence.

Poor Mr. Taylor, mused Raven. I feel sorry for him already. He has no idea what waits for him when he returns from his travels. And Melinda, if she does succeed with her wily schemes, surely she will not be happy with a man who is so easily dupped. "Oh, look. It's finally stopped raining. Let's go for a walk along the beach and see what treasures the waves have washed to shore."

Melinda touched her cheek with a vainglorious motion. "And risk this fair skin in that sweltering heat? You go on without me. I believe I shall retire to my room and begin my wedding plans."

## Chapter Twenty-Two

Never had Raven seen a more glorious rainbow as the one that arched high in the velvety, unruffled sky that afternoon. Gone were the heat-swollen, wind-driven clouds and the loud palpitating thunder. They were replaced with crystal, serene radiance and a colorful display of yellows and pinks and violets. Raven reclined on the beach, her weight resting on her elbows. Her skirt was pulled above her knees. The warmth of the glittering grains of sand beneath her and the balmy sensation of the sun penetrating her slender form made her skin tingle with a vibrant awareness. Her eyes were set in a hypnotic gaze, watching as the white-crested waves rushed to attack the shore, then slowly ease back out to sea, leaving behind a shaded imprint of their foamy outline that would be erased by the next surge. A solitary gull cackled noisily and glided just above the surface. His wings were in full span, and his sharp eye skimmed the water for any movement. He finally focused on a fish, swooped down, grasped it in his beak and then winged his way farther out to sea.

"Ahoy, lass!"

The voice startled her, and she rubbed the sleepiness from her eyes to discover her outstretched legs had barely escaped the sea's high tide.

"When I walked down earlier, ye were sleepin' so peaceful I couldn't bring myself to disturb ye, but I thought I'd best do so now afore the tide took ye out with it." He motioned for her to scoot back farther and sat down crosslegged beside her. "Captain Ahab at your service, ma'am. And who might ye be, if I may ask."

For a moment, Raven thought she must be dreaming, but she now realized that the gray-bearded figure beside her was indeed real. "I'm Raven Gatewood, sir. My father and I are guests of Mr. Taylor."

"I'm most pleased to make your 'quaintance, Miss Gatewood. I brought your father here from New Providence." His unmistakable cockney accent clearly revealed that he was from London's East side. "I captain the *Cotton Queen* for Mr. Taylor."

Perhaps Captain Ahab had been assigned that task temporarily, she reasoned, since Juan is unable to serve in both capacities. Of course! "How long have you worked for Mr. Taylor?" she asked, positive that his answer would clear up her questions.

"Close to ten years. Yep, ten years indeed. Ever since Mr Taylor decided to go into this sort of business." He scraped some burned particles of tobacco from his short-stemmed clay pipe.

"Ten years?"

"Yep," he replied, drawing on his pipe. "Ten years!"

But why did Juan tell me that he was the ship's captain? Or did he just say that he worked for Mr. Taylor on his ship. Perhaps Captain Ahab was his superior officer. "Excuse me, sir, what was that you just said?"

"I asked how your father's doing?"

"Oh, much, much better now, thank you. Captain Ahab, do you know a man here by the name of Juan Perez?"

The sun-aged mariner scratched his whiskers thoughtfully. "Juan Perez, hummm. No can't say that I do."

"I thought perhaps he was a member of your crew, but I must have been mistaken. He most likely works for another one of the planters here."

"I doubt that, missy. Mr. Taylor's the only planter on Eleuthera."

"Oh, well, it's getting late, sir. My father has probably already begun to worry about me," she said, pulling herself up.

"I'll walk ye as far as the path," he offered, brushing sand from his woolen trousers.

They plodded along in the damp softness of the water's edge.

"Good-bye, Captain Ahab."

"Bye, lass. It was a pleasure talkin' to ye."

Raven took her time walking up the pathway, for she was trying to sort out her muddled thoughts. Why would Juan have lied to me, she asked herself over and over. Surely he knew that once I had reached Eleuthera, I would discover the truth myself. How did he intend to explain his deception to me? Unless . . . unless he had no intention of ever coming here. If he does not work for Mr. Taylor, then why would he even need to return here? He most certainly lied to me concerning his job, so how am I to interpret anything he ever said as the truth? His declarations of love, and his marriage proposal . . . were they lies as well? Sunken in her dismal gloom, she sat down into the swing and swayed desolately back and forth.

Raven questioned Mama Bella, Jacob, the Tarltons and Ullah, praying that one of them would recognize the name of Juan Perez, but everyone had given her a blank stare and an unhesitant shake of their heads. Earlier, her father had admitted that his only knowledge of her rescuer stemmed from being aware of the governor commissioning Perez to apprehend Red Ames.

*I cannot allow myself to think about this any longer,* she determinedly resolved. *The only alternative I have is to wait until Mr. Taylor has arrived. Surely he can clear up this confusion over Juan. If he is as unfamiliar with the name as everyone else, then I will have to resign myself to being a foolish, naive girl who was indeed deceived by false declarations of love. If that is the case, then I will have to try my hardest to dissuade Papa from remaining here a moment longer than is necessary.*

"Come along, Raven!" ordered her father with stern playfullness. "You have been as moody as Melinda as of late. You've hardly even been outside this last week."

"I just haven't been feeling very well, Papa," she replied gloomily.

"You're sick? Why didn't you say so earlier? I'll have Captain Ahab sail us to Nassau immediately."

"No, no Papa. Not physically ill, just a bit depressed." She sighed.

"My poor, poor kitten," comforted her father. "It

must be more difficult for you than I had thought. I suppose I have been spending too much time at the Tarltons, but I didn't think you'd mind since you and Melinda seem to have resolved your differences."

"Oh, no Papa. Do not even think of giving up your afternoon chess matches with Mr. Tarlton's father. I know how much you respect having an admirable opponent." She grinned. "And truthfully, Melinda and I are getting along much better. She's been awfully busy of late with her wedding plans, and frankly I'm a bit bored listening to all of that." And, she thought grimly, every time Melinda starts singing the praises of her fiancé, it brings to mind too many memories about Juan, memories that would best be forgotten, at least until I learn the truth about him.

"Get up!" he insisted, energetically leaping to his feet. "I feel like a new man this morning, almost like the years have fallen away like fish scales. You and I are going to go spelunking. We will explore Preacher's Cave. It is quite near here, you know. I have had Mama Bella pack us a picnic lunch, and I refuse to take no for an answer."

"All right, Papa, perhaps an outing is just what I need to liven my senses. Let me go upstairs and get my walking shoes."

He reached for something behind the couch. "I took the liberty of fetching them myself," he said, holding up a pair of soft, white kidskin shoes. "I will get our basket, and we shall be off on our spelunking adventure."

She could not help but laugh at her father's merry antics, for she liked the change that had come over him. The slumped shouldered, downcast, solitary figure she had spotted wandering aimlessly on the beach no longer existed. In his place was the father of her childhood; a cheery, boyishly handsome man who was always thinking of new ways to entertain her. Most of the lined creases had disappeared from his face, but some were left on his forehead, a permanent reminder of his trying ordeal.

Jacob already had Prancer and Storm saddled for their outing when they arrived at the stalls.

"I see you and Storm have developed quite an attachment for each other," noted her father, as Storm's nose nuzzled close to Raven.

"He is just on such good behavior because he thinks I brought him a treat." She dug into her dress pocket and brought out a carrot and held it temptingly in front of the horse until he had nibbled most of the orange stalk away.

Little had changed since the day the two of them had walked down past the fields. Naked, dirt-smudged children still played their games while their mothers tended the gardens and their fathers worked in the fields. Mr. Tarlton waved to them, pausing long enough to wipe the sweat from his face with an orange kerchief he kept tied around his neck. Abreast, they rode past the fields and into a dense wooded area carpeted with pine needles. Casuarinas that seemed to stretch skyward surrounded them.

Sir Robert moved his finger to his lips. "Shh," he cautioned as they proceeded onward. "Up ahead is a lake full of most unusual birds."

"What are they?" asked Raven, trying to suppress her giggles once they paused beside the tranquil pond. She was captivated by the pinkish, long-necked creatures whose brightly plumaged bodies seemed far too plump for their skinny, stiltlike legs. Some were wading in the water, standing on one leg then shifting to the other as their black, pointed beaks darted into the water when something edible or interesting swam past. The females, who were not as colorful as the males, were nesting on the wet bank.

"The Spanish named them 'flamingoes,'" answered Sir Robert softly. "Come now, we should leave. They are extremely skittish creatures, and if the females sense our presence they will desert their eggs."

They made a wide semicircle around the pond, careful not to disturb the birds, and ventured on through the woodland until they were atop a grassy knoll. The contour of the coastline was not as smooth as she had expected. Instead, it alternated between high, steep cliffs whose rocky bases were washed with each surge of the tide, and exquisite pink-sanded, sun-kissed beaches similar to the one in front of the house.

Preacher's Cave was so named, explained her father as they approached it, because it was the site of the Eleutherian Adventurers' first religious service on their island of freedom. Raven and Sir Robert tied the horses to a lignum vitae branch at the entrance of the grass-smothered mouth. The inside of the cave was light and open.

"Oh, Papa, do you think there might be any pirates' treasures buried here?" she asked excitedly, quite enthralled by the spirit of adventure as they proceeded inside the sunlit interior.

He laughed in reply, then ducked a wasp nest, one of many hanging from the gnarled tree vines that had found their way inside. "I doubt us finding anything more than a few owls or a couple of bats in here. Next time, though, we shall bring our shovels."

She moved her hand along the side of the cave. "Look!" she exclaimed, holding up her palm to let him see the black soot that smudged it. "It looks as though someone has built a fire in here fairly recently."

He examined her hand closer. "Either that or what you have rubbed off the walls is a reminder of the Spanish, whose forces burned the Preacher's Cave settlement and Governor's Harbor back in 1684."

"So that is why so little remains of the colony on Cupid's Cay," deduced Raven. "When Henry sailed past it, it looked as though all of the houses were abandoned or in ruin."

"Such a shame, for I understand the structure of their church and homes was copied from the New England type of architecture found in Massachusetts. Apparently, Sayles was quite taken by their design when he ventured to Boston in search of aid for his struggling colony."

"The Spanish have done so much to prevent the development of settlements here. It seems they will never cease their rampage of burning and plundering."

"I fear not until the entire continent is claimed by them," he replied gravely. "Because of their greed and thirst for power and wealth, they have completely destroyed cultures even more advanced than their own; the Maya, Aztec, and Inca of Mexico and South America, and now the Indian villages and British settlements of the Bahamas."

"Even Maria said that the cruelness of the Spanish military leaders was appalling. She once told me that her own people have degenerated into loathsome beasts who seem to take pleasure in inflicting pain and suffering on their captors."

"Enough grim talk," requested her father cheerfully, wrapping his arm around his daughter's waist and leading her down five smooth stone steps that had been hewed into the rock's surface by nature. A flat-topped boulder stood at the far end of the cave. "It looks like a pulpit, doesn't it. Obviously that is why the adventurers held their first service of Thanksgiving here. I am sure they must have seen the stone and felt assured that it had been created especially for them. Even now, a serene, almost spiritual atmosphere prevails here."

After pausing for several moments of silent reverence, Sir Robert turned to leave. "I have always wanted to explore farther back in the cave, but the passageways are so narrow I felt they would cave right in on me. Perhaps back there is where your pirate treasure is buried. Let's go back outside. All of this spelunking has worked up an enormous appetite!"

"You are beginning to sound more and more like Henry," she told her father while spreading their picnic on a rock just outside the cave. Mama Bella's loaf of bread was still warm, and they attacked it and the fried chicken with ravenous vigor.

"After all of this food," said Sir Robert afterward, rubbing his stomach, "we should let the horses ride us back home!"

They led Prancer and Storm down a bush-lined path that winded down the hillside to the ocean, and walked along the tide dampened surf. Midway home, they met Captain Ahab, who after a bit of pleasant conversation, offered to take them sailing to the northern part of the island early the next day.

The following morning, Ahab breakfasted with them, and the trio left shortly afterward. Melinda had been invited to join their sight-seeing excursion, but she declined, using the "unbearable August weather" as her excuse.

In Taylor's sloop, *The Gay Dolphin,* with Captain Ahab at the helm and aided by a moderate, south-easterly breeze, they sailed up the northern coast to Hatchet Bay where the beaches and bays were sheltered by high ground, and the deep green water ran close inshore. Gradually the coastline began its rise into high precipices that had unusual sand markings eroded into their limestone cliffs. Situated at the peak of one of these cliffs was the settlement of Gregory Towne.

"That reminds me of a Cornish fishing village," observed Robert as they glided beneath it."

"Aye, that it does," agreed Ahab. "Except for the palms in the background.

Sheer, steep cliffs elevating to at least sixty feet marked their way toward Mutton Fish Point. To the west lay Current Island, a low, marshy cay, which was covered with thick scrub and palmettos.

"Back in 1709, began Ahab, his pipe dangling from between the corners of his wind-cracked lips, "the Spanish captured a British naval vessel. Instead of claiming the ship and its cargo and abandoning the crew on an island where they could be found, the commander decided to leave them on this God-forsaken island. He had them stripped and tied side by side to the trees in that swamp and left them to die the worst death imaginable."

Sir Robert shook his head bitterly. "Another example of Spanish cruelty. No one could last more than a few hours in such torrid heat with no fresh water and swarms of mosquitoes biting them."

"Aye," said Ahab. "And can you imagine what it must have been like to have watched the man beside you die, knowing that your fate was a similar one soon to come? At that time, I was the captain of a supply brig. We were en route to Harbour Island and something made me drop anchor offshore to this cay. Might have been one of those feelings a man gets sometimes when he knows somethin' just isn't right, or maybe the wind had carried those poor devils' pleas for help. By the time we waited to make certain the Spanish were a far distance away, all but two of the men had died. We cut down the survivors, and before we could stop them, they ran past us, screamin' like crazed men and plunged into the ocean. There was nothin' we could do to save them once they began a guzzlin' that salt water. In their delirious state, they drowned. Just as well, for they would have gone berserk shortly anyway."

"How did you come to work for Morgan?" asked Sir Robert, anxious to divert the topic of conversation, for it was evident that even though what Ahab had described had happened some time ago, it still weighed heavily on his mind.

"Shortly after what I just told you of, I gave up my command. I met Mr. Taylor in Nassau. He had just arrived from England, having recently completed his studies at the university. He had some outlandish idea about growing and exporting cotton, but no one took him very seriously. At first," he remembered, smiling, "even I thought him mad, but he offered me a sizeable sum of money for my services, and I would have been a fool not to have signed on with him."

"To the east of us, Captain Ahab," Raven pointed excitedly, "what is that?"

"It looks like some sort of an arched formation in the water," offered her father. "It appears to bridge the rocks beneath it."

"At first glance," said Ahab knowingly. "It does seem to divide that part of Eleuthera in half. See how the land suddenly drops to sea level. That's called the Glass Window. Sailors say that there the ocean kisses the sound. Look through the hold to the other side, lass."

"Why, it's like looking through a pane of glass . . . a mirror, for it appears that the other side is a reflection of this," marveled Raven as she watched the water blast against the rocky base of this natural phenomenon.

"Thus its name, the Glass Window," said Ahab.

He anchored the sloop at that spot, close enough to have a good view of the arch, but far enough away not to get caught in the swell in case the flow of the current changed. "Let's see what Mama Bella packed for our lunch."

After the food had been devoured and the pitcher of citronade emptied, he and Sir Robert pulled the anchor. "It will be dusk by the time we reach home, so we'd best get started now."

"Would it be possible to round the point and return home by way of the eastern coast?" inquired Raven, curious to see the other side of this island of freedom.

"Possible, but not very practical," answered the captain. "You see, we would have to cut across that channel over yonder, and even the most competent mariner avoids it whenever possible. The waters there are treacherously shallow. A jagged arrangement of rocks and connecting reefs lies just under the water's surface. They're called the Devil's Backbone. So the safest way home is the way we came."

The next day was Sunday, and for the first time in nearly a month, a provisions ship sailed from Nassau and docked at Governor's Harbor. The field workers and their families, singing their noisy chants, filed up the beach, dressed in their finest batiks. Raven, Sir Robert, and the Tarltons joined the brightly colored paraders.

The wharf was lined with vendors yelling prices for their straw merchandise and fresh fruits and vegetables. Cords of yard goods, barrels of flour, tea, and coffee, boxes of beaded trinkets, sewing notions, and casks of rum were displayed on the dock for the buyer's inspection. Sir Robert purchased several lengths of material for his daughter, and Mama Bella promised Raven that she would show her how to use indigo and braziletto dyes to obtain blue and red batiks.

Two letters were addressed in care of the Morgan plantation, one to Captain Ahab and one to Melinda. When Mama Bella handed Melinda hers that evening, she snatched it from her hand and darted upstairs to the privacy of her room. The Tarltons were invited to Sunday supper, and throughout the meal, Melinda flirted shamelessly with both of their sons. After they had left, Melinda pulled Raven aside and suggested that they go into the sitting room where "that infernal snooping Negress isn't under foot."

"Guess what?" she said, her face aglow and waving her letter. "This is from Aunt Sarah. Morgan has arrived in Nassau, and he will be coming home within the next few days."

"Why, that's wonderful, Melinda. I'm sure you must be very happy."

"Oh, I am Raven. But I'm not so sure that you're going to be."

"Whatever is that supposed to mean, Melinda?"

"Oh, nothing. Just that, well, with Morgan coming home, I guess you and your father will be going back to England soon, and I know how much you'll miss the Bahamas."

How I pray that Mr. Taylor will confirm all that Juan himself told me, she thought. If not, I must be strong enough to admit that I gave myself to a man who deliberately misled me, abused my emotions, and took advantage of a young girl's foolish thoughts of love.

Raven could not sleep that night, for she tossed fretfully from side to side, dreaming of Juan Perez lying in someone else's embrace and smirking at Raven's declarations of love. She would beg him over and over to leave his companion and marry her as he had promised, but he heartlessly pushed her aside, disclaiming that he had made any such promise to a shameless, willing hussy as she. Raven wakened herself with her own sobs and muffled pleas for his devotion.

I am too restless to sleep. My mind is conjuring up all sorts of horrible images while I am yet unsure as to Juan's motives for deceiving me. Perhaps I should go downstairs and find a book to distract me from such hateful thoughts.

She slipped a robe over her muslin chemise, and with her candle flickering against the dark, paneled corridor, tiptoed quietly down the stairs. As she pulled one book from its place, a second volume fell to the floor.

She bent down to pick it up and blew the dust from its cover. She reached up to return it to the book cabinet, but hesitated, for the title caught her eye: *Journal of Morgan Robert Taylor, 1648ñ1685.*

I have no business snooping in someone else's diary. After all, she reasoned, it is a record of very personal thoughts that were intended for no one but the author. She deliberated for a moment, but then succumbed to temptation and guiltily took it with her upstairs.

Perhaps I shall learn more about the mysterious Mr. Taylor, she thought, trying to justify her actions. Settling back on her pillow, she began with the first entry, July 1648.

Reading the hastily scribbled writing on the yellowed pages was a most difficult task, but from what she could decipher, the author was writing about leaving his home and parents in order to undertake some perilous sea voyage. At this point, he was nearing the end of his tumultuous travel at sea. Surely this was not Mr. Taylor's diary, for Papa said he was a man much younger than himself. Undoubtedly this belonged to the first Mr. Taylor, his father. She hurriedly skimmed the tattered pages, familiar words catching her eyes: "Sayle," "Eleuthera," and "Adventurers."

She anxiously thumbed through the succeeding pages until she found the last entry, which was dated November 14, 1685, and read it aloud:

"How foolish old men are! I was so jubilant upon first realizing my little Juanita was with child; our child. How I have longed all these years for a son. The stifled screams of Margaret and Samuel and baby Victor still haunt my sleep. Why does everything I love die? It seems as though all whom I touch, all those

397

dearest to me, are taken from me. First my parents, then my wife and sons, and now you, my precious Juanita. Am I forever doomed to a solitary life of unhappiness?

"Even now as I try to deaden my feelings with gin, I remember as though it were yesterday the day I found your lifeless body washed up on the shore. Even in your unconscious state, you were the epitome of loveliness; black hair lying upon the sand like drenched seaweed, the fine curve of your delicate nose and the aristocratic structure of your high, olive cheekbones. You looked as though you were immured within a peaceful slumber. I feared that you had already been visited by the angel of death, for never had I seen a living being so serene. Had it not been for the feel of the slightest wisp of a faint breath upon my hand, I would have buried you there on the beach where I found you. You seemed to sense my thoughts, and your eyes slowly opened. Oh, my darling one, the year of happiness I have shared with you has managed to compensate for the misery of my last fifty. And now, now that I have just learned that you, too, have been taken from me, I resign myself to the fact there is no end to my hellish punishment. What dastardly deed could I ever have committed to warrant such cruelty?

"I hear my newborn son screaming for his mother's breast, but there is no warm, life-giving nipple for him to suck. I cannot even look at my son, our son, without feeling anger. I almost hate the little whelp, despise my own flesh, for had he never been conceived, you, my darling, would still be here with me. Why could it not have been him and not you?

"These three hours since your death have seemed like

an eternity. I cannot close my ears to my son's cries; the screams are driving me mad! How can I live without you? The time for your burial draws near. I shall carry you myself down to the ocean, for that is the only appropriate way for you to leave this life. Those surging waves delivered you to me, and now I must return Neptune's bounty. Do not weep, dearest, for I do not intend to leave you alone in those waters. I know how you fear the sea. I shall hold you in my arms until my lungs are filled with water and we both sink to our grave along the ocean's floor."

Raven closed the journal; there was no need to read the preceeding entries, she already knew what was in them.

Morgan Robert Taylor, son of an Englishman of the same name and a shipwrecked Spanish señorita, Juanita—Juanita Perez most likely. Juan—Juanita, Roberto—Robert. Juan Roberto Perez.

Trying to hold back the flood of tears she knew would surely fall lest she struggle to control them, Raven closed the cover of the seventy-year-old journal and laid it on the table beside her bed. She blew out the candle and buried her head in the pillow. Only then did she release the flow of her feelings. She cried for the bitter man whose dying thoughts she had invaded, for the tiny babe who would never know a mother's caress or the sound of her laughter, and for the young man who grew into adolescence knowing that his own father could not bear the sight of him.

But most of all, the tears she shed were for herself. How could she face the man who had chosen to keep his true identity from her, even in their most intimate moments together? Would she be able to pretend never having seen her father's friend once he was introduced to her? And the hardest struggle of all to endure would be forcing a smile upon her face as the man she loved, the man she could never bring herself to forget, drew Melinda into his embrace and whispered the same vows of love that he had professed to her only months before.

hortly past nine the next morning Raven heard
Illah's timid rapping on her door, but pretending to be
oundly asleep, ignored it. An hour later Sir Robert
arged into the room, startled to find that his daughter
ad made no preparation to begin the morning's
ctivity.

"Good Lord, Raven. It is well past ten and still you
re not dressed. Did I not tell you that Morgan is to
rrive promptly at noon?" he asked, with a reprimand-
ng scowl. "You know we are to be at the harbor at
oon to greet him!"

"I am sorry, Papa," she apologized meekly, "but I
eally do not feel well this morning. You go on without
ne."

"Nonsense! Some sunlight and a few whiffs of that
alty air is all you need to cure you of your ailments.
Iurry along now," he ordered. "I shall wait for you in
he library."

Raven hesitated, her head lowered so her father
vould not notice the red puffiness rimming her eyes.
Please, Papa, I fear that would only magnify my
eadache. I am sure Mr. Taylor will understand if I am

not there."

"You have only half an hour to dress."

Raven knew by the unrelenting tone of his voice that she had little choice but to join him. She threw back the covers with a defeated, exasperative motion and forced herself into an upright position. She stumbled to the basin and angrily splashed her face with cold water.

Oh, I mustn't be so vexed with Papa, she told herself gazing disdainfully into the oval mirror above her dressing table. It is only natural for him to want me to accompny him to the harbor to greet his benefactor. He has no idea of how uncomfortable the introduction is going to be for me. How could he? For all he knows, my only association with Mr. Taylor is through one brief bit of correspondence.

I still find it hard to believe that Morgan and Juan are the same. Although I should have expected all along that something was amiss, the thought never crossed my mind. Such polished mannerisms and refined language as those possessed by Juan Perez were most assuredly not the traits of a sailor. How easily I was deluded by his magnificent performance. Very convincing he was! I dare say Mr. Taylor missed his calling. He's far better suited for the theater than the sea or a plantation.

Raven dressed with care, after having finally selected a dress of ivory muslin from her wardrobe. The intricate stitching below the bodice clinched her narrow waist and forced her breasts upward toward the fashionably low, eyelet-bordered neckline. She brushed her hair until it shone with a glossy luster and allowed it to cascade in loose curls over her proudly upright shoulders. How foolish I was to even consider

402

owering in my room. I intend to make that scoundrel
eel just as uncomfortable as I. Oh, I shudder to think
what may have happened had I not discovered his
father's journal in the library. I would surely have made
a blubbering idiot of myself in front of everyone. Now I
am much better prepared to deal with our meeting, and
it will be I who will be in complete control of this
situation.

On her way out of the room she paused for a second
glance in the mirror and nodded appreciatively at her
reflection. All traces of last night's anxiety had been
erased with cold compresses and a faint brush of
powder. You may have been made a fool once, Raven
Gatewood, she thought, forcing her pursed lips into a
congenial smile, but I will make certain that arrogant
Morgan Taylor never knows of the tormenting anguish
he has caused me. I refuse to give him such pleasure.
Next time, I will not be so easily persuaded by those
meaningless phrases of love.

She pulled a purple hibiscus from the vase on her
writing table and tucked it into her hair before rushing
down to meet her father.

"There now. Did I not tell you that you would feel
much better once you were up and out?" he asked,
giving his daughter an appraising smile as she
descended the stairs.

"I apologize for detaining you, Papa, but that
dreadful headache had me in a rather foul mood."

"I understand, Raven. Moodiness is a woman's
prerogative, just as long as she does not carry it to an
extreme. Speaking of which, Mama Bella and Melinda
are battling again."

"And what of this time?" asked Raven, eyeing the

empty space in the book cabinet. I must remember to return that book to its place, she thought.

Sir Robert shrugged his shoulders. "Who knows Probably some petty incident hardly worth anyone's attention. I certainly hope Morgan won't allow himsel to be overwhelmed by Melinda's seemingly benign disposition."

"I feel certain that Mr. Taylor will be most deserving of Melinda's attentions," she remarked bitterly.

Sir Robert gave his daughter a perplexed look, bu before he could ask her to explain such a peculia statement, Mama Bella stormed into the room. "Ah de de-clar! Dat gal is meaner dan a hol nest o' waspers. If' she don' watch her step, ah's gonna forgit jes who ah i: an' turn her 'crost my knee!"

"Don't let her upset you so, Bella. If she knows how much she provokes you, she will just continue he childish behavior," advised Sir Robert.

Mama Bella nodded in acquiescence and waddlec out of the room, hurling Melinda a threatening look as the girl came down the stairs.

Insipid bitch, cursed Melinda under her breath Upon seeing Raven and Sir Robert, she suddenly transformed her ire into melodious cheerfulness "Good morning, Sir Robert, Raven. It was so nice o you to wait for me. I just knew I would be late. Tha lazy Ullah waited until the very last minute to press my dress. Do you think I look all right?" she asked twirling slowly around in front of them so they coulc each admire her elegantly attired form. Her dress wa made of glimmering satin. Only her face was lef uncovered, and that would be shielded from the sun by a parasol trimmed with lace ruffles to match the trimming around her wrists and neck.

"You look lovely," praised Sir Robert, knowing that if her vanity were not appeased they might well miss Morgan's homecoming entirely.

"Yes, absolutely lovely. Just like a story-book princess," answered Raven with an unusual display of calmness. And I suspect that virginal image is just what you wish to convey to your returning suitor, she thought bitterly as a twinge of jealousy shot through her.

"Well then, let's not waste any more time. It would disappoint Morgan so if we were not there to greet him the moment his ship docks," said Melinda.

They arrived at the harbor promptly at noon and just as the *Gay Dolphin* rounded the tip of Cupid's Cay and glided gracefully up to the wharf. Even though Raven had vowed she would remain calm and indifferent throughout the entire ordeal, an uneasy queeziness fluttered in her stomach. Try as hard as she could, she was not able to dissuade her eyes from scanning the deck for Juan Perez. She caught a quick glimpse of him as he disembarked the vessel, and even though she deliberately averted her gaze out to sea, she was uncomfortably aware that in a few moments he would be alongside her.

The taut muscles of his upper legs flexed underneath the close-fitting linen breeches he wore as Morgan Taylor strode toward them with that same confident gait Raven had seen so often. She could not help but remember the solid firmness of his thigh as it had pressed against hers the night Captain Mabry had seated the dashing sea captain beside her.

Stop it! Stop it! She clenched her fists and gritted her

teeth. Do not make this any more difficult than it already is, she warned herself. If you choose to remember him at all, then remember the pain that his deception has caused you. Erase all else from your memory.

"And this is my daughter, Raven," Sir Robert proudly told his benefactor, their arms still clasped in a gentlemanly gesture of friendship. "After receiving your letter, it seems she thought it best to come nurse her father herself."

Even without the dark growth of whiskers shading his face, Taylor's identity was unmistakable—that full, sensuous mouth, regally straight nose, the square-set prominence of his jaw, the lofty arch of his well-curved brow, and those deeply penetrating, feline-like eyes.

"At last I have the pleasure of making your charming acquaintance, Miss Gatewood." The amusement in his tone was discernable only to Raven, and it made her slightly uncomfortable, for he stared boldly at her.

Raven swallowed nervously, hoping to get rid of the lump from the middle of her throat. "My . . . my father has told me so much about you, I feel I practically know you myself."

"Indeed?" He grinned. "The feeling is mutual, I assure you." He turned to Mama Bella and clasped her pudgy hands in his. "And my dear Mama Bella. How I have missed you these last six months. I do not believe I have had a decent meal since I left you."

Raven was sure she detected a crimson blush on the Negress's rounded cheeks. "Nah, Massah Morgan. Yo' knows you's jes sayin' dat ta makes me feel good. Welcome home, suh!" She flung her flabby arms around his neck. Her eyes sparkled with a joyous dampness.

Raven pondered for a moment on the touching reunion. Almost like that of a mother and her son, she thought. Could Bella be the woman whose milk gave life to the orphaned babe thirty-three years earlier. Of course, she decided, that would account for their familial closeness.

Melinda's lips were thrust out in pouting displeasure. Inside she was fuming. How dare he ignore me for that darkie! Why, I should have been the first one he greeted! I saw how Raven eyed him and the way he returned her brazen stare. I knew all along she would try and steal him from me.

Her thoughts were malicious, but her words were coated with honey when Taylor finally did acknowledge her. "Dear, dear Morgan. I cannot tell you how wonderful it is to see you again." She fluttered her blond lashes coquettishly. "I trust Uncle Woodes informed you of the circumstances leading to my being here."

Taylor was obviously uncomfortable. "That he did, Miss Nelson, and I assure you that you and your family are welcome guests at my home any time," he said with stiff politeness.

Melinda possessively looped her arm around his and shot Raven and Mama Bella a blazing look of triumph. "I am certain you must be simply exhausted after your trip, Morgan."

He managed to free himself from her tight hold and face the others; his features flushed with embarrassment. "Mama Bella has informed me that the workers have prepared an enormous feast in their village to

407

celebrate my return. I would be most honored, Robert, if you and your lovely daughter would share the festivities with me."

"Thank you, Morgan. It would be a pleasure."

"Fine, fine," he said, drawing Sir Robert up beside him. "Now, you must tell me of all that has transpired during my absence."

Melinda stubbornly refused to be pried from his side, even though she was deliberately excluded from his conversation and could barely keep step with the men's lengthy strides. Mama Bella snickered to herself, for it was obvious that Taylor could not rid himself of the fair-skinned woman too soon. She, Raven, and Captain Ahab followed behind as the group made its way up the beach to the village.

Upon reaching the chipped shell clearing of the native settlement, Mama Bella disappeared inside one of the palmetto frond huts, and Ahab managed to strike up a conversation with the Tarlton boys. Sir Robert stood talking with the elder Mr. Tarlton while Taylor conversed with his overseer about cotton productivity during his absence. Melinda was obviously infuriated at having been neglected by Taylor, so Raven joined her, suggesting that they watch the activity from one of the benches that had been placed in the shade underneath a soursop tree.

The air was filled with tempting aromas and the sounds of exhilarated vivacity. The field hands and their families all reveled in boisterous merriment. Kinky-haired, chestnut-colored children armed with sticks and stones and ready to defend the midday meal against the wild yellow mongrels who lurked in the woods encircled the fires where three of the village's largest hogs were being roasted to succulent tenderness in honor of the "bossman"'s return.

"Don't look so sullen. You've hardly said a word the entire time we've been sitting here. If you aren't careful your mouth will be permanently creased with that hideous frown," cautioned Raven, knowing that her comment would definitely bring some sort of reaction from the sulking Melinda.

"Why do you not just mind your own business?" snapped Melinda gloweringly. "I'm angry at you already, and don't pretend to be so innocent. You know good and well why I'm upset with you."

"Oh, hush, Melinda. This is a rather nice party, don't you agree? The field workers were very considerate to welcome him home in this way."

"No doubt those black devils will look for any excuse to keep them from their chores. I'm not even sure I want to be a part of this merrymaking anyway." She pouted haughtily. "Socializing with these darkies? Why, that's unheard of!"

Her indifferent attitude changed to one of personable warmth as the Tarlton boys sauntered hesitantly toward them, each carrying two plates of ribs, yams, and peas. "Why how sweet of you both to join us lonely girls. And I see you've brought us some of that deliciously tempting food," said Melinda sweetly, fluttering her eyes. "I was just commenting to Raven how nice it would be to see you two."

Although Geoffrey Tarlton was nearly two years older than his brother George, the two young men could easily have been mistaken for twins. Both had wavy auburn hair and an abundance of freckles sprinkled over their faces. They shared the same love for the sea as well and were constantly badgering Captain Ahab to let them work for him since they had no desire to follow their father's profession.

"If it is permissible with the two of you, my brother and I would be most honored to keep you company," offered Geoffrey, the more outspoken of the two, as he handed a plate to Raven and placed his own on the ground at her feet. "Come along, George, let's fetch some citronade for the ladies. Excuse us, please."

Melinda nodded graciously and watched as the brothers hurried back to the tables. "Did you see Morgan glaring at those two? What a look of jealousy! Serves him right! I'll teach him to leave me unaccompanied again," she said flippantly, tossing aside her blond curls.

"Oh, thank you so much, boys. Now you must sit down and eat before the food gets cold. Don't be so shy, George. Come on over here beside me. I'm not going to bite."

After they had finished their meals, Melinda, noticing that Morgan was still casting scowling frowns in their direction, suggested that they move in closer to the others and be a bit more sociable. She took George's arm, then linked her other hand to Geoffrey's elbow. "Such gaiety is simply marvelous," she said. "How I love dances and parties!"

Ten of the ebony-skinned men had lined up facing the center of the clearing. Opposite them stood an equal number of women. The drum music began with a monotonous staccato thumping on the tightly stretched cowhide covering. The tempo gradually grew faster until the wiry, stone-faced musician was pounding with frantic force. The dancers kept their eyes on him,

410

waiting for a signal for their dance to begin.

Two couples suddenly leaped into the center of the circle. One foot was put in front of the other, then drawn quickly back while the dancers tapped their toe and heel to the ground. The men raised and lowered their arms, careful to keep their elbows close to their sides while their partners, holding red bandannas above their heads, waved to the spectators. This was repeated until each couple had their turn in the center.

"It exhausts me just watching them," said Raven, fanning herself.

Geoffrey grabbed her arm. "Shall we try it?"

"No, no. I don't believe I've quite mastered the steps yet."

Melinda blinked enthusiastically. "Oh, I should love to try it, Geoff. Please, let's do." She held out her arm, and they joined the activity.

When it became their turn for the center dancing, Melinda held her handkerchief high above her head and gyrated her hips provocatively, her eyes never straying from Morgan's stunned face. When the dance ended, they were applauded loudly and surrounded by congratulating villagers. One of the women was holding a young baby on her hip. The child, never having seen silken strands of yellow hair, reached out to Melinda. Before he could be stopped the little fellow had entangled his sticky fist in Melinda's hair.

"Get away! Get away from me! Stop that, you little beast!" screamed Melinda.

Raven could not help but laugh at the befuddled expression on Melinda's face. "You should take that as a compliment," she said, trying to placate the rattled woman. "The only thing he wanted to do was touch you."

"You get away from me, too," she sniffed childishly.
Her eyes searched for Morgan, but he was too
engrossed in comforting the mother and infant to pay
her any attention. "Humph!" she said. Then realizing
how conspicuously silly she must look to everyone, she
pulled Geoffrey away from the group. "Please, I beg of
you, take me away from these . . . these animals."

Once Melinda had retreated to the main house, the
festive spirit resumed, and the incident was quickly
forgotten. Raven restlessly scanned the crowd for her
father, and upon finding him settled comfortably
beneath a palm involved in a chess match with the elder
Mr. Tarlton, she decided not to distract him.

"It appears that your handsome suitor has gone to
the aid of another damsel and left you to entertain
yourself."

"Oh! Mr. Taylor, you quite starltled me." Please do
not let him hear how rapidly my heart is thumping, she
pleaded silently. I cannot make a fool of myself again.

"I trust you are enjoying yourself."

She could not bring herself to return his bold gaze, so
instead she rested her eyes on the narrow scar on his
cheek. "Yes, yes I am," she answered with perfunctory
calmness. "It is a lovely party. You must feel honored
that your workers think so highly of you."

Her gaze shifted restlessly, first to her father, then
to a group of children nearby who were playing
*mayamba,* and then to Mama Bella who had donned
her ritual robes and was surrounded by a cluster of
young women.

"She's telling their fortune," explained Morgan,
having followed Raven's gaze. "By tossing those

412

stones, she can predict when they will marry and how many children will grace their households. Perhaps she would even consent to telling yours."

"No thank you. I prefer to discover things on my own, not with the aid of a mambo."

"You seem unusually uncomfortable," he said, lowering his voice. "Let us walk down to the shore. There is so much we need to discuss."

"No, no, really I—" she stammered. "Well, all right, as long as I am not gone too long. I don't want my father to worry."

"As you wish." He held out his arm for her, but she ignored his gesture, chattering nervously as they made their way through the boisterous crowd.

The instant they were out of sight and concealed by the wooded thicket, Taylor stepped ahead and pulled her against him. Their faces touched, and his lips searched for hers. "My dearest, dearest Raven. How I have missed you. I should never have left you alone in Nassau. Henry told me all about what happened to you. Thank God I am here with you now. I swear I will never again leave your side."

For one brief moment, Raven was lost in the past and almost allowed herself to return his passionate kiss. No, no I mustn't, she thought wildly. He is not the man I gave my love to not so long ago. He has changed! Her body stiffened with cold frigidity. Do not permit yourself to become entrapped by him again!

She jerked herself away abruptly, and with renewed strength stormed at him. Her face was livid with anger, and her tightly clenched fist pushed him away. "Just who do you think you are, Mr. Taylor? Just because you are responsible for saving my father's life is no

413

reason for you to think that payment of such a debt includes free liberties with me."

The dark thickness of his eyebrows twitched with startled amazement. "Raven! What has gotten into you? Not so long ago you vowed your love to me for eternity, and now you—"

"I haven't the slightest idea of what you're talking about," she said with disdainful indignation. "Now if you will excuse me." She whirled herself around. How she wanted him to hold her, to kiss her tenderly, and to offer a believable explanation for his actions. But no, she could not allow this to happen lest her defenses crumble and she fall into his embrace, and into his selfish trap once again.

He grabbed her arm with a savage roughness and swung her back around. His fingers dug deeper into her skin. "I do not enjoy these little charades, Raven. I am not some young whelp like Geoff Tarlton who can be dangled on a string," he told her with biting accusation. "I demand to know why your attitude toward me has changed so. Surely you have not forgotten the night we spent together in my cabin aboard the *Falcon,* or our last evening together at Henry's. Or were those just insignificant, meaningless encounters for you? Answer me!"

She managed to flash him a look of genuine awe. "Surely you must be mistaken, Mr. Taylor, for until this very afternoon, I have never set eyes on you before in my life." She raised her head proudly and returned his heated stare. "Now, if you will excuse me, I must be returning to the others. You may be certain that I will not mention any of this to my father, or to your fiancé!"

Taylor's lips twisted in a cruelly sardonic grin. "Yes,

by all means, go back to the celebration. I have no desire to tarnish the reputation of such a lady as yourself."

His parting words stung in her ears and put her mind in even more turmoil, for he had said exactly the same thing that evening on the deck of the *Fancy Free*. That time she had invited him to stay and talk with her longer, but this time she nodded curtly to her adversary and proceeded back up the path.

How dare he think that I will succumb so easily to his beckonings! Does he not realize that I am not a marionette to be dangled by strings and controlled by his whims. How dare he accuse me of such! Why do I feel as though I am being unfair? I must admit I did not give him a chance to explain his actions, but why should I have. What guarantee do I have that his explanations will not just be more lies to cover up the ones he has already told me?

She dwelt on such thoughts the remainder of the evening and well into the night, long after they had all returned to the house from the party. She could not sleep for wondering had she indeed been justified in pretending to not recognize him. Or was it a foolish thing to do, she questioned herself over and over.

I'm certain he saw through that farce. No matter how aloof I tried to appear, he knew I had weakened considerably when I accepted his kiss. I wonder if he experienced that same delicious tingling sensation as I when our lips pressed together after so long a time?

She sighed longingly and raised the edge of the netted pavilion to snuff out the candle. We would have made such an ideal pair, Juan and I—Morgan and I. Oh, I will never become accustomed to calling him by that name, for it sounds as though it is the name of a stranger, not the man with whom I am in love. Was once in love, she corrected herself quickly.

I must face the reality, no matter how hard or trying it may be; the man I knew as Juan Perez is forever gone. I wish he would vanish from my heart as well. I can never forget the humiliation his deceit has brought me. And to think, he accused me of perpetrating the charade. Not for one instant did I pretend to be something I was not.

Why can I not hate him? I've certainly good enough reason! Why do I still even think of him? I had best erase him completely from my memory, just pretend I have never known him . . . or his touch . . . or his kiss . . . or the feel of his body.

## Chapter Twenty-Four

For the remainder of the week her cold indifference toward Taylor continued, as did the miserable chagrin which daunted her during the few hours they were forced in each other's company. Luckily he and her father were usually up and out by the time she ventured from her room, but try as hard as she could to avoid any contact with him, certain encounters were inevitable. During the evening meals, she would feel his burning stare upon her, even when the conversation was not directed to her. Taylor seemed to enjoy making it a point to single her out from the others so she could answer his trivial questions. She was unable to control herself during these times and would stutter and stammer most uncomfortably in reply.

"Your father tells me a most remarkable story, Miss Gatewood, of how you were kidnapped by some sea bandits," he remarked one evening, shortly after Sir Robert had retired to his room, leaving Taylor to entertain the two young women.

She nodded hesitantly. "That is correct, Mr. Taylor."

"Please, dear girl, call me Morgan. Such formality is

not necessary. And I will call you Raven," he said, smiling with peculiar geniality.

"All right," she stiffly conceded.

"He also told me that you were rescued by some fellow who was out in search of this pirate named Ames. Now what was your hero's name. He was Spanish, I believe," he said, stroking his chin thoughtfully.

"Surely you remember his name, Morgan," interrupted Melinda. "Why, you must be as familiar with it as you are your own. I thought everyone knew of the heroic exploits of Juan Perez," she sneered pithily. "Some of us even know about his romantic tendencies as well, don't we Raven?"

"Ah, so you developed quite an attachment to your courageous hero, heh Raven?" he asked with deliberate smoothness. "Perhaps that is why you have been so solemn as of late. You long for the company of this dashing young man, do you not?"

Raven felt her face flush crimson with embarrassment. Then she met his intent look with an acrid glower. "An inexperienced young woman's infatuation could hardly be referred to as an attachment, Mr. Taylor. Until you mentioned him, I can assure you, I had quite forgotten all about Juan Perez. Now, I am sure there are other, more important things that need to be discussed between the two of you, so if you will excuse me, good evening!"

Just as she had managed to retreat to the stairs without allowing a single tear to fall, Mama Bella halted her hurried exit. "Cum in heah, chile." She prodded her gently into the cook room. "Ah kin sees you'ns 'bout ready to cry. Nah tell Mammy Bella

418

whut's deh matta."

Raven sniffed, determined not to let Mama Bella know the real reason for her anxiety. "I'm just tired, that's all. And I thought perhaps Mr. Taylor and Melinda could carry on their courtship ever so much better without the interference of a third person."

"So ah's right. Ah might haf knowed," said the Negress, seating herself beside the distressed girl. "If'n yo' wants hem, youh gotta fights fer hem. Don' give in s'easily to Miss Priss!"

"No, you don't understand. I don't want him. She can have him for all I care. They'd make a lovely bride and groom."

"Ah's seen de way yo' looks at hem and de way he stares at yo' when youse back is turned. Ah'm old 'nough to tell when two people's in love!"

"Love? Why I most certainly do not love him. He is without a doubt the most arrogant, conceited, the rudest and the brashest man I have ever—"

Mama Bella chuckled. "Jes' as ah spected. An ah haf jes' whut yo' needs tah makes shoah he feels de same way." She handed Raven a silver vial.

"What's this?" she asked, curiously opening the container's lid to peer inside. She poured out its powdery contents onto the table; leeks, rose petals, and corrinder seeds. Just as she did, Melinda's light footsteps were heard pattering up the stairs, followed a moment later by Morgan's heavier ones.

Mama Bella winked cunningly. "De day a leaf falls into de wata' not nec'sarly de day it sinks ta da bot'om."

"Which means?" asked Raven, amused by Mama Bella's funny proverb.

"De battle ain't ovah yet, chile. Dis heahs Mammy

Bella's love majik. Wheneva yo' can, sprinkle some of it on Massah Morgan when he ain't lookin'. Purty soon, he'll be askin' yo' pappy fer yo' hand."

Not wanting to offend the well-meaning old woman, Raven brushed the loose substance back into the vial, snapped the lid tight and stuck it in her pocket. "Thank you, Mama Bella. You're very sweet!"

The sturdy Negress gave her a wide-toothed grin. "An, if'n Miz Nelson's still mean to yo', ahs got 'nother poti'n jes' fer her."

Raven bent down and kissed her soft, rounded cheek. "Good night, Mama Bella."

"'Night, chile."

Raven was tempted to tiptoe on down the hallway and linger for a moment in front of Melinda's room and listen for any out-of-the-ordinary sounds, but she decided against such action for fear what she may hear would confirm her worst suspicions.

If he wants her, she decided, reprimanding herself for even considering such snoopy tactics, there is very little I can do to stop him. "A contemptible rogue and a pampered child," she said aloud. "What a pair they'll make. Why, they deserve each other!"

She removed her dress quickly, draped it across the dressing screen, and slipped her chemise over her head. The night was sultry and uncomfortably hot, not a wisp of air circulated in her room. I wish it would rain, she thought. My sleep has been fitful enough without this heat!

She stepped out onto the veranda and gazed up at the star-studded sky, but no relief from the torrid stickiness was in sight. An eerie feeling swept across her, almost as though someone were spying on her every move. Silly girl, she thought to herself. Who would be watching you. By now everyone is fast asleep or too engaged in their own frivolous frolic to pay me any attention.

Without taking her eyes from the veranda, she eased back into her room. The full moonlight shimmered against her nightgown and illuminated the sensual nakedness beneath the thin material.

A low, muffled gasp escaped her lips when she finally did turn around. "What, what are you doing in here?" she demanded callously, trying to hide her fright. She glared hatefully at the intruder.

Morgan moved toward her with stealthy silence, almost like a lion stalking its prey. Raven could feel the shameless lust in his catlike eyes as he peered appraisingly beneath her flimsy nightdress.

"I asked you a question! What gives you the right to barge into my room uninvited?" She felt the brass post of the bed against her back. Trapped! She could not get away from his muscular form as he edged closer, closing in on her. She tried to maintain her composure, for she was certain it would only make Morgan feel more manly if he knew that his presence were upsetting her.

"No, no please," she begged as he pulled her to him with one hand while the other cupped her chin and tilted her face back. "Please, don't hurt me any more," she said, almost in tears. "Please, I beg of you!"

Morgan brushed his lips over her reddened cheek, across her closed eyes and then rested on her mouth. When she finally did look up, he gazed mockingly into her emerald depths. "So that is how you return a man's kiss when you are but infatuated with him?" The

421

corners of his mouth turned up in a cruel grin. "You yourself admitted that is how you viewed our relationship."

"Please go now," she mumbled, eyes downcast on her bare feet. "Have you not humiliated me enough already. Must you make that pain even more unbearable?"

"So it is I who have humiliated you?" he asked reproachingly. "That is the way you see it? The blame all falls on my shoulders?"

"Yes, that is exactly the way I see it. You purposely allowed me to become enamoured of you, then you lied repeatedly to me. Obviously you had no concern for my feelings whatsoever."

"I told you no lies, Raven," he defended himself softly. "I would never have deliberately lied to you about my love or about anything else."

She felt herself weaken at his words, but drew herself up proudly. "Think very carefully, Mr. Morgan Taylor. Or would you prefer to be called Juan Perez?"

He gleamed with amusement. "So that is it. I thought as much. You are still angry because I kept my true identity secret."

"Of course that was only an oversight on your part, correct?" she asked, her strength gaining.

"Please sit down, Raven. My explanation is rather involved."

"I prefer to stand, thank you."

"Sit down," he said authoritatively. "Good Lord, woman, you did not used to be so difficult. Sit here, on the bed, beside me," he commanded as she moved to a bamboo chair in the corner. "If I have to shout my defense all the way across the room, I shall awaken everyone."

She reluctantly gave in to his command and sat down, careful that their bodies were separated by the bulky roll of bed covers.

"If you remember the evening we stood on the forward deck of the *Fancy Free* you asked me about my family, and I told you the entire truth." He nodded to the journal Raven had forgotten to return to the book cabinet. "That should vouch for my honesty. I admit there were one or two things I chose to omit, not because I wanted to deceive you but because I felt they were best to remain unmentioned. First was my name, and second was that I had spent considerable time in England. These two oversights were slight compared to the bulk of information you did discover about me that evening."

"Do not try to make atonements for yourself. There was no reason for you to lie to me as to who you really were. Even after I told you I had received a letter from a Mr. Taylor of Eleuthera explaining the circumstances of my father's four-year absence you pretended to be just an employee of his. You could have told me that you were my father's benefactor. There was no reason for such mystery. Surely you realized that once I arrived here I would discover the truth myself."

"Perhaps you are right, Raven. But I told you the circumstances surrounding my mission. Absolute secrecy was to be maintained if I were to be successful in capturing Ames. Only the governor and Henry knew that—"

"Henry knew as well?" blurted Raven. "And he

allowed me to think that—"

"Just calm down for a moment and let me continue. How impetuous you've become! There were two reasons for my maintaining such secrecy. First, I did not want Red Ames to burn and plunder Governor's Harbor in retaliation, and second my crew would be more apt to follow the commands of a man of Perez's background than they would a gentleman planter. Do you understand anything I'm saying?"

"But you could have confided in me. I would not have betrayed you."

"I know that Raven, but believe me, I thought I was doing the right thing. Tell me you believe me. You do, don't you?"

She nodded weakly. "What you have said does make sense, I suppose, but—"

"But what, Raven. I can see by your frown that you still doubt me."

"What about Melinda. Are you planning on marrying her?"

The question obviously took him by surprise. "Me, marry Melinda? What ever gave you such a ridiculous notion?"

"She did."

"And if I were planning on something so drastic, do you think I would be in your room this moment begging with you to understand my past actions?"

"Oh, Morgan. Are you telling me the truth?" she entreated.

He clasped both her hands in his. His words were spoken with such graveness that Raven could not help but believe them to be sincere. "I give you my word that what I have told you is the complete truth. I swear to you on my dead father's journal that I have not lied. I love you, Raven. No one but you. How will I ever convince you of that? You have been the only woman in my thoughts since we first met five months ago. From that time on I have belonged only to you. Until that moment we kissed on the *Fancy Free* I did not realize what true purpose there was to one's heart. Before that time I had only a void in my chest."

Raven was relieved. All of the worries and doubts had suddenly disappeared. "My feelings for you have never been just an infatuation, Morgan. I just said that because I was hurt. I was very bitter and angry this evening because I thought that you and Melinda were making fun of me. I have loved you all along. No matter how hard I tried to convince myself otherwise, the flutterings I feel inside when you touch me are so very, very real." She laid her head on his shoulder. "It is so wonderful to be beside you again."

He pulled her even closer and caressed her face with one hand while stroking her hair with the other. "You will never know how disturbed I was when you pretended not to recognize me. Sailing home I had envisioned you running toward the boat when it sailed into view, your skirt above your knees and your long, silky hair fluttering out behind you. Instead," he laughed good naturedly, "I was met by an icy, stone-faced woman, whom, I venture to say, had to be dragged to the harbor to meet me."

"Shhh. Let us not talk of such unpleasantries," she cooed murmurously, nuzzling against his face. "We are finally together now, and that is all that should matter."

"And together we will always be, for I never intend to

let you stray from my sight again," he vowed.

Wrapped up in each other's embrace, they fell back onto the bed. The flaming passions that had been restrained during their separation soared to consuming heights. He gently lifted her chemise over her head and unbuttoned his shirt so he could feel the welcoming soft warmth of her breasts against the hardness of his chest. His mouth longingly enveloped hers, and she felt as though her very breath would be extinguished by his fervent ardor. She clung to him with emulous zeal. They returned to reality only for a moment while he rid himself of his trousers and she tossed her wrinkled nightgown to the floor. He leaned over to blow out the candle, but she stopped him, saying that she wanted the light to illuminate his body as they made love.

Her legs parted at his touch, and he massaged the warmth between her thighs while his mouth sought the fullness of her heaving breasts. She moaned with ecstatic pleasure and pleaded, "Please, my darling, we have waited long enough already."

He moved gently across her outstretched nakedness, arousing more desire in Raven than she had ever dreamed possible. They were possessed with such a craving for each other that their bodies soon became one in unrestrained lust.

Afterward, they lay side by side in exhaustive silence. Finally, after several moments had elapsed, Raven turned to her lover and propped herself up on her elbow. He reached over and kissed the pinkness of her rounded nipples. "Such splendid beauty is all mine," he mumbled selfishly, cuddling closer to her breasts. "All mine!"

Raven smiled, pleased to have incited such passion

in him, and stroked Morgan's dark head. "Do you know something?"

"Mmm? What is it darling?" he asked tracing the line of her cleavage with his tongue.

She playfully pushed him away. "No, wait a moment."

"What? Tired of me already, are you?" He grinned impishly. "What happened to my wanton wench who could never get enough of my manliness."

"Believe me, darling, she has not disappeared," she assured him. "I was just wondering what ever happened to Red Ames. I have been so childish this last week I completely neglected to inquire of your success in that mission."

"I hardly think this is an appropriate time for your questions, but since you insist, and you know I can refuse you nothing, I shall be most happy to tell you of your betrothed's gallant battle with that infamous, red-haired rogue."

Raven clapped her hands joyously. "Then you did catch him? Good for you! Oh, I'm so proud of you," she said, giving his neck a roughly affectionate hug.

"If I get this sort of reception every time I capture a criminal I shall have to go to Nassau tomorrow and unlock all of the cells."

"Don't you dare! Now that you're here, you're not going anywhere for quite a while, Mr. Taylor! Now, tell me how you did it. I would have loved to have been there and seen the look on that monster's face. Please, you must give me a thorough account of all that happened. It isn't necessary to spare any of the horrible details, for Red Ames deserved every bit of punishment he received."

"You must not romanticize the event so," said Morgan. "It was not nearly as exciting as you might imagine. As a matter of fact, we came upon Ames quite by accident. After Jennings's ship went down, Ames decided to abort his plans to invade Nassau and decided to sail for the Florida Keys instead. We were on our way back to Nassau at the same time and luckily sighted his flag long before he took notice of ours.

"The moment we were within firing range, we bombarded his ship with cannon and musket fire. It was our good fortune that his crew was too drunk to do much more than stumble around on the deck, and *Le Bordeaux* burst into flames. There are two things sailors fear most, fire onboard their ship and having to jump into the ocean for fear of what lies beneath the surface. Well, he and his men were forced to abandon ship, and like most sailors, very few could swim. Most of them drowned, and the ones who did manage to reach the bow of the *Falcon* were brought aboard and cuffed in chains immediately."

"And what of Ames? Did he perish in the water or in the fire?"

"He was one of the few who were able to swim to the safety of our ship. When he crawled aboard, Horningold had the shackles and chains ready for him and didn't give him a chance to even cough up the water. We reached Nassau the next night, and the following day, Ames was tried and hanged along with the survivors of his mangy crew."

Raven breathed a sigh of relief. "Thanks to you, I shall never again have to worry about waking up and seeing his pock-marked face hovering above me. You know, Morgan, hanging seems like much too lenient a punishment," she said, remembering how he had tortured his prisoners so mercilessly before putting them out of their misery. "Thank God you were not injured."

"We were fortunate, indeed. Not one of my men was harmed, and the ship returned to port in excellent condition."

"What about Horningold and George and Cockram. What will they all do now?"

"They were all given property rights to good farming acreage for their part in helping to supress piracy once and for all, but I suspect most of the men will want to become involved in the whaling industry Woodes and I plan to promote. Their love of the sea far exceeds their love of the land, or their willingness to till the soil. But enough of such matters. We have something far more important to discuss."

"Oh, and that is?"

"My making a respectable woman out of you before your father has *me* hanged. After all, I was responsible for dishonoring you and so it is only fitting that I make atonements for my lusty greed."

"You still want to . . . to—"

"Yes, I want to make you my wife. Why the startled look? I told you all along my intentions were perfectly honorable, did I not?"

"Well, yes, but that was when you were Juan Perez. How was I to know that Morgan Taylor intended to carry out the promises made by his other identity?"

"I want to marry you more now than ever before. You see, my dearest, after I left you at Henry's and went back out to sea, I realized that without you, life held no meaning whatsoever for me. The thought of being in your arms again was my motivation. I wanted to complete my task and return to Eleuthera where I was certain I would find you waiting for me. A man needs far more than adventure and wealth, but only after I became acquainted with you did I realize this was true.

"Had I received news of Captain Jack's boat sinking, God knows what foolish moves I might have made against Ames; moves that would have endangered my ship and the men who trusted me. But as it was, I knew nothing of what had transpired during my absence until I returned to Nassau with Ames. So, dear girl, what is your answer? Do you think you can be happy living on an island in the middle of the Atlantic Ocean with a— What was it you called me? Oh, yes, with a contemptible rogue?"

"What a foolish question for you to ask! I could be happy anywhere as long as I knew you were by my side." All her misgivings and apprehensions about Taylor had been erased. There was no cause to worry about Melinda, for all doubts concerning their relationship had been banished as well. And Raven was no longer troubled about her father's reaction to such a union, for there no longer existed any reason for him to oppose their wedding. After all, he had hinted on several occasions that he wished they could remain on Eleuthera forever.

"So, my darling," he said, giving her a kiss on the cheek, "now that that is settled, I had best return to my own room."

"Must you leave so soon?" she asked disappointedly. "Why, you have spent only a few moments with me."

He drew her into his embrace once more, "I'm afraid

it is much later than you think, dearest. The downstairs clock just chimed five o'clock. What would my future father-in-law say if he were to see me sneaking out of his daughter's room at daybreak? We shall all have a leisurely breakfast together in a few hours, and I will approach Sir Robert for your hand then. Good-bye my darling." He said, blowing her a kiss on his way out.

## Chapter Twenty-Five

Three hours later as she was waiting for Morgan and her father to join her for breakfast, Raven's exhalted bliss faded to dispondent sorrow. "I don't understand, Melinda. What do you mean that you forgive me for my behavior last night?" she asked curiously as Melinda sat down at the mahogany table. "If you are upset about my excusing myself after that silly little comment you made about Juan Perez—"

"You know very well that's not what I'm referring to," she retorted accusingly, but with an insouciant manner. "I know all about your cozy tryst with Morgan last night."

Raven's bewildered silence implicated her guilt, as did the incriminating pallidness of her face.

Smoothing a nonexistent wrinkle from her skirt, Melinda continued smugly. "You see, Raven, Morgan told me all about it this morning. The poor man was so distraught. He came to my room before seven, confessed his wrong doing and begged me to forgive him. And of course, I told him that I would need time to contemplate the matter. Have you nothing to say for yourself, dear friend?"

"Surely you do not expect me to plead for your exoneration as well," she finally replied. "Besides, why should I even believe you?"

"My only desire, Raven, is that you and I harbor no malice toward each other. We were almost friends at one time," she said with convincing clemency. "I understand perfectly well your reasons for doubting what I say as the truth. I imagine that right now you must feel as though you have been made a fool of and your love as well as your body cruelly violated."

"And no doubt, my troubled feelings are the reason for your benign show of mercy?" asked Raven with bitter rancor. She was trying hard to not let the gnawing sorrow inside her become apparent, for Melinda would only enjoy her discomfort all the more.

Melinda clearly had the upper hand now, and she was determined to make the most of her superior position. "I suppose that I am as much to blame as you for Morgan's behavior last night," she admitted reluctantly. "You see, after you left us alone in the sitting room last night, things got a bit out of hand. It became increasingly difficult to control ourselves, and rather than submit to him before our wedding night, I left him all alone in his suffering. I did not suspect he would follow me to my room and threaten to go to you if I refused him. I had hoped he was making an idle, childish threat that was intended to coerce me into compromising myself to his whims. He taunted me with the fact that you two had been lovers before you came to Eleuthera; only then you knew him as Juan Perez."

"He . . . he told you of that?"

"Why of course. How else could I possibly have known?"

How else indeed, thought Raven with disheartened shame. "And what else did Morgan tell you?"

Melinda shrugged her shoulders with modest aloofness, secretly pleased that Raven had taken such an interest in her words. "Only that after he promised to marry you, you became quite receptive to his amorous advances."

"Oh, I see," choked Raven, her voice fading to a barely audible whisper.

"But now that he and I have resolved our differences and he's decided that he intends to proceed with our original plans, there is no reason why the three of us should not exercise the utmost civility in our relationship. After all, I shall be spending a good part of my honeymoon with you!"

"Your honeymoon? With me?" Up until now, Raven had managed to maintain her self-respect by feigning an air of aloofness, but with that last jab, she felt herself slowly begin to quaver.

"Why, yes. I know you cannot be too terribly pleased about it either, but it cannot be helped," she remarked with concise sharpness.

"I do not understand, Melinda. What are you talking about?"

"The four of us," she patiently explained. "You, your father, Morgan, and I shall sail to Nassau on the twentieth of this month to attend a gala celebration in Morgan's honor. We shall be married the following day by the minister there, and on Monday, the twenty-fifth, set sail for England. You and your father will return to your home once we reach Plymouth, and Morgan and I shall go on to my father's country estate in Devonshire for several days before going to London.

"Oh, please, Raven, don't look so dismal," she said with hypocritical soothingness. "One day, you, too, will find a suitable mate, only let this be a lesson to you that you should never submit to his carnal demands before that little band of gold is secure on your finger."

Not being able to listen to anymore of Melinda's biting comments, Raven jumped up from her chair, nearly knocking it back against the dish cabinet, and ran defeatedly from the room, leaving Melinda to gloat in her harsh victory.

She ran until her legs grew heavy and tired, until she thought they would collapse with another step, and still she ran. Her heart raced wildly, pounding against the bodice of her dress as though it were going to escape from her chest. Her head pulsated painfully with Melinda's vindictive words. Her very being was shattered. She wanted to get as far away from Morgan as possible.

She had no one to whom she could pour out her heart, no one to comfort her and tell her that all would work itself out in time, and that the pain she felt now would slowly heal as she got older.

How could she face her father after she had repeatedly disgraced herself so? She hated herself. She hated Morgan and all of the unforgivable agony he had intentionally caused her. His declarations of love, the way he kissed her, the ferocity of their lovemaking had all been lies. Lies! Lies! Lies! Wicked and vicious lies!

Will I never learn? she asked herself over and over. What a spectacle I have made of myself! Because I gave myself to a man I loved wholeheartedly, a man I believed loved me as well, is this to be my punishment forever. How pleased with herself Melinda must be knowing that she could have done no more damage to my heart had she pierced it with a cutlass. No doubt, I am the topic of their mindless humor this very instant. Poor silly girl, how easily she was swayed with a few meaningless words of love, she could hear Melinda say.

How righteous it was of her to so graciously pardon Morgan's indiscretion, especially since he came to me out of necessity to complete what she had already started. Damn! Damn! Damn them both! I should have had enough sense to see beyond his shallow words and barren embraces. Oh, why didn't I? Surely I cannot be doomed to a life of mistreatment by those I dare to love.

In her fury, Raven had ended up outside the stable. Storm and Prancer were already saddled, probably for Morgan and his sweet darling, she thought grimly. Such a shame I must spoil their lover's outing!

Storm's velvety ears perked up in warm recognition, and he nuzzled his damp nose against her shoulder and whinnied softly.

"Good boy, good boy," she whispered in his ear. "At least I have one friend on this island. You will never deceive me, will you boy? You may be an animal, but you are far more sensitive than your master. He's more of an animal than you."

Holding her skirt above her knees with one hand while the other gripped the saddle horn, she swung herself into the saddle. "Come along, boy . . . giddap!" she said, spurring him lightly in the side as they rode toward the beach.

Storm's sprightly caper quickened to a swift gallop as they reached the edge of the casuarinas. Aware of his restlessness, Raven gave him his head, and he bolted across the surf-smoothed shore in all of his ebony magnificence. Storm's hoofs tirelessly pounded the receding tide as he raced along the shell-spangled sands. The fiery, spirited steed vaulted gracefully over scattered branches of driftwood that had been washed upon the shore by the previous night's high tide.

Raven closed her eyes and confidently clung to his neck. She did not care where her mount took her or how fast his agile limbs traveled, just as long as he put a lengthy distance between her and Morgan. A sense of interminable freedom encompassed both horse and rider.

After a while, she felt her steed's powerful bulk stiffen with rigid hesitation. She opened her eyes. A low, wall-like mound of rocks blocked their path. "No! No! Storm!" she screamed, tightly jerking the reins.

Raven knew that jumping the obstacle ahead would be much too risky, for Storm could easily stumble and break a leg and hurl her against the barrier to an instant death.

The sudden pull of the reins made him jerk his head, and he became dangerously skittish. Only inches from the wall, his front legs lifted off the ground, and he reared high in protest. His astonished rider tumbled from the saddle, her head barely escaping the jagged edges of the threatening rocks. The horse slowly walked over to the sandy spot where his rider lay and nudged her face with his nose.

"It's all right, boy. I know you didn't mean to," she said, raising her head and struggling to regain the breath the fall had temporarily knocked from her. She made an effort to rise to her feet, but her ankle gave way beneath her. "My foot, I think it's broken," she said to Storm. "You must go back to the stable for help. Do you understand? Go back to the stable. Get Jacob!"

Storm tilted his head curiously to one side, then as though he understood her desperate plea, galloped off in the direction they came from.

I pray he knows the way back to the stable. Surely Jacob will come in search of me when Storm returns riderless.

The mid-morning sun blazed unrelentingly upon her. Using her hands, Raven awkwardly and slowly managed to crawl into the shadows of a cluster of palms. The heat parched her mouth, and she longed for water. She looked around her, hoping to find a coconut, but none had fallen from the trees. Hoardes of unusually large flies swarmed about her, alighting on her arms, her face, and her legs. They would beligerently return to their prey even after she had shooed them away. Their sting brought blood to the surface of Raven's skin, and only when an onshore breeze filtered through the trees did they leave her in peace.

She watched disconsolately as the sun moved in deathly slowness across the cloud-free sky. She knew that by the time it had reached its midday height, there would be no shadows of palms to protect her, and if no one came in search of her, she could easily perish.

"Raven, Raven, can you hear me?" a familiar voice pleaded as her cheeks were rubbed with a damp cloth. He held a container of water to her mouth. "Easy now, don't drink so much at one time. Just sip it."

Struggling against the glare of the sun, she finally pried her eyes open. She saw the face of her rescuer and tried to wriggle free from his hold. "No, no! Stay away from me! I hate you! Stay away!"

"Shhh, everything will be all right, darling," he assured her softly, holding her head in his lap. "I have already sent your father to get Ahab. They will bring the boat around shortly to pick us up."

"How did you find me?" she asked weakly.

"I was at the stable looking for you when Storm returned. I sent Jacob back to the house for your father, and he and I followed Storm's tracks."

"My foot, is it broken?"

"No, I don't think so, probably just a very nasty sprain," he answered, massaging her ankle.

She stiffened at his touch and tried to raise herself up. "Please, don't do that!"

He gently pushed her back down. "Just relax, Raven. I am afraid that some other bones may be bruised as well. Here, does it hurt when I push in on your ribs?" he asked, feeling her side.

She glared at him angrily and slapped his hand away. "It is not necessary that you feign such concern for my welfare, Mr. Taylor. You see, Melinda has already informed me of your plans to wed her. Don't you think having my father and I on your honeymoon is just a bit too much?" she asked venemously. "Must you constantly flaunt your infidelity in front of me. Do you not think I have feelings as well?"

"I understand your anger, Raven, but you must give me a chance to explain."

"That seems to be your favorite statement—along with, 'I shall never again let you out of my sight,'" she added caustically. "I am tired of your explanations. Lies seem to come quite natural to you. No, I will not give you a chance to explain those things that Melinda revealed to me this morning. You would just fabricate still another tale to defend yourself."

"I am sorry her lies subjected you to such pain, Raven. Believe me I am," he said sincerely. "But you know as well as I that Melinda will resort to any means to get her way. She is a jealous, vicious woman who is taking her anger out on you because I failed to return her affections."

"She was neither angry nor jealous this morning, Morgan," answered Raven sourly. "She was perfectly rational. Why should she not have been? She was gloating over my stupidity the entire time. I'm sure you two have had a good laugh at my expense."

"Just give me a chance to offer a logical explanation for her behavior."

"No," replied Raven stubbornly, covering her ears with her hands. "I am not interested in anything you have to say."

"I do not believe you have much of a choice. You have to listen to me; you certainly cannot get up and run away, and it will be yet another half hour before Ahab reaches us."

"You may talk as much as you wish, but I assure you it will make no difference as far as I am concerned," she replied with staunch directness.

"Last night, after you left me alone with her, she made it quite clear that I was welcomed to pay her a visit in her room later on. I scoffed at her offer, and she became angry and stormed upstairs."

"Of course she did. And you expect me to believe

that? Certainly I am not as naive as I may appear."

"There are several reasons I ignored her flirtation. First of all, her uncle and I are very close, and I do not want to endanger our friendship over his silly niece. Secondly, she thought for some strange reason that all she had to do was flaunt her pretty little body in my face and I would follow her like a panting dog. I refused to give her that satisfaction. And thirdly, and most importantly I might add, I have already by my own choice committed myself to a lifelong obligation with you, and I have no desire to risk losing you for a few sordid encounters with her. Do you understand now?"

"I know you expect me to," she answered with biting derision. "And while it is a most convincing story, it does not account for a few insignificant details."

"Which are?"

"First of all, how did Melinda know you were even in my room last night had you not told her?"

"I assume she saw me either entering last night or leaving this morning."

"All right then, how did she know about your adventures as Juan Perez? She was well informed of your escapades."

"Think carefully, Raven," he said complacently. "Who else knew of my disguise as a ship's captain?"

"The governor and Henry, but I really don't see the point you're trying to make."

"That's right, the governor and Henry. And the governor is married to Melinda's mother's sister. I am sure that aunt and niece have maintained a regular correspondence, and Melinda would resort to using any bit of information to her own advantage."

"Yes, I suppose that is feasible," she said, weakening.

She remembered the last letter Melinda got from her aunt, the one that arrived the day the provision ship came to Governor's Harbor. Since then, Melinda had acted even snider, she decided. And some of the insinuating comments she had made since then! "I just don't know what to think any more."

Taylor tousled her hair affectionately. "I know you've been put in a very difficult situation, but I assure you I am telling the truth. If you don't believe me, ask Mama Bella."

"What does she have to do with this?"

"She overheard the entire conversation. As a matter of fact, midway through it, she stormed into my room demanding that I give her an explanation for my treatment of you. She was furious. After I had calmed her down and explained everything to her satisfaction, I went downstairs and confronted Melinda. I intended to have her rectify matters with you then, but you had already run away. I went down to the stables, knowing that was probably where you were headed, and Jacob told me you had taken Storm out for a ride, which incidentally spoiled my plans for our going riding and having a romantic beach picnic later this afternoon."

Raven grinned ashamedly. "And I thought the horses were saddled for you and Melinda."

"If you have any doubt whatsoever in your mind, dearest Raven, please talk to Mama Bella. She can verify that what I have told you is the truth. You know, she's grown particularly fond of you. So have I for that matter."

"Oh, Morgan. I feel so ashamed for ever having doubted you," she said with remorse. "But Melinda really was convincing!"

"I'm sure she was," he laughingly agreed. "She told me some rather interesting stories about you and Geoffrey Tarlton."

"She wouldn't have dared!" stormed Raven. "Why the only time I've even spoken to him alone was at that party the day of your arrival."

"Shhh, don't let your temper flare so over her. I have learned to just overlook her childishness. You would do well to do likewise. She'll be out of our lives soon enough. As a matter of fact, she is probably packing this very minute. I intend to have Ahab take her to Nassau as soon as possible. Her presence here has caused both of us far too much sorrow."

"How will you explain your asking her to leave to the governor?"

"I'm sure I won't have any explanations to make. She was so humiliated by the time I finished giving her a thorough lashing, she'll be glad to get away."

"You're not angry with me, are you, Morgan?" she asked, leaning her head back on his chest and staring into the greenness of his eyes. "I vow that no matter what else happens, I will never again doubt anything that you tell me."

"I am afraid that your word is not good enough for me, Raven," he remarked, frowning somberly. "You must prove your love."

"Why Morgan, haven't I done that already?" she teased wickedly, sensing that he was only pretending to make a serious request.

"You must prove that you will never again doubt my word, and you must do so by marrying me this very afternoon," he insisted, continuing with his grave air.

"Marry you— This afternoon?" she stammered

confusedly. "But what about—?"

He hushed her questions. "All has been taken care of, I assure you. I asked your father's permission long before you and Melinda had your little chat, and I have already sent word to Reverend Maryville to be at my . . . at our home promptly at six this evening. And I'm sure that Mama Bella is planning a huge celebration for us. Whether you like it or not, dear girl, you are already committed. And frankly, I see no way out for you."

Raven was too surprised to speak.

Morgan continued. "And furthermore, Sir Robert is delighted with the prospect of having me as a son-in-law. You mustn't disappoint him! And did I tell you that the three of us are going to England next month to clear up that matter concerning your aunt and uncle. Oh, and by the way, afterward, Sir Robert will return to Eleuthera with us to try his skill at cultivating pineapples."

"If you will cease your ramblings long enough, sir, I may have a chance to answer your question."

"I didn't ask you anything. I only told you just how it is going to be. I don't see as you have much of a choice. Must I remind you that I was responsible for saving both you and your father's lives?"

"Oh, yes! Yes! Yes!" Raven was laughing, her smiles intermingled with tears. "Yes, I will marry you. I will!"

He gathered her in his strong arms and distributed kisses over her face. "Nothing again will ever cause us any worry or any bitterness. That, I promise! I will see to it that you are the most contented woman on earth. And I will be the doting husband."

"And I will strive to make you so very, very happy,

444

Morgan," she promised softly as she kissed his neck. "So very, very happy."

"Just as long as you don't try and tame me the way you did Storm," he joked in reply. He picked her up and carried her along the gleaming, sun-swept surf, never for a moment taking his eyes from the radiant loveliness of her smiling face.

Raven sighed contentedly. No longer must she relive the horrors she had witnessed earlier, for Morgan was there to protect her. Her father would not have to leave his beloved islands or his only child, and she, yes and she would forever be united with her handsome, dashing hero. Nothing would ever be able to sever the strong bindings of their love-filled union, for theirs was a love to overcome all obstacles.

# BESTSELLING ROMANCES BY JANELLE TAYLOR

**SAVAGE ECSTASY** (824, $3.50)

It was like lightning striking, the first time the Indian brave Gray Eagle looked into the eyes of the beautiful young settler Alisha. And from the moment he saw her, he knew that he must possess her — and make her his slave!

**DEFIANT ECSTASY** (931, $3.50)

When Gray Eagle returned to Fort Pierre's gates with his hundred warriors behind him, Alisha's heart skipped a beat: would Gray Eagle destroy her — or make his destiny her own?

**FORBIDDEN ECSTASY** (1014, $3.50)

Gray Eagle had promised Alisha his heart forever — nothing could keep him from her. But when Alisha woke to find her red-skinned lover gone, she felt abandoned and alone. Lost between two worlds, desperate and fearful of betrayal, Alisha hungered for the return of her FORBIDDEN ECSTASY.

# READ THESE PAGE-TURNING ROMANCES!